STAR WARS

COMPLETE CROSS-SECTIONS

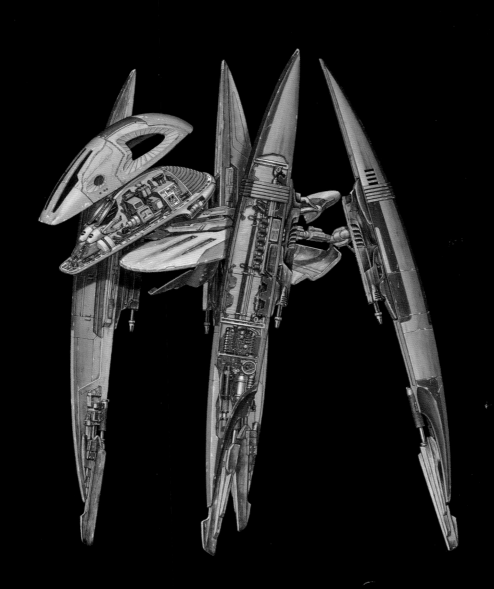

STAR WARS

COMPLETE CROSS-SECTIONS

Written by
David West Reynolds (Episodes I, IV–VI)
Curtis Saxton (Episodes II–III)

Extra material for this edition written by
Kerrie Dougherty

Illustrated by
Hans Jenssen and Richard Chasemore

Additional illustrations by
John Mullaney, Jon Hall

LUCAS BOOKS
www.starwars.com

www.dk.com

CONTENTS

FOREWORD

E VER SINCE CHILDHOOD, I've been a fan of cool hardware design. In the late 1960s, my father built a model kit of a nuclear submarine called the USS *Patrick Henry*. This model was cut-away on one side and included a detailed interior. I studied that model intently, trying to understand why everything was where it was and how the space was used. This fascination continued when I later came across sectional drawings of World War II aircraft carriers and battleships. I would marvel at their complexity, but I could see the logic of the design—form followed from function.

As I became interested in film, and science fiction films in particular, I also became fascinated by the internal workings of the hardware seen in these movies. I wanted to know how these futuristic spaceships were meant to work, and I appreciated it when it was clear that the movie designers had put some serious thought into the design of the vehicles. I spent many hours looking through *The Making of 2001–A Space Odyssey*, trying to piece together how all of the interior movie sets of the starship *Discovery* would fit together inside the fictional vessel's spherical hull.

And then came *Star Wars*. Here was a picture where everyone involved clearly cared about making the *Star Wars* universe look functional, believable, and real. Everything had an authentic look, one that was lived-in and used. It made sense to me when I later discovered that Ralph McQuarrie had worked for Boeing, and that Joe Johnston, John Dykstra, Grant McCune, and many of the first crew at Industrial Light & Magic (ILM) had industrial design backgrounds.

Twenty years later, I found myself working at ILM and participating in the *Star Wars* prequel trilogy. I now had the distinct pleasure of watching the design process from the inside. I got to see George Lucas's ideas go from written description to simple sketches, then to refined drawings, and finally to highly detailed miniatures or computer graphics.

Working very closely with the artists during all of this, I saw (and participated in) a number of little cheats to get through the required action with the approved designs. These were little things, like the fact that the landing gears for the Queen's Royal Starship were too tall to fold up into the underside of the craft, or that R2-D2's "shoulders" couldn't have fitted into a Naboo starfighter without making unsightly bulges in the hull.

Consequently, I really admire the thought, planning, and meticulous detail that Hans Jenssen and Richard Chasemore put into the drawings in this book. In many cases, with the help of the writers, they've resolved our design cheats—I especially like what they did with R2-D2's shoulders in the Naboo starfighter! They've taken the process that the concept designers started and painstakingly brought it to conclusion, filling in the millions of details we never had time to think about. In that sense, *Complete Cross-Section*s is the last chapter in the creation of the vehicles of the *Star Wars* saga.

JOHN KNOLL
VISUAL EFFECTS SUPERVISOR, ILM
EPISODES I–III

THE OLD REPUBLIC

Over 25,000 years ago, the introduction of hyperdrive technology made it possible for settlers to spread throughout the galaxy. After many millennia of exploration and colonization, a significant proportion of inhabited star systems were united to form a democratic Galactic Republic. The basic technology of starflight remained constant—in the Republic era, artistic expression and functional practicality are the drivers of vehicle design. Centuries of complacency and corruption, however, have led to political turmoil throughout the Republic. New and unusual technologies and designs begin to emerge as the Separatist movement entices many star systems to break away from the Republic. Greedy commercial organizations, aligned with the Separatist cause, create craft with dual military/commercial uses, often incorporating droid technologies, while the Republic counters the threat with new military vehicles to aid the Jedi in their attempt to maintain peace and stability.

NABOO DESIGN

The sleek and elegant lines of the Naboo N-1 starfighter exemplify the ancient traditions of artistic craftsmanship that are the hallmark of starship design in the Republic era. The people of Naboo work art into everything they make and their artist-engineers are highly respected. However, the N-1's aesthetic appeal does not supersede its practical capabilities, and the vehicle is well-suited to its role in the planet's Security Forces. When the need arises, this beautifully crafted vessel can be a fearsome adversary in combat.

DROID TECHNOLOGY

The droid tri-fighter symbolizes the demise of the Republic's traditions of artistic design. The droid vehicles and weaponry utilized by the Separatist movement are functional and expendable, mass-produced as cheaply as possible, and unaffected by human concerns for self-preservation. The bizarre design of Separatist craft—often based on the appearance of terrifying alien predators—represents the triumph of ruthless pragmatism over artistic expression.

DEFENDERS OF THE REPUBLIC

The Jedi Knights have maintained peace and security throughout the galaxy for millennia, using the diplomatic vessels of the Republic for transport and assistance with "aggressive negotiations." However, as the threat from the Separatist movement progresses into the galaxy-wide conflict known as the Clone Wars, the Jedi require new, deadly starfighters to defend the Republic. The fast, agile Jedi Interceptor combines elegant yet practical design with lethal effectiveness and has become a symbol of authority and hope for the Republic's forces.

COMMERCIAL FORCES

The Trade Federation is a leading power amongst the merchant factions seeking the overthrow of the Republic. The organization combines its commercial and military aims by making dual use of many of its craft, converting utilitarian cargo vessels into Droid Control Ships to transport and coordinate its droid armies. Foreshadowing the Empire's mass-production of spacecraft, the Trade Federation and its allies use modified versions of a small selection of vehicles for a wide range of applications. In this way, the greedy commercial interests achieve maximum effectiveness from each vehicle design with a minimum of cost.

THE GALACTIC EMPIRE

T HE REPUBLIC'S TRANSFORMATION INTO the Galactic Empire ends the chaos of the Clone Wars, but it also ushers in an oppressive new era in which the citizens of the galaxy are subjugated under a merciless, terrifying dictatorship. To help the Empire maintain its iron grip on the galaxy, the regime develops many new weapon technologies. The Rebel Alliance—a small army of united dissidents fighting against Imperial rule—poses a threat to the New Order. In order to restrict the Rebels' access to Imperial technologies, many manufacturers are brought under Imperial control or closed down, while other organizations become dominant due to lucrative Imperial contracts. As a result, the variety of spacecraft and vehicle designs produced under the Empire's rule is greatly reduced in comparison to the days of the Old Republic, as mass-production replaces the old traditions of craftsmanship and individuality.

REIGN OF TERROR

Imperial Star Destroyers—massive capital ships with enormous firepower—are used to maintain control across the Empire's star systems. The first Star Destroyers were developed by the Republic during the Clone Wars. The emergent Empire refined and developed the Star Destroyer design, augmenting its firepower and capacity to carry assault forces. The end result was an instrument of terror built to crush all opposition to Imperial rule.

IMPERIAL ENFORCER

The TIE bomber is an important component of the Empire's enforcement arsenal, utilized to bomb rebellious planets or communities into submission, or to destroy spacecraft in flight. This heavily armed spacecraft is a good example of the Imperial practice of utilizing a minimal selection of basic designs and adapting them for various purposes and functions. The versatile TIE (Twin Ion Engine) fighter-craft design is readily adaptable and has become a "workhorse" vehicle for the Galactic Empire.

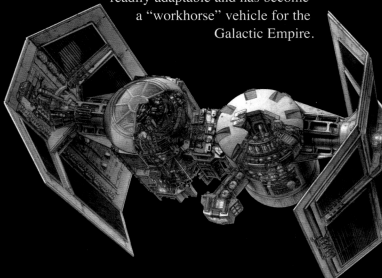

ASSAULT BEHEMOTH

In addition to its relentless space- and aerial-attack forces, the Empire also utilizes heavy ground-assault vehicles to crush its enemies into submission. Behemoth assault vehicles such as the AT-AT (All Terrain Armored Transport) walker are utilized across the galaxy as troop transports and attack craft. Their size and firepower exemplifies Emperor Palpatine's objective of total subjugation through the use of awe-inspiring military might.

THE REBEL RESPONSE

In the face of overwhelming Imperial forces, the Rebel Alliance fights back with an assortment of craft and weapons. Disaffected engineers and designers, who do not want to work under Imperial rule, join the Alliance and form the backbone of its military design capabilities. With limited access to components and manufacturing facilities, the Alliance designs and builds fast, well-armed, and maneuverable ships—including the T-65 X-wing—to battle against Imperial oppression.

TECHNOLOGY

THE TECHNOLOGY IN USE throughout the galaxy during both the era of the Old Republic and the reign of the Galactic Empire is the long-established product of millennia of scientific and technical research on many worlds. Hyperdrive technology, which makes interstellar spaceflight possible, has existed for 25,000 years and is highly refined, making space travel safe and routine. There are few completely new innovations, but myriad variations on the basic technological principles can be found across the star systems. Sophisticated devices incorporating computing technologies are integral to the operation of galactic society, as well as its vehicles and equipment. Mechatronics technologies have given the galaxy a cheap and expendable labor force—droids—which can be designed to perform virtually any task. In the upheaval created by the downfall of the Old Republic, the rise of the Empire, and the ensuing Galactic Civil War, military technologies come to the fore, as opposing parties create weapons and warcraft that will provide tactical and strategic advantage.

HYPERSPACE COMMUNICATIONS
Supralight hyperwaves, which travel through hyperspace, enable signals to be carried instantaneously across the galaxy. The public HoloNet uses hyperwaves to allow real-time communication between planets and starships. Military, Rebel, and pirate groups use their own secure hyperwave communication systems.

Communications an

Sensor computer

Primary sensory array

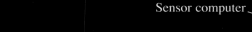

SENSOR SYSTEMS
Sensors analyze the environment around a vehicle for threats and hazards. Scanners and other instruments survey the surrounding area at different ranges, feeding back information that is processed by the sensor computer.

Repulsorlift

Proton torpedo

GRAVITY TECHNOLOGIES
Modern galactic civilization uses a variety of devices to manipulate gravity. Repulsorlift technology allows a craft to hover or fly over a planetary surface, and acceleration compensators enable spacecraft crews to carry out high-speed maneuvers without being pulverized by gravitational forces. Tractor beams manipulate gravitational forces to move or retrieve objects. All of these devices use subnuclear "knots" of space-time to exert control over gravity. These knots are the products of massive, automated power-refineries that surround black holes and process their space-time fields.

HYPERDRIVE AND SUBLIGHT ENGINES
A hyperdrive-equipped starship can accomplish faster-than-light travel, via the eerie realm of hyperspace. Hyperdrives utilize supralight "hypermatter" particles to allow a jump to lightspeed without changing the complex mass/energy configuration of the ship. The hyperdrive field, once generated, has to be projected around the starship to enable it to remain in hyperspace—a drive system failure will result in the ship dropping out of hyperspace back into real space in a potentially dangerous location, such as an asteroid belt or the heart of a star. Sublight engines propel spacecraft in real space. They are used for orbital operations, during space battles, and when traveling within planetary systems. The most common type of sublight engine is the ion drive, which produces thrust by projecting a stream of charged particles through the engine's exhaust port. Fuels can include pressurized radioactive gas, volatile composite mixtures, and explosive liquid metals.

POWER SOURCES

Starships and vehicles use a hierarchy of power technologies that were perfected in pre-Republic times. Domestic devices generally run on portable chemical, fission, and fusion reactors. These systems consume a variety of fuels, depending upon local resources. Most starships use fusion systems that contain more powerful hypermatter-annihilation cores.

ASTROMECH DROIDS

Specifically created to work with spacecraft, astromech droids are designed to operate both as an independent unit and as an integral part of the vehicle. They can function equally well inside the vessel or in the vacuum of space. As ship-units, astromechs interface with their craft's computer systems to augment the capabilities of ship and pilot. They monitor and diagnose flight performance, calculate and store hyperspace data, and pinpoint technical errors or faulty computer-coding. As independent units, most astromechs are programmed to repair a variety of different vehicles and are used as on-board and ground-based repair and maintenance crews.

Astromech droid

Sublight engine

Hyperdrive

Deflecror shield projectors

Power generator

Laser cannon

SHIELDS

Ships and vehicles are protected by force fields that repel solid objects or absorb energy. Constant power is required to dissipate the energy from impacts. Concussion shields are used to repel space debris, and deflector shields (ray and particle shields) help to protect craft during battle. Ray shields deflect or break up the beams from energy weapons. Particle shields protect against impact from high-velocity projectiles and proton weapons. Shield intensities diminish gradually with distance from the generator or projector, although shields projected in an atmosphere tend to have a defined outer surface. When a shield absorbs large energy blasts, the momentum can surge back to the ship or vehicle and affect its motion.

ARMAMENT

Laser cannons and turbolasers fire invisible energy beams that travel at lightspeed. A glowing pulse traveling along the beam at less than lightspeed marks the energy bolt's path. However, the light given off by this visible pulse depletes the overall energy content of the beam. Blasters and ion cannons are also classed as energy weapons—blasters fire powerful bolts created by the excitation of high-energy gas while ion cannons emit bursts of ionized energy. Proton weapons are physical ordnance, which cause destruction by releasing clouds of high-energy, high-velocity proton particles. Proton torpedoes are among the most powerful weapons carried by starfighters, but they are secondary to laser cannons, as only a limited number of torpedoes can be carried.

Episode I
The Phantom Menace

The Galactic Republic is engulfed by turmoil. Thousands of years of peace and prosperity are threatened by the greed of powerful new commercial organizations, such as the Trade Federation, which have risen to challenge the authority of the Galactic Senate. To resolve disputes, the Republic must call on the negotiating skills of its guardians of peace and justice, the Jedi Knights. During their efforts to resolve one such flash point—the blockade of the planet Naboo by the Trade Federation—Jedi Master Qui-Gon Jinn and his Padawan Obi-Wan Kenobi become embroiled in a complex plot that ultimately leads them to the desert planet Tatooine. There they discover a young slave, Anakin Skywalker, who shows amazing Force-potential. Qui-Gon believes he may be the "Chosen One" of Jedi lore, destined to bring balance to the Force.

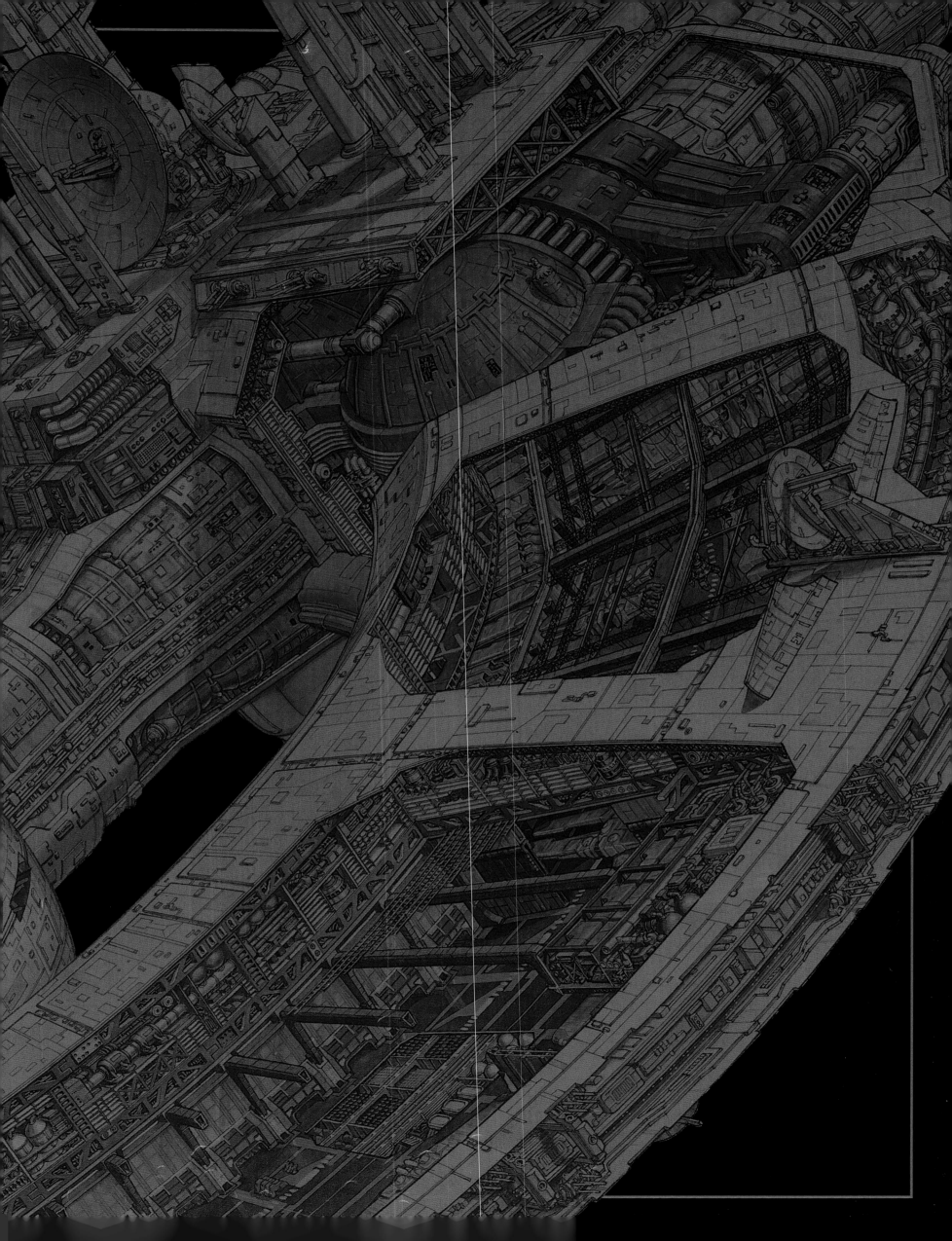

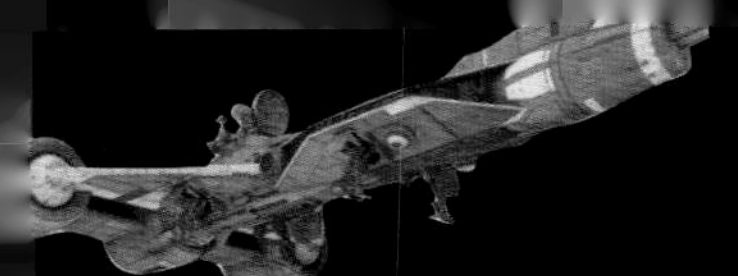

REPUBLIC CRUISER

CARRYING TWO JEDI KNIGHTS into the heart of danger, the Republic Cruiser is dispatched by Supreme Chancellor Valorum to the blockaded planet of Naboo. The direct predecessor to the well-armed Blockade Runner Corvette, the peaceful Republic Cruiser was assembled in the great orbital shipyards of Corellia, and serves as a testament to the quality and fame of Corellian spacecraft design. The *Radiant VII* is a veteran of 34 years in service of the diplomatic corps of Coruscant itself, capital world of the Galactic Republic. The ship has endured many adventures, bringing Jedi Knights, ambassadors, and diplomats to trouble spots around the galaxy on missions of security and vital political significance. Its interchangeable salon pods are well-armored and insulated against any kind of eavesdropping. In this safe haven, critical negotiations can take place and crises can be averted.

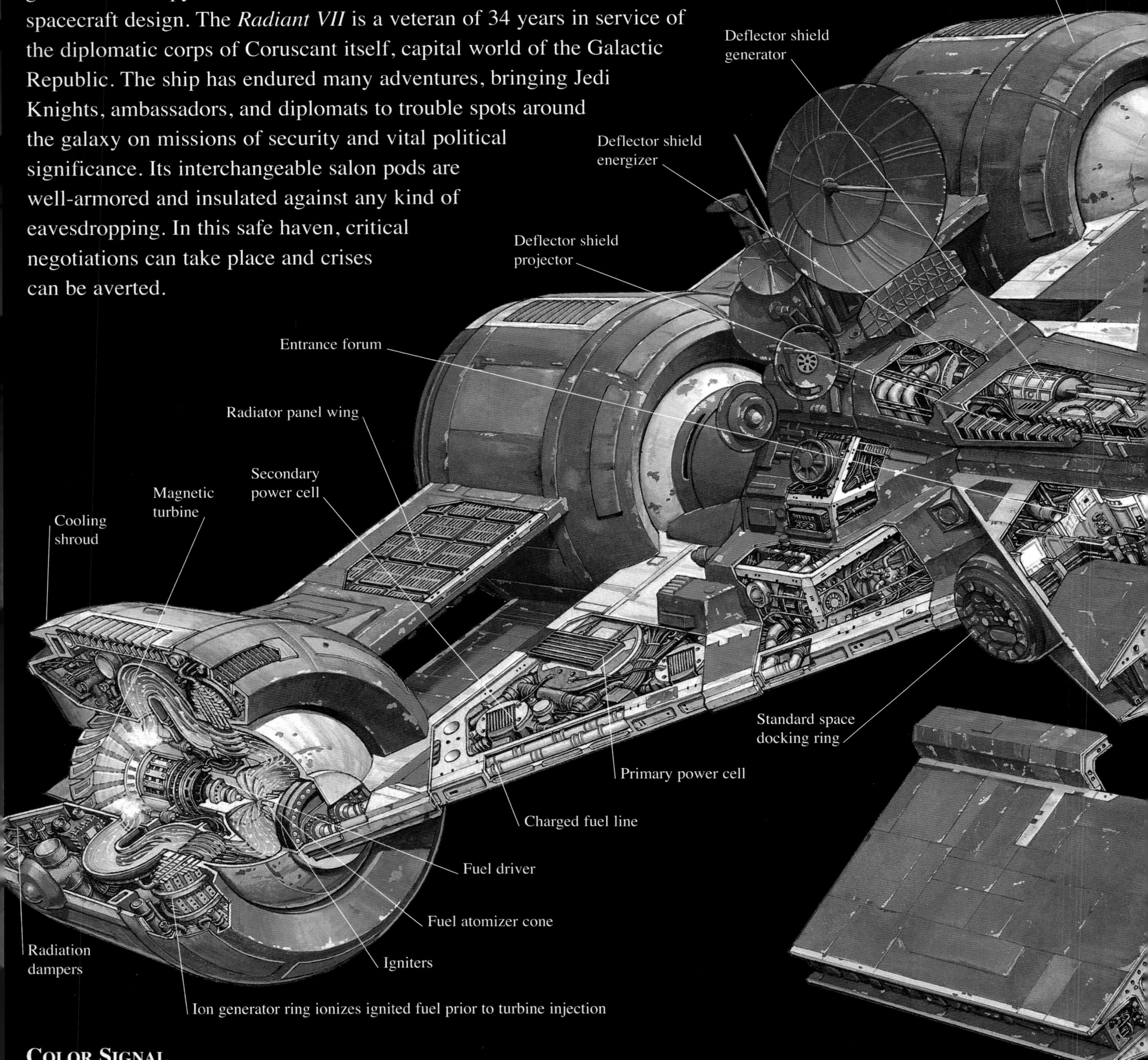

Dyne 577
sublight engine

Deflector shield
generator

Deflector shield
energizer

Deflector shield
projector

Entrance forum

Radiator panel wing

Secondary
power cell

Magnetic
turbine

Cooling
shroud

Standard space
docking ring

Primary power cell

Charged fuel line

Fuel driver

Fuel atomizer cone

Radiation
dampers

Igniters

Ion generator ring ionizes ignited fuel prior to turbine injection

8-person
escape pod

COLOR SIGNAL

The striking red color of the Republic Cruiser sends a message to all who see it. Scarlet declares the ship's diplomatic immunity and serves as a warning not to attack. Red is the color of ambassadorial relations and neutrality for spacecraft of the Galactic Republic, and has been for generations. The tradition will continue even into the days of the Empire: Princess Leia Organa's consular vessel *Tantive IV* of Alderaan is striped in red to indicate its special diplomatic status. The extraordinary full-red color scheme of the Republic Cruiser signifies that the ship comes straight from the great capital world of Coruscant.

THE SALON POD

The Republic Cruiser often serves as a neutral meeting ground for Republic officials and leaders of groups in conflict. To accommodate the many kinds of alien physiology in the galaxy, customized salon pods are available in the hangars on Coruscant, and the Republic Cruiser can be equipped with any of these. In emergency situations, the entire salon pod can eject from the cruiser with its own sensors and independent life-support gear ready to sustain the diplomatic party on board.

COMMUNICATING IN A DIVERSE GALAXY

In order to communicate with any culture it may visit, the Republic Cruiser sports a wide variety of dish and other communications antennas. (Years later, the Empire will standardize communications across the galaxy, making such an array unnecessary.) On board the cruiser, two communications officers specialize in operating the communication computers, deciphering strange languages, and decoding the complex signal pulses of unorthodox alien transmissions.

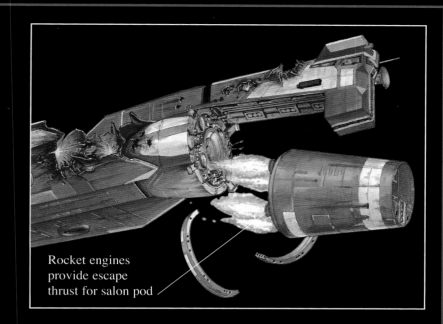

Rocket engines provide escape thrust for salon pod

Wiring and systems trunk

Crew lounge

Navigational sensor dish

Salon pod magnoclamps

Captain's storage

Formal dining room

Multi-comm station

Upper deck state rooms

Lift

Navigator's station

Automated docking signal receiver

Cockpit

Lounge

Escape pod access tunnel (from lower deck)

Salon vestibule

Salon pod breakaway cowling

Main salon pod airlock doors

Hologram pad

Main forward sensors

Captain's quarters

Interchangeable diplomatic salon pod

Seating for 16 beings

Salon pod independent sensors

Mid-deck corridor

Droid hold

TIGHT SECURITY

Civilian models of the Corellian Cruiser are used for straightforward transport purposes, but the scarlet Republic Cruisers are dedicated to the special objectives of galactic political service. To accomplish their missions, Republic Cruisers must often rely on their reputation as absolutely secure vessels for high-level diplomatic meetings and confrontations. For security reasons, crew is kept to a bare minimum, with many ship functions attended by simple utility droids.

DATA FILE

Manufacturer: Corellian Engineering Corporation
Make: Space Cruiser
Length: 115 m (380 ft)
Sublight engines: 3 Dyne 577 radial atomizers
Hyperdrive: Longe Voltrans tri-arc CD-3.2
Crew: 8 (captain, 2 co-pilots, 2 communications officers, 3 engineers)
Passenger capacity: 16
Armament: none (unarmed diplomatic vessel)
Escape pods: two 8-person pods plus salon pod

LANDING SHIP

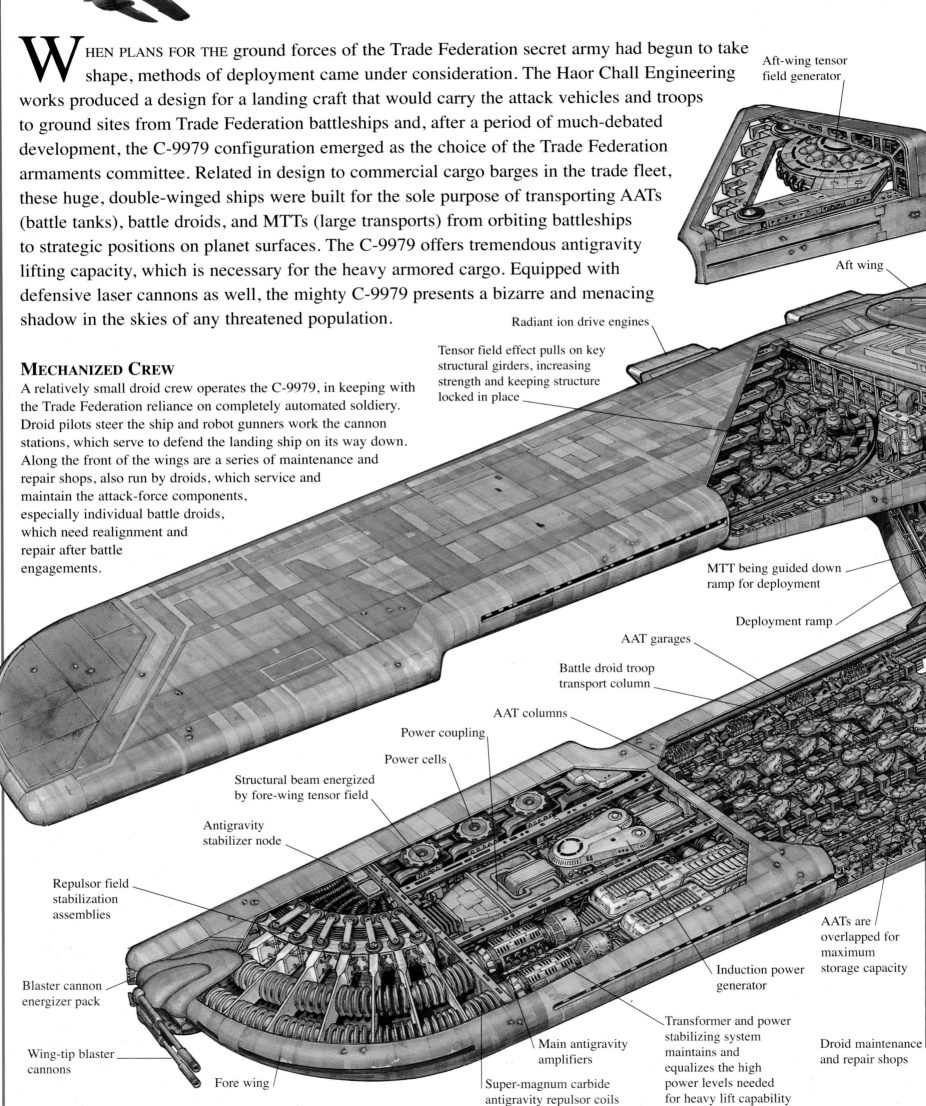

WHEN PLANS FOR THE ground forces of the Trade Federation secret army had begun to take shape, methods of deployment came under consideration. The Haor Chall Engineering works produced a design for a landing craft that would carry the attack vehicles and troops to ground sites from Trade Federation battleships and, after a period of much-debated development, the C-9979 configuration emerged as the choice of the Trade Federation armaments committee. Related in design to commercial cargo barges in the trade fleet, these huge, double-winged ships were built for the sole purpose of transporting AATs (battle tanks), battle droids, and MTTs (large transports) from orbiting battleships to strategic positions on planet surfaces. The C-9979 offers tremendous antigravity lifting capacity, which is necessary for the heavy armored cargo. Equipped with defensive laser cannons as well, the mighty C-9979 presents a bizarre and menacing shadow in the skies of any threatened population.

MECHANIZED CREW

A relatively small droid crew operates the C-9979, in keeping with the Trade Federation reliance on completely automated soldiery. Droid pilots steer the ship and robot gunners work the cannon stations, which serve to defend the landing ship on its way down. Along the front of the wings are a series of maintenance and repair shops, also run by droids, which service and maintain the attack-force components, especially individual battle droids, which need realignment and repair after battle engagements.

Aft-wing tensor field generator

Aft wing

Radiant ion drive engines

Tensor field effect pulls on key structural girders, increasing strength and keeping structure locked in place

MTT being guided down ramp for deployment

Deployment ramp

AAT garages

Battle droid troop transport column

AAT columns

Power coupling

Power cells

Structural beam energized by fore-wing tensor field

Antigravity stabilizer node

Repulsor field stabilization assemblies

AATs are overlapped for maximum storage capacity

Induction power generator

Blaster cannon energizer pack

Wing-tip blaster cannons

Fore wing

Main antigravity amplifiers

Super-magnum carbide antigravity repulsor coils

Transformer and power stabilizing system maintains and equalizes the high power levels needed for heavy lift capability

Droid maintenance and repair shops

LOADING

C-9979 landing ships are berthed in hidden hangar areas of the Trade Federation battleships. Here they are assembled, serviced, and maintained, and when ready for deployment they are loaded with MTTs, AATs, and troop carriers which have been prepared for combat. Landing ships are stored in an unloaded condition to reduce structural stress and so that the attack craft can be serviced individually.

DATA FILE

Design and manufacture: Haor Chall Engineering
Wingspan: 370 m (1,200 ft)
Hyperdrive: none
Max. atmospheric speed: 587 kph (365 mph)
Troop carrier capacity: 7 per wing; total 28
AAT (battle tank) capacity: 24 per fore wing, 33 per aft wing; total 114
MTT (large transport) capacity: 3 per fore wing, 3 in stage area, 2 in landing pedestal; total 11
Crew: 88 (droids only)
Armament: 2 pairs of wing-tip laser cannons, 4 turret-mounted cannons

Electromagnetic transport clamp-on rail will guide MTT down deployment ramp

Control center

MTT powers up its onboard repulsors in staging area

Control signal receiver picks up vital signal from the Droid Control Ship

Deflector shield projectors

Pressure charging turbine atmosphere intake

Cannon charging turret

Main defensive cannon

Wing-tip plating is an alloy composite transparent to repulsor effect

Staging area

Fore-wing tensor field generator

Radiator panel for tensor power system

Navigation sensors

Combat sensors

Forward tensor field generator increases load-bearing ability of wing mounts

MTT garage

Antigravity rails support MTTs

Center MTT has deployed and an AAT now follows into position

Main deployment doors include perimeter field sensors to detect possible land mines, electrical fields, and other hazards

Doors require clear landing area for opening clearance

Landing gear fairing

MTT preparing to back into position over deployment ramp

Foot ramp

Atmosphere pressure charging turbines

Tanks in escort position

MTT moving out for battle position

DEPLOYMENT

The wings of the landing ship contain rows of MTTs, AATs, and battle droid troop carriers racked in garage channels for maximum loading capacity. For deployment, the attack vehicles are guided along repulsor tracks to a staging platform. MTTs in particular require the assistance of the repulsors built into these tracks, because their onboard maneuvering equipment is not precise enough to negotiate the cramped confines of the garage zones without causing collision damage. At a staging platform, the vehicles are rotated into position and seized by transport clamps, which draw them aft and guide them down the drop ramp in the landing ship's "foot." The great clamshell doors of the "foot" then open wide to release the ground forces. Deployment of the full load of vehicles on board a C-9979 can take up to 45 minutes.

STORING THE TRANSPORT

C-9979s are built with removable wings so they can be stored efficiently. Powerful tensor fields bind the wings to the fuselage when the ship is assembled for use. The huge wings of the C-9979 would tax the load-bearing capabilities of even the strongest metal alloys, making tensor fields vital for the integrity of the ship. Forward-mounted tensor fields bind the wing mounts firmly to the fuselage, while wing-mounted tensor fields keep the span of the wings from sagging.

MTT (LARGE TRANSPORT)

THE TRADE FEDERATION'S Baktoid Armor Workshop has long designed armaments for Trade Federation customers. When called upon to design and build vehicles for the Trade Federation droid army, it easily turned its resources to the creation of deadly weapons made to ensure a long line of future customers. The Trade Federation MTT (Multi-Troop Transport, or simply large transport) was designed to convey platoons of ground troops to the battlefield and support them there. Its deployment on Naboo is its first use in major military action, and many large transports had seen only training exercises on remote worlds before being used there. They are designed for deployment in traditional battle lines, hence their heavy frontal armor. Reinforced and studded with case-hardened metal alloy studs, the MTT's face is designed to ram through walls so that troops may be deployed directly into enemy buildings (or "future customer buildings," as the Trade Federation often prefers to say). When ready to deploy, it opens its large front hatch to release the battle droid contingents from its huge storage rack, extended on a powerful hydraulic rail. Two droid pilots direct it according to instructions transmitted from the orbiting Droid Control Ship.

DATA FILE
Design and manufacture: Baktoid Armor Workshop
Troop capacity: 112 battle droids carrying standard blaster rifles
Armament: four 17 kv anti-personnel blasters twin-mounted in ball turrets
Length: 31 m (103 ft)
Height: 13 m (43 ft)
Max. ground speed: 35 kph (22 mph)
Max. lift altitude: 4 m (13 ft)
Deployment method: carried to planet surface in C-9979 landing ship

Control room escape hatch (at rear)

Lift

Repulsorlift sled

Drive unit adapted from civilian cargo sled

Deployment rack extensor drive

Rack operator droid

Rack drive heat exhaust vents

Rack extensor drive engine

TROOP CARRIER

The Trade Federation troop carrier conveys battle droid units to deployment zones behind the protection of ground armor, in secure conditions, or within occupied areas. A rack similar to that in the MTT contains a full complement of 112 battle droids folded into their space-saving configuration, ready for action on release.

Pressure equalizer valves

Power converter grids

HEAVY LIFTING

The MTT's engine works hard to power repulsorlifts that carry a very heavy load of troops and solid armor. The repulsorlift generator's exhaust and cooling system is vented straight down toward the ground through several large vents under the vehicle. This creates a billowing storm of wind around the MTT, which lends it a powerful and menacing air.

Kuat Premion Mk. II power generators

Repulsor motor gas cooling system exhaust

Heavy-duty repulsor cooling fins

THE BAKTOID SIGNATURE IN DESIGN

The MTT (large transport) was designed by the same Baktoid workshop that developed the AAT (battle tank) for the Trade Federation secret army. The distinctive Baktoid style gives both vehicles a look reminiscent of heavy, jungle-dwelling animals. Both are designed for use in formal battle lines and place vital equipment such as reactor and main engines at the rear, protected behind the heavy armor of the front surfaces.

Control signal receiver

Control room

Battle droid pilot

Battle droid engineer/gunner

THE DEPLOYMENT RACK

The original design of the MTT called for an open staging chamber inside it, but the Baktoid Armor Workshop is known for its original designs, and the MTT had the unusual job of conveying soldiers that were not living beings, but droids. The Baktoid engineers worked out a system that would load battle droids folded into very small configurations into a giant deployment rack. This rack would more than double the troop capacity of the MTT, extending to release the compressed troops which would then unfold into fighting configuration. At the conclusion of a battle, troops are reloaded into the rack and safely carried back to their base. The original open-staging chamber MTT design was retained for carrying wheel-like destroyer droids.

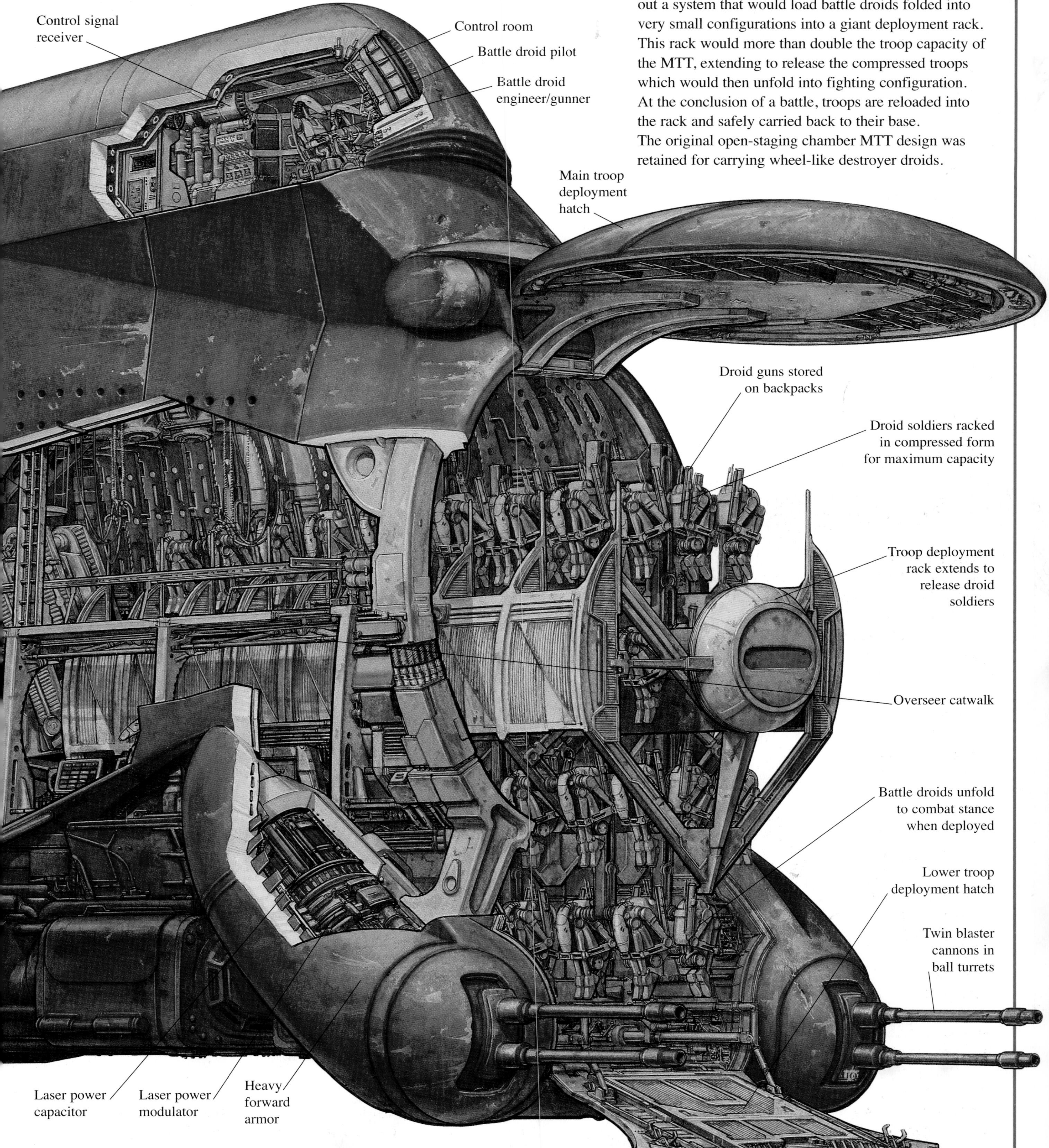

Main troop deployment hatch

Droid guns stored on backpacks

Droid soldiers racked in compressed form for maximum capacity

Troop deployment rack extends to release droid soldiers

Overseer catwalk

Battle droids unfold to combat stance when deployed

Lower troop deployment hatch

Twin blaster cannons in ball turrets

Laser power capacitor

Laser power modulator

Heavy forward armor

PROPULSION

The sub uses rotating fins to cycle water through an electromotive field that actually drives the ship. The fins contain flat, flexible electronic units linked in series, which send electrical impulses down their length, pushing the water along. Combined with the rotating fins, this electromotive field can grab onto and displace a great deal of water, hurtling the sub through the sea at great speed.

DATA FILE

Design and manufacture: Otoh Gunga Bongameken Cooperative
Make: tribubble bongo sub
Length: 15 m (50 ft)
Cargo capacity: 800 kg (1800 lb) in each of 2 cargo bubbles
Crew: 1 (with 2 passengers)
Special features: the forward cockpit can eject as an escape pod in emergencies, but can sustain its hydrostatic field only briefly, so it must race for the surface in case of a disaster before its power runs out

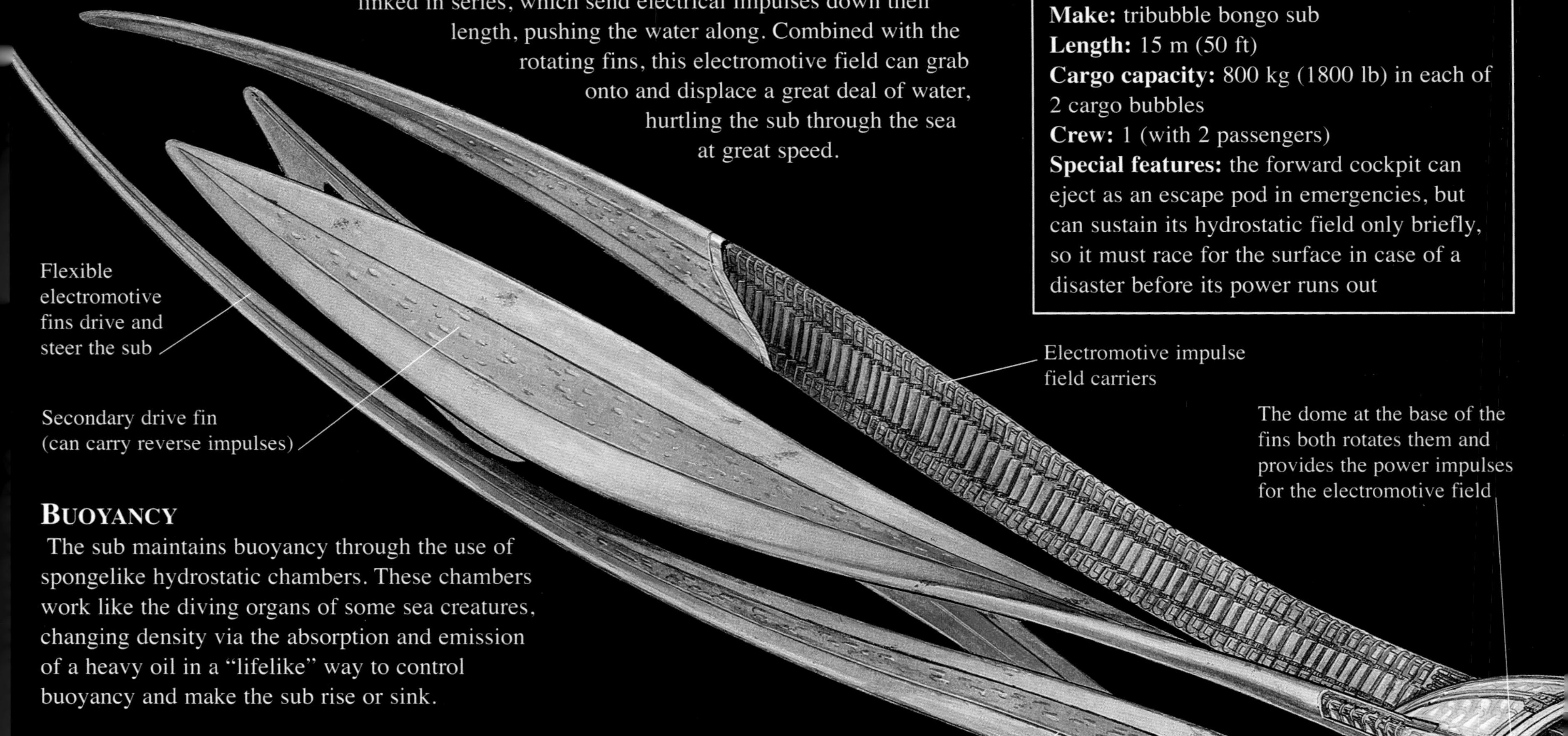

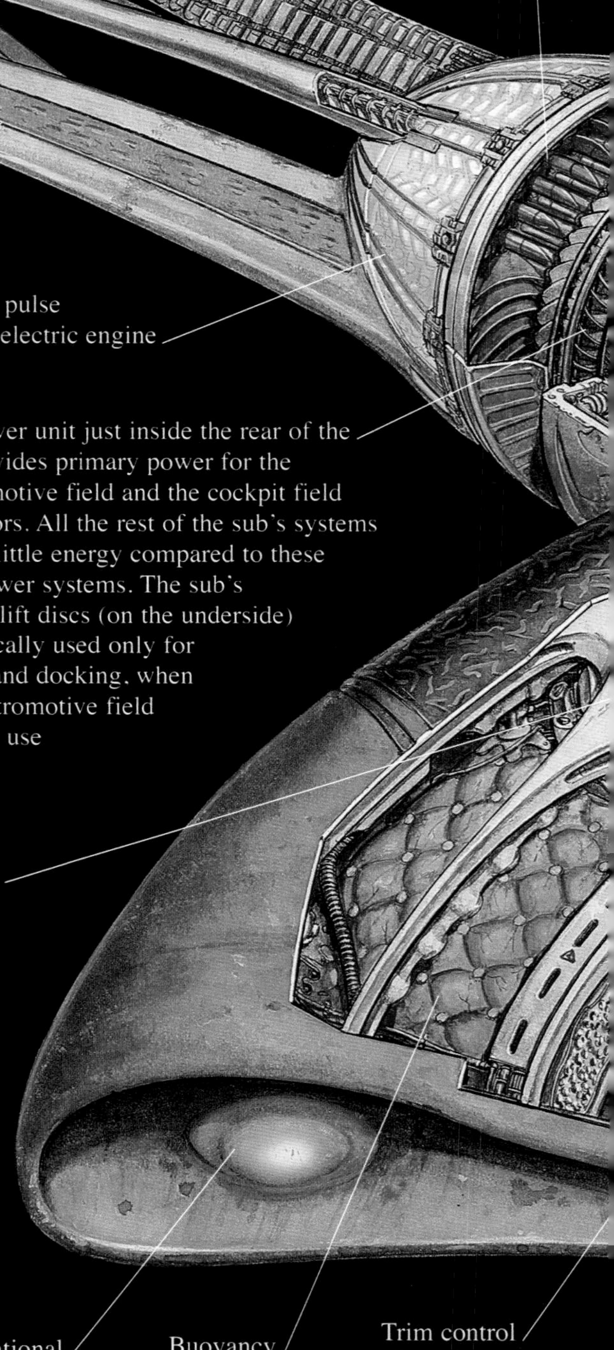

Flexible electromotive fins drive and steer the sub

Secondary drive fin (can carry reverse impulses)

Electromotive impulse field carriers

The dome at the base of the fins both rotates them and provides the power impulses for the electromotive field

BUOYANCY

The sub maintains buoyancy through the use of spongelike hydrostatic chambers. These chambers work like the diving organs of some sea creatures, changing density via the absorption and emission of a heavy oil in a "lifelike" way to control buoyancy and make the sub rise or sink.

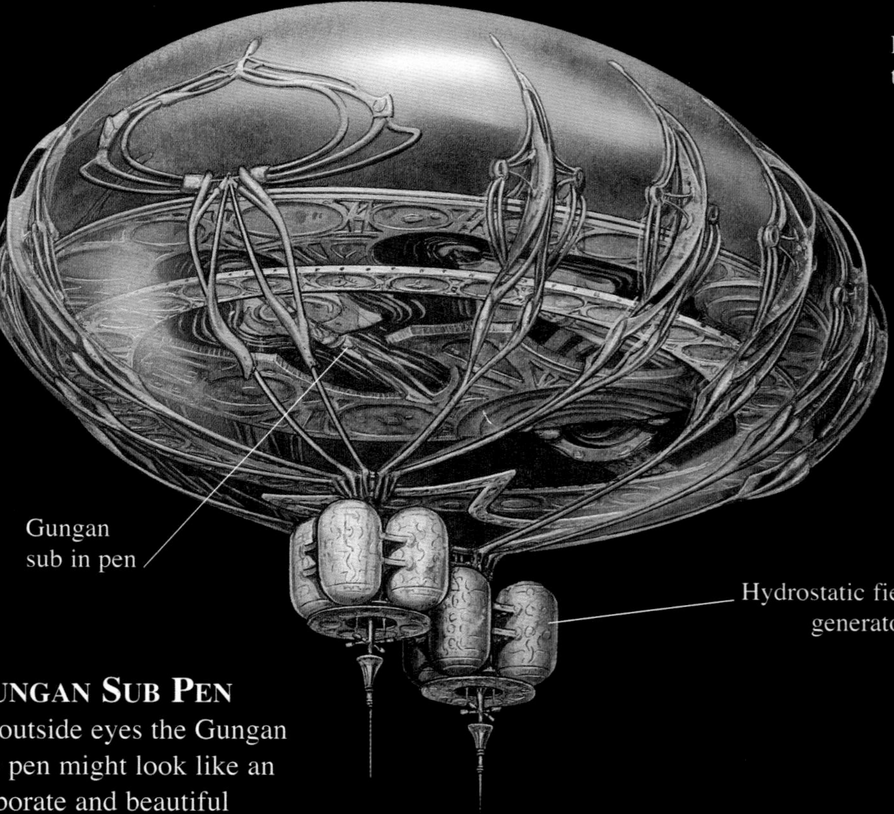

Fins are tough but flexible

Centrifugal pulse conversion electric engine

The power unit just inside the rear of the sub provides primary power for the electromotive field and the cockpit field generators. All the rest of the sub's systems require little energy compared to these high-power systems. The sub's repulsorlift discs (on the underside) are typically used only for launch and docking, when the electromotive field is not in use

Gungan sub in pen

Hydrostatic field generators

GUNGAN SUB PEN

To outside eyes the Gungan sub pen might look like an elaborate and beautiful structure of special significance; however, within Otoh Gunga it is just an ordinary docking port. Gungans believe that everything they make speaks of who they are, and that anything they construct should add to the beauty of their world.

Hydrostatic field receptors

HYDROSTATIC BUBBLES

The cockpit bubbles of the sub work on the same principle as the bubbles enclosing the underwater city of Otoh Gunga and the sub pen shown above. A hydrostatic field is projected between the prong over each cockpit and the margins where the bubble meets the sub body. The prong and the powerful receptors in the bubble margin act as opposing poles. A force current running between these two poles creates the hydrostatic field of the cockpit bubble that holds air in and water out, while still allowing solid objects to pass through.

Navigational light

Buoyancy chamber

Trim control oil cyclers

GUNGAN SUB

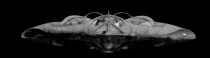

THIS KIND OF SUBMERSIBLE is a common utility transport in Otoh Gunga, designed to carry passengers, cargo, or both. The forward cockpit bubble carries only pilot and passengers, but the side bubbles can carry either passengers or cargo depending on whether they are fitted with seats. The sub's distinctive form originates from both the Gungans' construction methods and their love of artistic design. The Gungans produce many of their structures using a secret method that actually "grows" the basic skeletons or shells of buildings or vehicles. This gives Gungan constructions a distinctive organic look, which is then complemented by artistic detail, even on simple vehicles like the sub. Gungan organically generated shells can be combined to make complex constructions, and then modified and fitted with electronic and mechanical components to give them the needed functionality. The organic skeletons are exceptionally strong, though still susceptible to damage by some of the larger sea monsters encountered in deep waters.

THE ARM'S-LENGTH RELATIONSHIP

The rectangular cargo containers in the cargo pods of the sub are Naboo-made. While the leaders of Naboo and the Gungans have little contact, out of necessity a significant amount of trade goes on at the fringes of each society, and just as Naboo trade goods are vital in the underwater cities of the Gungans, Gungan products and food supplies are vital to the Naboo people. The two societies pretend not to need each other but are actually greatly intertwined.

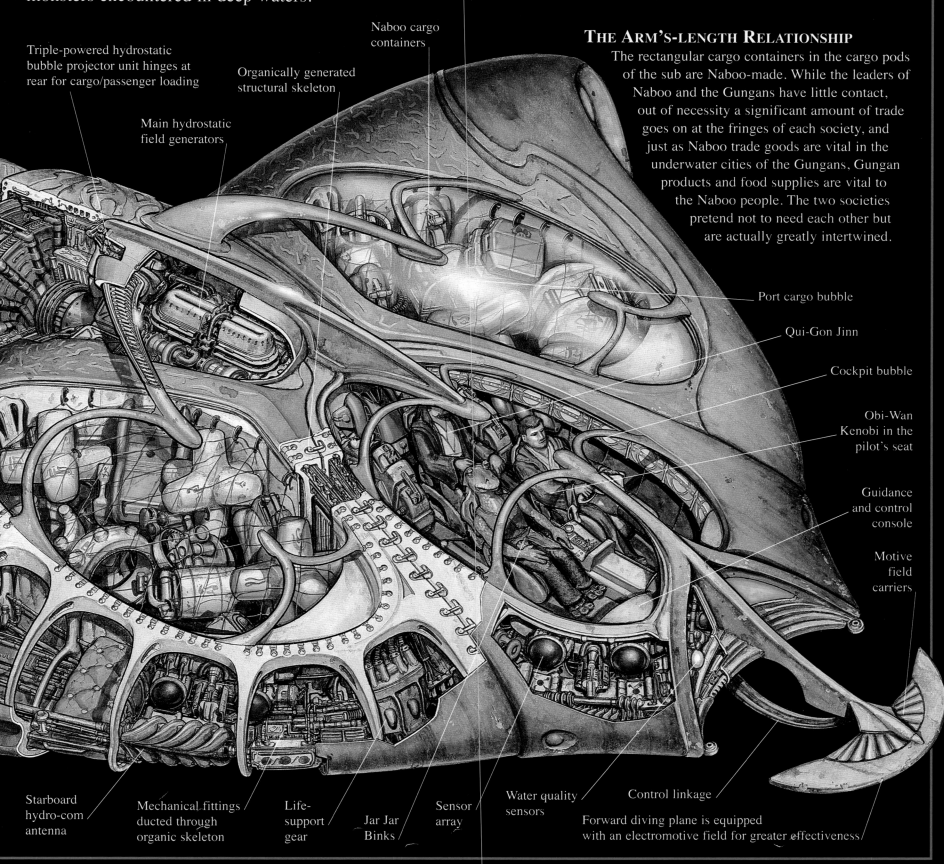

Naboo cargo containers

Triple-powered hydrostatic bubble projector unit hinges at rear for cargo/passenger loading

Organically generated structural skeleton

Main hydrostatic field generators

Port cargo bubble

Qui-Gon Jinn

Cockpit bubble

Obi-Wan Kenobi in the pilot's seat

Guidance and control console

Motive field carriers

Starboard hydro-com antenna

Mechanical fittings ducted through organic skeleton

Life-support gear

Jar Jar Binks

Sensor array

Water quality sensors

Control linkage

Forward diving plane is equipped with an electromotive field for greater effectiveness

NABOO QUEEN'S ROYAL STARSHIP

THE ROYAL STARSHIP of Queen Amidala of Naboo is a unique starship handcrafted by the Theed Palace Space Vessel Engineering Corps. Completed six years ago, the Royal Starship replaced the previous royal vessel before Queen Amidala came to office. The gleaming craft, usually helmed by the Queen's chief pilot Ric Olié, conveys Queen Amidala in matchless style to locations around Naboo for royal visitations, parades, and other observances. The ship also carries Amidala on formal state visits to other planetary rulers or to the Galactic Senate at the capital world of Coruscant itself. It is designed for short trips, and accordingly features limited sleeping facilities, primarily dedicated for the ruler and a customary entourage.

Expressing the Naboo love of beauty and art, the dreamlike shape of the Queen's ship, together with its extraordinary chromium finish, make it a distinctive presence in any setting. The starship is made to embody the glory of the Naboo royalty, symbol of the noble spirit of the Naboo people. Service to the Queen is a great honor, and the design of a Royal Starship is the highest goal to which a Naboo engineer can aspire. Every centimeter of the ship's wiring is laid out with exacting precision, neatly run in perfect parallel rows, making the ship a work of art in every respect.

ROYAL CHROMIUM

A mirrored chromium finish gleams over the entire surface of the Royal Starship from stem to stern. Purely decorative, this finish indicates the starship's royal nature. Only the Queen's own vessel may be entirely chromed. Royal starfighters are partly chromed, and non-royal Naboo ships bear no chrome at all. The flawless hand-polished chrome surface over the entire Royal Starship is extremely difficult to produce and is executed by traditional craftspeople, not by factory or droid equipment.

NUBIAN AT HEART

The starship's unique spaceframe was manufactured at Theed, yet the ship makes use of many standard galactic high-technology components that cannot be produced on Naboo. The ship is built around elegant Nubian 327 sublight and hyperdrive propulsion system components, giving it high performance and an exotic air. Nubian systems are often sought by galactic royalty and discriminating buyers who appreciate the distinctive design flair of Nubian components. Nubian equipment is easily acquired on civilized worlds but can be hard to obtain on more remote planets, as the Queen discovers during her forced landing on Tatooine.

Starboard sensor array dome

Main hold

Tech station

Jar Jar Binks

Lift to lower deck

Table

Hyperdrive bay (in floor)

Forward hold

Royal quarters

Navigation light recess

Extension boarding ramp to lower deck

Navigation floodlight

Forward maintenance station

Wiring throughout the ship is laid out with exacting care and precision to honor the Queen

Power node

Communications antennas

Forward bulkhead

Forward long-range sensor array

Navigational sensors

Forward deflector shield projector

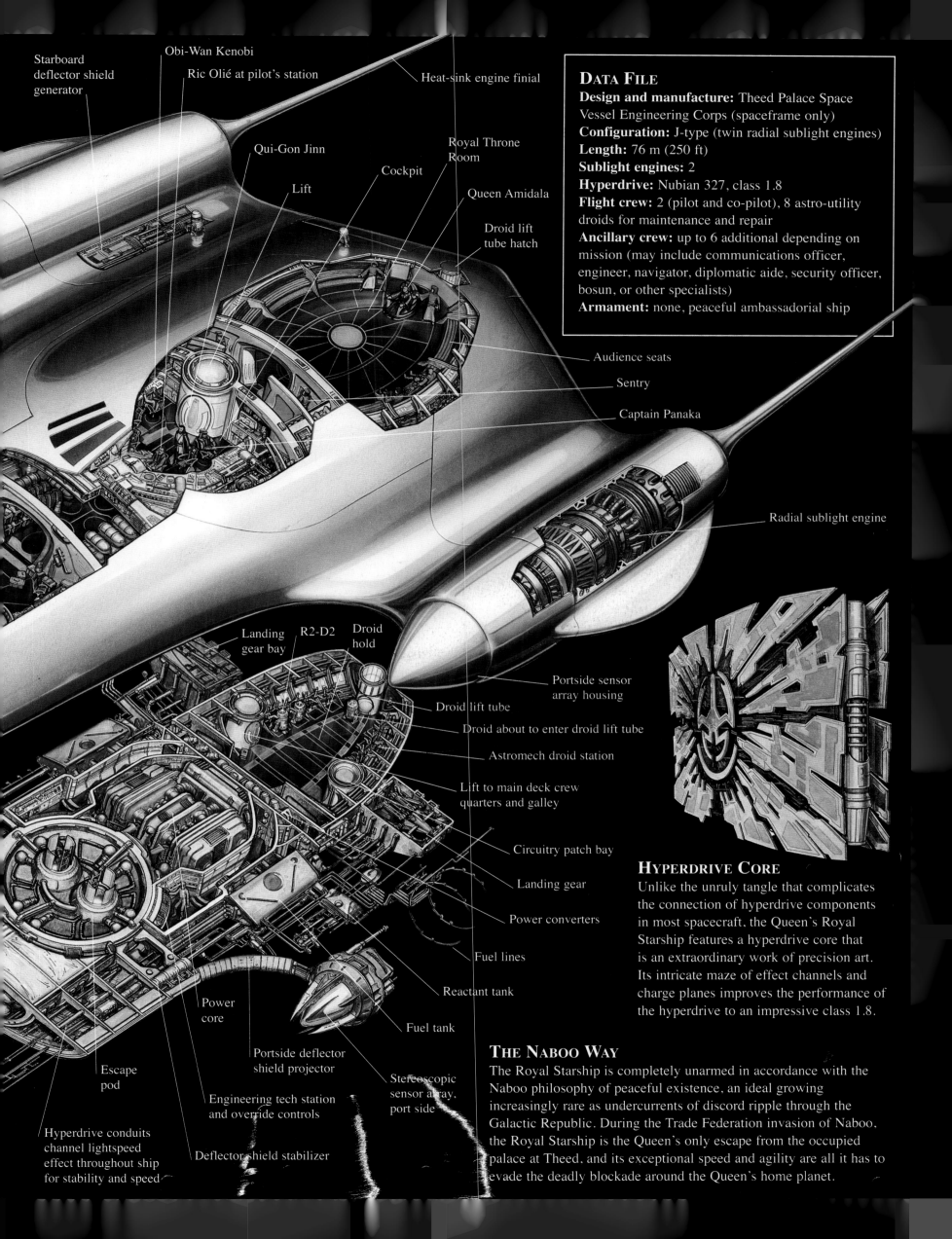

Starboard deflector shield generator

Obi-Wan Kenobi

Ric Olié at pilot's station

Heat-sink engine finial

Qui-Gon Jinn

Royal Throne Room

Cockpit

Lift

Queen Amidala

Droid lift tube hatch

DATA FILE

Design and manufacture: Theed Palace Space Vessel Engineering Corps (spaceframe only)
Configuration: J-type (twin radial sublight engines)
Length: 76 m (250 ft)
Sublight engines: 2
Hyperdrive: Nubian 327, class 1.8
Flight crew: 2 (pilot and co-pilot), 8 astro-utility droids for maintenance and repair
Ancillary crew: up to 6 additional depending on mission (may include communications officer, engineer, navigator, diplomatic aide, security officer, bosun, or other specialists)
Armament: none, peaceful ambassadorial ship

Audience seats

Sentry

Captain Panaka

Radial sublight engine

Landing gear bay

R2-D2

Droid hold

Portside sensor array housing

Droid lift tube

Droid about to enter droid lift tube

Astromech droid station

Lift to main deck crew quarters and galley

Circuitry patch bay

Landing gear

Power converters

Fuel lines

Reactant tank

Power core

Fuel tank

Escape pod

Portside deflector shield projector

Engineering tech station and override controls

Stereoscopic sensor array, port side

Hyperdrive conduits channel lightspeed effect throughout ship for stability and speed

Deflector shield stabilizer

HYPERDRIVE CORE

Unlike the unruly tangle that complicates the connection of hyperdrive components in most spacecraft, the Queen's Royal Starship features a hyperdrive core that is an extraordinary work of precision art. Its intricate maze of effect channels and charge planes improves the performance of the hyperdrive to an impressive class 1.8.

THE NABOO WAY

The Royal Starship is completely unarmed in accordance with the Naboo philosophy of peaceful existence, an ideal growing increasingly rare as undercurrents of discord ripple through the Galactic Republic. During the Trade Federation invasion of Naboo, the Royal Starship is the Queen's only escape from the occupied palace at Theed, and its exceptional speed and agility are all it has to evade the deadly blockade around the Queen's home planet.

PODRACERS

HIGH-SPEED PODRACING harkens back to primitive eras with its traditional Podracer designs and the mortal danger seen in racing spectacles. Pulled on flexible control cables by fearsomely powerful independent engines, a small open cockpit (the "Pod") carries a daring pilot at speeds that can exceed 800 kilometers (500 miles) per hour. Considered in its lightning-fast modern form too much for humans to manage, Podracing is almost exclusively carried on by other species that sport more limbs, more durable bodies, a wider range of sensory organs, or other biological advantages.

TEEMTO'S PODRACER

Teemto Pagalies' Podracer is typical of Podracers found in the Outer Rim: a unique design incorporating certain standard features. Its unusual circular shape is designed around an internal metal cycling ring which acts as a gyroscopic stabilizer for the non-aerodynamic Pod. Other components are standard: control line anchors, a brace of repulsors to float the Podracer safely off the ground, a complex engine sensor and telemetry computer package, and a variety of control levers and switches suited to the particular body shape of the race pilot himself.

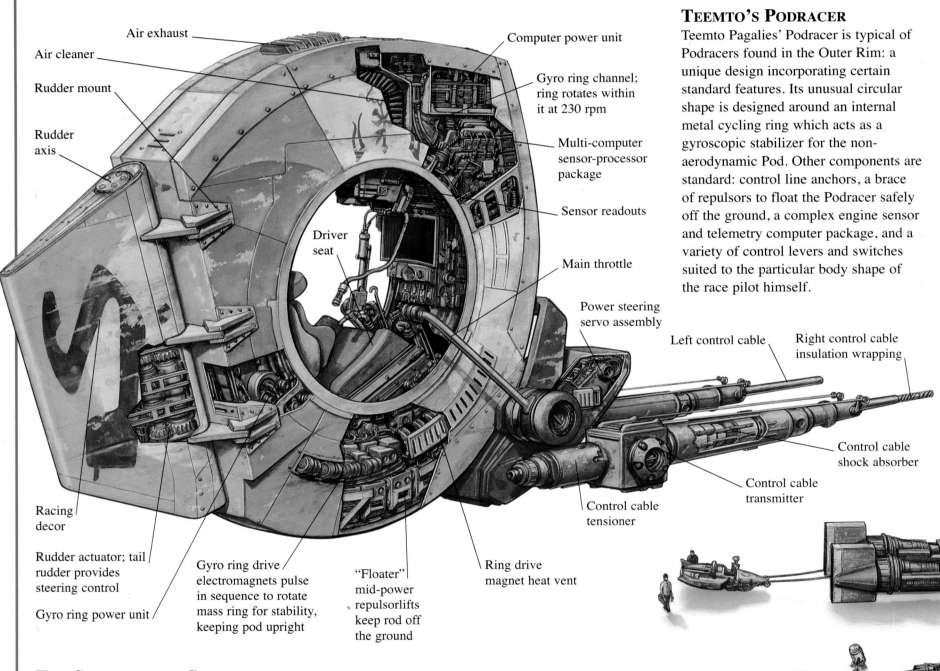

Air exhaust

Air cleaner

Rudder mount

Rudder axis

Computer power unit

Gyro ring channel; ring rotates within it at 230 rpm

Multi-computer sensor-processor package

Sensor readouts

Driver seat

Main throttle

Power steering servo assembly

Left control cable

Right control cable insulation wrapping

Control cable shock absorber

Control cable transmitter

Racing decor

Rudder actuator; tail rudder provides steering control

Gyro ring power unit

Gyro ring drive electromagnets pulse in sequence to rotate mass ring for stability, keeping pod upright

"Floater" mid-power repulsorlifts keep rod off the ground

Control cable tensioner

Ring drive magnet heat vent

THE STORY OF THE SPORT

Podracing has its origins in ancient contests of animal-drawn carts, of the kind still seen in extremely primitive systems far from the space lanes. Long ago a daring mechanic called Phoebos recreated the old arrangement with repulsorlift Pods and flaming jet engines for a whole new level of competition and risk. The famous first experimental race ensured Podracing's reputation as an incredibly dangerous and popular sport.

PODRACING TODAY

Long ago banned from most civilized systems, Podracing is still famous on Malastare and in a few other locales. Real Podracing aficionados, however, look beyond the Republic to the rugged worlds of the Outer Rim, where Podraces still serve as a spectacle for hundreds of thousands and vast gambling fortunes are made and lost. This naturally makes the Hutts an accessory to most racing venues.

A SPECTATOR'S GUIDE TO THE PODRACERS

Eighteen Podracers, many well known at Mos Espa, qualify for the great Boonta Eve Race, in which nine-year-old Anakin Skywalker enters his customized Radon-Ulzer. Notoriously fine-tuned machines, not all these Podracers make it as far as the starting line … and several more never make it to the finish. While mechanical breakdowns are not uncommon, the high-stakes Boonta is also menaced by discreet sabotage.

0   5
Scale in meters
(5 m = 16 1/2 ft)

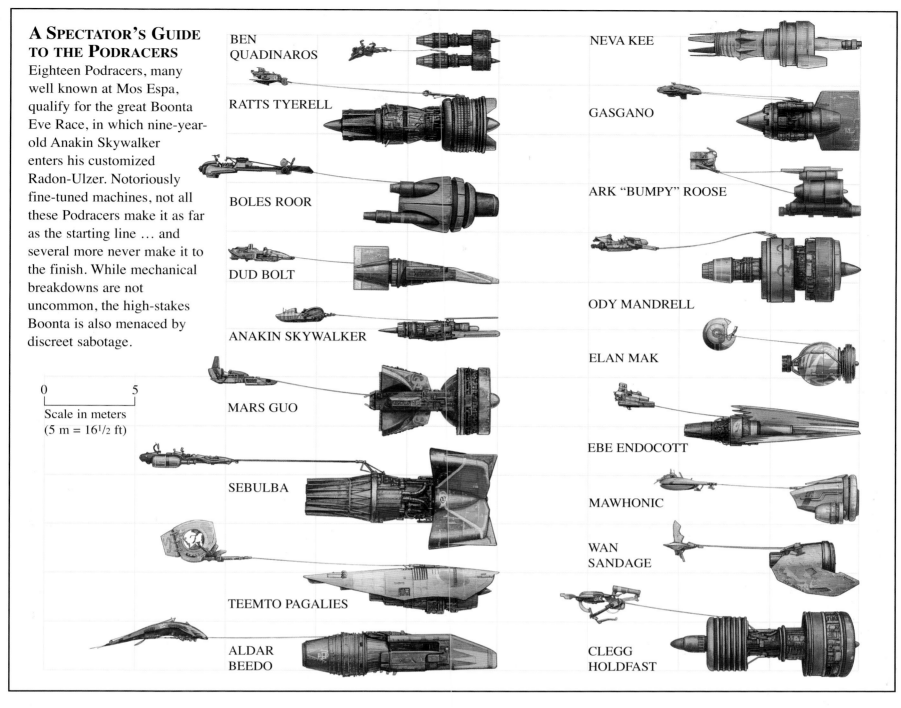

BEN QUADINAROS

RATTS TYERELL

BOLES ROOR

DUD BOLT

ANAKIN SKYWALKER

MARS GUO

SEBULBA

TEEMTO PAGALIES

ALDAR BEEDO

NEVA KEE

GASGANO

ARK "BUMPY" ROOSE

ODY MANDRELL

ELAN MAK

EBE ENDOCOTT

MAWHONIC

WAN SANDAGE

CLEGG HOLDFAST

THE RACE LINEUP

Racers qualify for starting positions at the Mos Espa arena via a complex set of traditions which involve a combination of past performance, popularity, and random chance. Most Podracers feature a distinctive ensign or decor scheme representing a race pilot's rich patron, family lineage, protective deity, supporting guild, or simply colors that appeal to them. Colorful flags bearing these emblems herald the beginning of the formal race ceremony, and dynamic racing graphics decorate the vehicles for visibility and good luck. As with the Podracer designs, the bewildering variety of ensign types seen at Mos Espa arena contributes to the dazzling spectacle of the races.

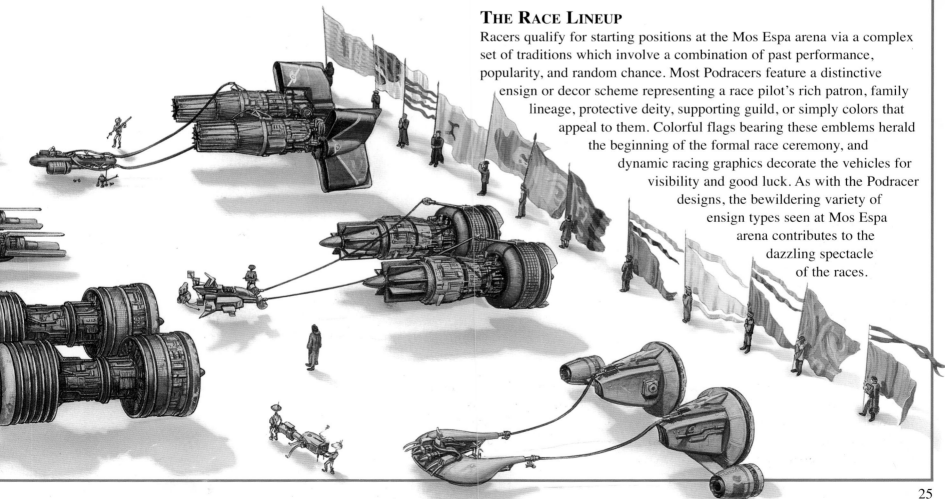

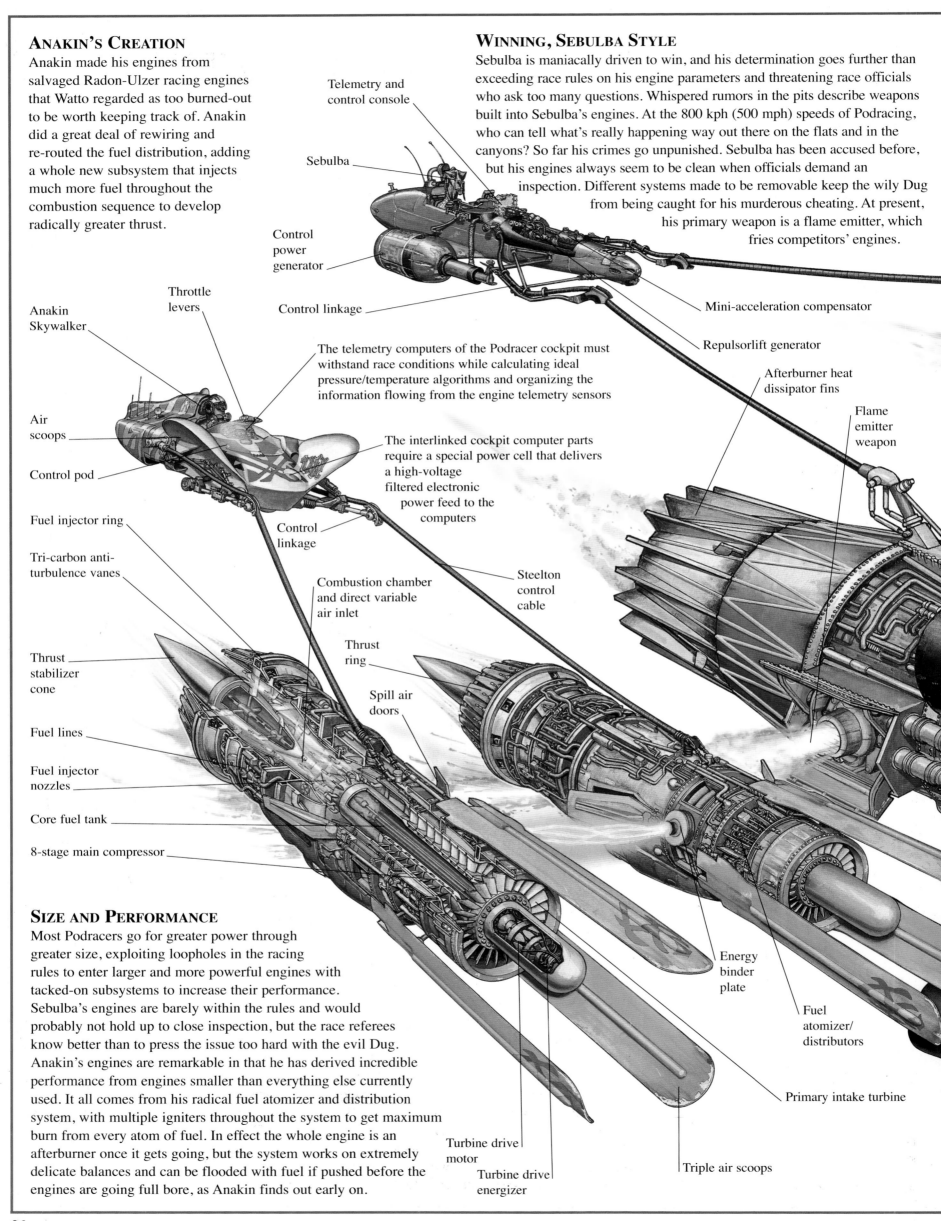

ANAKIN'S CREATION

Anakin made his engines from salvaged Radon-Ulzer racing engines that Watto regarded as too burned-out to be worth keeping track of. Anakin did a great deal of rewiring and re-routed the fuel distribution, adding a whole new subsystem that injects much more fuel throughout the combustion sequence to develop radically greater thrust.

WINNING, SEBULBA STYLE

Sebulba is maniacally driven to win, and his determination goes further than exceeding race rules on his engine parameters and threatening race officials who ask too many questions. Whispered rumors in the pits describe weapons built into Sebulba's engines. At the 800 kph (500 mph) speeds of Podracing, who can tell what's really happening way out there on the flats and in the canyons? So far his crimes go unpunished. Sebulba has been accused before, but his engines always seem to be clean when officials demand an inspection. Different systems made to be removable keep the wily Dug from being caught for his murderous cheating. At present, his primary weapon is a flame emitter, which fries competitors' engines.

Telemetry and control console

Sebulba

Control power generator

Control linkage

Throttle levers

Anakin Skywalker

Air scoops

Control pod

The telemetry computers of the Podracer cockpit must withstand race conditions while calculating ideal pressure/temperature algorithms and organizing the information flowing from the engine telemetry sensors

Mini-acceleration compensator

Repulsorlift generator

Afterburner heat dissipator fins

Flame emitter weapon

The interlinked cockpit computer parts require a special power cell that delivers a high-voltage filtered electronic power feed to the computers

Control linkage

Fuel injector ring

Tri-carbon anti-turbulence vanes

Combustion chamber and direct variable air inlet

Control linkage

Steelton control cable

Thrust ring

Spill air doors

Thrust stabilizer cone

Fuel lines

Fuel injector nozzles

Core fuel tank

8-stage main compressor

Energy binder plate

Fuel atomizer/ distributors

Primary intake turbine

SIZE AND PERFORMANCE

Most Podracers go for greater power through greater size, exploiting loopholes in the racing rules to enter larger and more powerful engines with tacked-on subsystems to increase their performance. Sebulba's engines are barely within the rules and would probably not hold up to close inspection, but the race referees know better than to press the issue too hard with the evil Dug. Anakin's engines are remarkable in that he has derived incredible performance from engines smaller than everything else currently used. It all comes from his radical fuel atomizer and distribution system, with multiple igniters throughout the system to get maximum burn from every atom of fuel. In effect the whole engine is an afterburner once it gets going, but the system works on extremely delicate balances and can be flooded with fuel if pushed before the engines are going full bore, as Anakin finds out early on.

Turbine drive motor

Turbine drive energizer

Triple air scoops

Anakin's & Sebulba's Podracers

The great Boonta Eve Race on Tatooine is a legend among Podracers. It is here that racers congregate from widespread star systems to match their skills and their engines against the best, in a setting largely unrefined by civilized society or its rules. Here are to be seen the most determined racers, the most extreme power ratios, the most exciting experimental engines that would be illegal elsewhere, and the most underhanded tactics to be found in the sport. And it is on this stage that a nine-year-old boy named Anakin Skywalker faces the highest possible stakes with a Podracer he built himself.

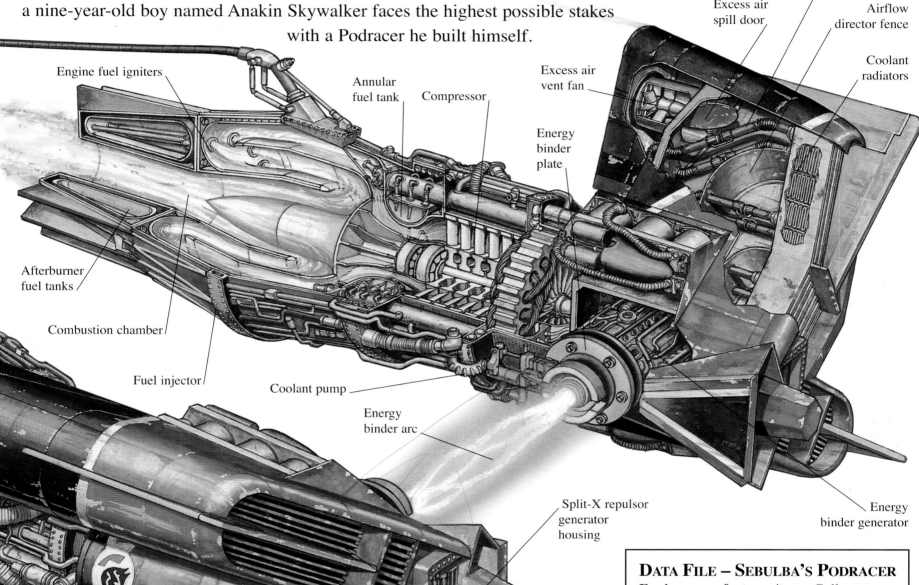

Engine fuel igniters

Annular fuel tank

Compressor

Excess air vent fan

Energy binder plate

Radiator hoses

Excess air spill door

Airflow director fence

Coolant radiators

Afterburner fuel tanks

Combustion chamber

Fuel injector

Coolant pump

Energy binder arc

Split-X repulsor generator housing

Energy binder generator

Upper Split-X air intake

Over-pressure system valve

Split-X stabilizing vane

Catching the Wind

One of Anakin's cleverest engine modifications is the set of triple air scoops ranged around each primary turbine intake. These "air brakes" provide additional control in cornering. Anakin had to wait a long time before he found metal plates and a hydraulic system that would be strong enough to make this idea work. The hydraulic struts are of Tyrian manufacture and came from a military surplus lot that Watto bought from Dreddon the Hutt, a crimelord known to make many arms deals in the star systems of the Outer Rim.

Data File – Sebulba's Podracer
Engine manufacturer/type: Collor Pondrat Plug-F Mammoth racing engines, fitted with Split-X ram air/radiator intakes
Engine length: 7.47 m (24 1/2 ft)
Max. speed: 829 kph (515 mph)
Max. repulsorlift altitude: 85 m (275 ft)
Fuel: Tradium power fluid pressurized with quold runium, activated with ionized injectrine

Data File – Anakin's Podracer
Engine manufacturer/type: Radon-Ulzer 620C racing engines, modified heavily by Anakin Skywalker
Engine length: 7 m (23 ft)
Max. speed: estimated 947 kph (588 mph)
Max. repulsorlift altitude: 105 m (350 ft)
Fuel: straight Tradium power fluid activated with injectrine, no additives

TOOLS OF EVIL

Built beneath the invisibility field projector are compartments containing equipment for Darth Maul's missions. Floating "dark eye" probe droids, a speeder bike, interrogator droids, prisoner torture devices, spying and surveillance gear, bombs, mines and eavesdropping technology are only part of the Sith Lord's inventory, and Darth Maul is never at a loss for equipment. Sith training has made Maul less reliant on technology and stronger in his inner abilities, but he keeps his Infiltrator fully equipped with the most advanced technology to maximize his power.

Cloak field generator

THE INVISIBLE ENEMY

Invisibility fields were considered theoretical until the discovery of the rare stygium crystals on the volcanically turbulent planet Aeten II in the Outer Rim. An invisibility field is a terrifying weapon, since it can defeat most security systems and make acts of theft, sabotage and assassination all but unstoppable.

Cloak generator hood

Stygium crystal mounts

Darth Maul's speeder bike is deployed through the underside cargo hatch

Storage for poisons, deadly weapons, blades, and other devices of evil intent

Swing bin

Access channel to cloak field generator and portions of cargo bay

"Dark eye" probe droids are remote activated

Cargo drop panel folds down to allow access to stored items

Landing gear

Radiator panels

Overload cache

SITH INFILTRATOR

DURING THEIR LONG CENTURIES of secret actions against the Jedi Order, Sith apprentices have maintained a tradition of special spacecraft suited to their evil missions, called Sith Infiltrators. Darth Maul's dreaded craft is the latest in this ancient line of dark vessels and is perhaps the most dangerous Infiltrator yet created. Able to appear and disappear with the ease of a shadow, it hides in its distinctive long prow a formidable full-effect cloaking device, a technological wonder that gives it invisibility on command. The Infiltrator is a customized version of an advanced armed star courier design from the workshop of the technological genius Raith Sienar, and features laser cannons, extensive sensor systems, and an experimental high-temperature ion engine system requiring large radiator panels, which fold inward during landings. Darth Maul uses the powerful capabilities of his Infiltrator to learn secret information, plant sabotage, and track targeted individuals anywhere in the galaxy. The evasive and deadly craft is an appropriate extension of the uncanny abilities of its Sith Lord pilot.

DATA FILE
Manufacturer: Sienar Design Systems, later customized in a secret laboratory
Make: armed star courier rebuilt as a unique 2-deck Sith Infiltrator
Length: 26.5 m (88 ft)
Sublight drive: high-temperature X-C 2 ion drive array
Hyperdrive: Sienar SSDS 11-A (class 3.0)
Crew: 1, with capacity for 6 passengers
Primary armament: 6 low-profile laser cannons (4 original, 2 added)

DROID STARFIGHTER

THE SPACE FIGHTERS deployed from the Trade Federation battleships are themselves droids, not piloted by any living being. Showered upon enemies in tremendous swarms, droid starfighters—also known as Vulture droids— dart through space in maddening fury, elusive targets and deadly opponents for living defenders. They are controlled by a continuously modulated signal from the central Droid Control Ship computer, which keeps track of every single fighter just as it pulses through the processor of every single battle droid. The signal receiver and onboard computer brain is in the "head" of the fighter and twin sensor pits serve as eyes. They are the most sophisticated automated starfighters ever built, carrying four laser cannons as well as two energy torpedo launchers, which pack them with firepower far beyond their size class.

Retracted walk mode claws

Composite shell cover antenna that receive control signa

Thrust exhaus nozzle

Landing repulsor bands

ATTACK AND FLIGHT MODES

To both protect and conceal its deadly laser cannons, the droid starfighter retracts its wings in flight mode (above). In this configuration, the droid can hide its military nature, enabling it to ambush the unwary. Covering the weapons when not in use, shielding them from micro-particles and atmospheric corrosion, can also improve their accuracy by a tiny degree, an effort at high precision typical of the Haor Chall engineer initiates.

Energy torpedo cannon

Engine module as removed for refueling

Solid fuel slug chamber

Solid fuel slug

Thrust dampers electromagnetically vector propulsion

Engine cooling fins

Thrust exhaust nozzles

Hydraulic wing/leg extension system

Walking leg struts (retracted)

Hydraulic and pneumatic charging systems for wing deployment and leg walking movement

Flight assault lasers

Antigravity generator

Laser muzzle brake

Power converter

Internal system cooling unit and demagnetizer

Light non-magnetic alclad alloy plating

Permanently installed power cells are recharged while droid is locked into war freighter power grid

SOLID FIRE FUEL

Unconventional solid fuel concentrate slugs give droid starfighters their powerful thrust. Expensive to manufacture, the slugs burn furiously when ignited, allowing the droid starfighter to hurtle through space with minimal engine mass. Thrust streams are vectored electromagnetically for steering. The solid fuel system limits the droids' fighting time, but the numerous droids are easily recycled back into their racks for recharge and refueling when spent.

DATA FILE

Design and manufacture: Xi Char cathedral factories, Charros IV
Length: 3.5 m (12 ft) wing tip to wing tip
Crew: permanent automated droid brain controlled by remote signal
Armament: 4 blaster cannons, 2 energy torpedo launchers
Flight time before refueling: 35 minutes

DROID CONTROL SHIP

FROM THE VERY FIRST STAGES of planning to build their secret army, the Trade Federation armaments committee had in mind the use of their great commercial fleet of giant cargo ships for transporting the weapons of war. Familiar to millions of officials and civilian personnel who dealt with them over the skies of numerous planets, the characteristic giant Trade Federation cargo ships had been built over many years, plying cargo among the far-flung stars of the galaxy as part of the extensive market of the Trade Federation. These seemingly harmless and slow-moving container ships would now hide, deep within their hangars, the tremendous army built to change the rules of commerce. Upon the first complete council approval of the secret army plan, the cargo fleet was brought under study, and by the end of the project's construction phase the Neimoidians had created from them a frightening fleet of battleships.

WAR CONVERSIONS

The converted battleships bear unusual equipment for cargo freighters, including powerful quad laser batteries designed to destroy opposition fighters launched against the secret army transports. These batteries are built to rotate inward while not in use, concealing their true nature until the Neimoidians wish to uncloak their military intentions to unsuspecting "future customers." While the cargo hangars and their ceiling racks in the inner hangar zones proved sufficient for the carriage of the secret army ground forces, additional large electrified racks were installed in the outermost hangar zones to quarter the dangerous colonies of droid starfighters, which draw power from the racks until launch.

CIVILIAN COMPROMISES

While the Trade Federation cargo fleet was ideal for hiding the existence of the secret army and carrying it unobtrusively to points of deployment, the commercial origins of the battleships leave them with shortcomings as "battleships." Fitted with numerous guns around the equatorial bands, the battleships carry considerable firepower with very limited coverage and so large areas of the ship are undefended by emplaced artillery. The onboard swarms of droid starfighters are thus essential for defense of the battleships from fighter attack.

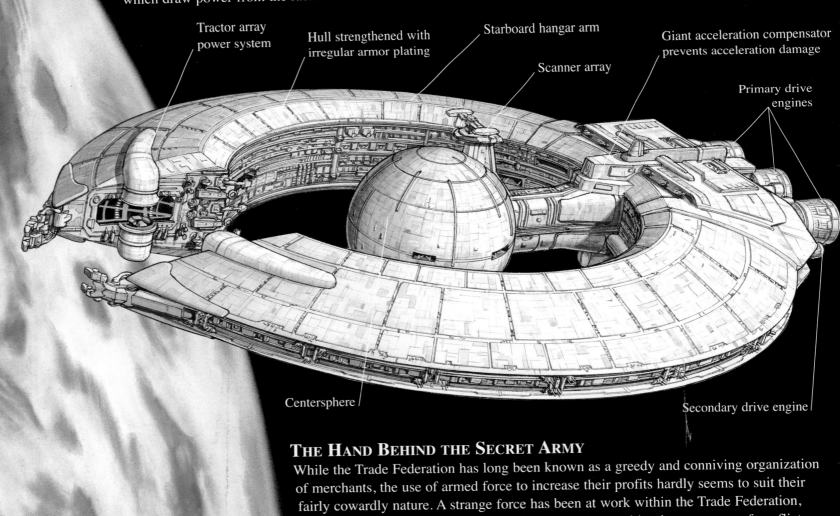

Tractor array power system

Hull strengthened with irregular armor plating

Starboard hangar arm

Scanner array

Giant acceleration compensator prevents acceleration damage

Primary drive engines

Centersphere

Secondary drive engine

THE HAND BEHIND THE SECRET ARMY

While the Trade Federation has long been known as a greedy and conniving organization of merchants, the use of armed force to increase their profits hardly seems to suit their fairly cowardly nature. A strange force has been at work within the Trade Federation, making it capable of extraordinary measures and commiting it to a course of conflict and outright war that will shake the very Galactic Republic. At its core, the Trade Federation's secret army appears to be the vision of a shadowy figure called Darth Sidious, who has been manipulating powerful Neimoidians to do his mysterious bidding. The Sith title of this dark lord holds menace for all, and no one can guess where this disturbing course of events will lead.

Secondary docking arms of several types support docking maneuvers with a wide variety of cargo craft

Hangars within the inner wall provide docking space for shuttles carrying officials, trade diplomats, merchants, and bureaucrats

Armored, sealed hangars hold shipments of highly toxic or dangerous materials stored well away from main hangar zones

Main tractor beam generator

Multiple tractor beam projectors guide craft of various sizes into safe landing in the outer hangar

Hangar landing target provides signal for automatic docking of visiting spacecraft

Reinforced bracing for primary docking claw

Primary docking claw rotator assembly

C-9979 landing ship, still under guidance from docking tractor beam array, starts onboard full propulsion at this point

Primary docking claws lock onto colossal freight barges for cargo transfer

Quad laser batteries in firing position

Rotators allow quad lasers to be withdrawn for concealment

Portside main hangar portals

Docking tractor beam housing

Fully loaded landing ship in launch-ready sequence

War freighters carry invasion forces yet lack control computer and its antennas

Typical triple quad laser battery

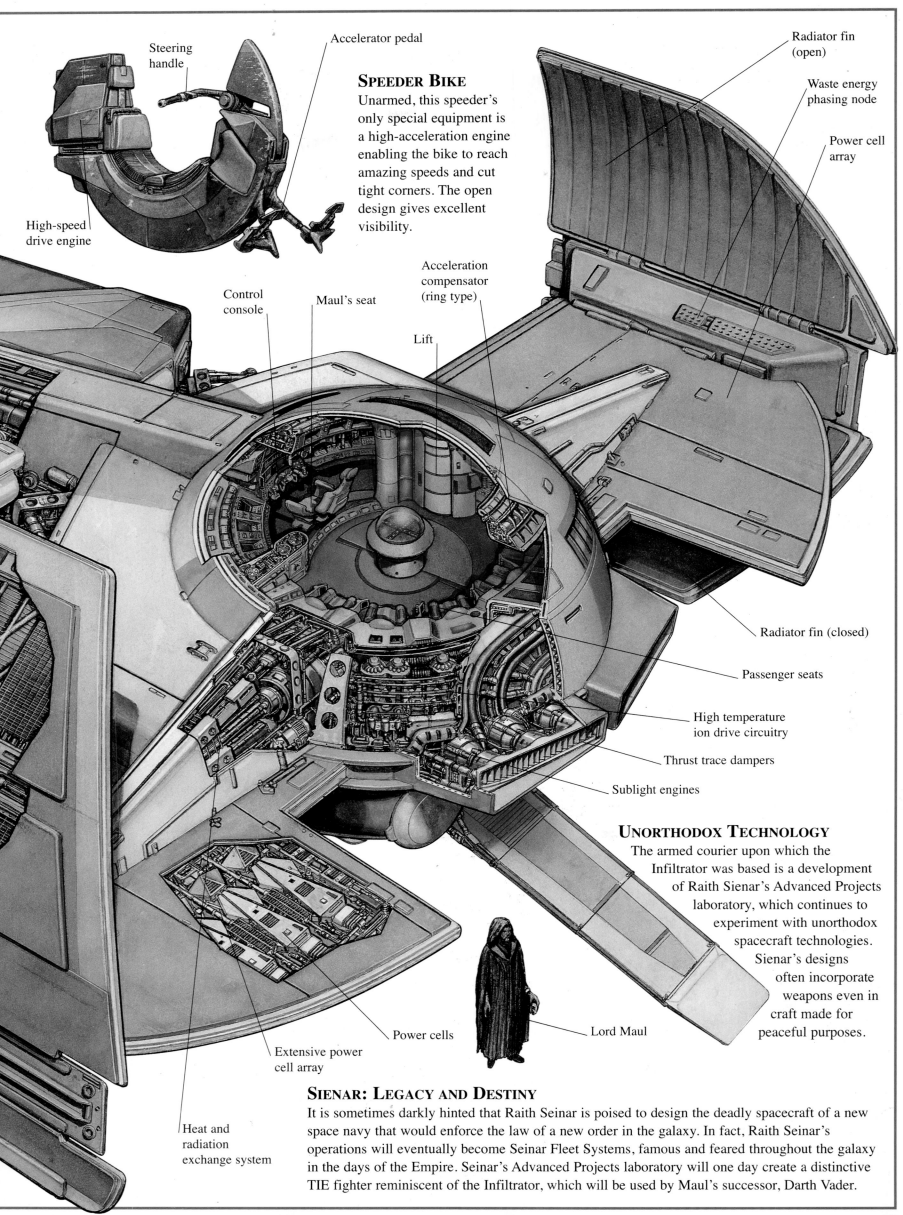

Steering handle

Accelerator pedal

High-speed drive engine

SPEEDER BIKE
Unarmed, this speeder's only special equipment is a high-acceleration engine enabling the bike to reach amazing speeds and cut tight corners. The open design gives excellent visibility.

Radiator fin (open)

Waste energy phasing node

Power cell array

Control console

Maul's seat

Acceleration compensator (ring type)

Lift

Radiator fin (closed)

Passenger seats

High temperature ion drive circuitry

Thrust trace dampers

Sublight engines

UNORTHODOX TECHNOLOGY
The armed courier upon which the Infiltrator was based is a development of Raith Sienar's Advanced Projects laboratory, which continues to experiment with unorthodox spacecraft technologies. Sienar's designs often incorporate weapons even in craft made for peaceful purposes.

Lord Maul

Power cells

Extensive power cell array

Heat and radiation exchange system

SIENAR: LEGACY AND DESTINY
It is sometimes darkly hinted that Raith Seinar is poised to design the deadly spacecraft of a new space navy that would enforce the law of a new order in the galaxy. In fact, Raith Seinar's operations will eventually become Seinar Fleet Systems, famous and feared throughout the galaxy in the days of the Empire. Seinar's Advanced Projects laboratory will one day create a distinctive TIE fighter reminiscent of the Infiltrator, which will be used by Maul's successor, Darth Vader.

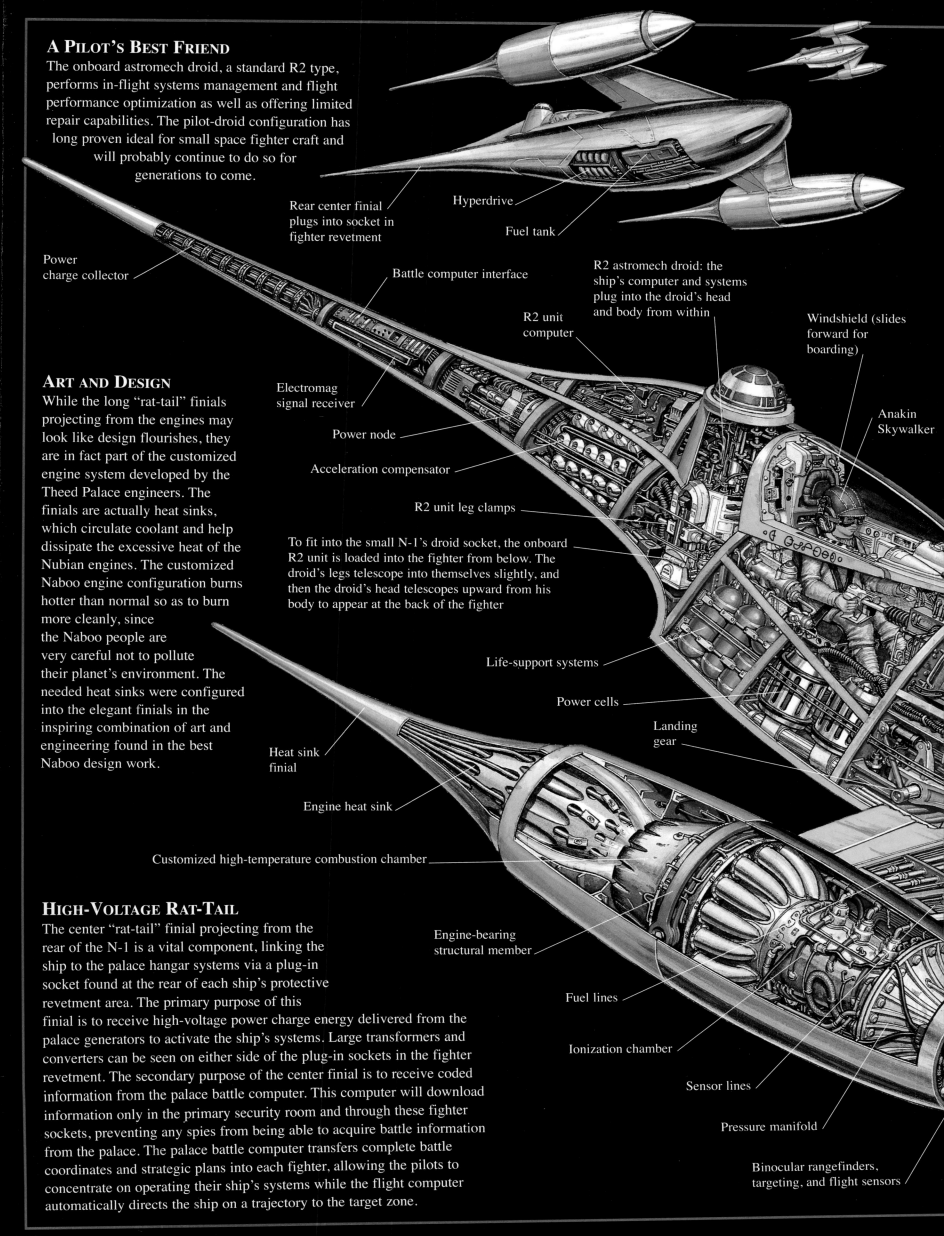

A Pilot's Best Friend

The onboard astromech droid, a standard R2 type, performs in-flight systems management and flight performance optimization as well as offering limited repair capabilities. The pilot-droid configuration has long proven ideal for small space fighter craft and will probably continue to do so for generations to come.

Rear center finial plugs into socket in fighter revetment

Hyperdrive

Fuel tank

Power charge collector

Battle computer interface

R2 astromech droid: the ship's computer and systems plug into the droid's head and body from within

R2 unit computer

Windshield (slides forward for boarding)

Anakin Skywalker

Art and Design

While the long "rat-tail" finials projecting from the engines may look like design flourishes, they are in fact part of the customized engine system developed by the Theed Palace engineers. The finials are actually heat sinks, which circulate coolant and help dissipate the excessive heat of the Nubian engines. The customized Naboo engine configuration burns hotter than normal so as to burn more cleanly, since the Naboo people are very careful not to pollute their planet's environment. The needed heat sinks were configured into the elegant finials in the inspiring combination of art and engineering found in the best Naboo design work.

Electromag signal receiver

Power node

Acceleration compensator

R2 unit leg clamps

To fit into the small N-1's droid socket, the onboard R2 unit is loaded into the fighter from below. The droid's legs telescope into themselves slightly, and then the droid's head telescopes upward from his body to appear at the back of the fighter

Life-support systems

Power cells

Landing gear

Heat sink finial

Engine heat sink

Customized high-temperature combustion chamber

High-Voltage Rat-Tail

The center "rat-tail" finial projecting from the rear of the N-1 is a vital component, linking the ship to the palace hangar systems via a plug-in socket found at the rear of each ship's protective revetment area. The primary purpose of this finial is to receive high-voltage power charge energy delivered from the palace generators to activate the ship's systems. Large transformers and converters can be seen on either side of the plug-in sockets in the fighter revetment. The secondary purpose of the center finial is to receive coded information from the palace battle computer. This computer will download information only in the primary security room and through these fighter sockets, preventing any spies from being able to acquire battle information from the palace. The palace battle computer transfers complete battle coordinates and strategic plans into each fighter, allowing the pilots to concentrate on operating their ship's systems while the flight computer automatically directs the ship on a trajectory to the target zone.

Engine-bearing structural member

Fuel lines

Ionization chamber

Sensor lines

Pressure manifold

Binocular rangefinders, targeting, and flight sensors

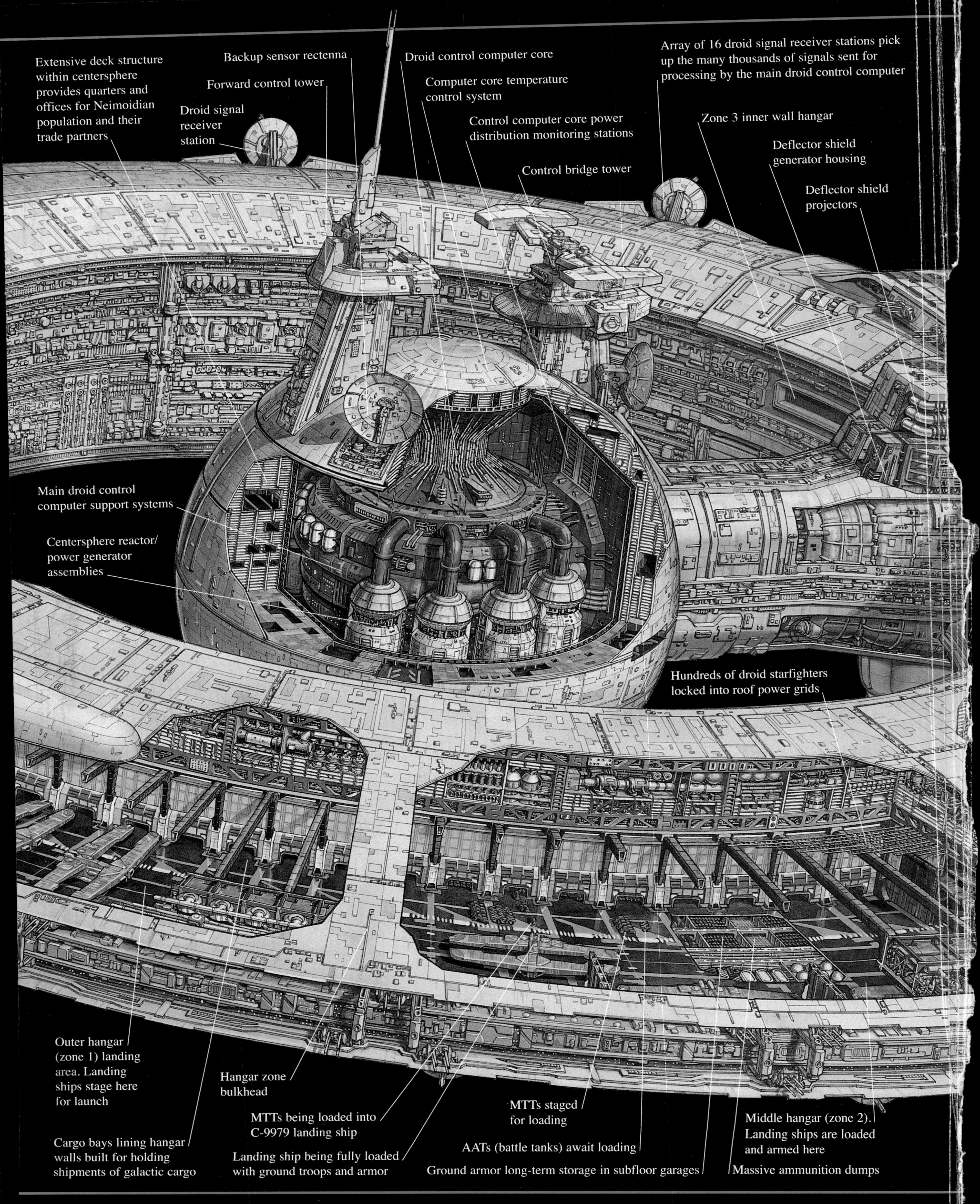

Extensive deck structure within centersphere provides quarters and offices for Neimoidian population and their trade partners

Backup sensor rectenna

Forward control tower

Droid signal receiver station

Droid control computer core

Computer core temperature control system

Control computer core power distribution monitoring stations

Control bridge tower

Array of 16 droid signal receiver stations pick up the many thousands of signals sent for processing by the main droid control computer

Zone 3 inner wall hangar

Deflector shield generator housing

Deflector shield projectors

Main droid control computer support systems

Centersphere reactor/ power generator assemblies

Hundreds of droid starfighters locked into roof power grids

Outer hangar (zone 1) landing area. Landing ships stage here for launch

Hangar zone bulkhead

MTTs being loaded into C-9979 landing ship

Landing ship being fully loaded with ground troops and armor

MTTs staged for loading

AATs (battle tanks) await loading

Ground armor long-term storage in subfloor garages

Middle hangar (zone 2). Landing ships are loaded and armed here

Massive ammunition dumps

Cargo bays lining hangar walls built for holding shipments of galactic cargo

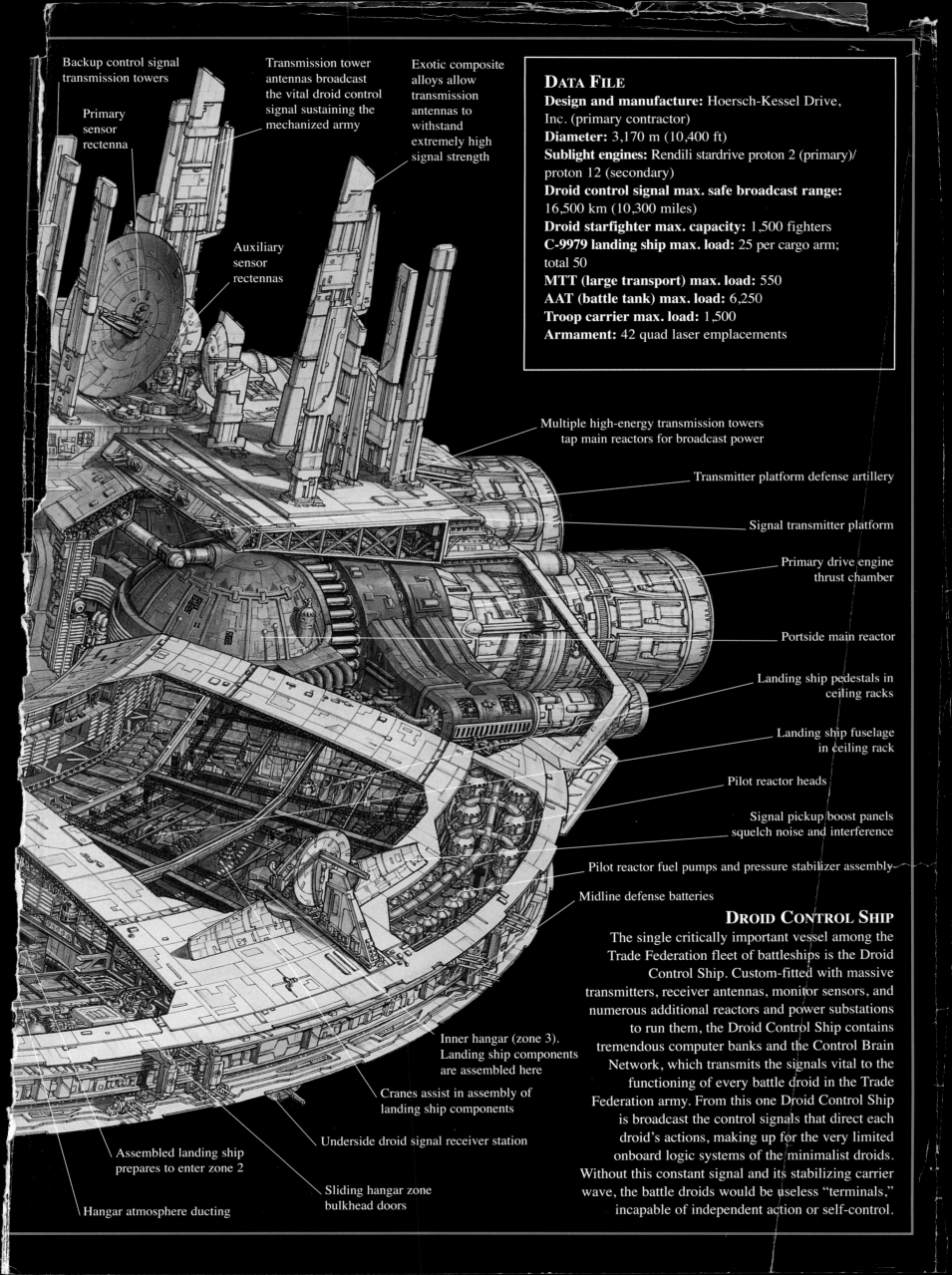

Backup control signal transmission towers

Primary sensor rectenna

Transmission tower antennas broadcast the vital droid control signal sustaining the mechanized army

Exotic composite alloys allow transmission antennas to withstand extremely high signal strength

Auxiliary sensor rectennas

DATA FILE
Design and manufacture: Hoersch-Kessel Drive, Inc. (primary contractor)
Diameter: 3,170 m (10,400 ft)
Sublight engines: Rendili stardrive proton 2 (primary)/ proton 12 (secondary)
Droid control signal max. safe broadcast range: 16,500 km (10,300 miles)
Droid starfighter max. capacity: 1,500 fighters
C-9979 landing ship max. load: 25 per cargo arm; total 50
MTT (large transport) max. load: 550
AAT (battle tank) max. load: 6,250
Troop carrier max. load: 1,500
Armament: 42 quad laser emplacements

Multiple high-energy transmission towers tap main reactors for broadcast power

Transmitter platform defense artillery

Signal transmitter platform

Primary drive engine thrust chamber

Portside main reactor

Landing ship pedestals in ceiling racks

Landing ship fuselage in ceiling rack

Pilot reactor heads

Signal pickup boost panels squelch noise and interference

Pilot reactor fuel pumps and pressure stabilizer assembly

Midline defense batteries

DROID CONTROL SHIP
The single critically important vessel among the Trade Federation fleet of battleships is the Droid Control Ship. Custom-fitted with massive transmitters, receiver antennas, monitor sensors, and numerous additional reactors and power substations to run them, the Droid Control Ship contains tremendous computer banks and the Control Brain Network, which transmits the signals vital to the functioning of every battle droid in the Trade Federation army. From this one Droid Control Ship is broadcast the control signals that direct each droid's actions, making up for the very limited onboard logic systems of the minimalist droids. Without this constant signal and its stabilizing carrier wave, the battle droids would be useless "terminals," incapable of independent action or self-control.

Inner hangar (zone 3). Landing ship components are assembled here

Cranes assist in assembly of landing ship components

Underside droid signal receiver station

Assembled landing ship prepares to enter zone 2

Sliding hangar zone bulkhead doors

Hangar atmosphere ducting

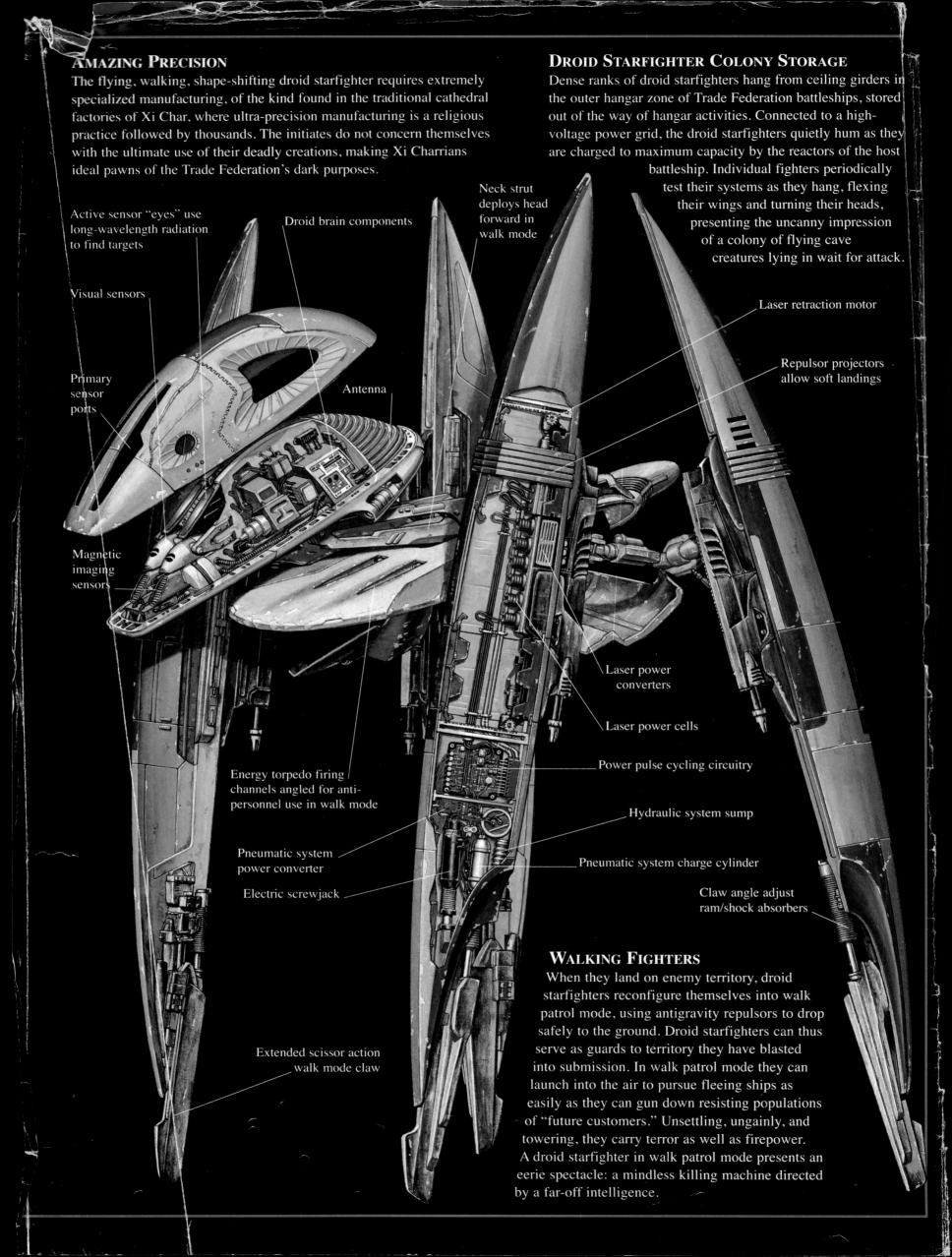

AMAZING PRECISION

The flying, walking, shape-shifting droid starfighter requires extremely specialized manufacturing, of the kind found in the traditional cathedral factories of Xi Char, where ultra-precision manufacturing is a religious practice followed by thousands. The initiates do not concern themselves with the ultimate use of their deadly creations, making Xi Charrians ideal pawns of the Trade Federation's dark purposes.

DROID STARFIGHTER COLONY STORAGE

Dense ranks of droid starfighters hang from ceiling girders in the outer hangar zone of Trade Federation battleships, stored out of the way of hangar activities. Connected to a high-voltage power grid, the droid starfighters quietly hum as they are charged to maximum capacity by the reactors of the host battleship. Individual fighters periodically test their systems as they hang, flexing their wings and turning their heads, presenting the uncanny impression of a colony of flying cave creatures lying in wait for attack.

Active sensor "eyes" use long-wavelength radiation to find targets

Droid brain components

Visual sensors

Neck strut deploys head forward in walk mode

Laser retraction motor

Primary sensor ports

Antenna

Repulsor projectors allow soft landings

Magnetic imaging sensors

Laser power converters

Energy torpedo firing channels angled for anti-personnel use in walk mode

Laser power cells

Power pulse cycling circuitry

Pneumatic system power converter

Hydraulic system sump

Electric screwjack

Pneumatic system charge cylinder

Claw angle adjust ram/shock absorbers

WALKING FIGHTERS

When they land on enemy territory, droid starfighters reconfigure themselves into walk patrol mode, using antigravity repulsors to drop safely to the ground. Droid starfighters can thus serve as guards to territory they have blasted into submission. In walk patrol mode they can launch into the air to pursue fleeing ships as easily as they can gun down resisting populations of "future customers." Unsettling, ungainly, and towering, they carry terror as well as firepower. A droid starfighter in walk patrol mode presents an eerie spectacle: a mindless killing machine directed by a far-off intelligence.

Extended scissor action walk mode claw

NABOO N-1 STARFIGHTER

THE SINGLE PILOT NABOO ROYAL N-1 STARFIGHTER was developed by the Theed Palace Space Vessel Engineering Corps for the volunteer Royal Naboo Security Forces. Sleek and agile, the small N-1 faces aggressors with twin blaster cannons and a double magazine of proton torpedoes. Found only on Naboo and rarely seen even there, the N-1, like the Queen's Royal Starship, uses many galactic standard internal components in a custom-built spaceframe that reflects the Naboo people's love of handcrafted, elegant shapes. The Naboo engineers fabricate some of their own parts such as fuel tanks and sensor antennas, but most of the high-technology gear is acquired through trade from other, more industrialized worlds. The Theed Palace engineers developed a customized engine system, however, based on a standard Nubian drive motor but modified significantly to release fewer emissions into the atmosphere. The Naboo being a peaceful people, the Space Fighter Corps is maintained as much through tradition as for military defense, and primarily serves as an honor guard for the Queen's Royal Starship. Nonetheless, the Royal Naboo Security Forces train in the N-1s on a regular basis, prepared for the honor of serving the Queen in combat if necessary, since service to the Queen symbolizes service to the great free people of Naboo themselves.

THAT GLEAMING ROYAL LOOK
The N-1 fighter sports a gleaming chromium finish on its forward surfaces. Purely decorative, this finish indicates the ship's royal allegiance. Early Naboo spacecraft required a chromelike finish for protection from harmful rays in the planet's upper atmosphere. Now that spacecraft and their pilots are fully shielded from such rays by electromagnetic field technology, the chrome finish is retained for tradition and kept as a royal symbol. Only royal ships may carry the hand-finished royal chromium treatment.

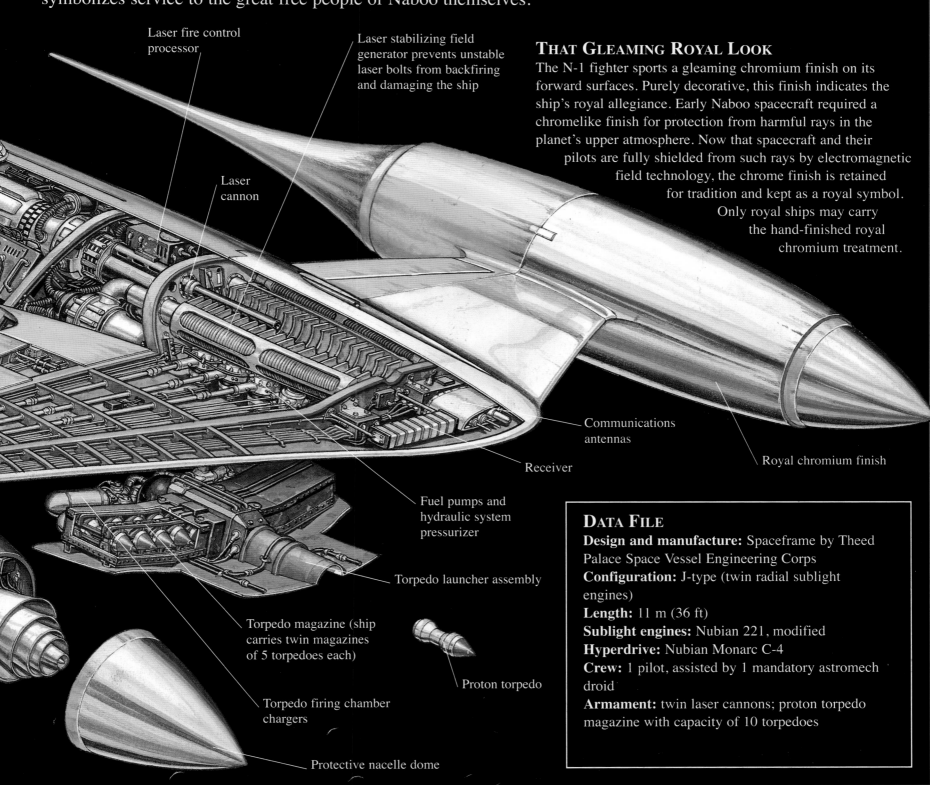

Laser fire control processor

Laser stabilizing field generator prevents unstable laser bolts from backfiring and damaging the ship

Laser cannon

Communications antennas

Receiver

Fuel pumps and hydraulic system pressurizer

Royal chromium finish

Torpedo launcher assembly

Torpedo magazine (ship carries twin magazines of 5 torpedoes each)

Proton torpedo

Torpedo firing chamber chargers

Protective nacelle dome

DATA FILE
Design and manufacture: Spaceframe by Theed Palace Space Vessel Engineering Corps
Configuration: J-type (twin radial sublight engines)
Length: 11 m (36 ft)
Sublight engines: Nubian 221, modified
Hyperdrive: Nubian Monarc C-4
Crew: 1 pilot, assisted by 1 mandatory astromech droid
Armament: twin laser cannons; proton torpedo magazine with capacity of 10 torpedoes

AAT (BATTLE TANK)

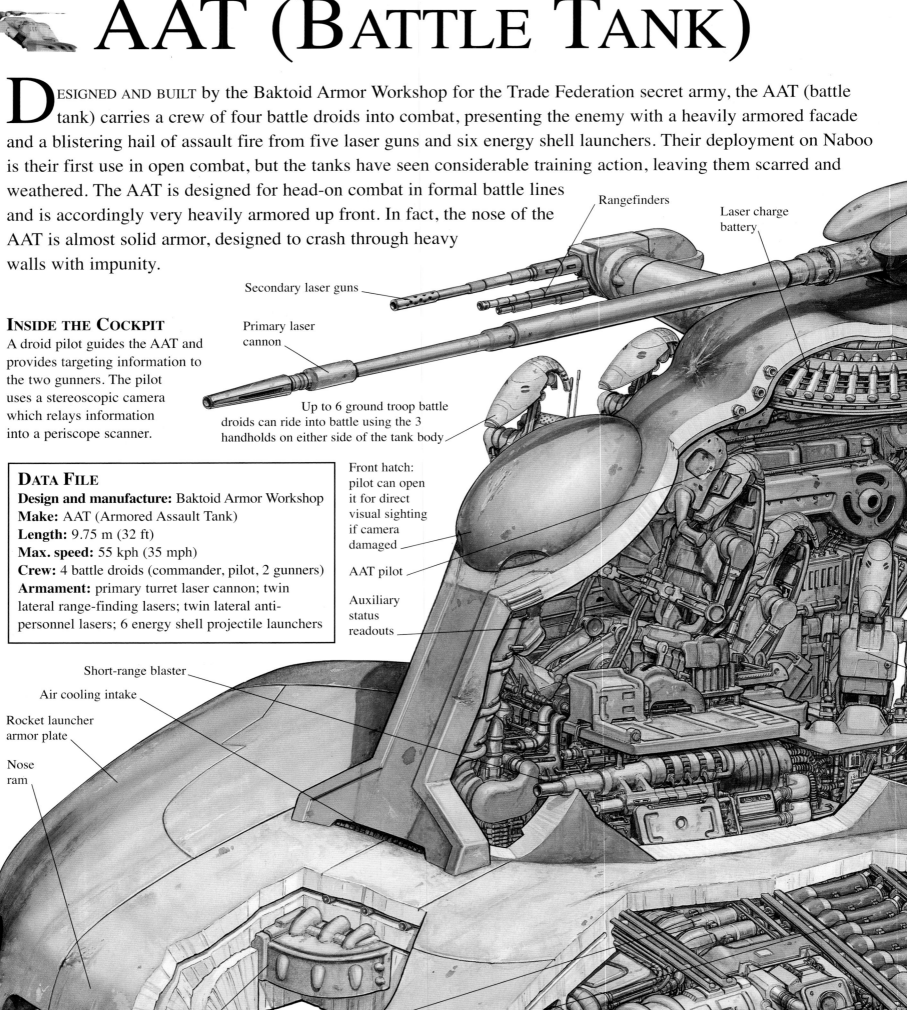

DESIGNED AND BUILT by the Baktoid Armor Workshop for the Trade Federation secret army, the AAT (battle tank) carries a crew of four battle droids into combat, presenting the enemy with a heavily armored facade and a blistering hail of assault fire from five laser guns and six energy shell launchers. Their deployment on Naboo is their first use in open combat, but the tanks have seen considerable training action, leaving them scarred and weathered. The AAT is designed for head-on combat in formal battle lines and is accordingly very heavily armored up front. In fact, the nose of the AAT is almost solid armor, designed to crash through heavy walls with impunity.

INSIDE THE COCKPIT

A droid pilot guides the AAT and provides targeting information to the two gunners. The pilot uses a stereoscopic camera which relays information into a periscope scanner.

DATA FILE

Design and manufacture: Baktoid Armor Workshop
Make: AAT (Armored Assault Tank)
Length: 9.75 m (32 ft)
Max. speed: 55 kph (35 mph)
Crew: 4 battle droids (commander, pilot, 2 gunners)
Armament: primary turret laser cannon; twin lateral range-finding lasers; twin lateral anti-personnel lasers; 6 energy shell projectile launchers

Rangefinders

Laser charge battery

Secondary laser guns

Primary laser cannon

Up to 6 ground troop battle droids can ride into battle using the 3 handholds on either side of the tank body

Front hatch: pilot can open it for direct visual sighting if camera damaged

AAT pilot

Auxiliary status readouts

Short-range blaster

Air cooling intake

Rocket launcher armor plate

Nose ram

Heavy solid plate armor

Forward repulsor disc

Bunker-busting shells

Armor-piercing shells

Energy cocooning chamber

Launch tube

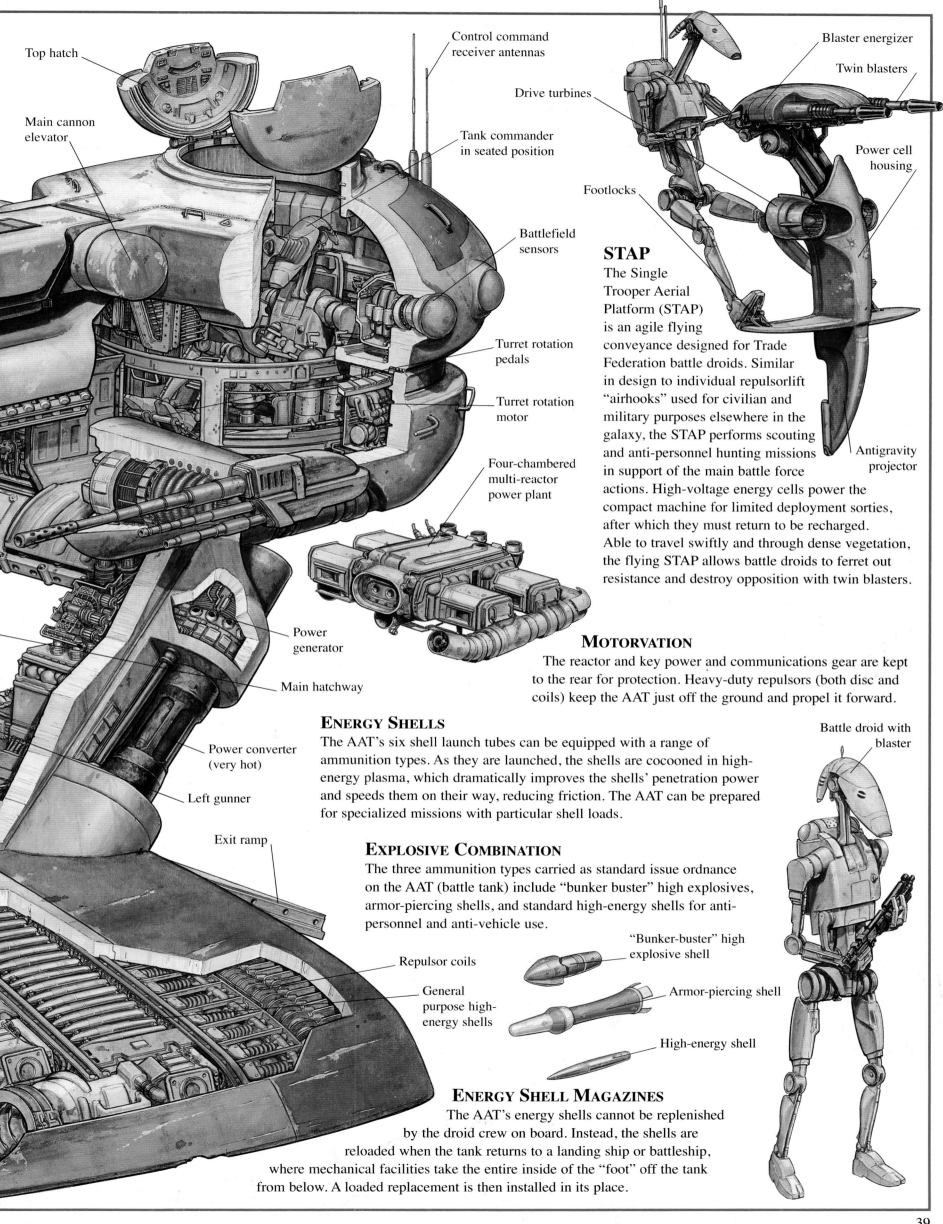

Top hatch

Main cannon
elevator

Control command
receiver antennas

Drive turbines

Tank commander
in seated position

Footlocks

Battlefield
sensors

Turret rotation
pedals

Turret rotation
motor

Four-chambered
multi-reactor
power plant

Power
generator

Main hatchway

Power converter
(very hot)

Left gunner

Exit ramp

Repulsor coils

General
purpose high-
energy shells

Blaster energizer

Twin blasters

Power cell
housing

Antigravity
projector

STAP

The Single
Trooper Aerial
Platform (STAP)
is an agile flying
conveyance designed for Trade
Federation battle droids. Similar
in design to individual repulsorlift
"airhooks" used for civilian and
military purposes elsewhere in the
galaxy, the STAP performs scouting
and anti-personnel hunting missions
in support of the main battle force
actions. High-voltage energy cells power the
compact machine for limited deployment sorties,
after which they must return to be recharged.
Able to travel swiftly and through dense vegetation,
the flying STAP allows battle droids to ferret out
resistance and destroy opposition with twin blasters.

MOTORVATION

The reactor and key power and communications gear are kept
to the rear for protection. Heavy-duty repulsors (both disc and
coils) keep the AAT just off the ground and propel it forward.

ENERGY SHELLS

The AAT's six shell launch tubes can be equipped with a range of
ammunition types. As they are launched, the shells are cocooned in high-
energy plasma, which dramatically improves the shells' penetration power
and speeds them on their way, reducing friction. The AAT can be prepared
for specialized missions with particular shell loads.

Battle droid with
blaster

EXPLOSIVE COMBINATION

The three ammunition types carried as standard issue ordnance
on the AAT (battle tank) include "bunker buster" high explosives,
armor-piercing shells, and standard high-energy shells for anti-
personnel and anti-vehicle use.

"Bunker-buster" high
explosive shell

Armor-piercing shell

High-energy shell

ENERGY SHELL MAGAZINES

The AAT's energy shells cannot be replenished
by the droid crew on board. Instead, the shells are
reloaded when the tank returns to a landing ship or battleship,
where mechanical facilities take the entire inside of the "foot" off the tank
from below. A loaded replacement is then installed in its place.

NABOO SPEEDERS

T HE SMALL GROUND CRAFT of the Naboo Royal Security volunteers are only lightly armed and armored, since they patrol a fairly peaceful society. They are designed for rapid pursuit and capture of troublemakers rather than combat with an armed enemy. The Flash and Gian speeders are the most common Naboo ground security craft, both vehicles bearing mounts for laser weapons which are sent into action only when such force is absolutely necessary. The Flash speeder is an agile general-use craft with thrust engines finely tuned to give the pilot good control on narrow city streets. The Gian speeder is a heavier and less maneuverable vehicle, which is used for forays outside the cities against more serious foes. Extra underside plating protects the Gian speeder from unexpected land mines and rugged ground obstacles.

DATA FILE – FLASH SPEEDER
Length: 4.5 m (14$\frac{1}{2}$ ft)
Crew: 1
Passengers: 1
Armament: 1 laser blaster

DATA FILE – GIAN SPEEDER
Length: 5.7 m (18$\frac{1}{2}$ ft)
Crew: 1 pilot, 1 gunner
Passengers: 2
Armament: 3 laser blasters

FLASH SPEEDERS
One of several small ground vehicles used by the Royal Naboo Security Forces, the Flash landspeeder serves for street patrol and high-speed pursuit of malefactors. The craft normally flies less than a meter off the ground and at maximum can attain a "float" of a couple of meters, but no more is necessary on the paved streets and level grasslands of Naboo. Only slightly modified from the civilian model of the Flash speeder, the craft is nonetheless patrol-grade and built of reliable and sturdy construction.

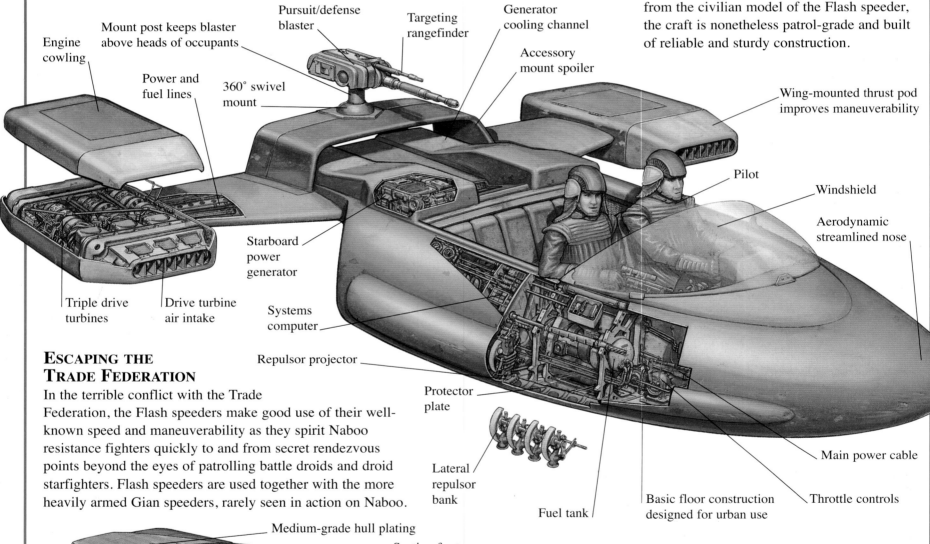

Engine cowling

Mount post keeps blaster above heads of occupants

Pursuit/defense blaster

Targeting rangefinder

Generator cooling channel

Accessory mount spoiler

Power and fuel lines

360° swivel mount

Wing-mounted thrust pod improves maneuverability

Pilot

Windshield

Aerodynamic streamlined nose

Starboard power generator

Triple drive turbines

Drive turbine air intake

Systems computer

Repulsor projector

Protector plate

Lateral repulsor bank

Fuel tank

Basic floor construction designed for urban use

Main power cable

Throttle controls

ESCAPING THE TRADE FEDERATION
In the terrible conflict with the Trade Federation, the Flash speeders make good use of their well-known speed and maneuverability as they spirit Naboo resistance fighters quickly to and from secret rendezvous points beyond the eyes of patrolling battle droids and droid starfighters. Flash speeders are used together with the more heavily armed Gian speeders, rarely seen in action on Naboo.

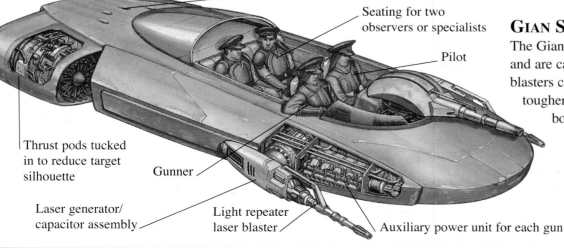

Medium-grade hull plating

Seating for two observers or specialists

Pilot

Thrust pods tucked in to reduce target silhouette

Gunner

Laser generator/ capacitor assembly

Light repeater laser blaster

Auxiliary power unit for each gun

GIAN SPEEDERS
The Gian speeders are heavier vehicles than the Flash speeders and are called out only for serious situations. Their three laser blasters can easily disable non-military vehicles. They have tougher hulls than ordinary civilian craft and their reinforced bodies allow them to withstand glancing hits. Their compact forward silhouette, with thrust pods tucked in behind rather than out on wing struts, makes the Gian less maneuverable but a harder target for enemies both in front and behind. To assist in tactical deployments, these speeders can be equipped with customized holographic planning systems.

CORUSCANT TAXI

THE AIR TAXI SHOOTING THROUGH the vast open spaces between the high skyscrapers is one of the most characteristic sights of the famous metropolis world of Coruscant. These air taxis are allowed unrestricted "free travel" and can thus leave the autonavigating skylanes to take the most direct routes to their destination. Skylanes confine most vehicles on long-distance journeys along defined corridors, without which there would be unmanageable chaos in the air. To rate "free travel," air taxi pilots must pass demanding tests that prove their ability to navigate the unique cityscape with skill and safety. They depend on their scanners, keen eyes, and instinct to avoid crashing into other craft, sending passengers plunging into the street canyons far below.

DATA FILE
Length: 8 m (25 ft)
Top speed: 191 kph (115 mph)
Max. altitude: 3.4 km (2.1 miles)
Normal max. trip range: 210 km (131 miles)
Crew: 1
Passengers: depends on species
Armament: none

Communications antenna

Turbine allows rapid acceleration

Efficient drive engine requires a minimum of fuel

Forward motion engine

Guidance computer balances navigational control between lift repulsors, steering repulsors, and drive engines

Luggage can be stored in crossbar compartments

Seats emit mild tractor field in flight to hold passengers securely inside without belts

Headlight circuitry varies spectrum output of beams

Simple construction designed for easy maintenance and repair

Drive engine housing

Multi-spectrum headlights

Side-mounted, low-power repulsors prevent collision and cushion docking

Signal receivers built into body frame pick up air traffic control transmissions

Lift repulsor carries taxi to great skyscraper heights

Precision stabilizing and steering radial repulsor array helps taxi navigate in crowded urban skylanes

WELL-EQUIPPED AIR TAXIS

The standard modern Coruscant air taxi uses a compact, focused, medium-grade repulsor to elevate it to the very highest skyscraper peaks. A radial battery of lower-powered antigravity devices gives it good navigational control in the open air, allowing it to swoop with accuracy around the aerial architecture, docking gently at its final destination. A refined, relatively quiet thrust engine propels the craft with surprising acceleration. Excellent receiver equipment monitors the many channels of Coruscant Air Traffic Control, allowing the pilot to use autonavigation or manual control at any time.

ABOVE AND BELOW

All significant traffic on Coruscant is air traffic – the original ground levels and roads having long ago been abandoned. Sealed tunnels in the lower realms allow for the transport of goods and materials through the city, as bulk shipments are barred by law from the crowded skylanes reserved for travelers.

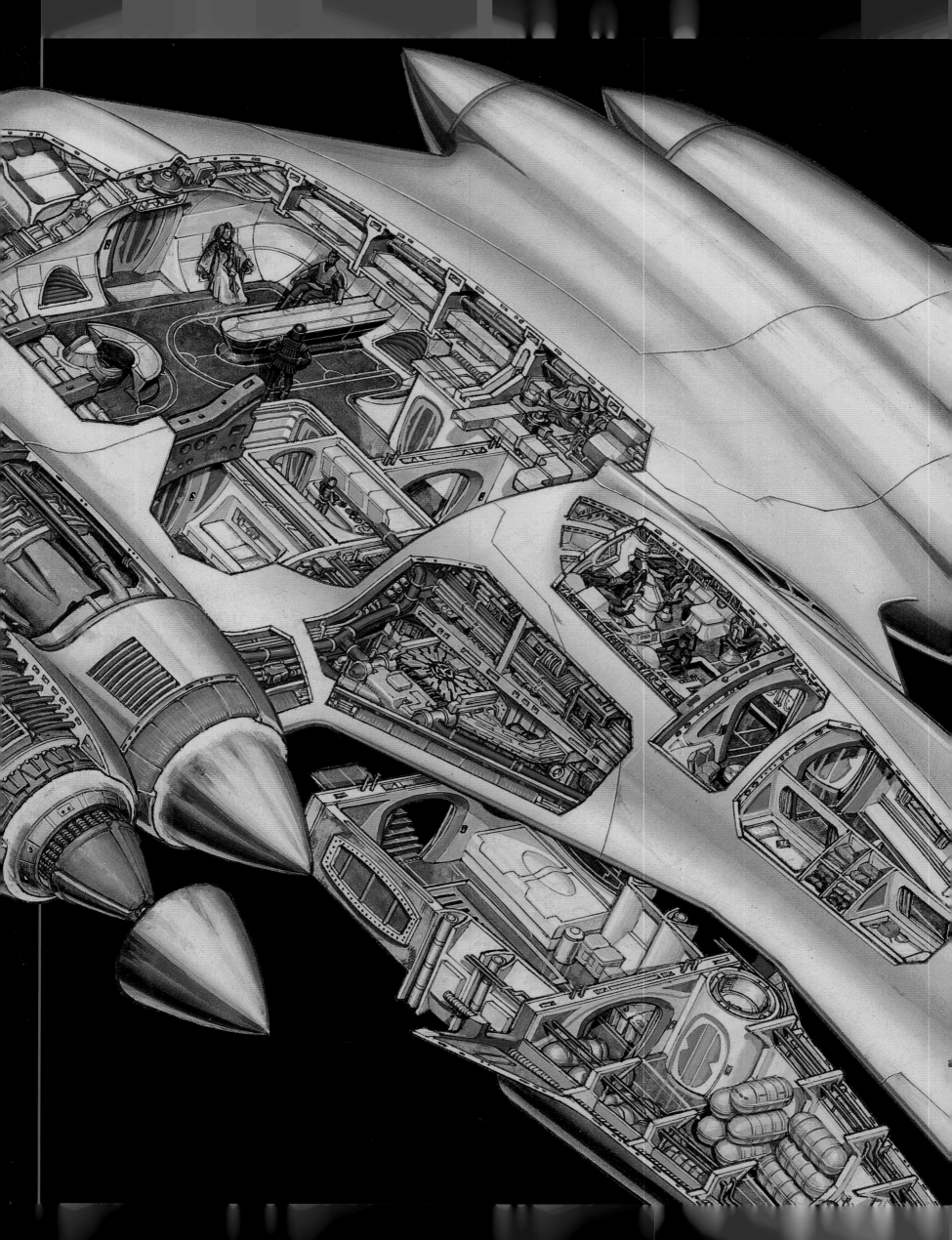

EPISODE II
ATTACK OF THE CLONES

A DECADE HAS PASSED since the Trade Federation's blockade of Naboo. The unity of the galaxy is under threat as thousands of star systems break away from the Republic to join the Separatist movement, an organization led by the enigmatic Count Dooku. The Separatists' actions have made it difficult for the limited number of Jedi Knights to maintain peace and order in the galaxy. After a divisive debate, the Senate passes the Military Creation Act, legitimizing the Republic's use of a clone army to counter the Separatist threat. Anakin Skywalker, now a Jedi Padawan, is apprenticed to Obi-Wan Kenobi, but Anakin's impatient nature is a source of much frustration to his Jedi mentor. Supreme Chancellor Palpatine takes an interest in Kenobi's apprentice, nurturing Anakin's growing dissatisfaction with the Jedi order. And as the galaxy teeters on the brink of war, the friendship between Anakin and Senator Padmé Amidala blossoms into a secret, forbidden love.

NABOO CRUISER

FEW ARE SURPRISED when Padmé Amidala descends from the throne of Naboo into the wider responsibilities of an appointment to the Senate. In fact, her esteem at the Naboo court remains so high that she continues to use a starship that features the highly distinctive chrome plating and sleek sculpting previously reserved exclusively for monarchs. Befitting one of the latest models from Theed Hangar, the Naboo Cruiser is so finely polished that only the intentionally decorative seams remain visible. Though not armed itself, the Cruiser travels with a guard convoy of starfighters, which escorts the ship to its ill-fated arrival on Coruscant.

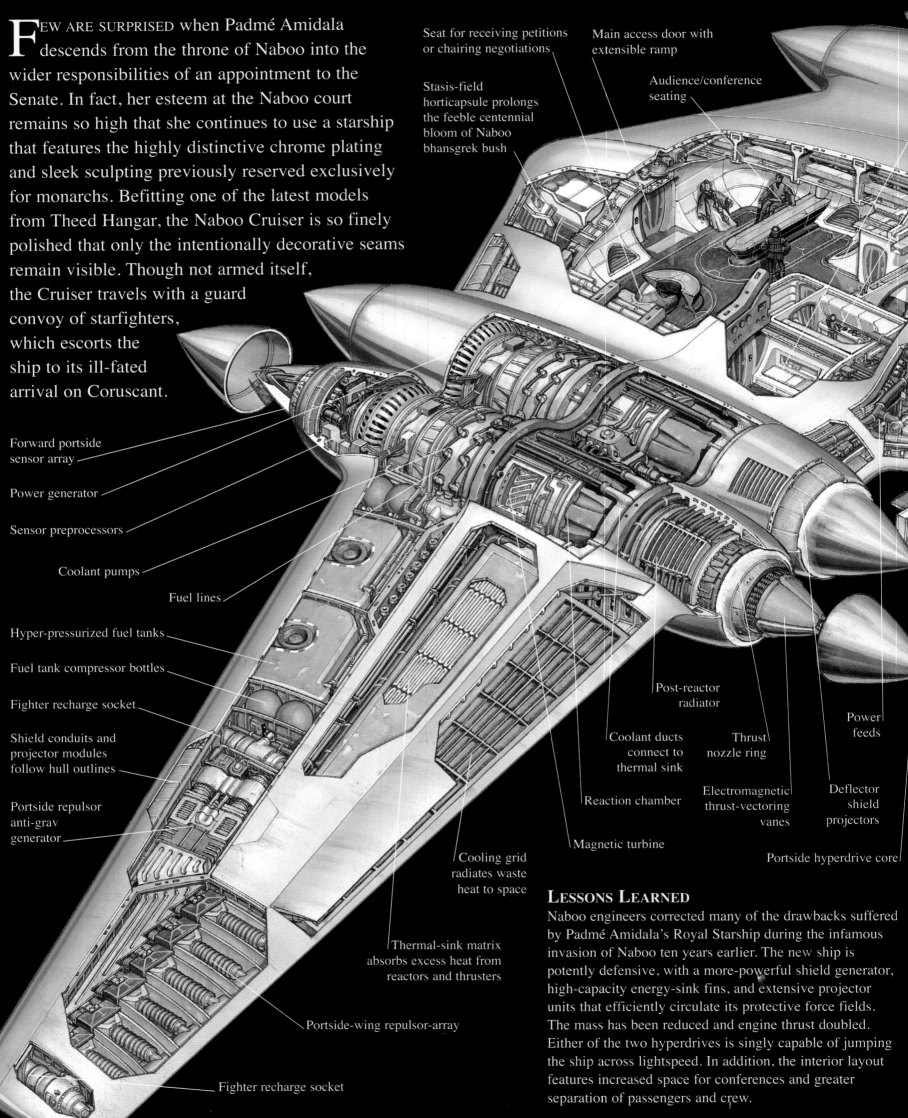

Seat for receiving petitions or chairing negotiations

Main access door with extensible ramp

Stasis-field horticapsule prolongs the feeble centennial bloom of Naboo bhansgrek bush

Audience/conference seating

Forward portside sensor array

Power generator

Sensor preprocessors

Coolant pumps

Fuel lines

Hyper-pressurized fuel tanks

Fuel tank compressor bottles

Fighter recharge socket

Shield conduits and projector modules follow hull outlines

Portside repulsor anti-grav generator

Post-reactor radiator

Power feeds

Coolant ducts connect to thermal sink

Thrust nozzle ring

Reaction chamber

Electromagnetic thrust-vectoring vanes

Deflector shield projectors

Magnetic turbine

Portside hyperdrive core

Cooling grid radiates waste heat to space

Thermal-sink matrix absorbs excess heat from reactors and thrusters

Portside-wing repulsor-array

Fighter recharge socket

LESSONS LEARNED

Naboo engineers corrected many of the drawbacks suffered by Padmé Amidala's Royal Starship during the infamous invasion of Naboo ten years earlier. The new ship is potently defensive, with a more-powerful shield generator, high-capacity energy-sink fins, and extensive projector units that efficiently circulate its protective force fields. The mass has been reduced and engine thrust doubled. Either of the two hyperdrives is singly capable of jumping the ship across lightspeed. In addition, the interior layout features increased space for conferences and greater separation of passengers and crew.

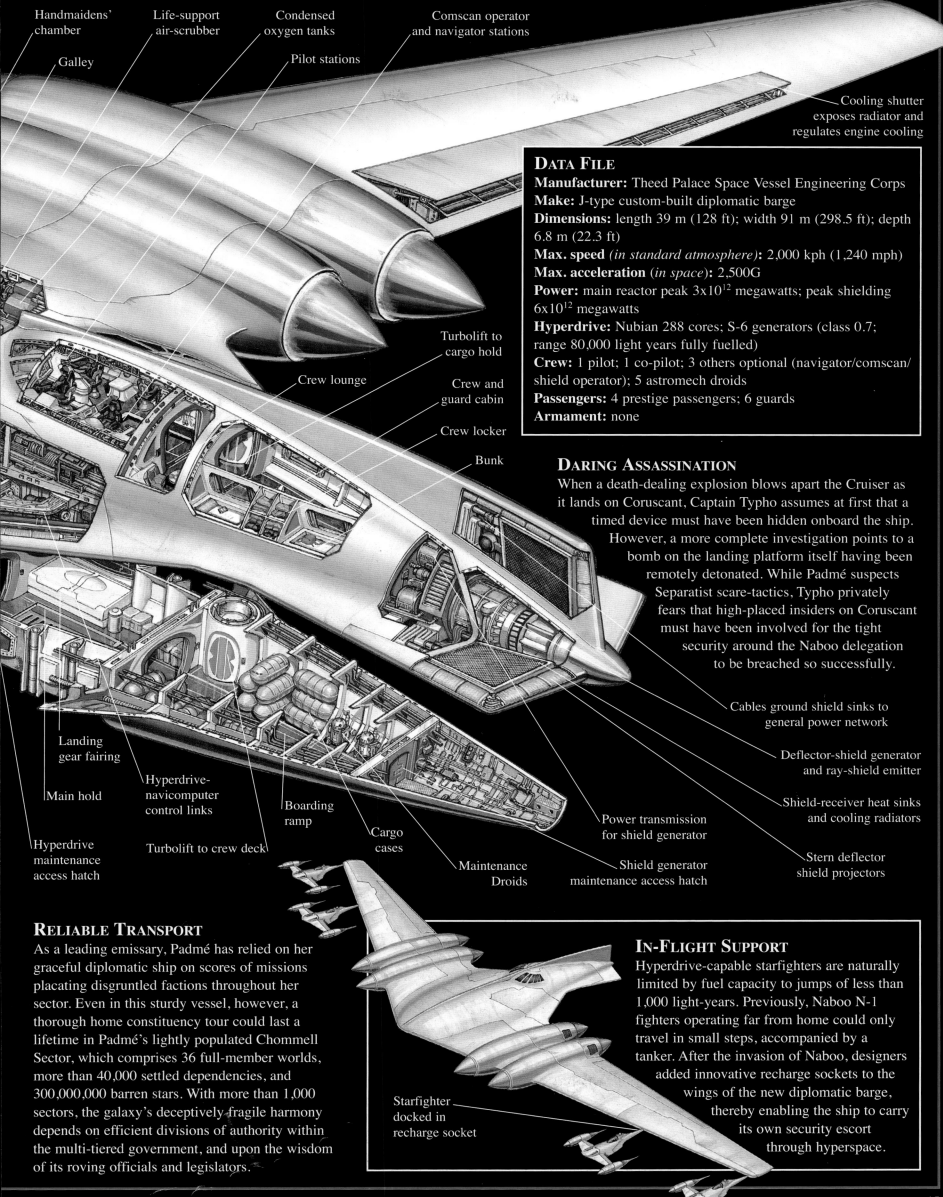

Handmaidens'
chamber

Life-support
air-scrubber

Condensed
oxygen tanks

Comscan operator
and navigator stations

Galley

Pilot stations

Cooling shutter
exposes radiator and
regulates engine cooling

Turbolift to
cargo hold

Crew lounge

Crew and
guard cabin

Crew locker

Bunk

DATA FILE

Manufacturer: Theed Palace Space Vessel Engineering Corps
Make: J-type custom-built diplomatic barge
Dimensions: length 39 m (128 ft); width 91 m (298.5 ft); depth 6.8 m (22.3 ft)
Max. speed (*in standard atmosphere*)**:** 2,000 kph (1,240 mph)
Max. acceleration (*in space*)**:** 2,500G
Power: main reactor peak 3×10^{12} megawatts; peak shielding 6×10^{12} megawatts
Hyperdrive: Nubian 288 cores; S-6 generators (class 0.7; range 80,000 light years fully fuelled)
Crew: 1 pilot; 1 co-pilot; 3 others optional (navigator/comscan/shield operator); 5 astromech droids
Passengers: 4 prestige passengers; 6 guards
Armament: none

DARING ASSASSINATION

When a death-dealing explosion blows apart the Cruiser as it lands on Coruscant, Captain Typho assumes at first that a timed device must have been hidden onboard the ship. However, a more complete investigation points to a bomb on the landing platform itself having been remotely detonated. While Padmé suspects Separatist scare-tactics, Typho privately fears that high-placed insiders on Coruscant must have been involved for the tight security around the Naboo delegation to be breached so successfully.

Cables ground shield sinks to
general power network

Deflector-shield generator
and ray-shield emitter

Shield-receiver heat sinks
and cooling radiators

Stern deflector
shield projectors

Landing
gear fairing

Main hold

Hyperdrive
maintenance
access hatch

Hyperdrive-
navicomputer
control links

Turbolift to crew deck

Boarding
ramp

Cargo
cases

Maintenance
Droids

Power transmission
for shield generator

Shield generator
maintenance access hatch

RELIABLE TRANSPORT

As a leading emissary, Padmé has relied on her graceful diplomatic ship on scores of missions placating disgruntled factions throughout her sector. Even in this sturdy vessel, however, a thorough home constituency tour could last a lifetime in Padmé's lightly populated Chommell Sector, which comprises 36 full-member worlds, more than 40,000 settled dependencies, and 300,000,000 barren stars. With more than 1,000 sectors, the galaxy's deceptively fragile harmony depends on efficient divisions of authority within the multi-tiered government, and upon the wisdom of its roving officials and legislators.

Starfighter
docked in
recharge socket

IN-FLIGHT SUPPORT

Hyperdrive-capable starfighters are naturally limited by fuel capacity to jumps of less than 1,000 light-years. Previously, Naboo N-1 fighters operating far from home could only travel in small steps, accompanied by a tanker. After the invasion of Naboo, designers added innovative recharge sockets to the wings of the new diplomatic barge, thereby enabling the ship to carry its own security escort through hyperspace.

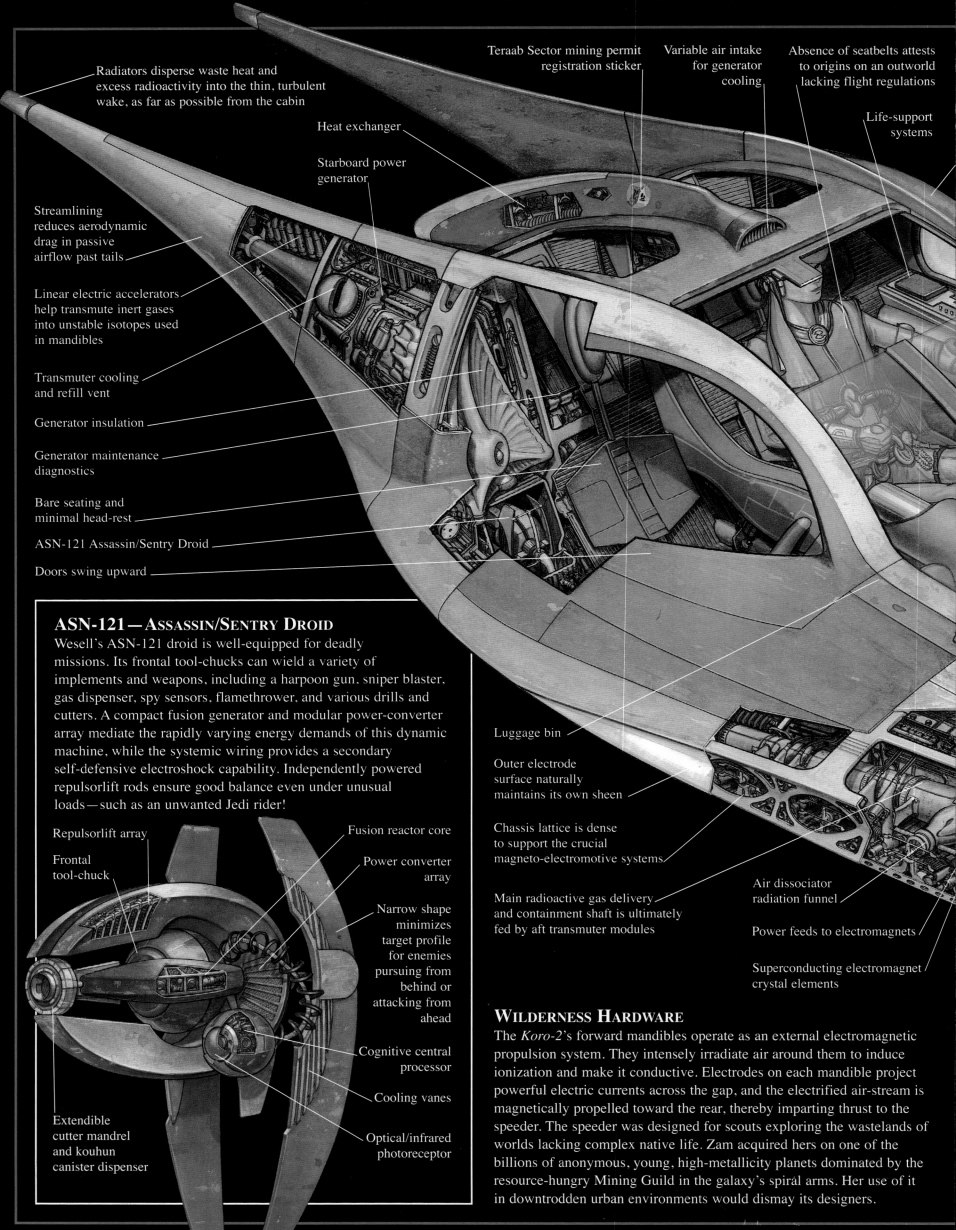

Radiators disperse waste heat and excess radioactivity into the thin, turbulent wake, as far as possible from the cabin

Heat exchanger

Starboard power generator

Teraab Sector mining permit registration sticker

Variable air intake for generator cooling

Absence of seatbelts attests to origins on an outworld lacking flight regulations

Life-support systems

Streamlining reduces aerodynamic drag in passive airflow past tails

Linear electric accelerators help transmute inert gases into unstable isotopes used in mandibles

Transmuter cooling and refill vent

Generator insulation

Generator maintenance diagnostics

Bare seating and minimal head-rest

ASN-121 Assassin/Sentry Droid

Doors swing upward

ASN-121—ASSASSIN/SENTRY DROID

Wesell's ASN-121 droid is well-equipped for deadly missions. Its frontal tool-chucks can wield a variety of implements and weapons, including a harpoon gun, sniper blaster, gas dispenser, spy sensors, flamethrower, and various drills and cutters. A compact fusion generator and modular power-converter array mediate the rapidly varying energy demands of this dynamic machine, while the systemic wiring provides a secondary self-defensive electroshock capability. Independently powered repulsorlift rods ensure good balance even under unusual loads—such as an unwanted Jedi rider!

Repulsorlift array

Frontal tool-chuck

Fusion reactor core

Power converter array

Narrow shape minimizes target profile for enemies pursuing from behind or attacking from ahead

Cognitive central processor

Cooling vanes

Optical/infrared photoreceptor

Extendible cutter mandrel and kouhun canister dispenser

Luggage bin

Outer electrode surface naturally maintains its own sheen

Chassis lattice is dense to support the crucial magneto-electromotive systems

Main radioactive gas delivery and containment shaft is ultimately fed by aft transmuter modules

Air dissociator radiation funnel

Power feeds to electromagnets

Superconducting electromagnet crystal elements

WILDERNESS HARDWARE

The *Koro-2*'s forward mandibles operate as an external electromagnetic propulsion system. They intensely irradiate air around them to induce ionization and make it conductive. Electrodes on each mandible project powerful electric currents across the gap, and the electrified air-stream is magnetically propelled toward the rear, thereby imparting thrust to the speeder. The speeder was designed for scouts exploring the wastelands of worlds lacking complex native life. Zam acquired hers on one of the billions of anonymous, young, high-metallicity planets dominated by the resource-hungry Mining Guild in the galaxy's spiral arms. Her use of it in downtrodden urban environments would dismay its designers.

ZAM'S AIRSPEEDER

Hired assassin Zam Wesell flies an airspeeder that is as unusual and exotic as she is herself. The totally self-enclosed craft has no external thrusters and few air intakes because it was built for use on hostile, primitive worlds. Its repulsorlift units provide anti-gravity support, while other mechanisms generate radiation and electromagnetic fields that move the craft by dragging upon the air. This system is versatile enough for use in a huge variety of atmospheres. However, in urban areas, outdoor power lines can snag the propulsion fields and confound the steering—although this merely provides an extra means of traction to a cunning mercenary like Wesell.

Airstream is mostly neutralized as it passes the cabin surface

Steering yokes control repulsorlift balance for banking turns

Compartment holds special oils for shape-shifting Clawdites

Dashboard navigation controls

Status lights indicate cabin non-contamination

Control displays

Pedals control power to mandible propulsion systems

Repulsorlift elements (under floor)

Fluorescent elements under translucent skin sense activity levels within operational ranges

Propulsion power systems, expanded upon standard model, protrude into mandible gap

Elongated storage bin for sniper rifle

Maintenance log capsule

Inner electrode surface

Re-transmuter refreshes radioactivity during idle periods

Pump circulates radioactive fluid

Propulsion system power cells

Vertical internal radiation shield

Irradiation gas distributor pipes

Shielded data cables connect frontal instruments to cabin controls

Adaptive tuner regulates performance of right mandible propulsion systems

Forward power cells

Forward-scanner ranging device

Inner electrode anti-surge sink

Isolation shroud protects scanner

Inner front surfaces have maximum piping density to provide the most intense irradiation

DATA FILE

Manufacturer: Desler Gizh Outworld Mobility Corp.
Make: *Koro-2* all-environment exodrive airspeeder
Dimensions: length 6.6 m (21.7 ft); width 2.1 m (7 ft); depth 0.9 m (3 ft)
Max. speed: 800 kph (496 mph)
Cargo capacity: 80 kg (176 lbs) or 0.04 m³ (1.4 ft³) in cabin and storage bins
Consumables: approx. five years' gas for irradiation system; two weeks' cabin air supply
Passengers: 1 (excluding driver)
Armament: none

DIRTY TECHNOLOGY

Zam's speeder creates some hazardous side-effects that amuse the callous hunter. Irradiation zones are constrained around the mandibles, but can sicken unknowing bystanders along the vehicle's path. Furthermore, drag-stream ions recombine chemically into unpleasant forms as they pass the cabin. In breathable atmospheres the products can include noxious gases that leave a foul reek in the speeder's wake.

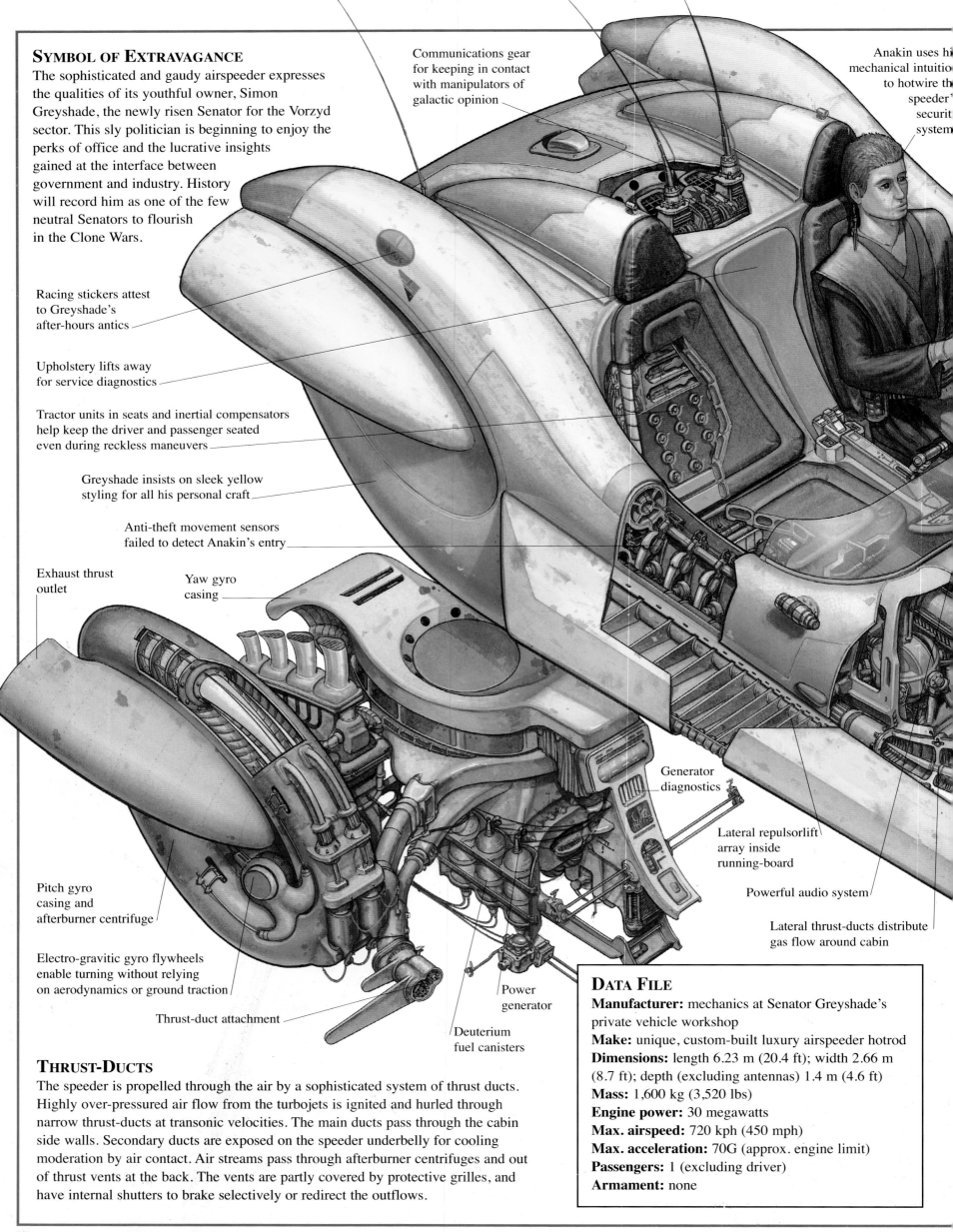

SYMBOL OF EXTRAVAGANCE

The sophisticated and gaudy airspeeder expresses the qualities of its youthful owner, Simon Greyshade, the newly risen Senator for the Vorzyd sector. This sly politician is beginning to enjoy the perks of office and the lucrative insights gained at the interface between government and industry. History will record him as one of the few neutral Senators to flourish in the Clone Wars.

Communications gear for keeping in contact with manipulators of galactic opinion

Anakin uses hi mechanical intuitio to hotwire th speeder' securit system

Racing stickers attest to Greyshade's after-hours antics

Upholstery lifts away for service diagnostics

Tractor units in seats and inertial compensators help keep the driver and passenger seated even during reckless maneuvers

Greyshade insists on sleek yellow styling for all his personal craft

Anti-theft movement sensors failed to detect Anakin's entry

Exhaust thrust outlet

Yaw gyro casing

Pitch gyro casing and afterburner centrifuge

Electro-gravitic gyro flywheels enable turning without relying on aerodynamics or ground traction

Thrust-duct attachment

Power generator

Deuterium fuel canisters

Generator diagnostics

Lateral repulsorlift array inside running-board

Powerful audio system

Lateral thrust-ducts distribute gas flow around cabin

THRUST-DUCTS

The speeder is propelled through the air by a sophisticated system of thrust ducts. Highly over-pressured air flow from the turbojets is ignited and hurled through narrow thrust-ducts at transonic velocities. The main ducts pass through the cabin side walls. Secondary ducts are exposed on the speeder underbelly for cooling moderation by air contact. Air streams pass through afterburner centrifuges and out of thrust vents at the back. The vents are partly covered by protective grilles, and have internal shutters to brake selectively or redirect the outflows.

DATA FILE
Manufacturer: mechanics at Senator Greyshade's private vehicle workshop
Make: unique, custom-built luxury airspeeder hotrod
Dimensions: length 6.23 m (20.4 ft); width 2.66 m (8.7 ft); depth (excluding antennas) 1.4 m (4.6 ft)
Mass: 1,600 kg (3,520 lbs)
Engine power: 30 megawatts
Max. airspeed: 720 kph (450 mph)
Max. acceleration: 70G (approx. engine limit)
Passengers: 1 (excluding driver)
Armament: none

ANAKIN'S AIRSPEEDER

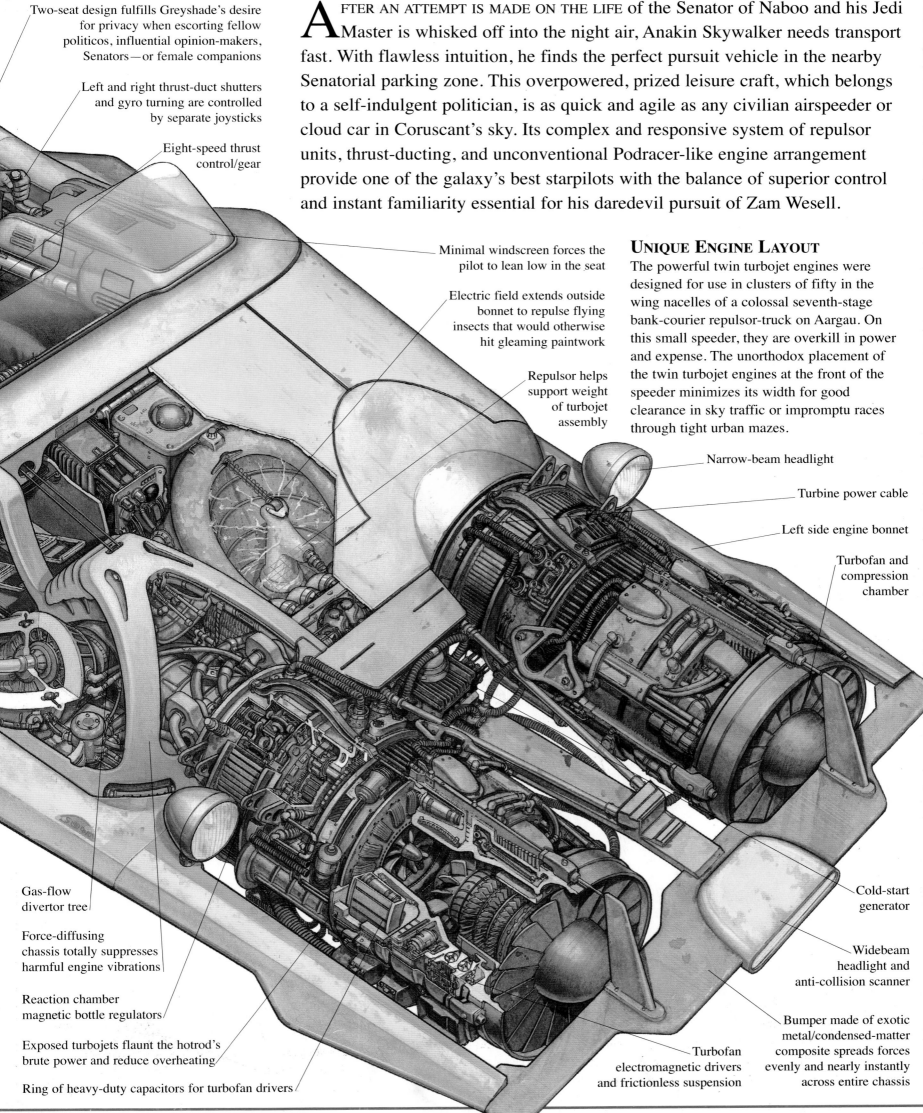

AFTER AN ATTEMPT IS MADE ON THE LIFE of the Senator of Naboo and his Jedi Master is whisked off into the night air, Anakin Skywalker needs transport fast. With flawless intuition, he finds the perfect pursuit vehicle in the nearby Senatorial parking zone. This overpowered, prized leisure craft, which belongs to a self-indulgent politician, is as quick and agile as any civilian airspeeder or cloud car in Coruscant's sky. Its complex and responsive system of repulsor units, thrust-ducting, and unconventional Podracer-like engine arrangement provide one of the galaxy's best starpilots with the balance of superior control and instant familiarity essential for his daredevil pursuit of Zam Wesell.

Two-seat design fulfills Greyshade's desire for privacy when escorting fellow politicos, influential opinion-makers, Senators—or female companions

Left and right thrust-duct shutters and gyro turning are controlled by separate joysticks

Eight-speed thrust control/gear

Minimal windscreen forces the pilot to lean low in the seat

Electric field extends outside bonnet to repulse flying insects that would otherwise hit gleaming paintwork

Repulsor helps support weight of turbojet assembly

UNIQUE ENGINE LAYOUT
The powerful twin turbojet engines were designed for use in clusters of fifty in the wing nacelles of a colossal seventh-stage bank-courier repulsor-truck on Aargau. On this small speeder, they are overkill in power and expense. The unorthodox placement of the twin turbojet engines at the front of the speeder minimizes its width for good clearance in sky traffic or impromptu races through tight urban mazes.

Narrow-beam headlight

Turbine power cable

Left side engine bonnet

Turbofan and compression chamber

Cold-start generator

Widebeam headlight and anti-collision scanner

Bumper made of exotic metal/condensed-matter composite spreads forces evenly and nearly instantly across entire chassis

Turbofan electromagnetic drivers and frictionless suspension

Gas-flow divertor tree

Force-diffusing chassis totally suppresses harmful engine vibrations

Reaction chamber magnetic bottle regulators

Exposed turbojets flaunt the hotrod's brute power and reduce overheating

Ring of heavy-duty capacitors for turbofan drivers

JEDI STARFIGHTER

When OBI-WAN KENOBI DEPARTS on his quest to Kamino, he requisitions one of the Jedi Temple's modified Delta-7 *Aethersprite* light interceptors. This ultra-light fighter is well shielded against impacts and blasts, and is equipped with two dual laser cannons that can unleash a withering frontal assault. Its sleek, blade-like form simplifies shield distribution and affords excellent visibility, especially in forward and lateral directions. A fighter of this size normally cannot travel far into deep space on its own, but the customized Jedi version features a socket for a truncated droid navigator and can dock with an external hyperdrive ring. Its design assumes dominance over any foe—essential for a prescient Jedi or any steely-nerved pilot trained for frontal assaults.

STOICAL DROID

Originally an R4-series astromech droid, R4-P17 was crushed while repairing trash compactor faults in the KDY research shipyards over Gyndine. While inspecting the Jedi customizations of the Delta-7 design, Anakin Skywalker found R4's wreck and rebuilt her with an R2-series dome. Now Temple property, R4 is the prototype for other integrated droid navigators in Jedi Delta-7 ships.

DATA FILE

Manufacturer: Kuat Systems Engineering, subsidiary of Kuat Drive Yards (fighter); TransGalMeg Industries Inc. (hyperdrive ring)
Make: Delta-7 *Aethersprite* light interceptor; Syliure-31 long-range hyperdrive module
Dimensions: length 8 m (26 ft); width 3.92 m (12.8 ft); depth 1.44 m (4.7 ft)
Max. speed (*in standard atmosphere*): 12,000 kph (7,400 mph)
Max. acceleration (*linear, in open space*): 5,000G
Hyperdrive: Class 1.0 (effective range 150,000 light-years)
Cargo capacity (*in cockpit*): 60 kg (132 lbs) or 0.03 m³ (1.06 ft³)
Consumables: five hours' fuel and air in normal sublight operation (air supply prolonged if pilot uses Jedi hibernation trance)
Crew: 1 pilot and 1 modified, integrated astromech droid
Armament: 2 dual laser cannons (1 kiloton per shot max.)

ANCIENT ICON

The starboard wing of Obi-Wan's craft is marked with a symbol of a disc with eight spokes. This ancient icon dates to the Bendu monks' study of numerology wherein the number nine (eight spokes joined to one disc) signifies the beneficent presence of the Force in a unitary galaxy. After the fall of the Galactic Republic 1,000 generations later, the Emperor will personalize this symbol by defacing the icon with the removal of two spokes.

The fighter's tiny profile makes it difficult to detect and easy to hide from long-range sensors

Red coloration indicates Jedi plenipotentiary status and diplomatic immunity

Transformers and power cells for bow hardware

Firing groove

Power feeds to bow deflectors

Ancient roundel with eight spokes

Deflector shield power hub

Comscan processor

Communications and scanning reflector dish

Multi-mode scanning and communications transceiver

Landing pad is a descending hull panel

Forward landing gear bay

Port landing light

Forward deflector shield projectors

Main reactor bulb

Ventral landing claw enables docking in zero-gravity environments, such as on planetary ring boulders

Laser cannon capacitors

Forward ventral power tree

Dual laser cannon emitter muzzles

PRIVILEGED NETWORK SCOUT

In an emergency, Kenobi's ship can relay encrypted signals via any suitably powerful hyperwave transceiver located in the same planetary system. During the mission to Geonosis, Obi-Wan uses a powerful interstellar relay station in the Geonosis system to communicate with Anakin on Tatooine.

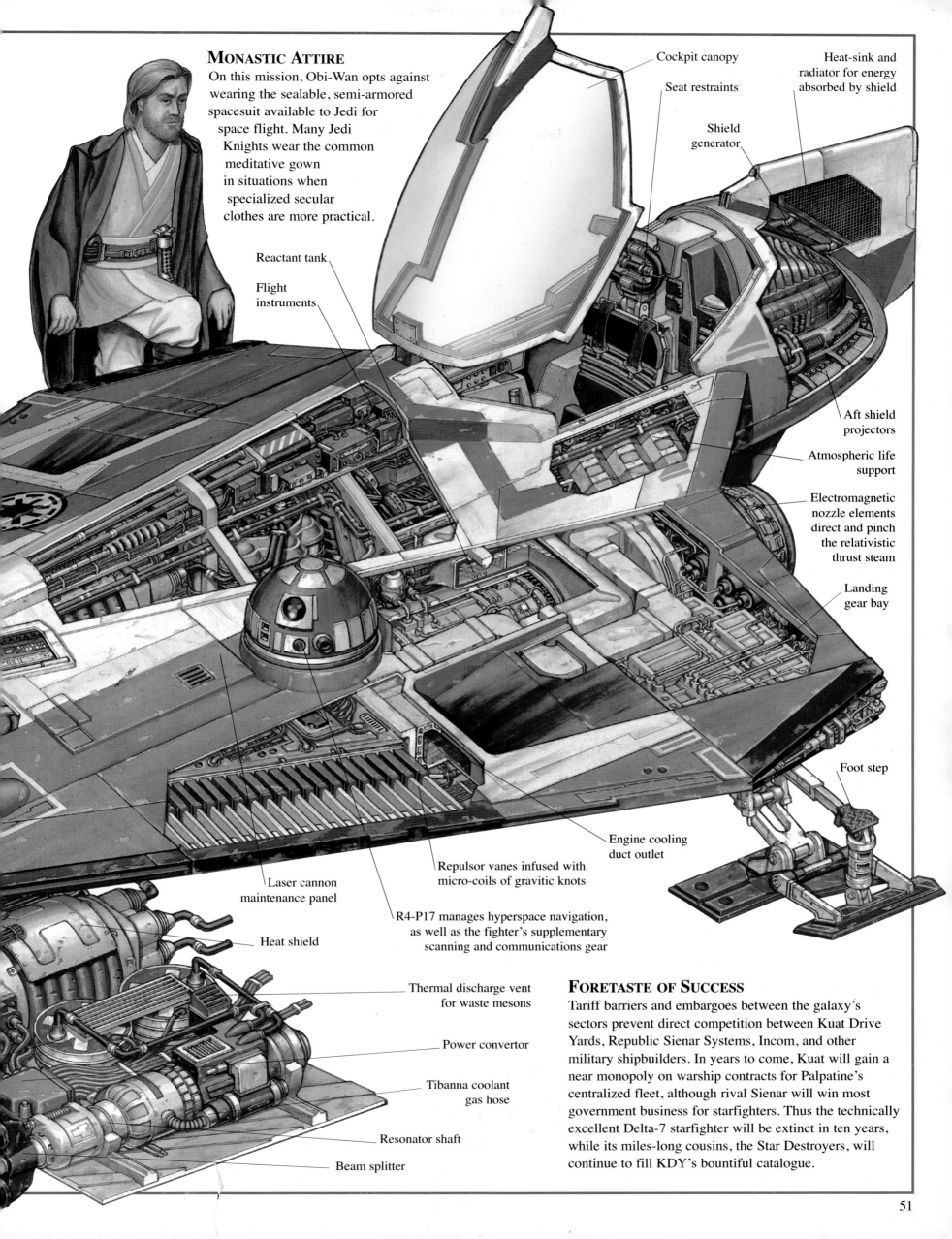

MONASTIC ATTIRE

On this mission, Obi-Wan opts against wearing the sealable, semi-armored spacesuit available to Jedi for space flight. Many Jedi Knights wear the common meditative gown in situations when specialized secular clothes are more practical.

Cockpit canopy

Seat restraints

Shield generator

Heat-sink and radiator for energy absorbed by shield

Reactant tank

Flight instruments

Aft shield projectors

Atmospheric life support

Electromagnetic nozzle elements direct and pinch the relativistic thrust steam

Landing gear bay

Foot step

Engine cooling duct outlet

Repulsor vanes infused with micro-coils of gravitic knots

Laser cannon maintenance panel

R4-P17 manages hyperspace navigation, as well as the fighter's supplementary scanning and communications gear

Heat shield

Thermal discharge vent for waste mesons

Power convertor

Tibanna coolant gas hose

Resonator shaft

Beam splitter

FORETASTE OF SUCCESS

Tariff barriers and embargoes between the galaxy's sectors prevent direct competition between Kuat Drive Yards, Republic Sienar Systems, Incom, and other military shipbuilders. In years to come, Kuat will gain a near monopoly on warship contracts for Palpatine's centralized fleet, although rival Sienar will win most government business for starfighters. Thus the technically excellent Delta-7 starfighter will be extinct in ten years, while its miles-long cousins, the Star Destroyers, will continue to fill KDY's bountiful catalogue.

JANGO FETT'S SLAVE I

JANGO FETT PILOTS A VICIOUSLY EFFECTIVE, CUSTOMIZED STARSHIP with superior shielding combined with high endurance levels, and a heavy arsenal of overt and hidden weapons. At first glance, the rugged vessel is recognizable as an ordinary *Firespray*-class law-enforcement patrol ship.

However, fine inspection reveals a montage of patched, rebuilt, and enhanced equipment attesting to its unsavory usage. Jango favors this uncommon but un-exotic craft for the element of disguise it affords him; as one of the galaxy's most proficient mercenaries, he nonetheless chooses to work in discreet obscurity, remaining unrecognized by most highly placed security officers and criminals alike.

When Jango's son Boba inherits *Slave I*, he will make some changes to suit his greater infamy and more aggressive style, including increased interstellar range and fuel capacity, installation of superior sensor jammers, and other stealth hardware.

DATA FILE

Manufacturer: Kuat Systems Engineering
Make: *Firespray*-class patrol and attack ship
Dimensions: length 21.5 m (70.5 ft); wingspan 21.3 m (70 ft); depth (excluding guns) 7.8 m (25.6 ft)
Max. speed *(in standard atmosphere)*: 1,000 kph (620 mph)
Max. acceleration *(linear, in open space)*: 2,500G
Hyperdrive: class 1.0
Crew: 1 pilot; up to 2 co-pilots/navigator/gunners
Passengers: 2 seated (immobilized captives are stored in lockers)
Armament: 2 laser cannons (600 gigajoules per shot); 2 blaster cannons (8×10^{12} joules per shot); missile-launcher (8×10^{17} joules per shot); minelayer (5×10^{19} joules per shot); other unknown weapons

INTERIOR REFIT

Originally stolen by Jango on the asteroid prison Oovo IV, *Slave I* has been extensively modified after a few harsh space battles. Jango has added spartan crew quarters for long hunts, since the original *Firespray* was furnished for shorter-term patrols. In addition, the police-regulation prisoner cages have been converted into less-humane, coffin-like wall cabinets to ensure control of captives.

Energy-shield shroud

Ladder to lower level

Corridor segment scavenged from a derelict Corellian starliner

Boba Fett

Fins contain repulsor grilles for landing maneuvers

Jango Fett

Cockpit console originally rotated to allow internal maintenance and observation of prisoner hold

Each deck's artificial gravity re-orients depending on flight mode

Flight instruments console

Expansion grid for future hardware (Boba will install stealth gear)

Upper portside inertial compensator

Sublight communications antenna

Shield generator main power conduit

Forward shield generator destined for relocation to make room for larger power cells and fuel tanks

Atmospheric life-support

Bunk sliding shutter

Jango's bunk

Navigator station

Forward starboard reactant tank

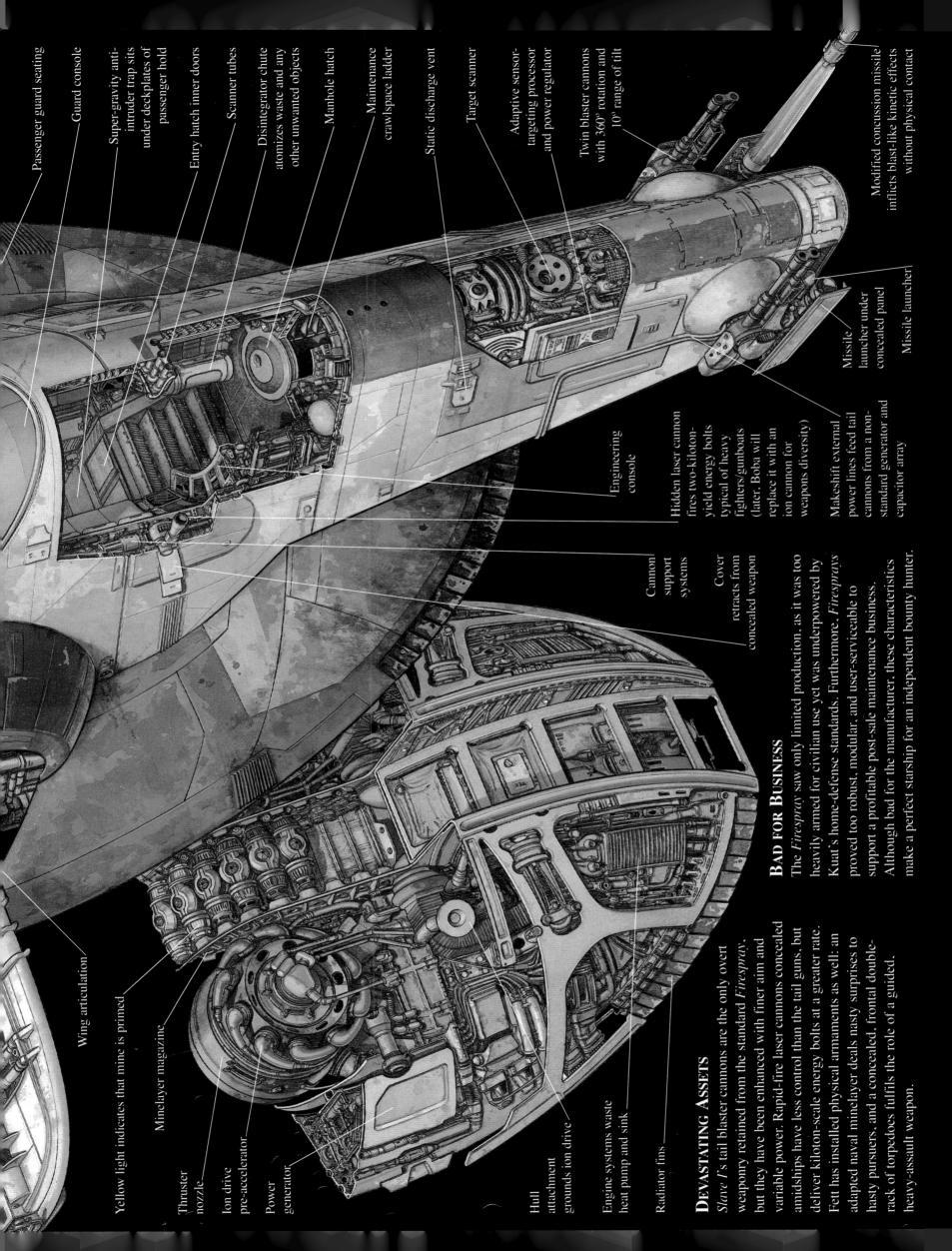

Passenger guard seating

Guard console

Super-gravity anti-intruder trap sits under deckplates of passenger hold

Entry hatch inner doors

Scanner tubes

Disintegrator chute atomizes waste and any other unwanted objects

Manhole hatch

Maintenance crawlspace ladder

Static discharge vent

Target scanner

Adaptive sensor-targeting processor and power regulator

Twin blaster cannons with 360° rotation and 10° range of tilt

Modified concussion missile inflicts blast-like kinetic effects without physical contact

Missile launcher under concealed panel

Missile launcher

Engineering console

Hidden laser cannon fires two-kiloton-yield energy bolts typical of heavy fighters/gunboats (later, Boba will replace it with an ion cannon for weapons diversity)

Makeshift external power lines feed tail cannons from a non-standard generator and capacitor array

Cannon support systems

Cover retracts from concealed weapon

Yellow light indicates that mine is primed

Minelayer magazine

Wing articulation

Thruster nozzle

Ion drive pre-accelerator

Power generator

Hull attachment grounds ion drive

Engine systems waste heat pump and sink

Radiator fins

DEVASTATING ASSETS

Slave I's tail blaster cannons are the only overt weaponry retained from the standard *Firespray*, but they have been enhanced with finer aim and variable power. Rapid-fire laser cannons concealed amidships have less control than the tail guns, but deliver kiloton-scale energy bolts at a greater rate. Fett has installed physical armaments as well: an adapted naval minelayer deals nasty surprises to hasty pursuers, and a concealed, frontal double-rack of torpedoes fulfils the role of a guided, heavy-assault weapon.

BAD FOR BUSINESS

The *Firespray* saw only limited production, as it was too heavily armed for civilian use yet was underpowered by Kuat's home-defense standards. Furthermore, *Firesprays* proved too robust, modular, and user-serviceable to support a profitable post-sale maintenance business. Although bad for the manufacturer, these characteristics make a perfect starship for an independent bounty hunter.

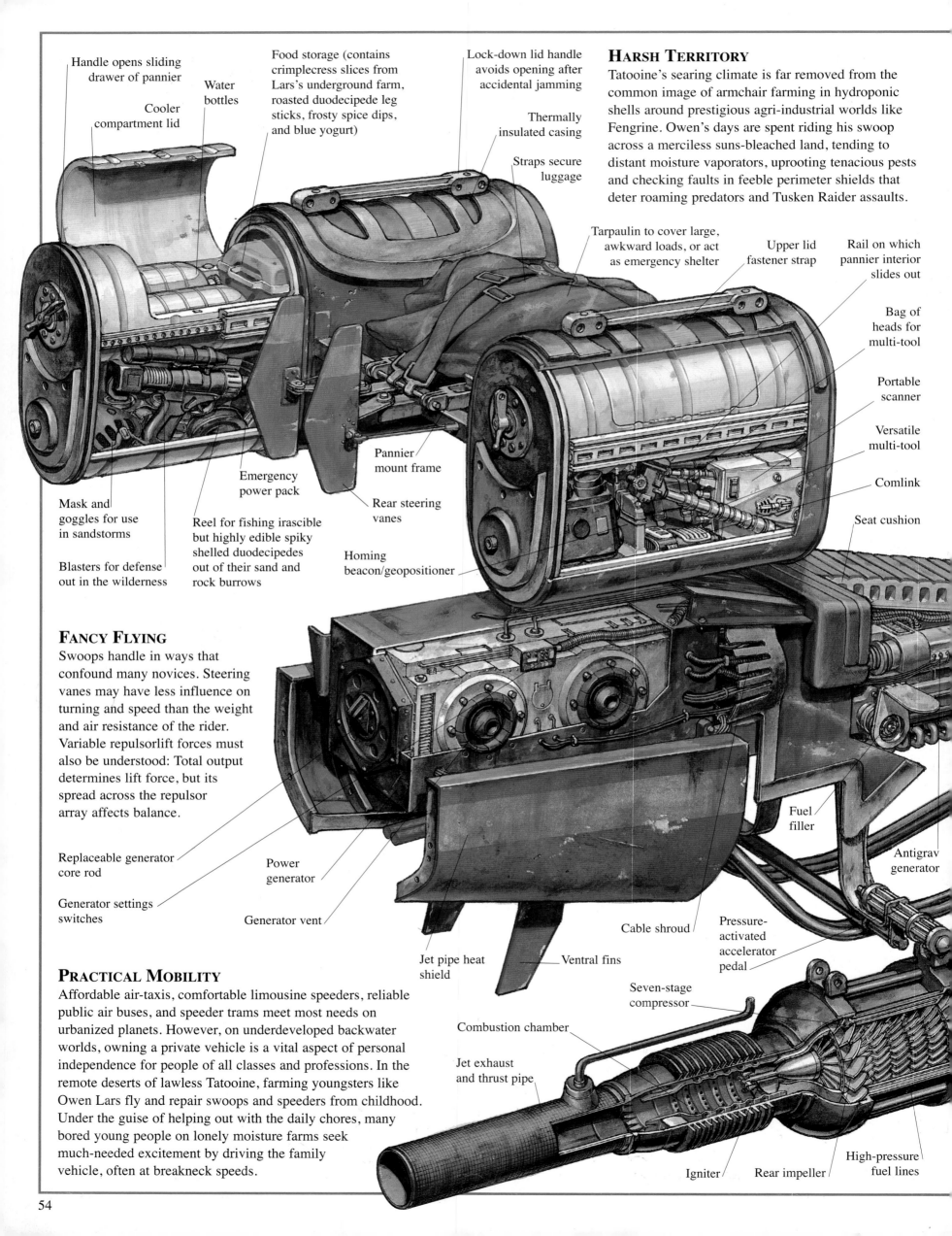

Handle opens sliding
drawer of pannier

Cooler
compartment lid

Water
bottles

Food storage (contains
crimplecress slices from
Lars's underground farm,
roasted duodecipede leg
sticks, frosty spice dips,
and blue yogurt)

Lock-down lid handle
avoids opening after
accidental jamming

Thermally
insulated casing

Straps secure
luggage

Harsh Territory

Tatooine's searing climate is far removed from the
common image of armchair farming in hydroponic
shells around prestigious agri-industrial worlds like
Fengrine. Owen's days are spent riding his swoop
across a merciless suns-bleached land, tending to
distant moisture vaporators, uprooting tenacious pests
and checking faults in feeble perimeter shields that
deter roaming predators and Tusken Raider assaults.

Tarpaulin to cover large,
awkward loads, or act
as emergency shelter

Upper lid
fastener strap

Rail on which
pannier interior
slides out

Bag of
heads for
multi-tool

Portable
scanner

Versatile
multi-tool

Comlink

Seat cushion

Mask and
goggles for use
in sandstorms

Blasters for defense
out in the wilderness

Emergency
power pack

Reel for fishing irascible
but highly edible spiky
shelled duodecipedes
out of their sand and
rock burrows

Pannier
mount frame

Rear steering
vanes

Homing
beacon/geopositioner

Fancy Flying

Swoops handle in ways that
confound many novices. Steering
vanes may have less influence on
turning and speed than the weight
and air resistance of the rider.
Variable repulsorlift forces must
also be understood: Total output
determines lift force, but its
spread across the repulsor
array affects balance.

Replaceable generator
core rod

Generator settings
switches

Power
generator

Generator vent

Jet pipe heat
shield

Ventral fins

Fuel
filler

Antigrav
generator

Cable shroud

Pressure-
activated
accelerator
pedal

Seven-stage
compressor

Combustion chamber

Jet exhaust
and thrust pipe

Igniter

Rear impeller

High-pressure
fuel lines

Practical Mobility

Affordable air-taxis, comfortable limousine speeders, reliable
public air buses, and speeder trams meet most needs on
urbanized planets. However, on underdeveloped backwater
worlds, owning a private vehicle is a vital aspect of personal
independence for people of all classes and professions. In the
remote deserts of lawless Tatooine, farming youngsters like
Owen Lars fly and repair swoops and speeders from childhood.
Under the guise of helping out with the daily chores, many
bored young people on lonely moisture farms seek
much-needed excitement by driving the family
vehicle, often at breakneck speeds.

OWEN LARS'S SWOOP BIKE

OF ALL PEOPLE ON DESOLATE TATOOINE, the implacable moisture farmers have the most pragmatic appreciation of vehicular technology, upon which they depend for daily survival. Young Owen Lars epitomizes this principle, as he patrols the family property on his fast, sand-beaten swoop.

Though not especially reliable, this farm vehicle is used more heavily than the homestead's dozen other semi-restored craft because it is fuel-efficient and easy to repair using Jawa-supplied parts. Owen bought his high-powered swoop from a Revwien merchant at an auction in remote Mos Nytram. Originally a racing vehicle, he immediately saw its durable, practical use. Townsfolk might scoff at the sight of a onetime sports vehicle hauling water trailers or vermin traps, but as far as Owen is concerned, utility is the true essence of grace.

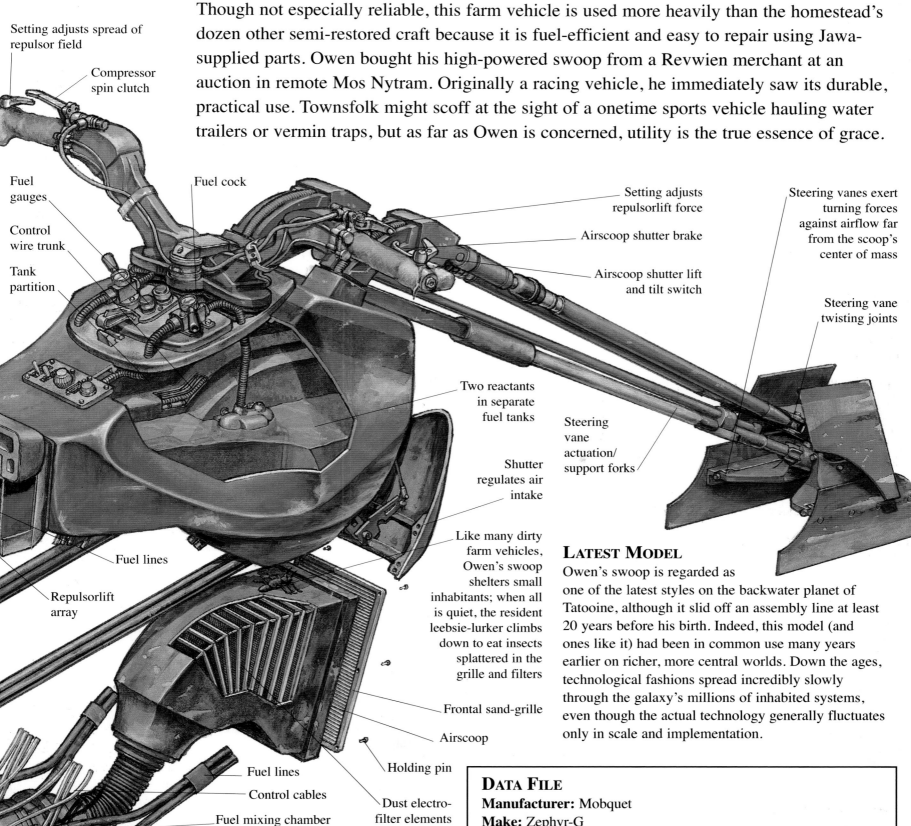

Setting adjusts spread of repulsor field

Compressor spin clutch

Fuel gauges

Fuel cock

Setting adjusts repulsorlift force

Airscoop shutter brake

Airscoop shutter lift and tilt switch

Steering vanes exert turning forces against airflow far from the scoop's center of mass

Steering vane twisting joints

Control wire trunk

Tank partition

Two reactants in separate fuel tanks

Steering vane actuation/ support forks

Shutter regulates air intake

Fuel lines

Repulsorlift array

Like many dirty farm vehicles, Owen's swoop shelters small inhabitants; when all is quiet, the resident leebsie-lurker climbs down to eat insects splattered in the grille and filters

Frontal sand-grille

Airscoop

Holding pin

Fuel lines

Control cables

Fuel mixing chamber

Front impeller

Dust electro-filter elements

LATEST MODEL

Owen's swoop is regarded as one of the latest styles on the backwater planet of Tatooine, although it slid off an assembly line at least 20 years before his birth. Indeed, this model (and ones like it) had been in common use many years earlier on richer, more central worlds. Down the ages, technological fashions spread incredibly slowly through the galaxy's millions of inhabited systems, even though the actual technology generally fluctuates only in scale and implementation.

SWOOP ENGINE

In its functional simplicity, the swoop is a tube. At the front, an airscoop feeds a turbojet in which fuel is mixed and ignited. At the rear, a tail-piped exhaust stream provides thrust. A repulsor array under the seat keeps the bike aloft, and is sustained by basic power cells and a generator. The only moving parts are the fans and gears of the compressor. These mechanisms are protected from abrasive sand and dust contaminants by a coarse grille at the airscoop mouth, followed by multiple layers of fast-acting electrostatic filters.

DATA FILE
Manufacturer: Mobquet
Make: Zephyr-G
Dimensions: length 3.68 m (12 ft); width 0.66 m (2 ft); depth 0.72 m (2.4 ft)
Max. airspeed: 350 kph (217 mph)
Max. acceleration: 2G (no inertial compensator; limited only by rider's grip and stamina!)
Cargo capacity: 50 kg (110 lbs) per pannier; 200 kg (440 lbs) lifting capacity including rider
Consumables: approx. 3,000 km (1,860 miles) worth of fuel
Crew: 1 (and 1 passenger, in discomfort)
Armament: none

PADMÉ'S STARSHIP

THIS SLIM YACHT FROM THE ROYAL HANGARS of Naboo is not a spacious diplomatic platform for long-range tours and conferences. It is a relatively fast ship suited to discreet getaways. Its security features include a powerful Naboo-style shield system, electronic countermeasures, and a last-resort passenger escape capsule. Queen Jamillia's royal starships normally sit idle since she prefers to concentrate on Naboo's domestic affairs, entrusting her external powers to Senator Padmé Amidala. Thus, the smallest royal yacht is available and ideally suited for Padmé's undercover travels as the galaxy's most threatened political target. Its small crew requirements minimize the risk of sabotage, allowing Padmé and Anakin to pilot the ship alone with back-up flight assistance from the droids C-3P0 and R2-D2. The yacht serves Padmé and Anakin well in their dangerous journey from Tatooine to the neighboring Geonosis system.

Coolant pump circulates a superfluid with enormous heat capacity to moderate the shield matrix during critical power spikes that cannot be radiated away quickly

Gleaming hull plating acts as passive physical radiation shielding

Deflector shield projector modules

Shield heat-sink and radiator matrix converts unusable energy surges into heat for disposal

Shield generator

INCONSPICUOUS TRANSPORT

The yacht is the smallest non-fighter vessel kept in the hangars of Theed Palace. Its simplified systems reduce maintenance time, making it ideal for secretive, unsupported excursions. It is much faster than most other civilian ships, and its narrow profile and sheltered engines amount to a small sensor signature. Thus the ship is well suited for evading the grasp of shadowy pursuers.

Orderly and aesthetically arranged Naboo circuitry

Astromech droid hold (two stations)

Connection to main reactor above

Starboard antigrav generator

Power node

Power trunk starboard fork

Extended boarding ramp

Tube containing turbolift platform connects upper and lower deck for fast access

Auxiliary comscan station

Ship's manual

Main reactor

Galley

Anakin's crew bunk

Toolkit

Navicomputer housing and power trunk

Navigator station

Anakin

Stores

Airlock

Hull substrate

R2-D2's station (unused)

Starboard stern repulsor coils

Reactor fuel tank

Fuel baffles

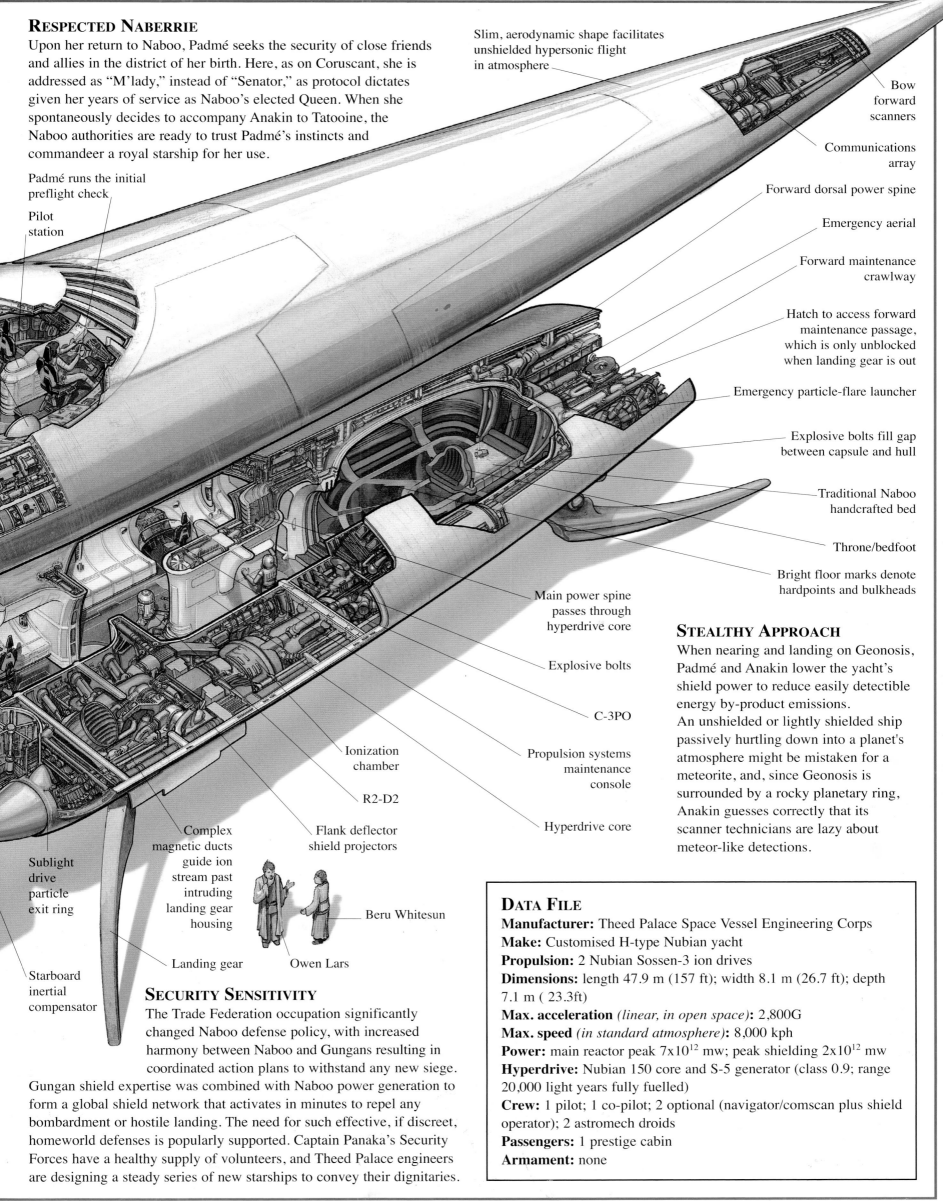

RESPECTED NABERRIE

Upon her return to Naboo, Padmé seeks the security of close friends and allies in the district of her birth. Here, as on Coruscant, she is addressed as "M'lady," instead of "Senator," as protocol dictates given her years of service as Naboo's elected Queen. When she spontaneously decides to accompany Anakin to Tatooine, the Naboo authorities are ready to trust Padmé's instincts and commandeer a royal starship for her use.

Padmé runs the initial preflight check

Pilot station

Slim, aerodynamic shape facilitates unshielded hypersonic flight in atmosphere

Bow forward scanners

Communications array

Forward dorsal power spine

Emergency aerial

Forward maintenance crawlway

Hatch to access forward maintenance passage, which is only unblocked when landing gear is out

Emergency particle-flare launcher

Explosive bolts fill gap between capsule and hull

Traditional Naboo handcrafted bed

Throne/bedfoot

Bright floor marks denote hardpoints and bulkheads

Main power spine passes through hyperdrive core

Explosive bolts

C-3PO

Propulsion systems maintenance console

Hyperdrive core

Ionization chamber

R2-D2

Flank deflector shield projectors

Complex magnetic ducts guide ion stream past intruding landing gear housing

Beru Whitesun

Landing gear

Owen Lars

Sublight drive particle exit ring

Starboard inertial compensator

STEALTHY APPROACH

When nearing and landing on Geonosis, Padmé and Anakin lower the yacht's shield power to reduce easily detectible energy by-product emissions.
An unshielded or lightly shielded ship passively hurtling down into a planet's atmosphere might be mistaken for a meteorite, and, since Geonosis is surrounded by a rocky planetary ring, Anakin guesses correctly that its scanner technicians are lazy about meteor-like detections.

SECURITY SENSITIVITY

The Trade Federation occupation significantly changed Naboo defense policy, with increased harmony between Naboo and Gungans resulting in coordinated action plans to withstand any new siege. Gungan shield expertise was combined with Naboo power generation to form a global shield network that activates in minutes to repel any bombardment or hostile landing. The need for such effective, if discreet, homeworld defenses is popularly supported. Captain Panaka's Security Forces have a healthy supply of volunteers, and Theed Palace engineers are designing a steady series of new starships to convey their dignitaries.

DATA FILE
Manufacturer: Theed Palace Space Vessel Engineering Corps
Make: Customised H-type Nubian yacht
Propulsion: 2 Nubian Sossen-3 ion drives
Dimensions: length 47.9 m (157 ft); width 8.1 m (26.7 ft); depth 7.1 m (23.3ft)
Max. acceleration *(linear, in open space)*: 2,800G
Max. speed *(in standard atmosphere)*: 8,000 kph
Power: main reactor peak 7×10^{12} mw; peak shielding 2×10^{12} mw
Hyperdrive: Nubian 150 core and S-5 generator (class 0.9; range 20,000 light years fully fuelled)
Crew: 1 pilot; 1 co-pilot; 2 optional (navigator/comscan plus shield operator); 2 astromech droids
Passengers: 1 prestige cabin
Armament: none

TRADE FEDERATION CORE SHIP

W ITH ITS FLEETS OF FREIGHTER-BATTLESHIPS, the Trade Federation is well-equipped to be one of the powerful merchant factions behind the advent of the Clone Wars. The heart and brain of each battleship is a detachable Core Ship, which comprises a massive, central computer and multiple power systems. These huge ships are serviced in special landing pits on planets affiliated to the Trade Federation, while the delicate cargo arms and engine blocks remain in orbit.

The Core Ships' ion-drive nozzles provide basic steering and slow acceleration, allowing them to dock in powerful, anti-gravity repulsorlift cushions with eight landing legs for stability. Scores of these ships are grounded on Geonosis, where they are being upgraded for coordination with the newly enhanced Baktoid droid armies. During the battle on Geonosis, the Core Ships are ringed with land and air defenses, allowing a good number to retreat safely to the skies.

DATA FILE

Manufacturer: Hoersch-Kessel Drive Inc. (basic Core Ship); Baktoid Combat Automata (droid-army control core)

Model: *Lucrehulk*-class modular control core (LH-1740)

Dimensions: diameter 696 m (2285 ft); depth (when landed, minus transmission mast) 914 m (3,000 ft)

Max. acceleration *(linear, in open space)*: 300G

Power: reactor peak 3×10^{24} watts; peak shield capacity 6×10^{23} watts

Cargo capacity: approx. 66 million m³ (2.3 billion ft³)

Consumables: 3 years supplies

Crew: 60 Trade Federation supervisors; 3,000 Droid Crew; 200,000 Maintenance Droids

Passengers: stateroom capacity for 60,000 trade representatives

Armament: 280 point-defense light laser cannons (8 kilotons per shot max.)

VERTICAL ORGANIZATION

The hierarchical arrangement of habitable areas on the Core Ships matches that of Neimoidian hives. Control bridges, executive suites, and treasuries are concentrated in globe's upper pole and towers, and resemble Neimoidia's luxurious surface palaces. Deeper levels are for junior managers, publicists, brokers, and droid storage. The lowest decks contain engineering areas and conference rooms for meeting outsiders; like the unfavorably dry and hot basements of Neimoidian warrens, frequented by subterranean scavengers and parasites, these decks are shunned by high-ranking officials.

Military Droid-feedback rectenna

Locking ridges on hull fit sockets on different classes of Trade Federation freighters and warships

Compact hypermatter-annihilation reactor

Newly upgraded AAT tanks loaded into equatorial bay

Transmitter tuning cells

Radiator cools transmission generators

Power generator supports transmitter sub-systems

Military control towers (now installed on most Core Ships)

STANDARD PART

Core-Ship design has changed little in the last century. In a typical display of Neimoidian thrift, the spheres can serve a variety of craft: The split-ring freighter-battleships of the Naboo blockade; larger, unarmed container vessels and tankers; and newer warships of the post-Naboo period, including cruisers with improved weapons placement and smaller, faster destroyers that defend the fleets and chase down blockade runners.

Docking ring for Corellian-standard boarding tubes and airlocks

Luxury executive suites

Command bridge

Scanner array

Executive escape-pod bay

VIP treasury

Upgraded computer core allows coordination of droid armies via Officer Droids and neighboring droid-control ships

New secondary fuel silos improve reactor overload containment systems

Transmission mast for military feedback and control signals

Ancillary reactors

Reactor-support assemblies are independent fusion-powered triggers and confinement-field generators for the hypermatter main-reactor core

Trench shield projectors channel their energies in synchronous sheaths

Thermal exhaust-vent safely moderates heat surges in core

Shield generator

Ceremonial hall for signing treaties and planetary protectorship leases

Lower decks are mostly uninhabited but patrolled by security droids

MTT troop transports

Defensive artillery

C-9979 landing ship parts

Droid battalions

Boarding ramp

New storage holds added after full militarization

Heavy cargo lift

Retractable maintenance gantry

Power feeds recharge ship systems

Landing gear retractors

Faster-than-light "hyperwave" transceiver reaches any part of the galaxy directly without using public HoloNet relays

Hull sections from leg socket cover

Waste fluid vent

Artillery power generator 58

Observation stations and workshops

Lift shaft

Walls are lined with gravitational reflectors for the ship's repulsors to act against

Particle shields cycle and intensify in trenches

Small, point-defense turrets

Thruster blast and radiation are harmlessly channeled into 6.4-km (4-mile) deep shaft

Anti-gravity repulsorlift suspensors

Foot-pads have never been tested to support the ship's full weight without repulsorlift assistance for more than an hour

Ventral thruster extends out of a lower hatch

Rings project one-way force-field that contains harmful radiation from the ship's exhaust in the blast shaft

HYPERLANE CONTROL

Core Ships' navicomputers contain precious interstellar data charts. In bygone ages, governments and private agencies shared such information publicly, but now the Trade Federation aggressively protects the coordinates it owns. As changes in astronomical conditions can make routes unsafe, the Trade Federation is gaining a virtual transport monopoly over patches of the galaxy. Now, only the Jedi and the Office of the Supreme Chancellor can afford to maintain more comprehensive charts.

NEW ALLY

After more than a decade of promoting its own trade interests by underhand means, the Trade Federation recognizes the strategic value of Count Dooku. As a persuasive orator with a zealous following on thousands of Separatist worlds, including Geonosis (home to the Federation's favorite dockyards and armorers), he is serving to increase disunity through the galaxy—and, as Nute Gunray knows, weak governments are good for business.

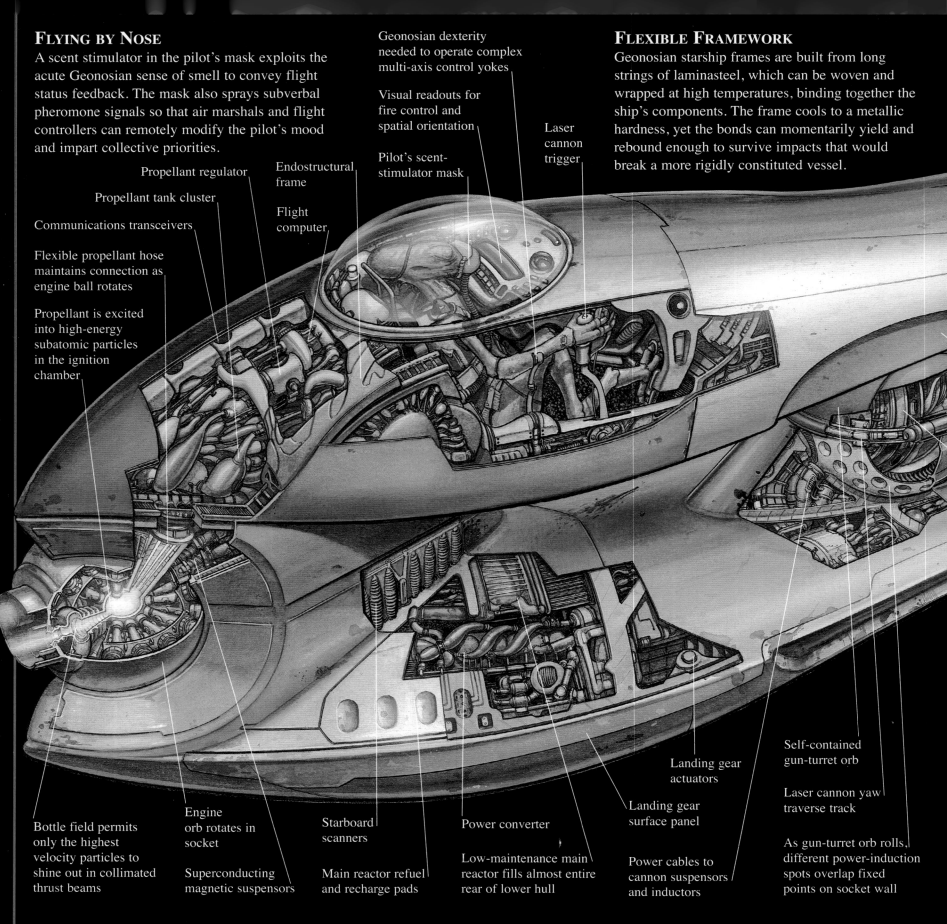

FLYING BY NOSE

A scent stimulator in the pilot's mask exploits the acute Geonosian sense of smell to convey flight status feedback. The mask also sprays subverbal pheromone signals so that air marshals and flight controllers can remotely modify the pilot's mood and impart collective priorities.

FLEXIBLE FRAMEWORK

Geonosian starship frames are built from long strings of laminasteel, which can be woven and wrapped at high temperatures, binding together the ship's components. The frame cools to a metallic hardness, yet the bonds can momentarily yield and rebound enough to survive impacts that would break a more rigidly constituted vessel.

Geonosian dexterity needed to operate complex multi-axis control yokes

Visual readouts for fire control and spatial orientation

Pilot's scent-stimulator mask

Laser cannon trigger

Propellant regulator

Propellant tank cluster

Communications transceivers

Endostructural frame

Flight computer

Flexible propellant hose maintains connection as engine ball rotates

Propellant is excited into high-energy subatomic particles in the ignition chamber

Bottle field permits only the highest velocity particles to shine out in collimated thrust beams

Engine orb rotates in socket

Superconducting magnetic suspensors

Starboard scanners

Main reactor refuel and recharge pads

Power converter

Low-maintenance main reactor fills almost entire rear of lower hull

Landing gear actuators

Landing gear surface panel

Power cables to cannon suspensors and inductors

Self-contained gun-turret orb

Laser cannon yaw traverse track

As gun-turret orb rolls, different power-induction spots overlap fixed points on socket wall

GEONOSIAN FIGHTER

D URING THE CLIMACTIC BATTLE WITH THE REPUBLIC, the Geonosian faction launches thousands of standby fighters to break the Republic's orbital cordon blocking Corporate Alliance ground reinforcements. These fightercraft combine high linear acceleration with phenomenal maneuverability as a result of the frictionless rotating mount of their thrusters. Despite their superior agility, few fighters are exported, since Geonosian senses and articulation differ from the galaxy's majority humanoid population. Furthermore, Geonosian policy has become fervently isolationist as the Republic stagnates, and their wary Archduke, Poggle the Lesser, believes that the hoarding of technical advantages is insurance of power and security.

REPUBLIC ASSAULT SHIP

The arrival of massive *ACCLAMATOR*-class troopships above Geonosis is a pivotal moment in galactic military history. The Separatists, working with nefarious corporate organizations, are stunned not only by the decisiveness of the hitherto stagnant Republic, but moreover by its use of a trained and well-equipped clone army—the first time the Republic has deployed an army since its inception. At the battle's turning point, the troopships land to disgorge swarms of armed transport gunships under the cover of turbolaser fire. The ships are accompanied by heavy ground vehicles and thousands of well-trained, dedicated clone troops.

BORN FROM BETRAYAL

The new Galactic Army's arsenal was secretly built by a mighty corporation that could have led the Separatists if not for bloody treachery. Leading Kuati executives were assassinated when Neimoidians took over the Trade Federation at the notorious Eriadu Conference a decade earlier. The outraged industrialists have since aligned with the Supreme Chancellery. Meanwhile, the pace of clandestine construction accelerates in Kuat's cordoned shipyards and factories on Rothana.

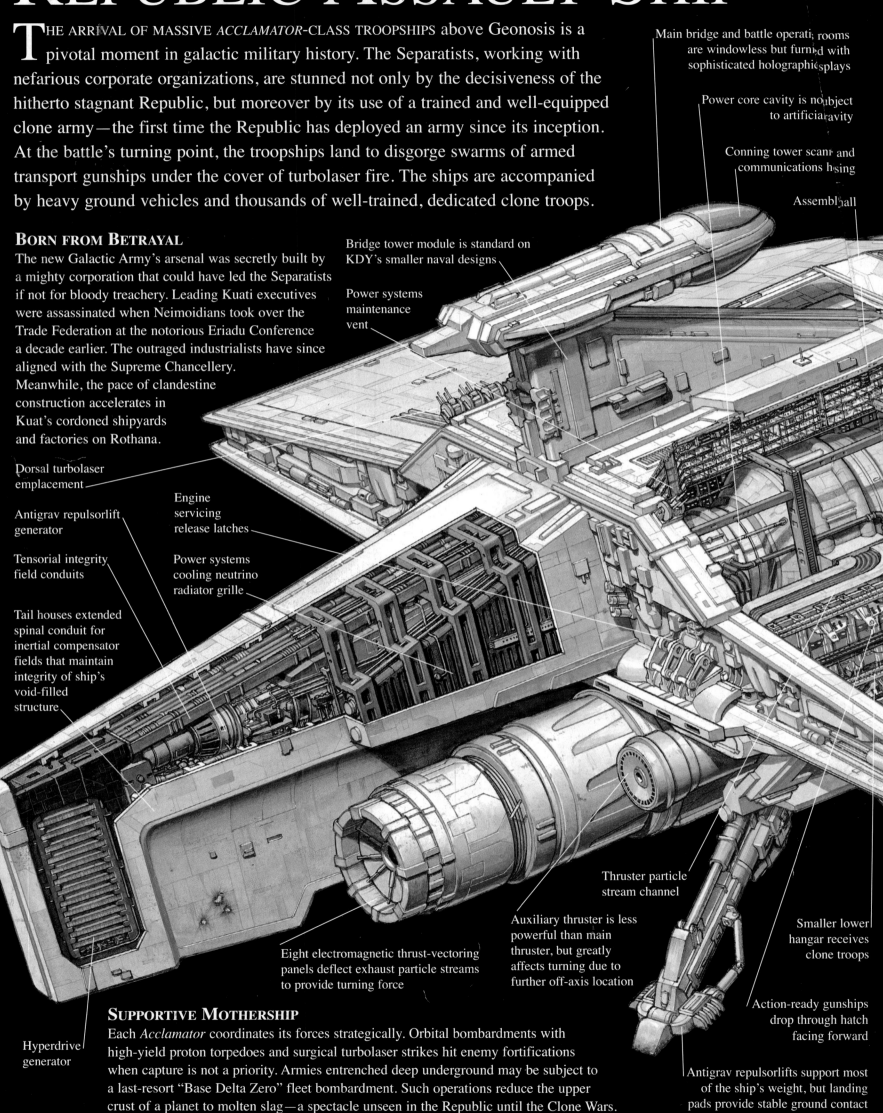

Main bridge and battle operations rooms are windowless but furnished with sophisticated holographic displays

Power core cavity is not subject to artificial gravity

Conning tower scanner and communications housing

Assembly hall

Bridge tower module is standard on KDY's smaller naval designs

Power systems maintenance vent

Dorsal turbolaser emplacement

Antigrav repulsorlift generator

Tensorial integrity field conduits

Tail houses extended spinal conduit for inertial compensator fields that maintain integrity of ship's void-filled structure

Engine servicing release latches

Power systems cooling neutrino radiator grille

Thruster particle stream channel

Auxiliary thruster is less powerful than main thruster, but greatly affects turning due to further off-axis location

Smaller lower hangar receives clone troops

Eight electromagnetic thrust-vectoring panels deflect exhaust particle streams to provide turning force

Action-ready gunships drop through hatch facing forward

Hyperdrive generator

SUPPORTIVE MOTHERSHIP

Each *Acclamator* coordinates its forces strategically. Orbital bombardments with high-yield proton torpedoes and surgical turbolaser strikes hit enemy fortifications when capture is not a priority. Armies entrenched deep underground may be subject to a last-resort "Base Delta Zero" fleet bombardment. Such operations reduce the upper crust of a planet to molten slag—a spectacle unseen in the Republic until the Clone Wars.

Antigrav repulsorlifts support most of the ship's weight, but landing pads provide stable ground contact

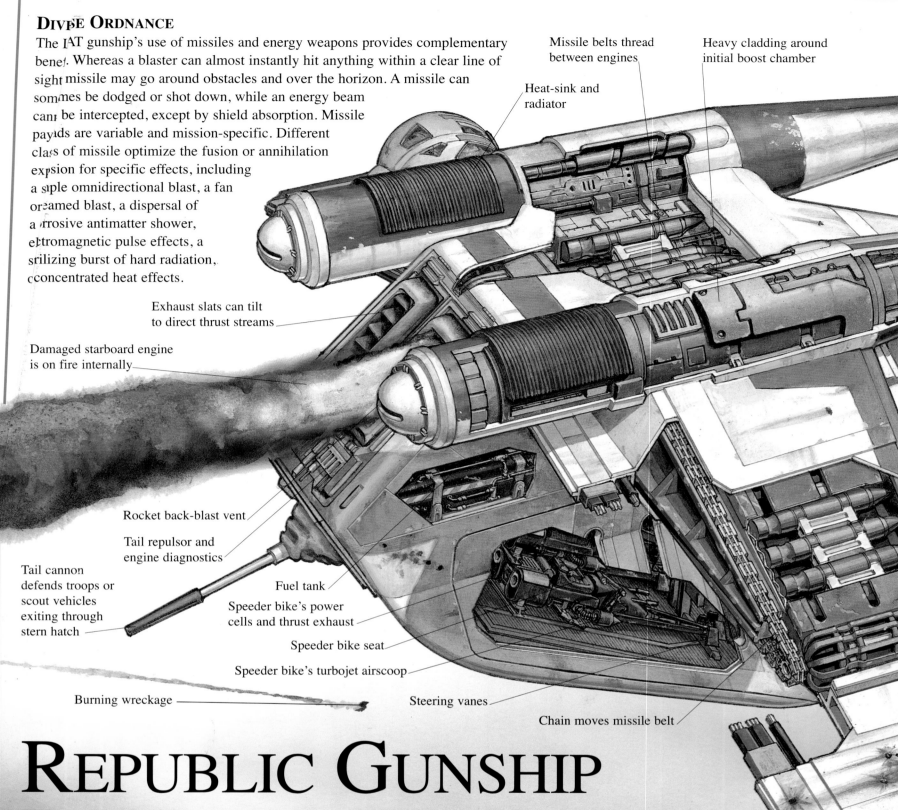

DIVIDE ORDNANCE

The LAAT gunship's use of missiles and energy weapons provides complementary benefit. Whereas a blaster can almost instantly hit anything within a clear line of sight, a missile may go around obstacles and over the horizon. A missile can sometimes be dodged or shot down, while an energy beam cannot be intercepted, except by shield absorption. Missile payloads are variable and mission-specific. Different classes of missile optimize the fusion or annihilation explosion for specific effects, including a simple omnidirectional blast, a fan or beamed blast, a dispersal of a corrosive antimatter shower, electromagnetic pulse effects, a sterilizing burst of hard radiation, or concentrated heat effects.

Missile belts thread between engines

Heavy cladding around initial boost chamber

Heat-sink and radiator

Exhaust slats can tilt to direct thrust streams

Damaged starboard engine is on fire internally

Rocket back-blast vent

Tail repulsor and engine diagnostics

Tail cannon defends troops or scout vehicles exiting through stern hatch

Fuel tank

Speeder bike's power cells and thrust exhaust

Speeder bike seat

Speeder bike's turbojet airscoop

Burning wreckage

Steering vanes

Chain moves missile belt

Power feeds to wing repulsors and turret

REPUBLIC GUNSHIP

THE GALACTIC REPUBLIC'S LAAT/i (Low-Altitude Assault Transport/infantry) aerial gunships play a vital role in the battle on Geonosis. These tactical transport craft and their variants can cross impassibly rough terrain to swiftly and safely disgorge an entire platoon of clone troopers or haul a slower armored vehicle into position. Enemy fighters must either remain at high altitudes or surrender their speed advantage when pursuing gunships below the mountain level. A military transport ship's entire gunship complement can deliver more than 2,000 soldiers in each of several repeated waves. However, these flying troop carriers are versatile gun platforms in their own right, too. They are lighter and faster than mobile artillery and most ground vehicles, yet still carry a considerable arsenal. Massive twin missile launchers allow concerted over-the-horizon strikes on slow or fixed targets such as enemy artillery and fortifications, in support of the advancing ground forces. Two pairs of widely rotating blaster cannons defend the gunship with bolts of deadly precision.

Finally, three chin- and tail-mounted laser cannons swivel and depress to devastate enemy infantry and other light ground assets. These guns are vital for clearing a path to deploy troops and vehicles—the fundamental function at which the LAAT-series gunships excel.

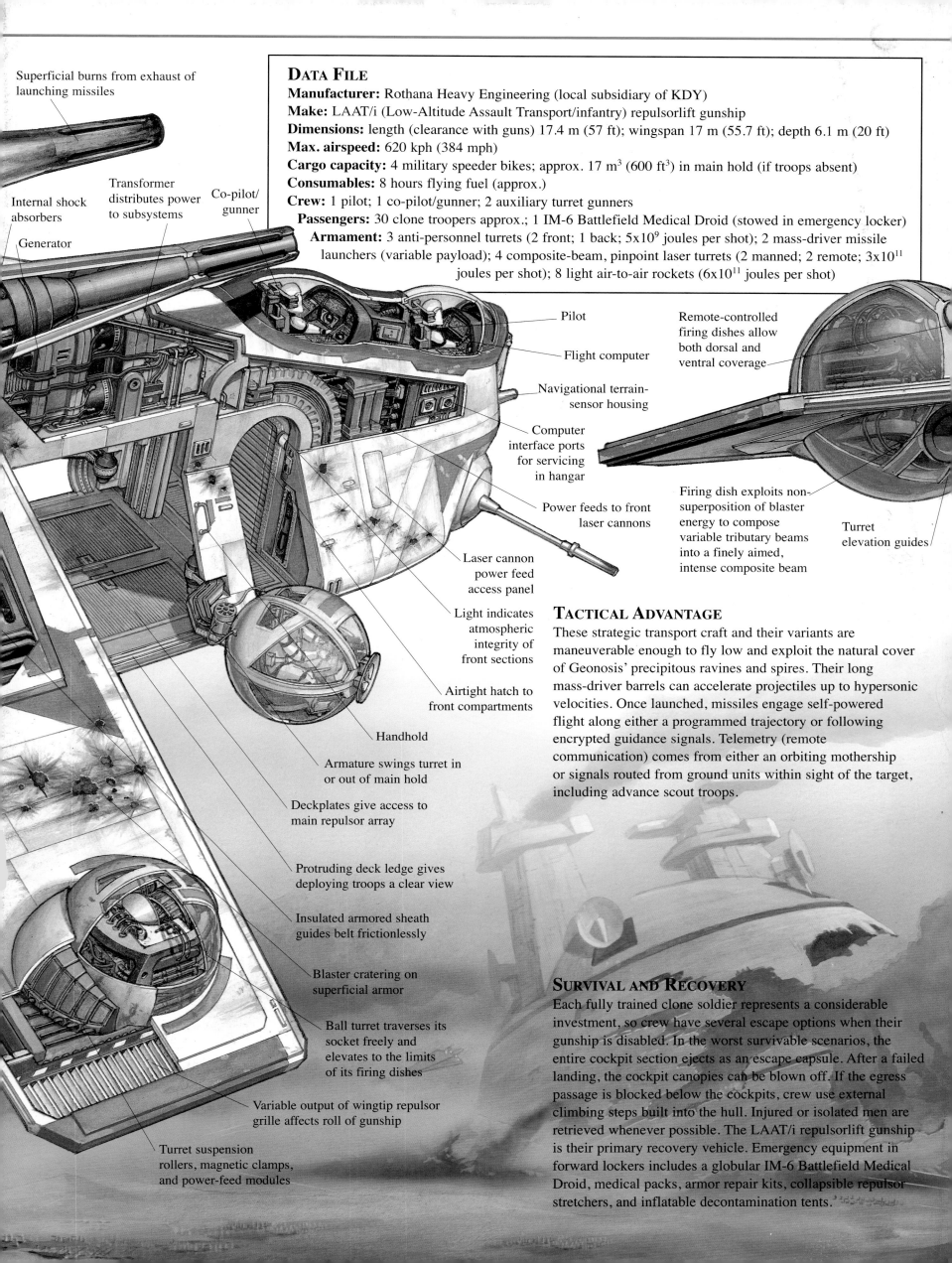

Superficial burns from exhaust of launching missiles

Internal shock absorbers

Transformer distributes power to subsystems

Co-pilot/ gunner

Generator

DATA FILE
Manufacturer: Rothana Heavy Engineering (local subsidiary of KDY)
Make: LAAT/i (Low-Altitude Assault Transport/infantry) repulsorlift gunship
Dimensions: length (clearance with guns) 17.4 m (57 ft); wingspan 17 m (55.7 ft); depth 6.1 m (20 ft)
Max. airspeed: 620 kph (384 mph)
Cargo capacity: 4 military speeder bikes; approx. 17 m^3 (600 ft^3) in main hold (if troops absent)
Consumables: 8 hours flying fuel (approx.)
Crew: 1 pilot; 1 co-pilot/gunner; 2 auxiliary turret gunners
Passengers: 30 clone troopers approx.; 1 IM-6 Battlefield Medical Droid (stowed in emergency locker)
Armament: 3 anti-personnel turrets (2 front; 1 back; 5×10^9 joules per shot); 2 mass-driver missile launchers (variable payload); 4 composite-beam, pinpoint laser turrets (2 manned; 2 remote; 3×10^{11} joules per shot); 8 light air-to-air rockets (6×10^{11} joules per shot)

Pilot

Flight computer

Remote-controlled firing dishes allow both dorsal and ventral coverage

Navigational terrain-sensor housing

Computer interface ports for servicing in hangar

Power feeds to front laser cannons

Firing dish exploits non-superposition of blaster energy to compose variable tributary beams into a finely aimed, intense composite beam

Turret elevation guides

Laser cannon power feed access panel

Light indicates atmospheric integrity of front sections

Airtight hatch to front compartments

Handhold

Armature swings turret in or out of main hold

Deckplates give access to main repulsor array

Protruding deck ledge gives deploying troops a clear view

Insulated armored sheath guides belt frictionlessly

Blaster cratering on superficial armor

Ball turret traverses its socket freely and elevates to the limits of its firing dishes

Variable output of wingtip repulsor grille affects roll of gunship

Turret suspension rollers, magnetic clamps, and power-feed modules

TACTICAL ADVANTAGE

These strategic transport craft and their variants are maneuverable enough to fly low and exploit the natural cover of Geonosis' precipitous ravines and spires. Their long mass-driver barrels can accelerate projectiles up to hypersonic velocities. Once launched, missiles engage self-powered flight along either a programmed trajectory or following encrypted guidance signals. Telemetry (remote communication) comes from either an orbiting mothership or signals routed from ground units within sight of the target, including advance scout troops.

SURVIVAL AND RECOVERY

Each fully trained clone soldier represents a considerable investment, so crew have several escape options when their gunship is disabled. In the worst survivable scenarios, the entire cockpit section ejects as an escape capsule. After a failed landing, the cockpit canopies can be blown off. If the egress passage is blocked below the cockpits, crew use external climbing steps built into the hull. Injured or isolated men are retrieved whenever possible. The LAAT/i repulsorlift gunship is their primary recovery vehicle. Emergency equipment in forward lockers includes a globular IM-6 Battlefield Medical Droid, medical packs, armor repair kits, collapsible repulsor stretchers, and inflatable decontamination tents.

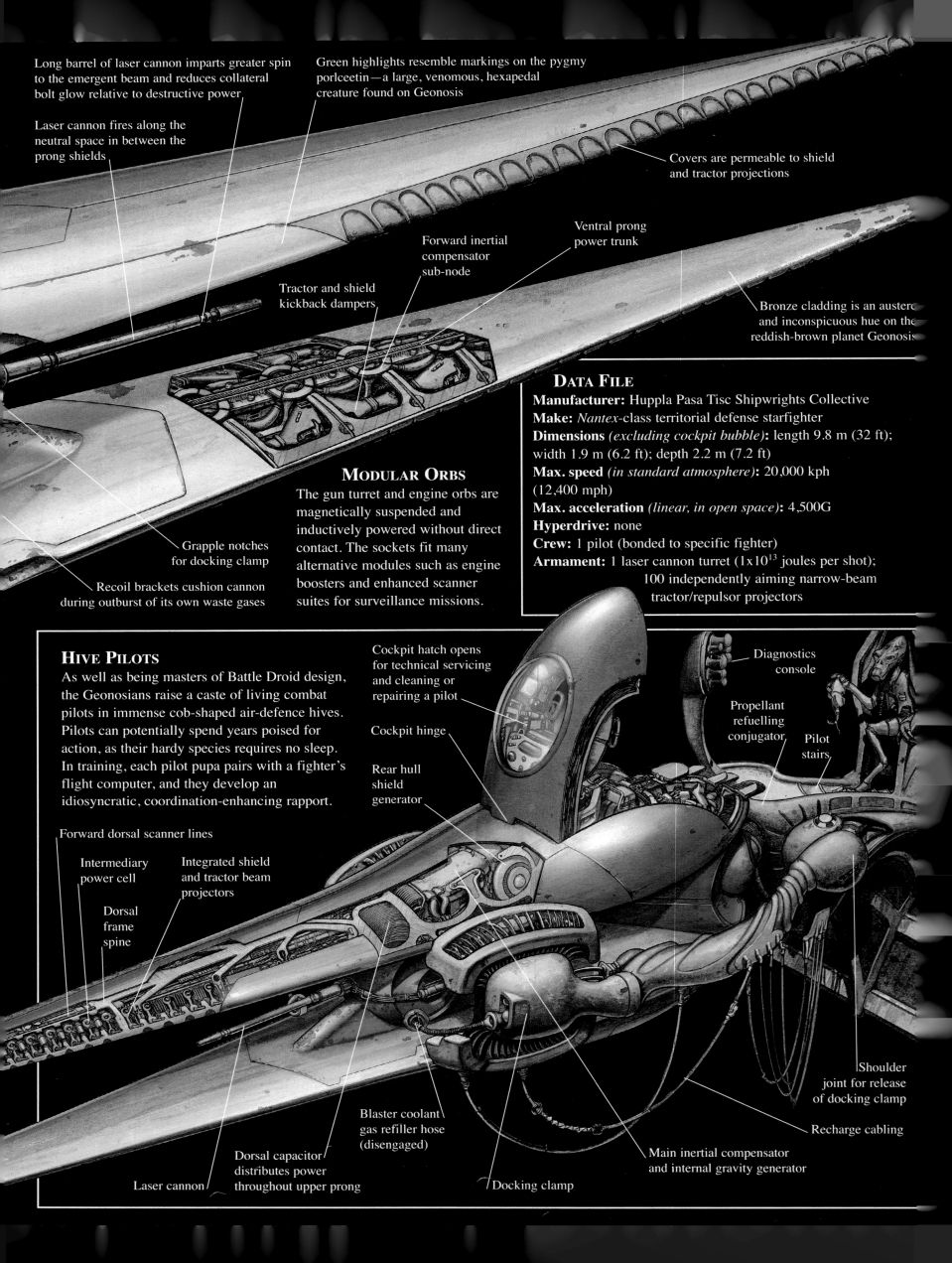

Long barrel of laser cannon imparts greater spin to the emergent beam and reduces collateral bolt glow relative to destructive power

Green highlights resemble markings on the pygmy porlceetin—a large, venomous, hexapedal creature found on Geonosis

Laser cannon fires along the neutral space in between the prong shields

Covers are permeable to shield and tractor projections

Ventral prong power trunk

Forward inertial compensator sub-node

Tractor and shield kickback dampers

Bronze cladding is an austere and inconspicuous hue on the reddish-brown planet Geonosis

Grapple notches for docking clamp

Recoil brackets cushion cannon during outburst of its own waste gases

MODULAR ORBS

The gun turret and engine orbs are magnetically suspended and inductively powered without direct contact. The sockets fit many alternative modules such as engine boosters and enhanced scanner suites for surveillance missions.

DATA FILE

Manufacturer: Huppla Pasa Tisc Shipwrights Collective
Make: *Nantex*-class territorial defense starfighter
Dimensions *(excluding cockpit bubble)*: length 9.8 m (32 ft); width 1.9 m (6.2 ft); depth 2.2 m (7.2 ft)
Max. speed *(in standard atmosphere)*: 20,000 kph (12,400 mph)
Max. acceleration *(linear, in open space)*: 4,500G
Hyperdrive: none
Crew: 1 pilot (bonded to specific fighter)
Armament: 1 laser cannon turret (1×10^{13} joules per shot); 100 independently aiming narrow-beam tractor/repulsor projectors

HIVE PILOTS

As well as being masters of Battle Droid design, the Geonosians raise a caste of living combat pilots in immense cob-shaped air-defence hives. Pilots can potentially spend years poised for action, as their hardy species requires no sleep. In training, each pilot pupa pairs with a fighter's flight computer, and they develop an idiosyncratic, coordination-enhancing rapport.

Cockpit hatch opens for technical servicing and cleaning or repairing a pilot

Diagnostics console

Cockpit hinge

Propellant refuelling conjugator

Pilot stairs

Rear hull shield generator

Forward dorsal scanner lines

Intermediary power cell

Integrated shield and tractor beam projectors

Dorsal frame spine

Shoulder joint for release of docking clamp

Recharge cabling

Blaster coolant gas refiller hose (disengaged)

Dorsal capacitor distributes power throughout upper prong

Main inertial compensator and internal gravity generator

Laser cannon

Docking clamp

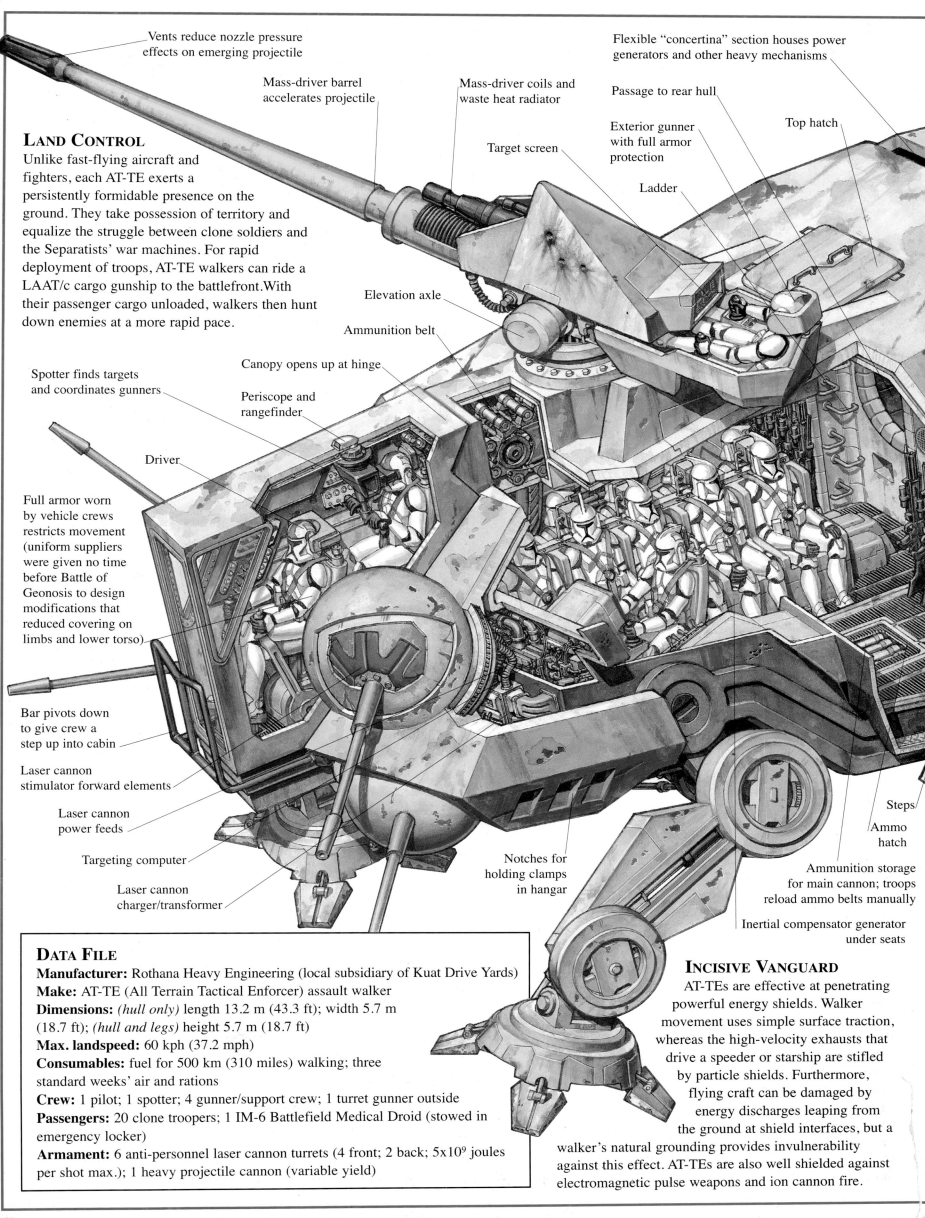

Vents reduce nozzle pressure
effects on emerging projectile

Flexible "concertina" section houses power
generators and other heavy mechanisms

Mass-driver barrel
accelerates projectile

Mass-driver coils and
waste heat radiator

Passage to rear hull

Top hatch

Target screen

Exterior gunner
with full armor
protection

Ladder

LAND CONTROL

Unlike fast-flying aircraft and
fighters, each AT-TE exerts a
persistently formidable presence on the
ground. They take possession of territory and
equalize the struggle between clone soldiers and
the Separatists' war machines. For rapid
deployment of troops, AT-TE walkers can ride a
LAAT/c cargo gunship to the battlefront. With
their passenger cargo unloaded, walkers then hunt
down enemies at a more rapid pace.

Elevation axle

Ammunition belt

Canopy opens up at hinge

Spotter finds targets
and coordinates gunners

Periscope and
rangefinder

Driver

Full armor worn
by vehicle crews
restricts movement
(uniform suppliers
were given no time
before Battle of
Geonosis to design
modifications that
reduced covering on
limbs and lower torso)

Bar pivots down
to give crew a
step up into cabin

Laser cannon
stimulator forward elements

Steps

Ammo
hatch

Laser cannon
power feeds

Notches for
holding clamps
in hangar

Ammunition storage
for main cannon; troops
reload ammo belts manually

Targeting computer

Laser cannon
charger/transformer

Inertial compensator generator
under seats

DATA FILE

Manufacturer: Rothana Heavy Engineering (local subsidiary of Kuat Drive Yards)
Make: AT-TE (All Terrain Tactical Enforcer) assault walker
Dimensions: *(hull only)* length 13.2 m (43.3 ft); width 5.7 m
(18.7 ft); *(hull and legs)* height 5.7 m (18.7 ft)
Max. landspeed: 60 kph (37.2 mph)
Consumables: fuel for 500 km (310 miles) walking; three
standard weeks' air and rations
Crew: 1 pilot; 1 spotter; 4 gunner/support crew; 1 turret gunner outside
Passengers: 20 clone troopers; 1 IM-6 Battlefield Medical Droid (stowed in
emergency locker)
Armament: 6 anti-personnel laser cannon turrets (4 front; 2 back; 5×10^9 joules
per shot max.); 1 heavy projectile cannon (variable yield)

INCISIVE VANGUARD

AT-TEs are effective at penetrating
powerful energy shields. Walker
movement uses simple surface traction,
whereas the high-velocity exhausts that
drive a speeder or starship are stifled
by particle shields. Furthermore,
flying craft can be damaged by
energy discharges leaping from
the ground at shield interfaces, but a
walker's natural grounding provides invulnerability
against this effect. AT-TEs are also well shielded against
electromagnetic pulse weapons and ion cannon fire.

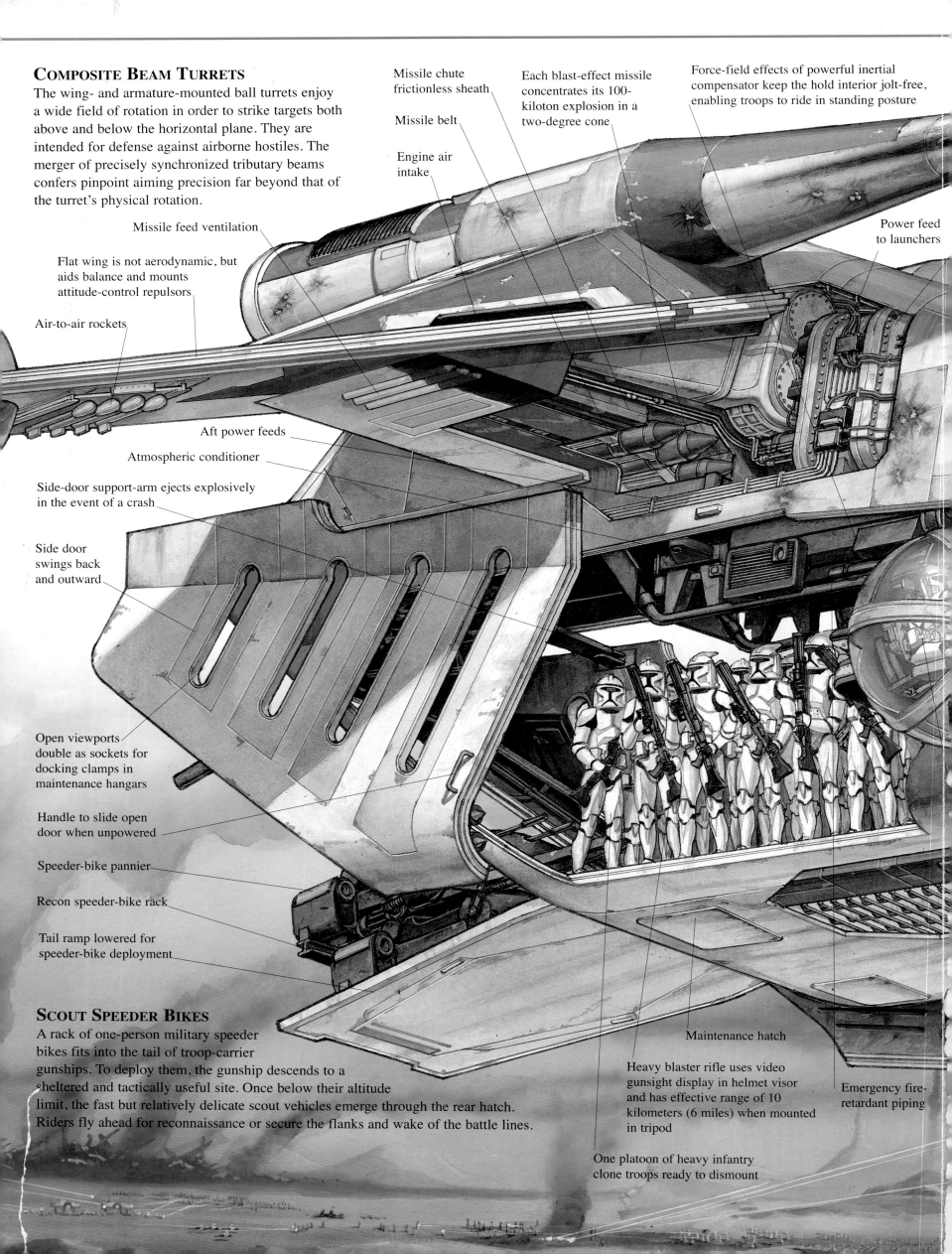

COMPOSITE BEAM TURRETS

The wing- and armature-mounted ball turrets enjoy a wide field of rotation in order to strike targets both above and below the horizontal plane. They are intended for defense against airborne hostiles. The merger of precisely synchronized tributary beams confers pinpoint aiming precision far beyond that of the turret's physical rotation.

Missile feed ventilation

Flat wing is not aerodynamic, but aids balance and mounts attitude-control repulsors

Air-to-air rockets

Missile chute frictionless sheath

Missile belt

Engine air intake

Each blast-effect missile concentrates its 100-kiloton explosion in a two-degree cone

Force-field effects of powerful inertial compensator keep the hold interior jolt-free, enabling troops to ride in standing posture

Power feed to launchers

Aft power feeds

Atmospheric conditioner

Side-door support-arm ejects explosively in the event of a crash

Side door swings back and outward

Open viewports double as sockets for docking clamps in maintenance hangars

Handle to slide open door when unpowered

Speeder-bike pannier

Recon speeder-bike rack

Tail ramp lowered for speeder-bike deployment

SCOUT SPEEDER BIKES

A rack of one-person military speeder bikes fits into the tail of troop-carrier gunships. To deploy them, the gunship descends to a sheltered and tactically useful site. Once below their altitude limit, the fast but relatively delicate scout vehicles emerge through the rear hatch. Riders fly ahead for reconnaissance or secure the flanks and wake of the battle lines.

Maintenance hatch

Heavy blaster rifle uses video gunsight display in helmet visor and has effective range of 10 kilometers (6 miles) when mounted in tripod

Emergency fire-retardant piping

One platoon of heavy infantry clone troops ready to dismount

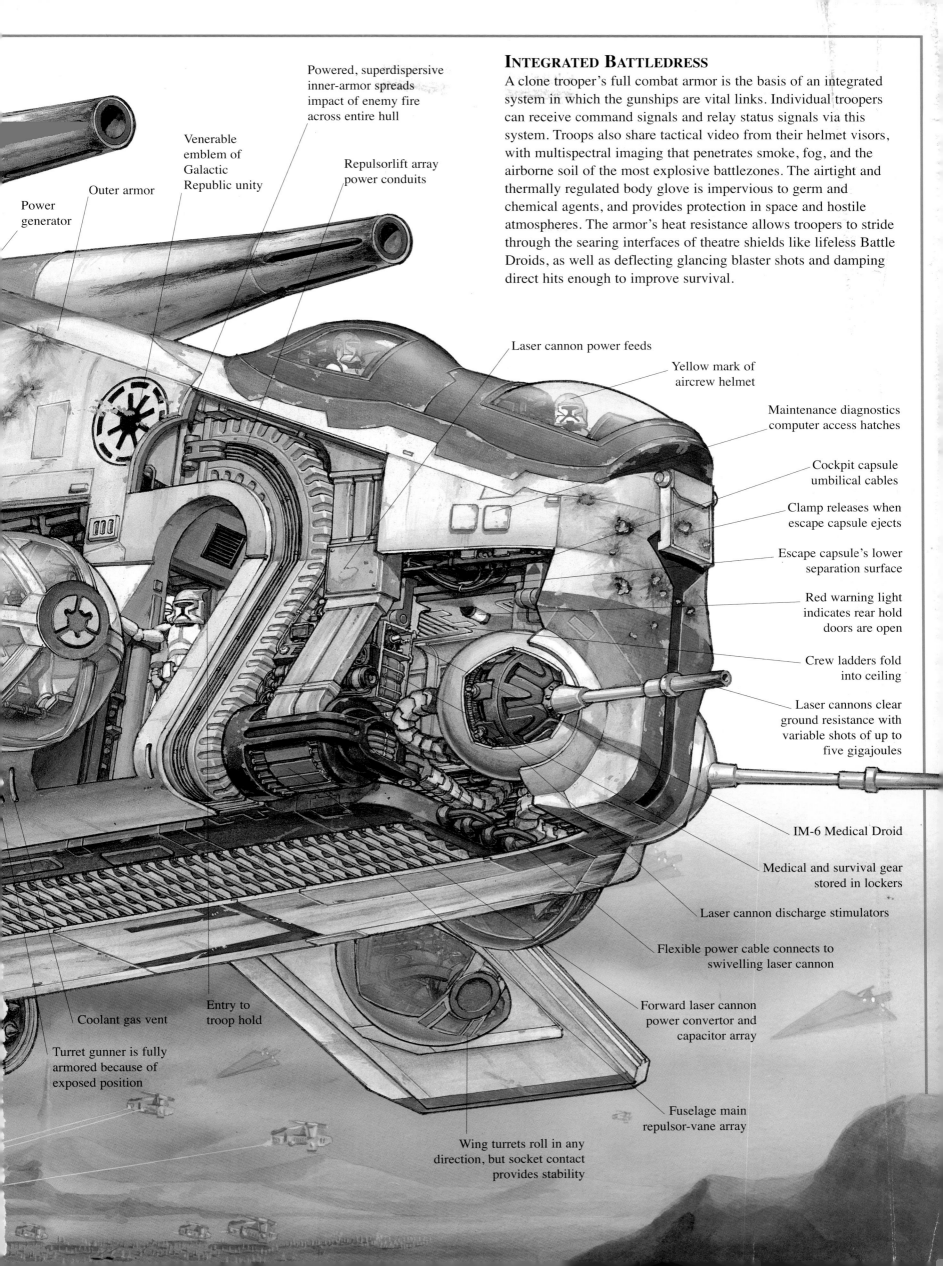

Power
generator

Outer armor

Venerable
emblem of
Galactic
Republic unity

Powered, superdispersive
inner-armor spreads
impact of enemy fire
across entire hull

Repulsorlift array
power conduits

INTEGRATED BATTLEDRESS

A clone trooper's full combat armor is the basis of an integrated system in which the gunships are vital links. Individual troopers can receive command signals and relay status signals via this system. Troops also share tactical video from their helmet visors, with multispectral imaging that penetrates smoke, fog, and the airborne soil of the most explosive battlezones. The airtight and thermally regulated body glove is impervious to germ and chemical agents, and provides protection in space and hostile atmospheres. The armor's heat resistance allows troopers to stride through the searing interfaces of theatre shields like lifeless Battle Droids, as well as deflecting glancing blaster shots and damping direct hits enough to improve survival.

Laser cannon power feeds

Yellow mark of
aircrew helmet

Maintenance diagnostics
computer access hatches

Cockpit capsule
umbilical cables

Clamp releases when
escape capsule ejects

Escape capsule's lower
separation surface

Red warning light
indicates rear hold
doors are open

Crew ladders fold
into ceiling

Laser cannons clear
ground resistance with
variable shots of up to
five gigajoules

IM-6 Medical Droid

Medical and survival gear
stored in lockers

Laser cannon discharge stimulators

Flexible power cable connects to
swivelling laser cannon

Forward laser cannon
power convertor and
capacitor array

Fuselage main
repulsor-vane array

Wing turrets roll in any
direction, but socket contact
provides stability

Entry to
troop hold

Coolant gas vent

Turret gunner is fully
armored because of
exposed position

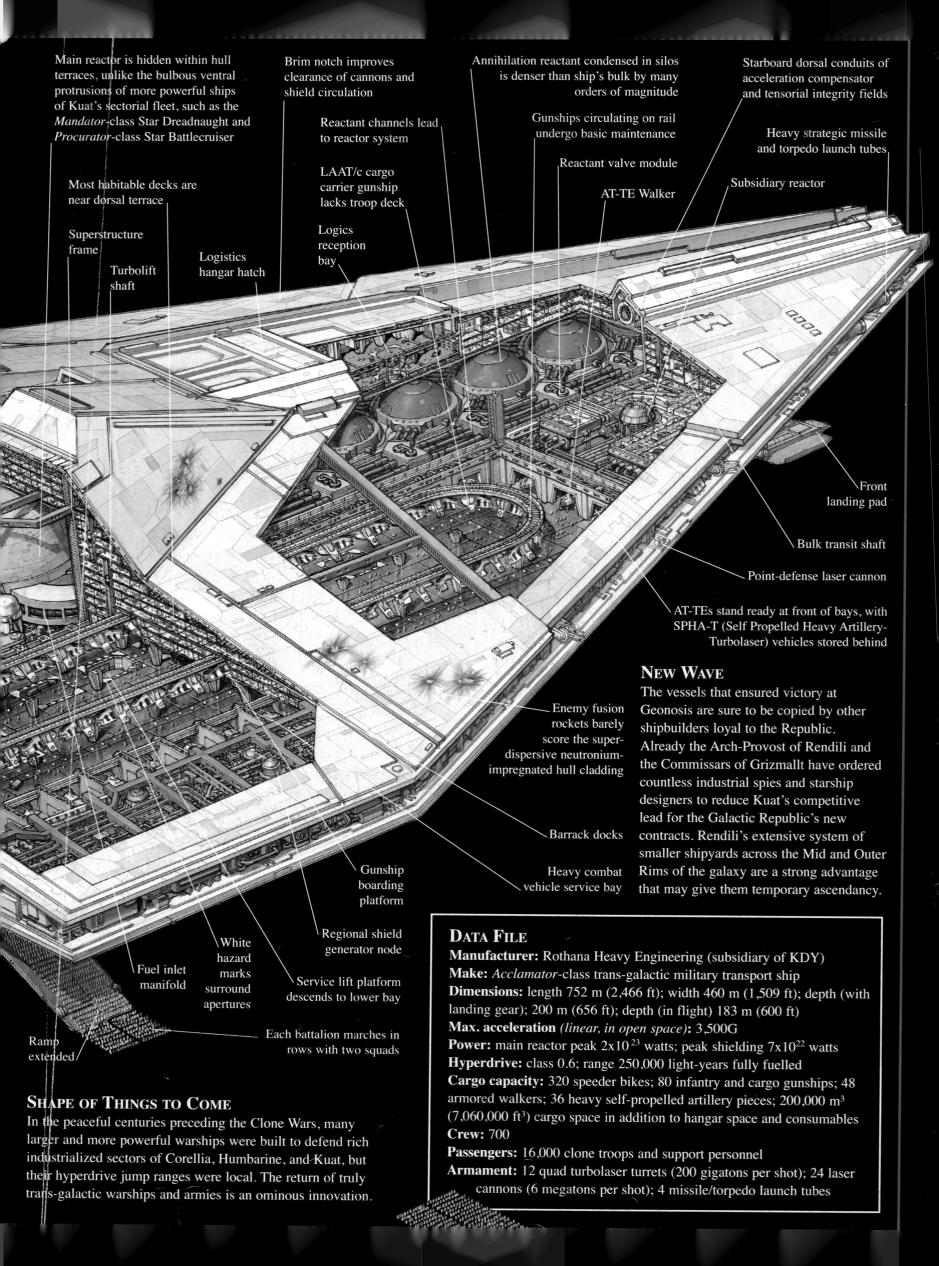

Main reactor is hidden within hull terraces, unlike the bulbous ventral protrusions of more powerful ships of Kuat's sectorial fleet, such as the *Mandator*-class Star Dreadnaught and *Procurator*-class Star Battlecruiser

Brim notch improves clearance of cannons and shield circulation

Annihilation reactant condensed in silos is denser than ship's bulk by many orders of magnitude

Starboard dorsal conduits of acceleration compensator and tensorial integrity fields

Most habitable decks are near dorsal terrace

Reactant channels lead to reactor system

Gunships circulating on rail undergo basic maintenance

Heavy strategic missile and torpedo launch tubes

Superstructure frame

LAAT/c cargo carrier gunship lacks troop deck

Reactant valve module

Subsidiary reactor

Turbolift shaft

Logistics hangar hatch

Logics reception bay

AT-TE Walker

Front landing pad

Bulk transit shaft

Point-defense laser cannon

AT-TEs stand ready at front of bays, with SPHA-T (Self Propelled Heavy Artillery-Turbolaser) vehicles stored behind

Enemy fusion rockets barely score the super-dispersive neutronium-impregnated hull cladding

NEW WAVE

The vessels that ensured victory at Geonosis are sure to be copied by other shipbuilders loyal to the Republic. Already the Arch-Provost of Rendili and the Commissars of Grizmallt have ordered countless industrial spies and starship designers to reduce Kuat's competitive lead for the Galactic Republic's new contracts. Rendili's extensive system of smaller shipyards across the Mid and Outer Rims of the galaxy are a strong advantage that may give them temporary ascendancy.

Barrack docks

Heavy combat vehicle service bay

Gunship boarding platform

White hazard marks surround apertures

Regional shield generator node

Fuel inlet manifold

Service lift platform descends to lower bay

Ramp extended

Each battalion marches in rows with two squads

SHAPE OF THINGS TO COME

In the peaceful centuries preceding the Clone Wars, many larger and more powerful warships were built to defend rich industrialized sectors of Corellia, Humbarine, and Kuat, but their hyperdrive jump ranges were local. The return of truly trans-galactic warships and armies is an ominous innovation.

DATA FILE

Manufacturer: Rothana Heavy Engineering (subsidiary of KDY)
Make: *Acclamator*-class trans-galactic military transport ship
Dimensions: length 752 m (2,466 ft); width 460 m (1,509 ft); depth (with landing gear); 200 m (656 ft); depth (in flight) 183 m (600 ft)
Max. acceleration *(linear, in open space)*: 3,500G
Power: main reactor peak 2×10^{23} watts; peak shielding 7×10^{22} watts
Hyperdrive: class 0.6; range 250,000 light-years fully fuelled
Cargo capacity: 320 speeder bikes; 80 infantry and cargo gunships; 48 armored walkers; 36 heavy self-propelled artillery pieces; 200,000 m³ (7,060,000 ft³) cargo space in addition to hangar space and consumables
Crew: 700
Passengers: 16,000 clone troops and support personnel
Armament: 12 quad turbolaser turrets (200 gigatons per shot); 24 laser cannons (6 megatons per shot); 4 missile/torpedo launch tubes

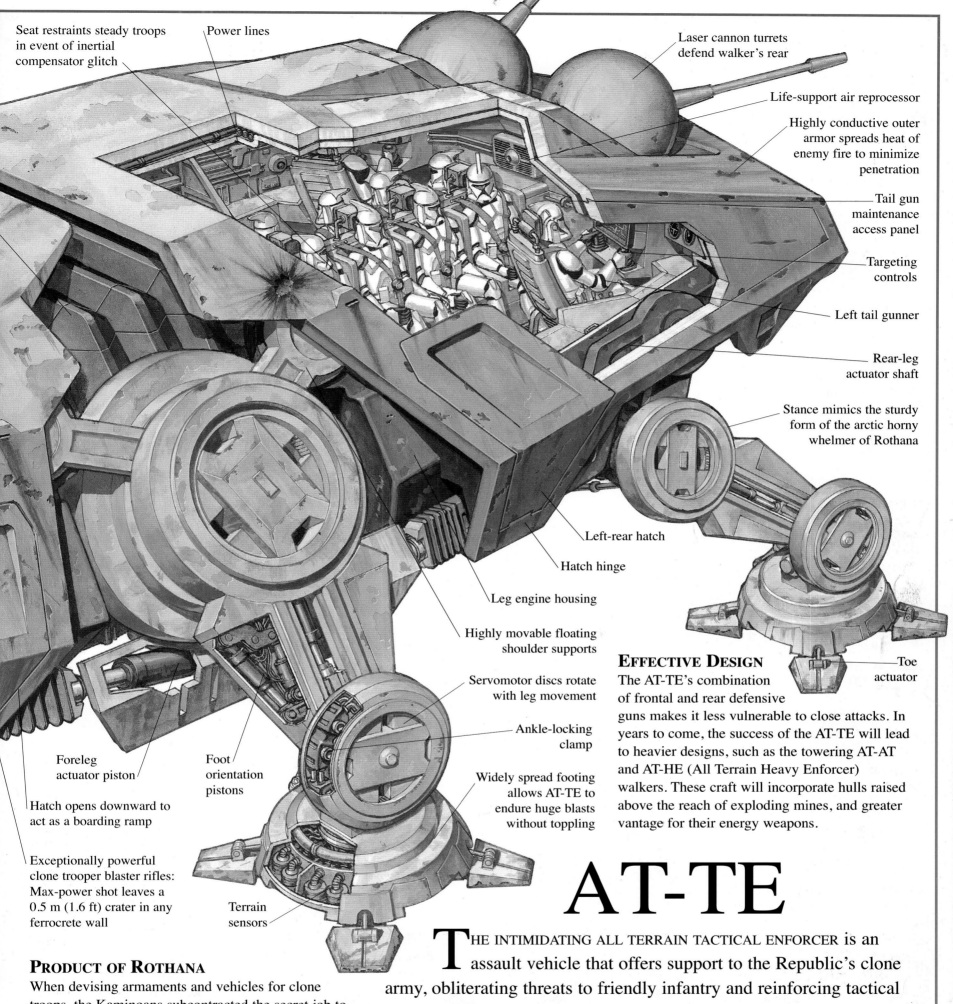

Seat restraints steady troops in event of inertial compensator glitch

Power lines

Laser cannon turrets defend walker's rear

Life-support air reprocessor

Highly conductive outer armor spreads heat of enemy fire to minimize penetration

Tail gun maintenance access panel

Targeting controls

Left tail gunner

Rear-leg actuator shaft

Stance mimics the sturdy form of the arctic horny whelmer of Rothana

Left-rear hatch

Hatch hinge

Leg engine housing

Highly movable floating shoulder supports

Toe actuator

Servomotor discs rotate with leg movement

Ankle-locking clamp

Foreleg actuator piston

Foot orientation pistons

Widely spread footing allows AT-TE to endure huge blasts without toppling

Hatch opens downward to act as a boarding ramp

Exceptionally powerful clone trooper blaster rifles: Max-power shot leaves a 0.5 m (1.6 ft) crater in any ferrocrete wall

Terrain sensors

EFFECTIVE DESIGN

The AT-TE's combination of frontal and rear defensive guns makes it less vulnerable to close attacks. In years to come, the success of the AT-TE will lead to heavier designs, such as the towering AT-AT and AT-HE (All Terrain Heavy Enforcer) walkers. These craft will incorporate hulls raised above the reach of exploding mines, and greater vantage for their energy weapons.

AT-TE

THE INTIMIDATING ALL TERRAIN TACTICAL ENFORCER is an assault vehicle that offers support to the Republic's clone army, obliterating threats to friendly infantry and reinforcing tactical control. Wading through the savage din of battle, the walker's sure-footed, six-legged stance allows it to cross crevices and climb otherwise impassably rugged slopes. Its massive turret-mounted missile-launcher bombards fixed emplacements or smites slow-moving aircraft, while six laser-cannon turrets swivel quickly to devastate faster line-of-sight targets. In the event of a close assault by enemy infantry, an AT-TE can dismount its two squads of troops to enter the fray and secure the immediate surroundings.

PRODUCT OF ROTHANA

When devising armaments and vehicles for clone troops, the Kaminoans subcontracted the secret job to Rothana Heavy Engineering, a subsidiary of Kuat Drive Yards—and no friend of the Trade Federation or Techno Union. Toiling in immense underground factories and honeycombed orbital shipyards, RHE's workforce is famed for its diligence. Their star system is uniquely clear of Trade Federation espionage, due to factors ranging from the impenetrably complex Rothanian etiquette (which makes outsiders stand out) to a sizeable KDY corporate-security starfleet and inventively deployed mines in Rothana's inbound hyperlanes.

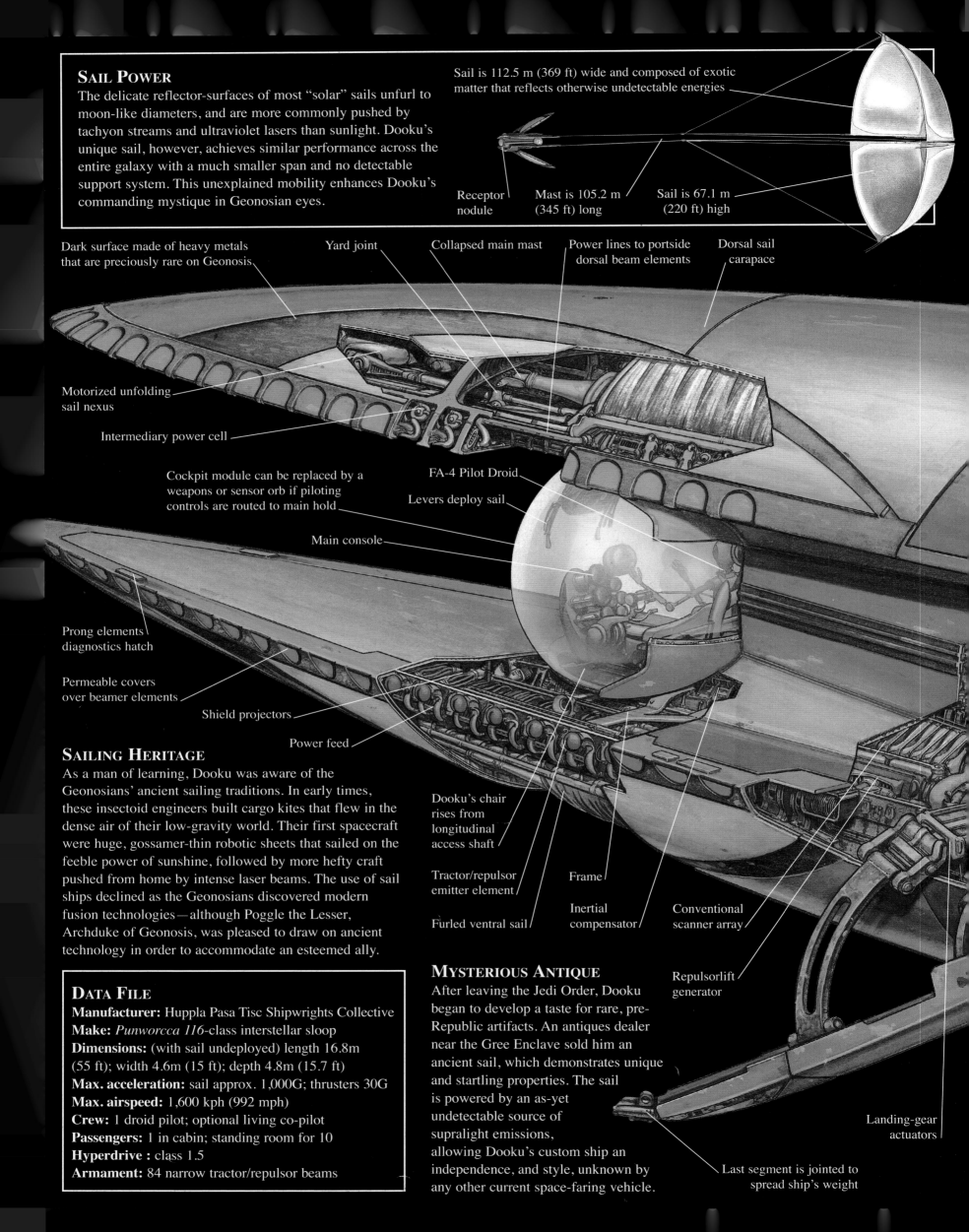

SAIL POWER

The delicate reflector-surfaces of most "solar" sails unfurl to moon-like diameters, and are more commonly pushed by tachyon streams and ultraviolet lasers than sunlight. Dooku's unique sail, however, achieves similar performance across the entire galaxy with a much smaller span and no detectable support system. This unexplained mobility enhances Dooku's commanding mystique in Geonosian eyes.

Sail is 112.5 m (369 ft) wide and composed of exotic matter that reflects otherwise undetectable energies

Receptor nodule

Mast is 105.2 m (345 ft) long

Sail is 67.1 m (220 ft) high

Dark surface made of heavy metals that are preciously rare on Geonosis

Yard joint

Collapsed main mast

Power lines to portside dorsal beam elements

Dorsal sail carapace

Motorized unfolding sail nexus

Intermediary power cell

Cockpit module can be replaced by a weapons or sensor orb if piloting controls are routed to main hold

FA-4 Pilot Droid

Levers deploy sail

Main console

Prong elements diagnostics hatch

Permeable covers over beamer elements

Shield projectors

Power feed

SAILING HERITAGE

As a man of learning, Dooku was aware of the Geonosians' ancient sailing traditions. In early times, these insectoid engineers built cargo kites that flew in the dense air of their low-gravity world. Their first spacecraft were huge, gossamer-thin robotic sheets that sailed on the feeble power of sunshine, followed by more hefty craft pushed from home by intense laser beams. The use of sail ships declined as the Geonosians discovered modern fusion technologies—although Poggle the Lesser, Archduke of Geonosis, was pleased to draw on ancient technology in order to accommodate an esteemed ally.

Dooku's chair rises from longitudinal access shaft

Tractor/repulsor emitter element

Furled ventral sail

Frame

Inertial compensator

Conventional scanner array

Repulsorlift generator

DATA FILE

Manufacturer: Huppla Pasa Tisc Shipwrights Collective
Make: *Punworcca 116*-class interstellar sloop
Dimensions: (with sail undeployed) length 16.8m (55 ft); width 4.6m (15 ft); depth 4.8m (15.7 ft)
Max. acceleration: sail approx. 1,000G; thrusters 30G
Max. airspeed: 1,600 kph (992 mph)
Crew: 1 droid pilot; optional living co-pilot
Passengers: 1 in cabin; standing room for 10
Hyperdrive : class 1.5
Armament: 84 narrow tractor/repulsor beams

MYSTERIOUS ANTIQUE

After leaving the Jedi Order, Dooku began to develop a taste for rare, pre-Republic artifacts. An antiques dealer near the Gree Enclave sold him an ancient sail, which demonstrates unique and startling properties. The sail is powered by an as-yet undetectable source of supralight emissions, allowing Dooku's custom ship an independence, and style, unknown by any other current space-faring vehicle.

Landing-gear actuators

Last segment is jointed to spread ship's weight

SOLAR SAILER

A GIFT FROM HIS GEONOSIAN COLLEAGUES, Dooku's ship is a unique melding of a *Punworcca 116*-class sloop with an elegant sail supplied by the Count himself. On Dooku's instructions, Geonosian engineers attached this enigmatic accessory to the ship to provide independent power without the need to carry fuel (apart from guide thrusters). The ship's interior is tailored to Dooku's sense of refinement, with an extensive databook library and ornate decorations. When the tide of battle turns, the Count flees to his escape vessel and slips away....

BOW PRONGS

Geonosian starships typically feature two or more multi-functional bow prongs. Rows of narrow-beam tractor/repulsor emitters along the prongs act as offensive grapples or steering aids when there are surrounding objects to pull and push against. Also, the spread of ray-shield energies around the prongs can be selectively adjusted to give the ship extra maneuverablity.

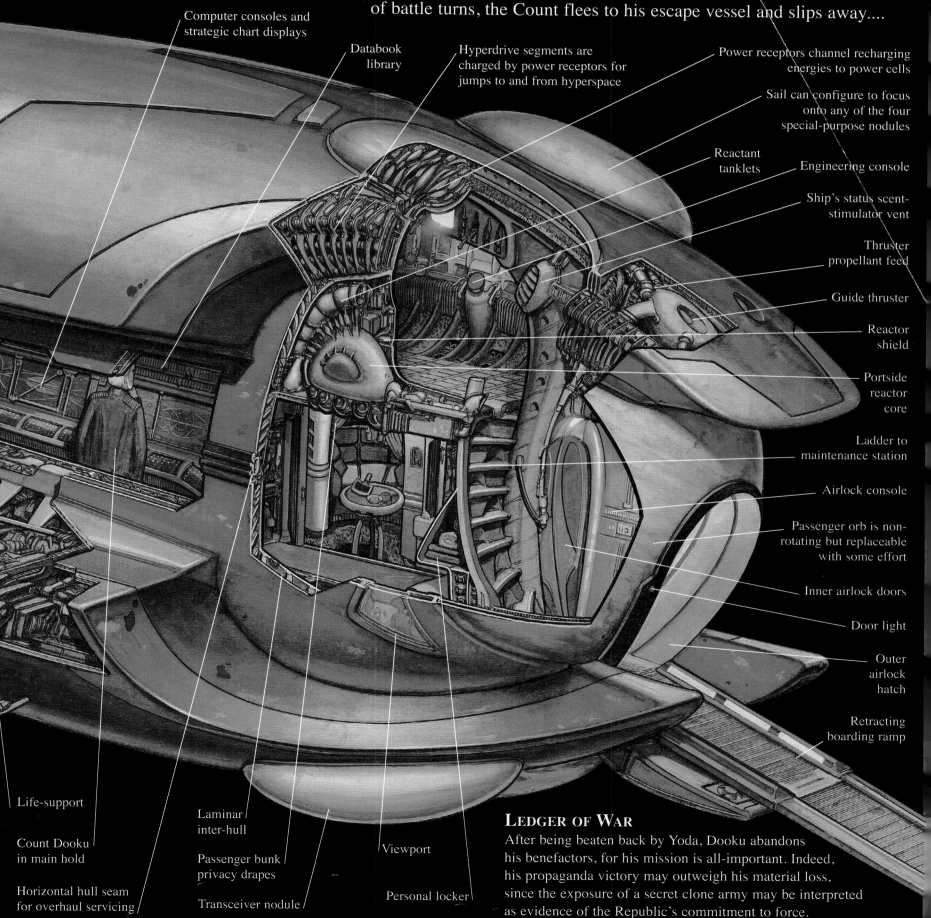

Computer consoles and strategic chart displays

Databook library

Hyperdrive segments are charged by power receptors for jumps to and from hyperspace

Power receptors channel recharging energies to power cells

Sail can configure to focus onto any of the four special-purpose nodules

Reactant tanklets

Engineering console

Ship's status scent-stimulator vent

Thruster propellant feed

Guide thruster

Reactor shield

Portside reactor core

Ladder to maintenance station

Airlock console

Passenger orb is non-rotating but replaceable with some effort

Inner airlock doors

Door light

Outer airlock hatch

Retracting boarding ramp

Life-support

Count Dooku in main hold

Horizontal hull seam for overhaul servicing

Laminar inter-hull

Passenger bunk privacy drapes

Transceiver nodule

Viewport

Personal locker

LEDGER OF WAR

After being beaten back by Yoda, Dooku abandons his benefactors, for his mission is all-important. Indeed, his propaganda victory may outweigh his material loss, since the exposure of a secret clone army may be interpreted as evidence of the Republic's commitment to force.

EPISODE III
REVENGE OF THE SITH

THE CLONE WARS HAVE escalated into a cataclysmic conflict, thousands of times vaster than the opening battle on Geonosis. Most of the Republic's Jedi Knights and clone troops are engaged in desperate campaigns across the galaxy. The Separatist movement, now known as the Confederacy of Independent Systems, is encircling the crumbling Galactic Republic, advancing ever-nearer to the star systems of the Galactic Core. Neither side, however, is aware that their leaders are secretly in league with each other. The Republic's Supreme Chancellor Palpatine is really the Sith Lord Darth Sidious, and his apprentice is Darth Tyranus, otherwise known as Count Dooku, the leader of the Separatists. Sidious is merely playing for time until he is ready to replace Tyranus with a new, more powerful apprentice, who will help him to achieve his ultimate aim: utter subjugation of the galaxy under Sith rule and the formation of a merciless new order—the Galactic Empire.

STAR DESTROYER-*VENATOR* CLASS

THE GALACTIC REPUBLIC's new *Venator*-class Star Destroyer is fast enough to chase down blockade runners and big enough to lead independent missions such as the liberation of Utapau. A flotilla of these medium-weight, versatile multi-role warships can blast through the shields of a Trade Federation battleship with ease. The hangars of the *Venator*-class are much larger than older Star Destroyers like the *Victory*-class, and can support hundreds of fightercraft. The ship is also capable of planetary landings as a military transport and can be an escort for battleships in the Republic armada. However, the primary function of the *Venator*-class is its role as a fighting ship and starfighter carrier, making it a firm favorite with Jedi fighter aces.

DATA FILE

Manufacturer: Kuat Drive Yards
Make: *Venator*-class Star Destroyer
Dimensions: length 1,137 m (3,729 ft); wingspan 548 m (1,797 ft); height (in flight) 268 m (87.9 ft)
Max. acceleration (*linear, in open space*): 3,000G
Hyperdrive: class 1.0; 60,000 light year effective range
Crew: 7,400
Armament: 8 heavy turbolaser turrets; 2 medium dual turbolaser cannons; 52 point-defense laser cannons; 4 proton torpedo tubes; 6 tractor beam projectors
Complement: 192 V-wing fighters; 192 Eta-2 *Actis* Interceptors; 36 ARC-170 fighters; 24 military walkers; 40 LAAT/i (Low Altitude Assault Transport/infantry) gunships; miscellaneous shuttles

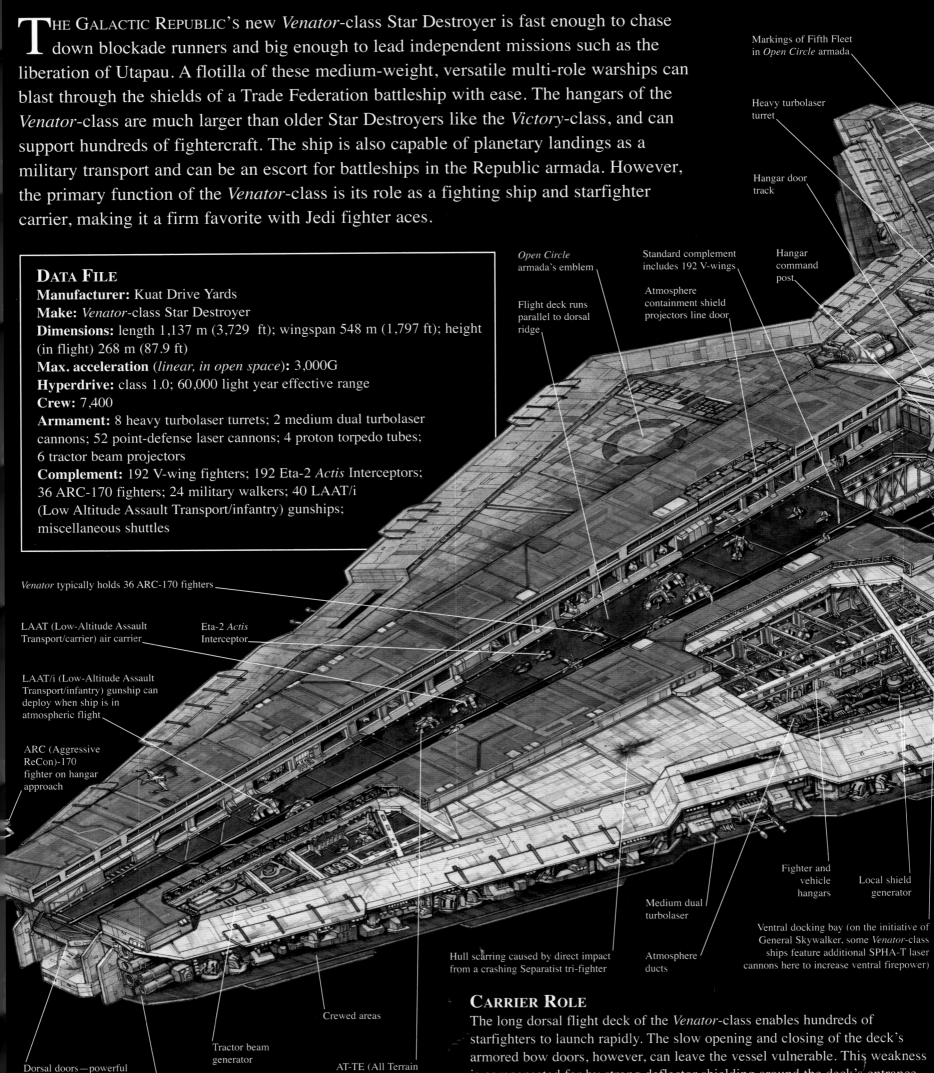

Markings of Fifth Fleet in *Open Circle* armada

Heavy turbolaser turret

Hangar door track

Open Circle armada's emblem

Standard complement includes 192 V-wings

Hangar command post

Flight deck runs parallel to dorsal ridge

Atmosphere containment shield projectors line door

Venator typically holds 36 ARC-170 fighters

LAAT (Low-Altitude Assault Transport/carrier) air carrier

Eta-2 *Actis* Interceptor

LAAT/i (Low-Altitude Assault Transport/infantry) gunship can deploy when ship is in atmospheric flight

ARC (Aggressive ReCon)-170 fighter on hangar approach

Fighter and vehicle hangars

Local shield generator

Medium dual turbolaser

Atmosphere ducts

Ventral docking bay (on the initiative of General Skywalker, some *Venator*-class ships feature additional SPHA-T laser cannons here to increase ventral firepower)

Hull scarring caused by direct impact from a crashing Separatist tri-fighter

Crewed areas

Tractor beam generator

AT-TE (All Terrain Tactical Enforcer) walker

Dorsal doors—powerful deflector shields also protect the ship's interior

Bow tractor beam projector

CARRIER ROLE

The long dorsal flight deck of the *Venator*-class enables hundreds of starfighters to launch rapidly. The slow opening and closing of the deck's armored bow doors, however, can leave the vessel vulnerable. This weakness is compensated for by strong deflector shielding around the deck's entrance, but the design flaw will be eliminated in future Star Destroyers.

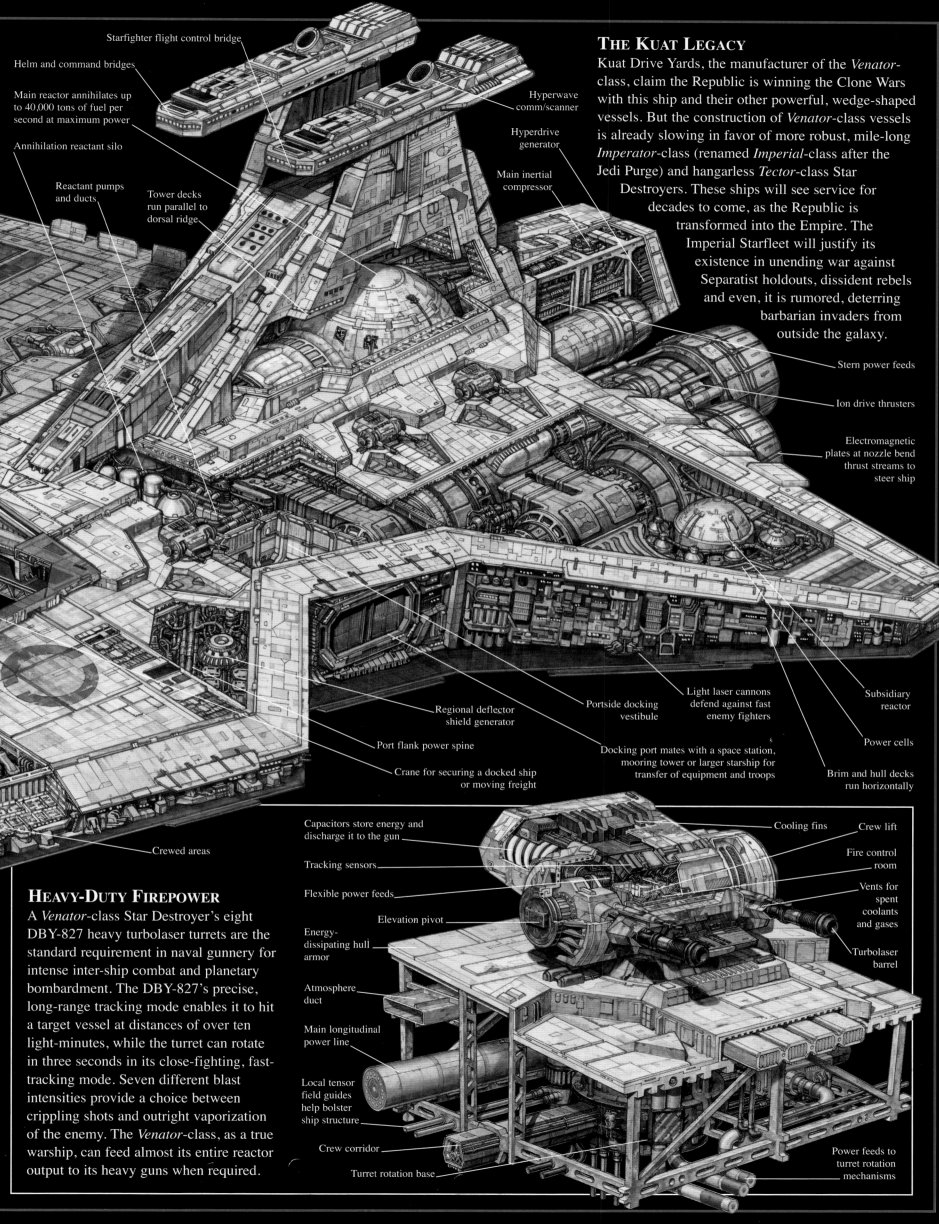

Starfighter flight control bridge

Helm and command bridges

Main reactor annihilates up to 40,000 tons of fuel per second at maximum power

Annihilation reactant silo

Reactant pumps and ducts

Tower decks run parallel to dorsal ridge

Hyperwave comm/scanner

Hyperdrive generator

Main inertial compressor

THE KUAT LEGACY

Kuat Drive Yards, the manufacturer of the *Venator*-class, claim the Republic is winning the Clone Wars with this ship and their other powerful, wedge-shaped vessels. But the construction of *Venator*-class vessels is already slowing in favor of more robust, mile-long *Imperator*-class (renamed *Imperial*-class after the Jedi Purge) and hangarless *Tector*-class Star Destroyers. These ships will see service for decades to come, as the Republic is transformed into the Empire. The Imperial Starfleet will justify its existence in unending war against Separatist holdouts, dissident rebels and even, it is rumored, deterring barbarian invaders from outside the galaxy.

Stern power feeds

Ion drive thrusters

Electromagnetic plates at nozzle bend thrust streams to steer ship

Subsidiary reactor

Power cells

Brim and hull decks run horizontally

Regional deflector shield generator

Portside docking vestibule

Light laser cannons defend against fast enemy fighters

Port flank power spine

Docking port mates with a space station, mooring tower or larger starship for transfer of equipment and troops

Crane for securing a docked ship or moving freight

Crewed areas

Capacitors store energy and discharge it to the gun

Tracking sensors

Flexible power feeds

Elevation pivot

Energy-dissipating hull armor

Atmosphere duct

Main longitudinal power line

Local tensor field guides help bolster ship structure

Crew corridor

Turret rotation base

Cooling fins

Crew lift

Fire control room

Vents for spent coolants and gases

Turbolaser barrel

Power feeds to turret rotation mechanisms

HEAVY-DUTY FIREPOWER

A *Venator*-class Star Destroyer's eight DBY-827 heavy turbolaser turrets are the standard requirement in naval gunnery for intense inter-ship combat and planetary bombardment. The DBY-827's precise, long-range tracking mode enables it to hit a target vessel at distances of over ten light-minutes, while the turret can rotate in three seconds in its close-fighting, fast-tracking mode. Seven different blast intensities provide a choice between crippling shots and outright vaporization of the enemy. The *Venator*-class, as a true warship, can feed almost its entire reactor output to its heavy guns when required.

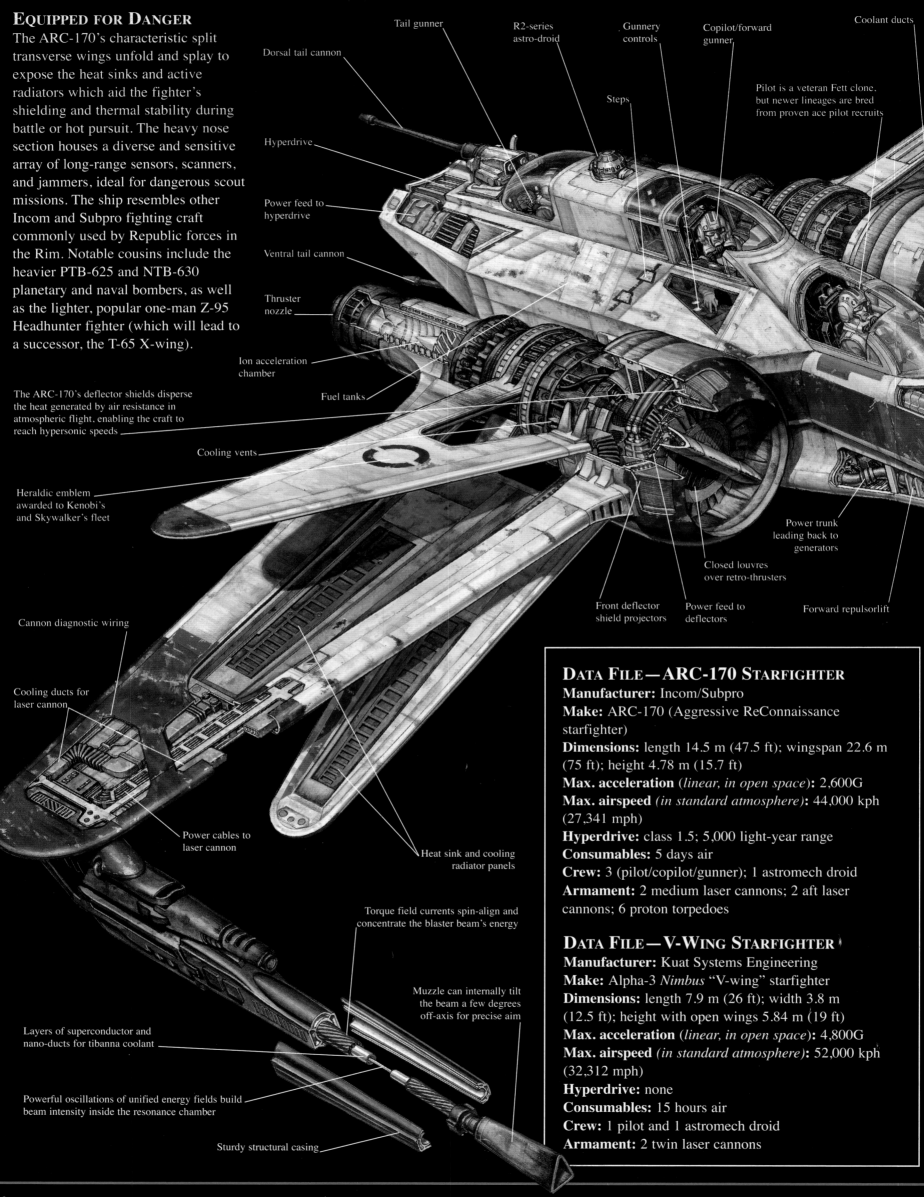

EQUIPPED FOR DANGER

The ARC-170's characteristic split transverse wings unfold and splay to expose the heat sinks and active radiators which aid the fighter's shielding and thermal stability during battle or hot pursuit. The heavy nose section houses a diverse and sensitive array of long-range sensors, scanners, and jammers, ideal for dangerous scout missions. The ship resembles other Incom and Subpro fighting craft commonly used by Republic forces in the Rim. Notable cousins include the heavier PTB-625 and NTB-630 planetary and naval bombers, as well as the lighter, popular one-man Z-95 Headhunter fighter (which will lead to a successor, the T-65 X-wing).

Tail gunner

Dorsal tail cannon

R2-series astro-droid

Gunnery controls

Copilot/forward gunner

Coolant ducts

Hyperdrive

Steps

Pilot is a veteran Fett clone, but newer lineages are bred from proven ace pilot recruits

Power feed to hyperdrive

Ventral tail cannon

Thruster nozzle

Ion acceleration chamber

Fuel tanks

The ARC-170's deflector shields disperse the heat generated by air resistance in atmospheric flight, enabling the craft to reach hypersonic speeds

Cooling vents

Heraldic emblem awarded to Kenobi's and Skywalker's fleet

Power trunk leading back to generators

Closed louvres over retro-thrusters

Front deflector shield projectors

Power feed to deflectors

Forward repulsorlift

Cannon diagnostic wiring

Cooling ducts for laser cannon

Power cables to laser cannon

Heat sink and cooling radiator panels

Torque field currents spin-align and concentrate the blaster beam's energy

Muzzle can internally tilt the beam a few degrees off-axis for precise aim

Layers of superconductor and nano-ducts for tibanna coolant

Powerful oscillations of unified energy fields build beam intensity inside the resonance chamber

Sturdy structural casing

DATA FILE—ARC-170 STARFIGHTER

Manufacturer: Incom/Subpro
Make: ARC-170 (Aggressive ReConnaissance starfighter)
Dimensions: length 14.5 m (47.5 ft); wingspan 22.6 m (75 ft); height 4.78 m (15.7 ft)
Max. acceleration (*linear, in open space*): 2,600G
Max. airspeed (*in standard atmosphere*): 44,000 kph (27,341 mph)
Hyperdrive: class 1.5; 5,000 light-year range
Consumables: 5 days air
Crew: 3 (pilot/copilot/gunner); 1 astromech droid
Armament: 2 medium laser cannons; 2 aft laser cannons; 6 proton torpedoes

DATA FILE—V-WING STARFIGHTER

Manufacturer: Kuat Systems Engineering
Make: Alpha-3 *Nimbus* "V-wing" starfighter
Dimensions: length 7.9 m (26 ft); width 3.8 m (12.5 ft); height with open wings 5.84 m (19 ft)
Max. acceleration (*linear, in open space*): 4,800G
Max. airspeed (*in standard atmosphere*): 52,000 kph (32,312 mph)
Hyperdrive: none
Consumables: 15 hours air
Crew: 1 pilot and 1 astromech droid
Armament: 2 twin laser cannons

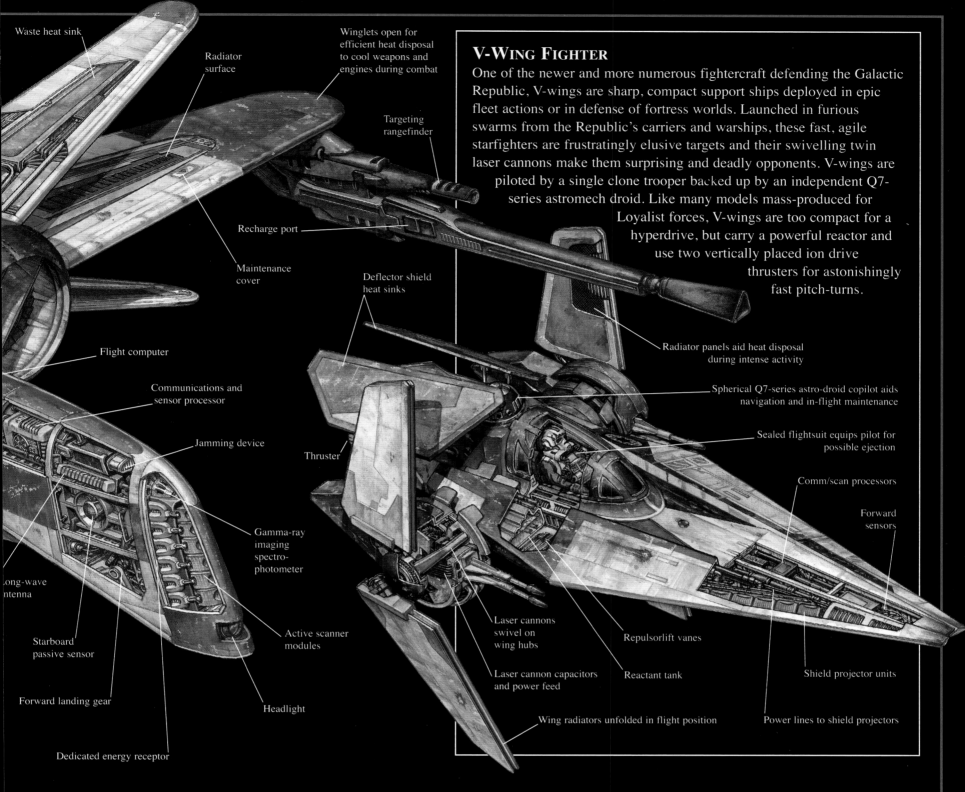

Waste heat sink

Radiator surface

Winglets open for efficient heat disposal to cool weapons and engines during combat

Targeting rangefinder

Recharge port

Maintenance cover

Deflector shield heat sinks

Flight computer

Communications and sensor processor

Jamming device

Thruster

Long-wave antenna

Gamma-ray imaging spectro-photometer

Starboard passive sensor

Active scanner modules

Forward landing gear

Headlight

Dedicated energy receptor

Laser cannons swivel on wing hubs

Laser cannon capacitors and power feed

Reactant tank

Wing radiators unfolded in flight position

V-Wing Fighter

One of the newer and more numerous fightercraft defending the Galactic Republic, V-wings are sharp, compact support ships deployed in epic fleet actions or in defense of fortress worlds. Launched in furious swarms from the Republic's carriers and warships, these fast, agile starfighters are frustratingly elusive targets and their swivelling twin laser cannons make them surprising and deadly opponents. V-wings are piloted by a single clone trooper backed up by an independent Q7-series astromech droid. Like many models mass-produced for Loyalist forces, V-wings are too compact for a hyperdrive, but carry a powerful reactor and use two vertically placed ion drive thrusters for astonishingly fast pitch-turns.

Radiator panels aid heat disposal during intense activity

Spherical Q7-series astro-droid copilot aids navigation and in-flight maintenance

Sealed flightsuit equips pilot for possible ejection

Comm/scan processors

Forward sensors

Repulsorlift vanes

Shield projector units

Power lines to shield projectors

Best of the Brave

The Open Circle fleet, led by Generals Kenobi and Skywalker, carries thousands of ARC-170s and other fighters that have endured harrowing months of continual war in the cruel Outer Rim sieges. Amongst the most experienced of ARC-170 squadrons is Squad Seven, a disciplined team of veteran aviators known for their unwavering courage. Squad Seven are clones of Jango Fett, the bounty hunter who was the genetic model for the first clone troops. However, an increasing number of units are formed from rigorously selected volunteers. Over the coming years, the most accomplished volunteer aces will be honored as stock for new clone lineages, and distinguished with all-black dress uniforms.

ARC-170 Fighter

Rugged and durable, the ARC-170 (Aggressive ReConnaissance) fighter is designed to undertake the loneliest, independent, manned patrols or daring raids, as it penetrates deeply into hostile sectors. With its inbuilt hyperdrive and capacity for a droid navigator, this long-range craft is built for days of unsupported interstellar missions, which vitally extends the reach of the Jedi and their starfleet beyond warships and carrier-dependent fighters. The ARC-170's main laser cannons are uncommonly large and blazingly effective against larger opponents. Robust armor, shields, and tail guns improve the odds of survival when the ship is surrounded by dozens or even hundreds of light, evasive droid fighters. When they're piloted into battle amid agile V-wings and Jedi Interceptors, the heavy-punching ARC-170 squadrons complete a formidable strike-force mix.

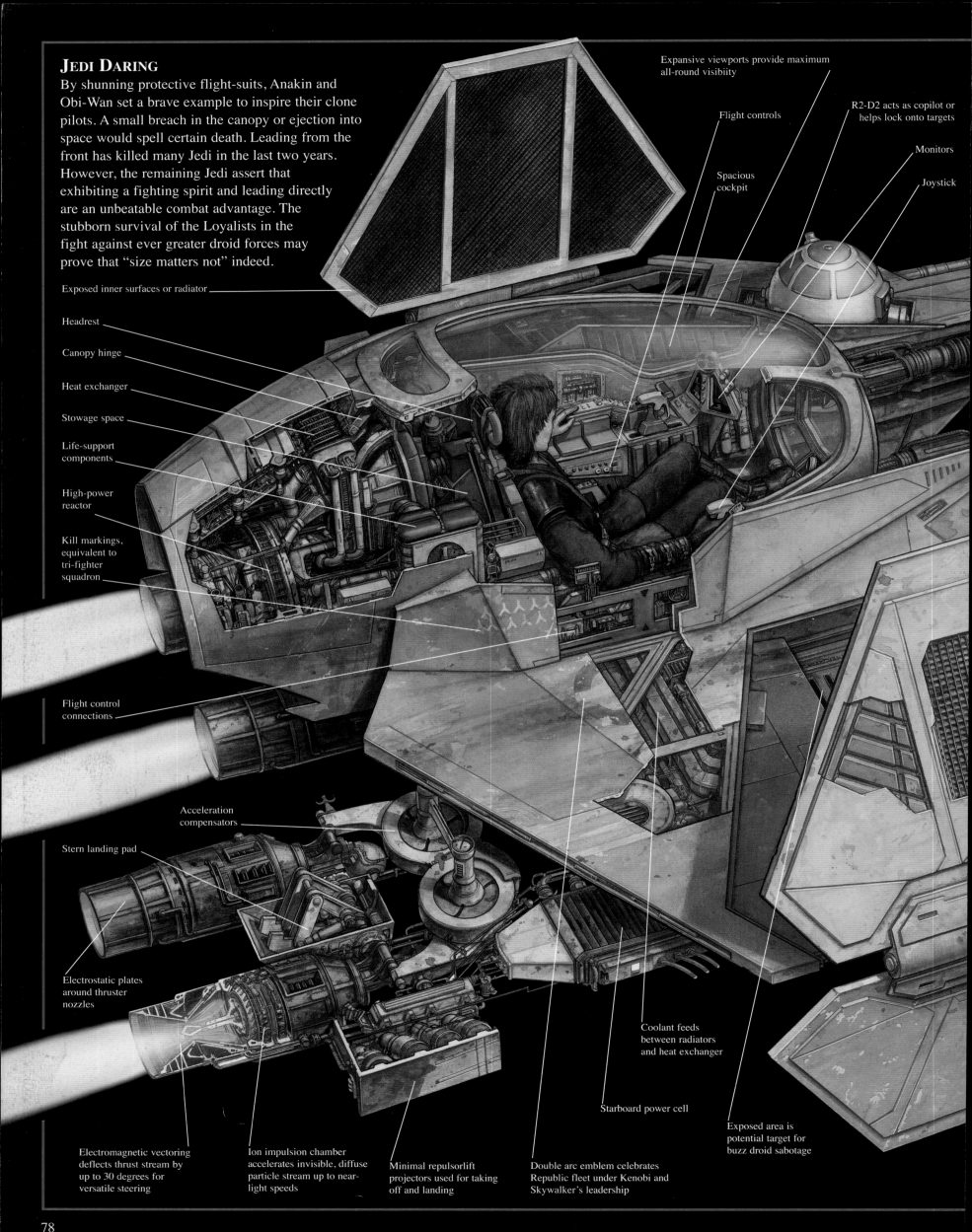

JEDI DARING

By shunning protective flight-suits, Anakin and Obi-Wan set a brave example to inspire their clone pilots. A small breach in the canopy or ejection into space would spell certain death. Leading from the front has killed many Jedi in the last two years. However, the remaining Jedi assert that exhibiting a fighting spirit and leading directly are an unbeatable combat advantage. The stubborn survival of the Loyalists in the fight against ever greater droid forces may prove that "size matters not" indeed.

Exposed inner surfaces or radiator

Headrest

Canopy hinge

Heat exchanger

Stowage space

Life-support components

High-power reactor

Kill markings, equivalent to tri-fighter squadron

Flight control connections

Acceleration compensators

Stern landing pad

Electrostatic plates around thruster nozzles

Expansive viewports provide maximum all-round visibiity

Flight controls

R2-D2 acts as copilot or helps lock onto targets

Monitors

Joystick

Spacious cockpit

Coolant feeds between radiators and heat exchanger

Starboard power cell

Exposed area is potential target for buzz droid sabotage

Electromagnetic vectoring deflects thrust stream by up to 30 degrees for versatile steering

Ion impulsion chamber accelerates invisible, diffuse particle stream up to near-light speeds

Minimal repulsorlift projectors used for taking off and landing

Double arc emblem celebrates Republic fleet under Kenobi and Skywalker's leadership

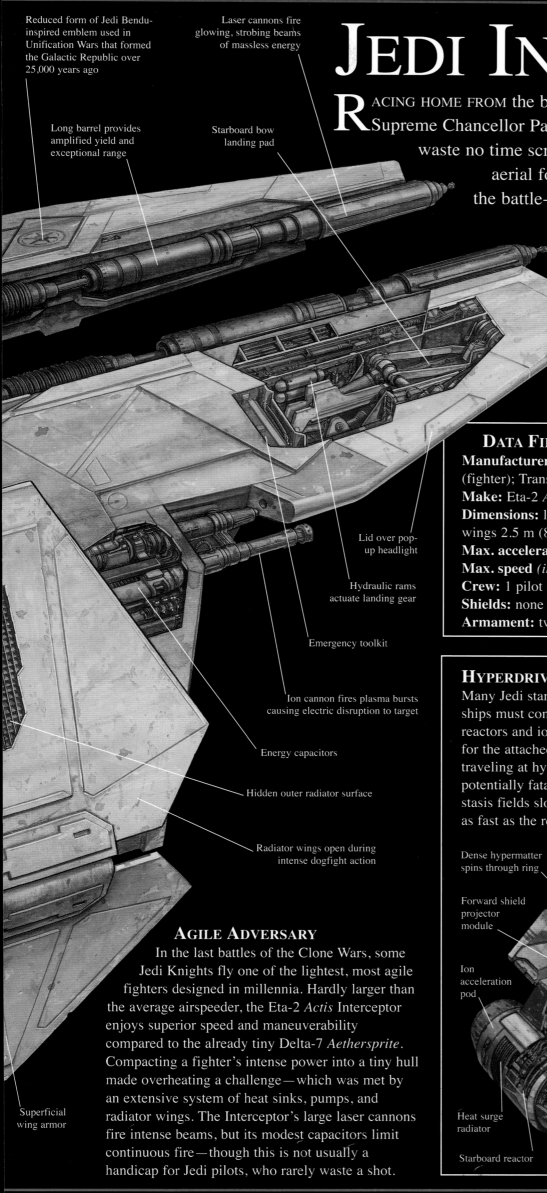

Reduced form of Jedi Bendu-inspired emblem used in Unification Wars that formed the Galactic Republic over 25,000 years ago

Laser cannons fire glowing, strobing beams of massless energy

Long barrel provides amplified yield and exceptional range

Starboard bow landing pad

Lid over pop-up headlight

Hydraulic rams actuate landing gear

Emergency toolkit

Ion cannon fires plasma bursts causing electric disruption to target

Energy capacitors

Hidden outer radiator surface

Radiator wings open during intense dogfight action

Superficial wing armor

JEDI INTERCEPTOR

Racing home from the brutal Outer Rim sieges to rescue the kidnapped Supreme Chancellor Palpatine, Obi-Wan Kenobi and Anakin Skywalker waste no time scrambling to their fighters. Leading the Republic's aerial forces in their Jedi Interceptors, they flit through the battle-zone with imp-like agility. Their spacecraft's compact design is suited to the Force-assisted tactical abilities of Jedi pilots—heavy flight instruments, sensors, and shields are unnecessary. Over the last three years, the distinctive Interceptor profile has become a symbol of authority and hope for the Republic's clone forces, and a frustrating apparition to the Separatists.

DATA FILE

Manufacturer: Kuat Systems Engineering, subsidiary of Kuat Drive Yards (fighter); TransGalMeg Industries Inc. (hyperdrive ring)
Make: Eta-2 *Actis* Interceptor; Syliure-45 hyperdrive module
Dimensions: length 5.47 m (18 ft); width 4.3 m (14.1 ft); height with open wings 2.5 m (8.2 ft)
Max. acceleration *(linear, in open space)*: 5,200G
Max. speed *(in standard atmosphere)*: 15,000 kph (9,321 mph)
Crew: 1 pilot and 1 astromech droid
Shields: none
Armament: two dual laser cannons; 2 secondary ion cannons

HYPERDRIVE BOOSTER

Many Jedi starfighters are too small to safely contain a hyperdrive, so the ships must connect to an external booster ring. Usually powered by twin reactors and ion drives, the ring contains "hypermatter," providing ballast for the attached starfighter during the jump to hyperspace. When traveling at hyperspeed, shields protect the ship and booster against potentially fatal collisions with interstellar gas and dark particles, while stasis fields slow the passage of onboard time, so that the pilot ages only as fast as the rest of the galaxy.

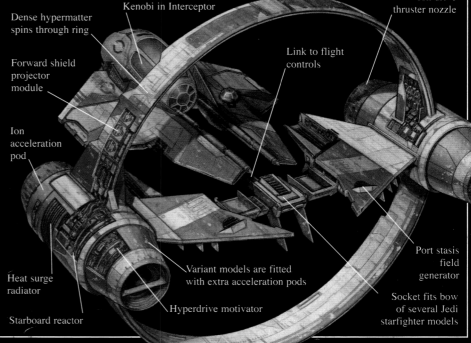

Kenobi in Interceptor

Ion drive thruster nozzle

Dense hypermatter spins through ring

Forward shield projector module

Link to flight controls

Ion acceleration pod

Port stasis field generator

Heat surge radiator

Variant models are fitted with extra acceleration pods

Socket fits bow of several Jedi starfighter models

Starboard reactor

Hyperdrive motivator

AGILE ADVERSARY

In the last battles of the Clone Wars, some Jedi Knights fly one of the lightest, most agile fighters designed in millennia. Hardly larger than the average airspeeder, the Eta-2 *Actis* Interceptor enjoys superior speed and maneuverability compared to the already tiny Delta-7 *Aethersprite*. Compacting a fighter's intense power into a tiny hull made overheating a challenge—which was met by an extensive system of heat sinks, pumps, and radiator wings. The Interceptor's large laser cannons fire intense beams, but its modest capacitors limit continuous fire—though this is not usually a handicap for Jedi pilots, who rarely waste a shot.

TRI-FIGHTER

CUNNING AND EERILY determined, droid tri-fighters are frightening new defenders of the Separatist battle fleets. These fast, agile space-superiority fighters are built to excel in dogfighting. Equipped with more advanced droid brains than common Trade Federation Vulture droid fighters, tri-fighters pose a challenge to even the best living starpilots. They may be outrun by high-speed Jedi Interceptors, but they are bulkier and more heavily armed, which makes them a force to be reckoned with.

COLICOID DESIGN

The tri-fighter's fearsome appearance and predatory programming is the work of the Colicoids—the creators of the Trade Federation's droideka heavy infantry. The ridged, three-armed design is based on the skull features of a terrifying prehistoric predator native to the planet Colla IV. Three independent thrusters give the craft its agility, and a powerful reactor and control/comms transceiver provide unusual range for a droid fighter.

Wing laser cannons can fire together or independently (cannon can tilt or slide on rail slightly to improve its deadly converging aim)

Support clamps lock cannon in place if fighter is firing while flying a twisting course

Continually charging capacitor feeds the laser cannon's rapid bursts of fire

Propellant delivery

Power and propellant regulation computer

Chain of power cells line inside of wing

Ionization reactor

Initial ion acceleration chamber

Electrodes

Secondary accelerator adds spin to ion stream

Particle stream exits thrust nozzle at near-light speed

Heat sinks grille inside radiator fin

Sensitive communications dish maintains a strong fix on mothership signal

Cables from power cells to weapon capacitor

Sturdy internal frame

Fuel tank

Main reactor core

Rotating frame holds reactor ball

Radiator surface

Repulsorlift aids flying over planetary surfaces

Reactor's magnetic confinement elements

Nose laser cannon is fixed in place

Barrel cooling blades

Left-eye photoreceptor

Discharge unit

Target scanner

Crafty and aggressive droid brain surrounding nose cannon's capacitor

Six re-arranged triangles from the Confederacy emblem signify the tri-fighter's squadron

Missile support rods fold out from wing

Clamps holding portside buzz-droid missile

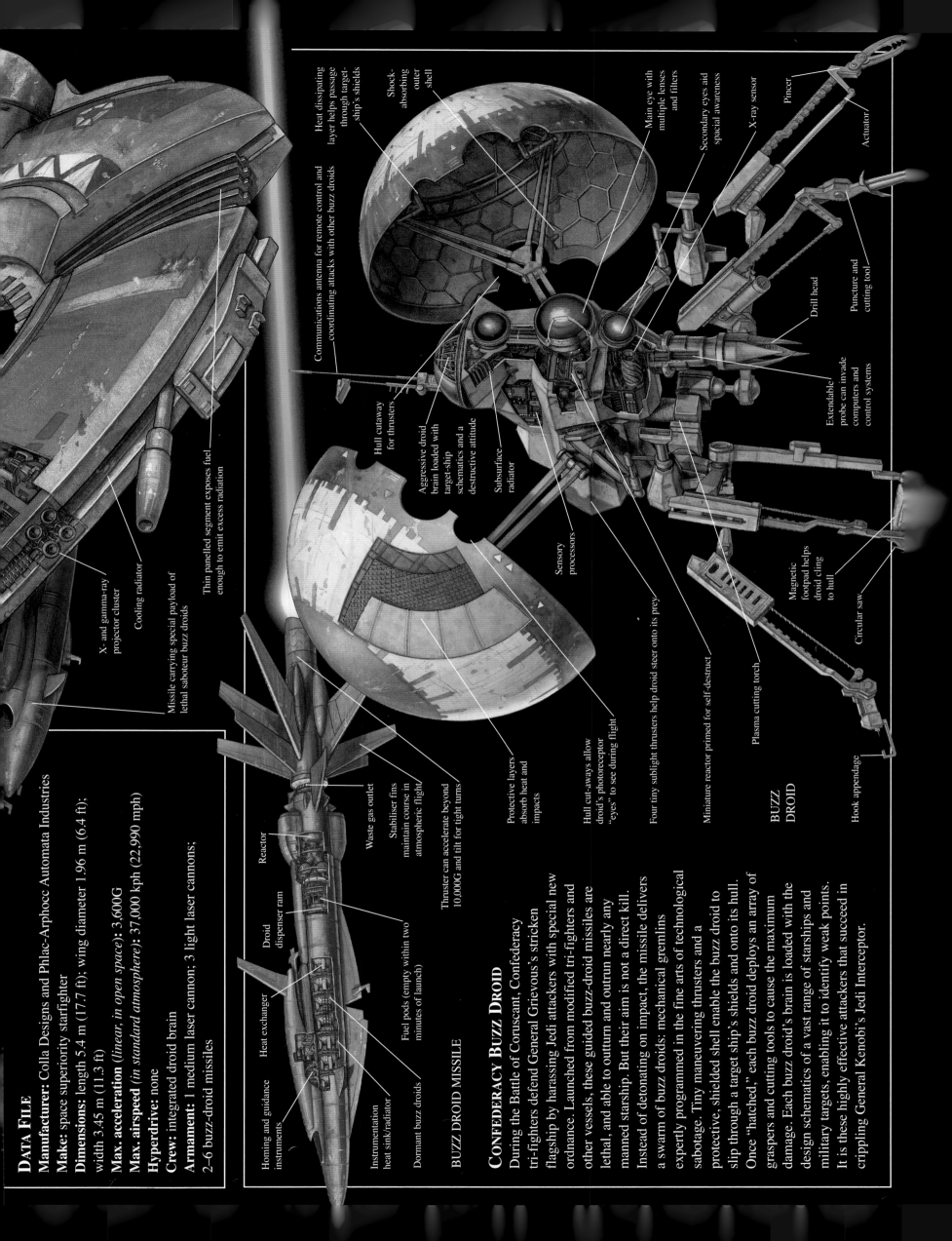

DATA FILE

Manufacturer: Colla Designs and Phlac-Arphocc Automata Industries

Make: space superiority starfighter

Dimensions: length 5.4 m (17.7 ft); wing diameter 1.96 m (6.4 ft); width 3.45 m (11.3 ft)

Max. acceleration (*linear, in open space*)**:** 3,600G

Max. airspeed (*in standard atmosphere*)**:** 37,000 kph (22,990 mph)

Hyperdrive: none

Crew: integrated droid brain

Armament: 1 medium laser cannon; 3 light laser cannons; 2–6 buzz-droid missiles

Heat dissipating layer helps passage through target-ship's shields

Shock-absorbing outer shell

Communications antenna for remote control and coordinating attacks with other buzz droids

Main eye with multiple lenses and filters

Secondary eyes aid spacial awareness

X-ray sensor

Pincer

Actuator/

Drill head

Hull cutaway for thrusters

Aggressive droid brain loaded with target-ship schematics and a destructive attitude

Extendable probe can invade computers and control systems

Subsurface radiator

Puncture and cutting tool

Sensory processors

Magnetic footpad helps droid cling to hull

Circular saw

Hull cut-aways allow droid's photoreceptor "eyes" to see during flight

Four tiny sublight thrusters help droid steer onto its prey

Plasma cutting torch

Miniature reactor primed for self-destruct

BUZZ DROID

Hook appendage

X- and gamma-ray projector cluster

Cooling radiator

Missile carrying special payload of lethal saboteur buzz droids

Thin panelled segment exposes fuel enough to emit excess radiation

Protective layers absorb heat and impacts

Thruster can accelerate beyond 10,000G and tilt for tight turns

Stabiliser fins maintain course in atmospheric flight

Waste gas outlet

Reactor

Droid dispenser ram

Heat exchanger

Fuel pods (empty within two minutes of launch)

Instrumentation heat sink/radiator

Dormant buzz droids

Homing and guidance instruments

BUZZ DROID MISSILE

CONFEDERACY BUZZ DROID

During the Battle of Coruscant, Confederacy tri-fighters defend General Grievous's stricken flagship by harassing Jedi attackers with special new ordnance. Launched from modified tri-fighters and other vessels, these guided buzz-droid missiles are lethal, and able to outrun and outrun nearly any manned starship. But their aim is not a direct kill. Instead of detonating on impact, the missile delivers a swarm of buzz droids: mechanical gremlins expertly programmed in the fine arts of technological sabotage. Tiny maneuvering thrusters and a protective, shielded shell enable the buzz droid to slip through a target ship's shields and onto its hull. Once "hatched," each buzz droid deploys an array of graspers and cutting tools to cause the maximum damage. Each buzz droid's brain is loaded with the design schematics of a vast range of starships and military targets, enabling it to identify weak points. It is these highly effective attackers that succeed in crippling General Kenobi's Jedi Interceptor.

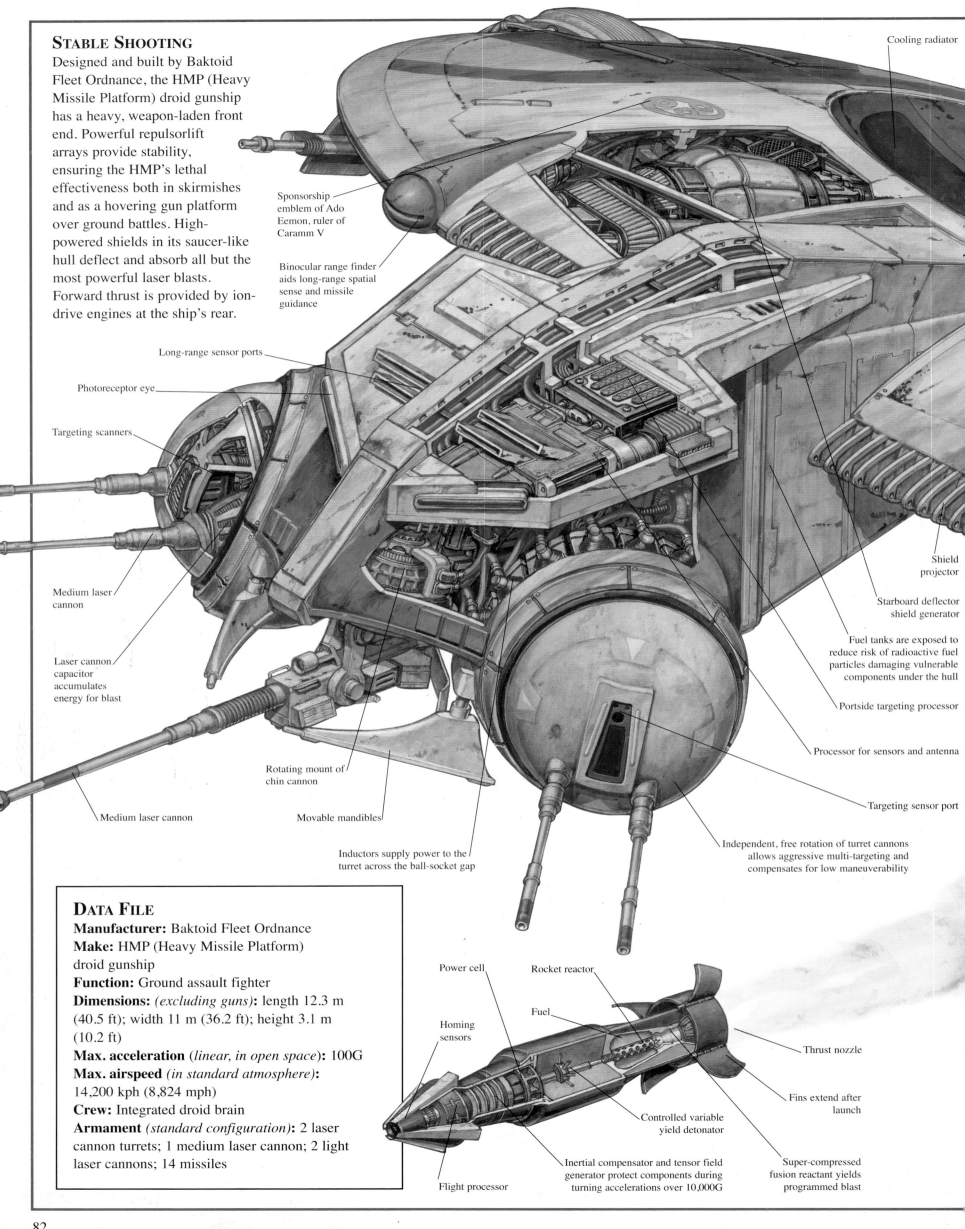

STABLE SHOOTING

Designed and built by Baktoid Fleet Ordnance, the HMP (Heavy Missile Platform) droid gunship has a heavy, weapon-laden front end. Powerful repulsorlift arrays provide stability, ensuring the HMP's lethal effectiveness both in skirmishes and as a hovering gun platform over ground battles. High-powered shields in its saucer-like hull deflect and absorb all but the most powerful laser blasts. Forward thrust is provided by ion-drive engines at the ship's rear.

Cooling radiator

Sponsorship emblem of Ado Eemon, ruler of Caramm V

Binocular range finder aids long-range spatial sense and missile guidance

Long-range sensor ports

Photoreceptor eye

Targeting scanners

Medium laser cannon

Laser cannon capacitor accumulates energy for blast

Medium laser cannon

Rotating mount of chin cannon

Movable mandibles

Inductors supply power to the turret across the ball-socket gap

Shield projector

Starboard deflector shield generator

Fuel tanks are exposed to reduce risk of radioactive fuel particles damaging vulnerable components under the hull

Portside targeting processor

Processor for sensors and antenna

Targeting sensor port

Independent, free rotation of turret cannons allows aggressive multi-targeting and compensates for low maneuverability

DATA FILE

Manufacturer: Baktoid Fleet Ordnance
Make: HMP (Heavy Missile Platform) droid gunship
Function: Ground assault fighter
Dimensions: *(excluding guns)*: length 12.3 m (40.5 ft); width 11 m (36.2 ft); height 3.1 m (10.2 ft)
Max. acceleration *(linear, in open space)*: 100G
Max. airspeed *(in standard atmosphere)*: 14,200 kph (8,824 mph)
Crew: Integrated droid brain
Armament *(standard configuration)*: 2 laser cannon turrets; 1 medium laser cannon; 2 light laser cannons; 14 missiles

Power cell

Rocket reactor

Homing sensors

Fuel

Thrust nozzle

Fins extend after launch

Controlled variable yield detonator

Super-compressed fusion reactant yields programmed blast

Inertial compensator and tensor field generator protect components during turning accelerations over 10,000G

Flight processor

DROID GUNSHIP

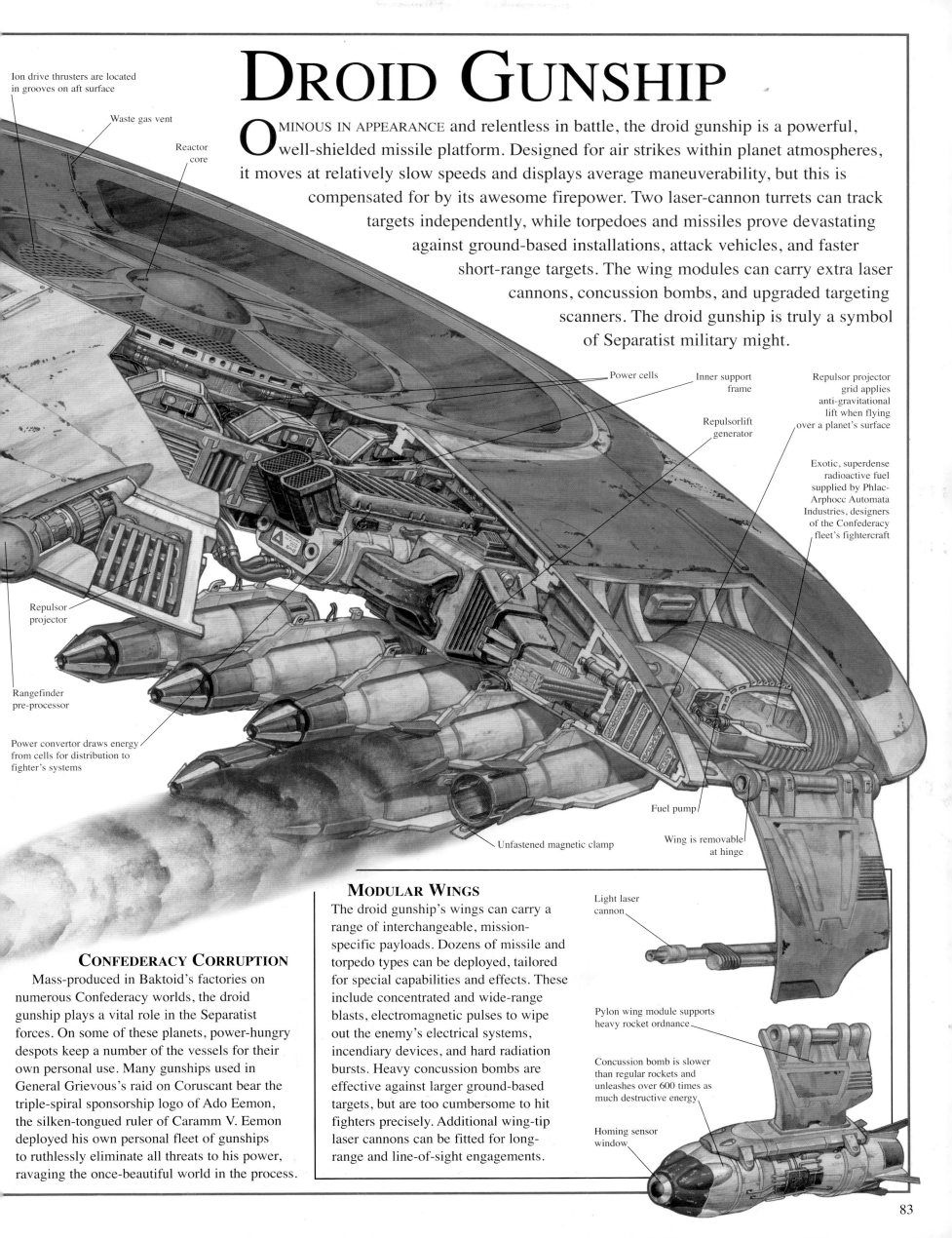

Ominous in appearance and relentless in battle, the droid gunship is a powerful, well-shielded missile platform. Designed for air strikes within planet atmospheres, it moves at relatively slow speeds and displays average maneuverability, but this is compensated for by its awesome firepower. Two laser-cannon turrets can track targets independently, while torpedoes and missiles prove devastating against ground-based installations, attack vehicles, and faster short-range targets. The wing modules can carry extra laser cannons, concussion bombs, and upgraded targeting scanners. The droid gunship is truly a symbol of Separatist military might.

Ion drive thrusters are located in grooves on aft surface

Waste gas vent

Reactor core

Power cells

Inner support frame

Repulsor projector grid applies anti-gravitational lift when flying over a planet's surface

Repulsorlift generator

Exotic, superdense radioactive fuel supplied by Phlac-Arphocc Automata Industries, designers of the Confederacy fleet's fightercraft

Repulsor projector

Rangefinder pre-processor

Power convertor draws energy from cells for distribution to fighter's systems

Fuel pump

Unfastened magnetic clamp

Wing is removable at hinge

CONFEDERACY CORRUPTION

Mass-produced in Baktoid's factories on numerous Confederacy worlds, the droid gunship plays a vital role in the Separatist forces. On some of these planets, power-hungry despots keep a number of the vessels for their own personal use. Many gunships used in General Grievous's raid on Coruscant bear the triple-spiral sponsorship logo of Ado Eemon, the silken-tongued ruler of Caramm V. Eemon deployed his own personal fleet of gunships to ruthlessly eliminate all threats to his power, ravaging the once-beautiful world in the process.

MODULAR WINGS

The droid gunship's wings can carry a range of interchangeable, mission-specific payloads. Dozens of missile and torpedo types can be deployed, tailored for special capabilities and effects. These include concentrated and wide-range blasts, electromagnetic pulses to wipe out the enemy's electrical systems, incendiary devices, and hard radiation bursts. Heavy concussion bombs are effective against larger ground-based targets, but are too cumbersome to hit fighters precisely. Additional wing-tip laser cannons can be fitted for long-range and line-of-sight engagements.

Light laser cannon

Pylon wing module supports heavy rocket ordnance

Concussion bomb is slower than regular rockets and unleashes over 600 times as much destructive energy

Homing sensor window

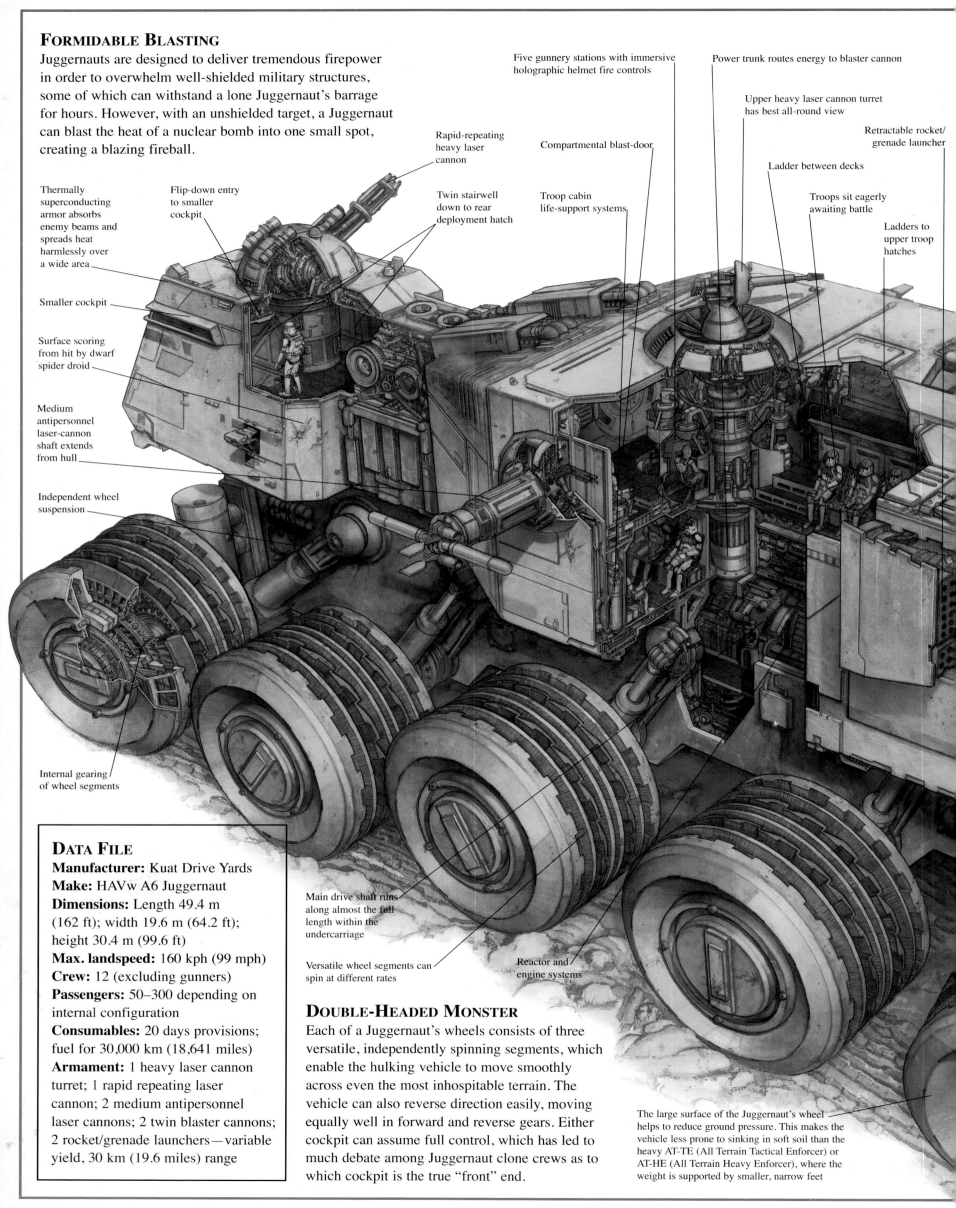

FORMIDABLE BLASTING

Juggernauts are designed to deliver tremendous firepower in order to overwhelm well-shielded military structures, some of which can withstand a lone Juggernaut's barrage for hours. However, with an unshielded target, a Juggernaut can blast the heat of a nuclear bomb into one small spot, creating a blazing fireball.

Thermally superconducting armor absorbs enemy beams and spreads heat harmlessly over a wide area

Flip-down entry to smaller cockpit

Smaller cockpit

Surface scoring from hit by dwarf spider droid

Medium antipersonnel laser-cannon shaft extends from hull

Independent wheel suspension

Internal gearing of wheel segments

Rapid-repeating heavy laser cannon

Twin stairwell down to rear deployment hatch

Five gunnery stations with immersive holographic helmet fire controls

Compartmental blast-door

Troop cabin life-support systems

Power trunk routes energy to blaster cannon

Upper heavy laser cannon turret has best all-round view

Retractable rocket/ grenade launcher

Ladder between decks

Troops sit eagerly awaiting battle

Ladders to upper troop hatches

Main drive shaft runs along almost the full length within the undercarriage

Versatile wheel segments can spin at different rates

Reactor and engine systems

DATA FILE
Manufacturer: Kuat Drive Yards
Make: HAVw A6 Juggernaut
Dimensions: Length 49.4 m (162 ft); width 19.6 m (64.2 ft); height 30.4 m (99.6 ft)
Max. landspeed: 160 kph (99 mph)
Crew: 12 (excluding gunners)
Passengers: 50–300 depending on internal configuration
Consumables: 20 days provisions; fuel for 30,000 km (18,641 miles)
Armament: 1 heavy laser cannon turret; 1 rapid repeating laser cannon; 2 medium antipersonnel laser cannons; 2 twin blaster cannons; 2 rocket/grenade launchers—variable yield, 30 km (19.6 miles) range

DOUBLE-HEADED MONSTER

Each of a Juggernaut's wheels consists of three versatile, independently spinning segments, which enable the hulking vehicle to move smoothly across even the most inhospitable terrain. The vehicle can also reverse direction easily, moving equally well in forward and reverse gears. Either cockpit can assume full control, which has led to much debate among Juggernaut clone crews as to which cockpit is the true "front" end.

The large surface of the Juggernaut's wheel helps to reduce ground pressure. This makes the vehicle less prone to sinking in soft soil than the heavy AT-TE (All Terrain Tactical Enforcer) or AT-HE (All Terrain Heavy Enforcer), where the weight is supported by smaller, narrow feet.

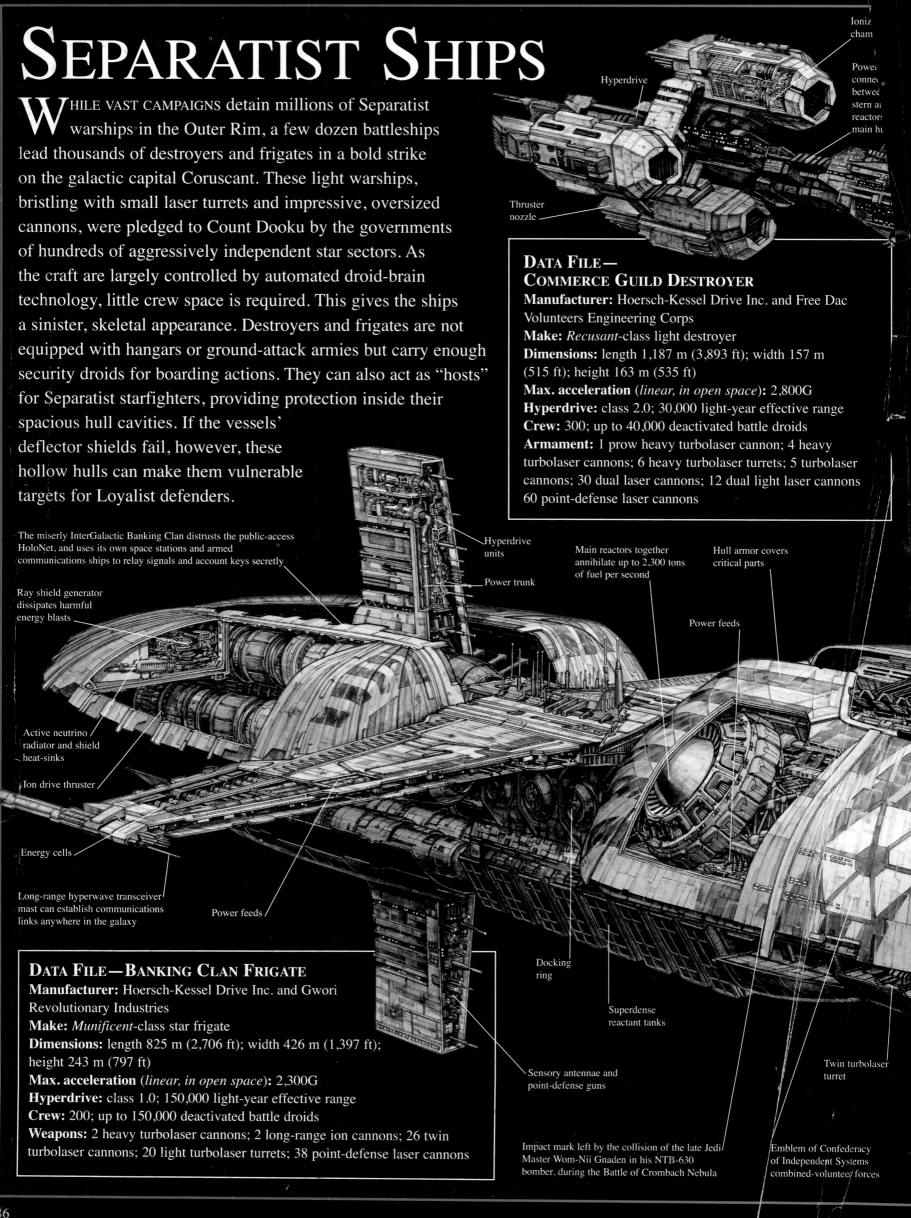

SEPARATIST SHIPS

WHILE VAST CAMPAIGNS detain millions of Separatist warships in the Outer Rim, a few dozen battleships lead thousands of destroyers and frigates in a bold strike on the galactic capital Coruscant. These light warships, bristling with small laser turrets and impressive, oversized cannons, were pledged to Count Dooku by the governments of hundreds of aggressively independent star sectors. As the craft are largely controlled by automated droid-brain technology, little crew space is required. This gives the ships a sinister, skeletal appearance. Destroyers and frigates are not equipped with hangars or ground-attack armies but carry enough security droids for boarding actions. They can also act as "hosts" for Separatist starfighters, providing protection inside their spacious hull cavities. If the vessels' deflector shields fail, however, these hollow hulls can make them vulnerable targets for Loyalist defenders.

Ioniz
cham

Power
conne
betwe
stern a
reactor
main hu

Hyperdrive

Thruster
nozzle

DATA FILE— COMMERCE GUILD DESTROYER
Manufacturer: Hoersch-Kessel Drive Inc. and Free Dac Volunteers Engineering Corps
Make: *Recusant*-class light destroyer
Dimensions: length 1,187 m (3,893 ft); width 157 m (515 ft); height 163 m (535 ft)
Max. acceleration (*linear, in open space*): 2,800G
Hyperdrive: class 2.0; 30,000 light-year effective range
Crew: 300; up to 40,000 deactivated battle droids
Armament: 1 prow heavy turbolaser cannon; 4 heavy turbolaser cannons; 6 heavy turbolaser turrets; 5 turbolaser cannons; 30 dual laser cannons; 12 dual light laser cannons 60 point-defense laser cannons

The miserly InterGalactic Banking Clan distrusts the public-access HoloNet, and uses its own space stations and armed communications ships to relay signals and account keys secretly

Ray shield generator dissipates harmful energy blasts

Active neutrino radiator and shield heat-sinks

Ion drive thruster

Energy cells

Long-range hyperwave transceiver mast can establish communications links anywhere in the galaxy

Hyperdrive units

Power trunk

Main reactors together annihilate up to 2,300 tons of fuel per second

Hull armor covers critical parts

Power feeds

Power feeds

Docking ring

Superdense reactant tanks

Sensory antennae and point-defense guns

Twin turbolaser turret

Impact mark left by the collision of the late Jedi Master Wom-Nii Gnaden in his NTB-630 bomber, during the Battle of Crombach Nebula

Emblem of Confederacy of Independent Systems combined-volunteer forces

DATA FILE—BANKING CLAN FRIGATE
Manufacturer: Hoersch-Kessel Drive Inc. and Gwori Revolutionary Industries
Make: *Munificent*-class star frigate
Dimensions: length 825 m (2,706 ft); width 426 m (1,397 ft); height 243 m (797 ft)
Max. acceleration (*linear, in open space*): 2,300G
Hyperdrive: class 1.0; 150,000 light-year effective range
Crew: 200; up to 150,000 deactivated battle droids
Weapons: 2 heavy turbolaser cannons; 2 long-range ion cannons; 26 twin turbolaser cannons; 20 light turbolaser turrets; 38 point-defense laser cannons

INVISIBLE HAND

I N A BOLD STRIKE at the galactic capital Coruscant, raiders from the Separatist flagship *Invisible Hand* have abducted Supreme Chancellor Palpatine. The vessel waits in orbit with the Confederacy fleet as the droid kidnappers return with their valuable prize—but before they can flee, thousands of Republic battleships engage the craft, trapping it in an upper atmospheric combat within the planet's defensive shield. *Invisible Hand* is badly damaged by superior enemy guns, so Jedi rescuers Obi-Wan Kenobi and Anakin Skywalker must find Palpatine in a rapidly decaying spacewreck. Ruptured compartments are flooded with fluidic coolants and propellants laced with invisible, exotic hypermatter fuels. Artificial gravity, tensor fields, and inertial compensators all begin to fail, as the crippled ship threatens to tear itself apart. The battle wages on, until *Invisible Hand* begins its meteoric fall toward the surface of Coruscant.

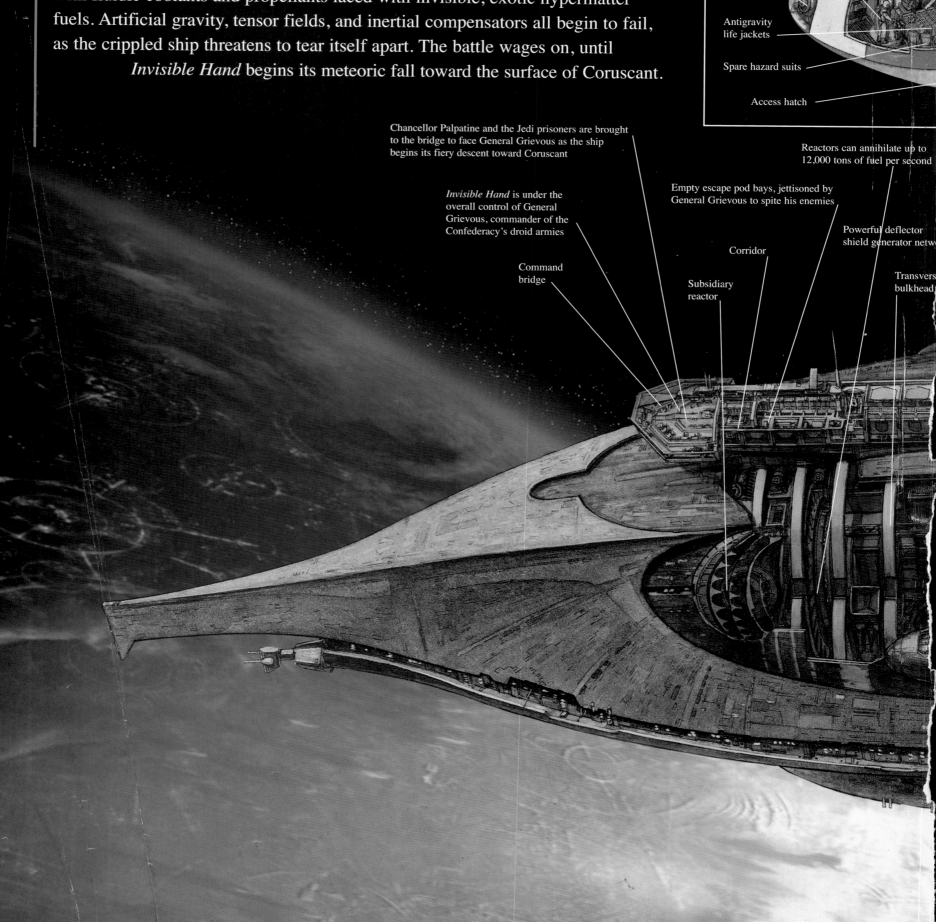

Fireship captain Jikesh Valia flies to the aid of the failing Separatist flagship

Medical bay door

Fu ta

Vertical access to upper deck

Fireman Pont Edisser readies his repulsorlift disk platform for flying rescues

Manuevering thruster

Antigravity life jackets

Spare hazard suits

Access hatch

Chancellor Palpatine and the Jedi prisoners are brought to the bridge to face General Grievous as the ship begins its fiery descent toward Coruscant

Invisible Hand is under the overall control of General Grievous, commander of the Confederacy's droid armies

Command bridge

Subsidiary reactor

Corridor

Empty escape pod bays, jettisoned by General Grievous to spite his enemies

Reactors can annihilate up to 12,000 tons of fuel per second

Powerful deflector shield generator netwo

Transvers bulkhead

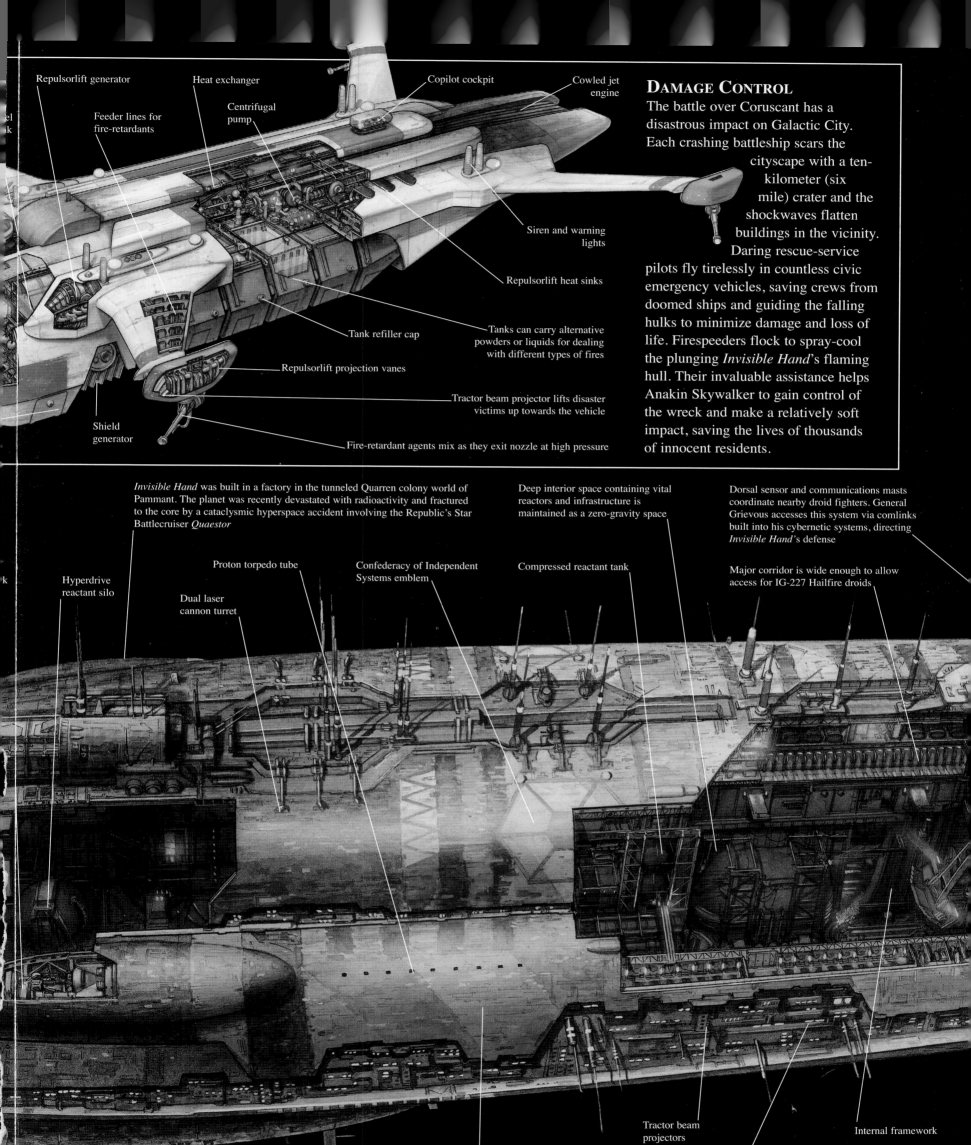

Repulsorlift generator

Heat exchanger

Copilot cockpit

Cowled jet engine

Feeder lines for fire-retardants

Centrifugal pump

Siren and warning lights

Repulsorlift heat sinks

Tank refiller cap

Tanks can carry alternative powders or liquids for dealing with different types of fires

Repulsorlift projection vanes

Tractor beam projector lifts disaster victims up towards the vehicle

Shield generator

Fire-retardant agents mix as they exit nozzle at high pressure

DAMAGE CONTROL

The battle over Coruscant has a disastrous impact on Galactic City. Each crashing battleship scars the cityscape with a ten-kilometer (six mile) crater and the shockwaves flatten buildings in the vicinity. Daring rescue-service pilots fly tirelessly in countless civic emergency vehicles, saving crews from doomed ships and guiding the falling hulks to minimize damage and loss of life. Firespeeders flock to spray-cool the plunging *Invisible Hand*'s flaming hull. Their invaluable assistance helps Anakin Skywalker to gain control of the wreck and make a relatively soft impact, saving the lives of thousands of innocent residents.

Invisible Hand was built in a factory in the tunneled Quarren colony world of Pammant. The planet was recently devastated with radioactivity and fractured to the core by a cataclysmic hyperspace accident involving the Republic's Star Battlecruiser *Quaestor*

Deep interior space containing vital reactors and infrastructure is maintained as a zero-gravity space

Dorsal sensor and communications masts coordinate nearby droid fighters. General Grievous accesses this system via comlinks built into his cybernetic systems, directing *Invisible Hand*'s defense

Proton torpedo tube

Confederacy of Independent Systems emblem

Compressed reactant tank

Major corridor is wide enough to allow access for IG-227 Hailfire droids

Hyperdrive reactant silo

Dual laser cannon turret

Tractor beam projectors

Internal framework

Dual laser cannon

Main hull is thicker and more extensive than those found on most small- and medium-sized Separatist warships

Viewing portals are not necessary for a ship with an all-droid crew, but are retained for the benefit of occasional living passengers

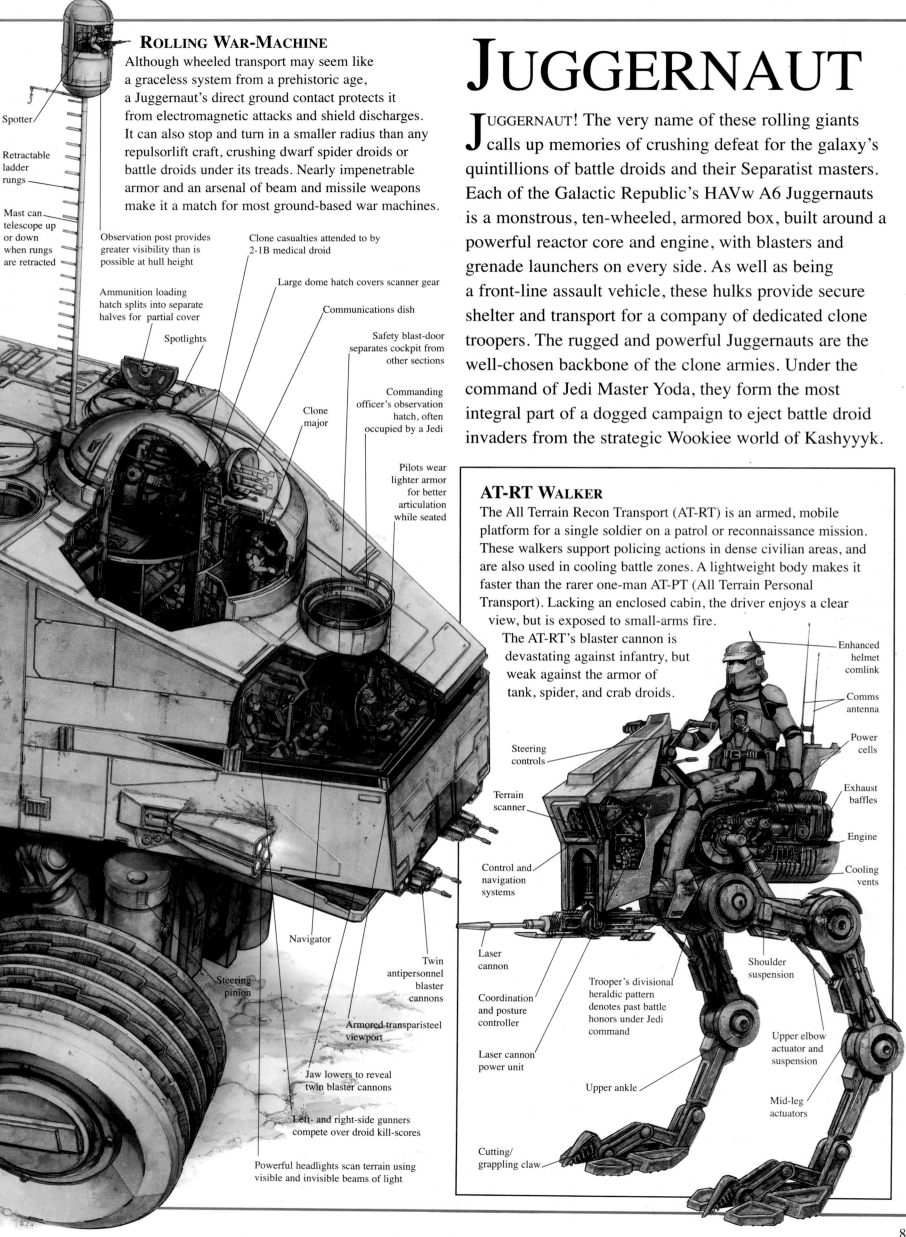

ROLLING WAR-MACHINE

Although wheeled transport may seem like a graceless system from a prehistoric age, a Juggernaut's direct ground contact protects it from electromagnetic attacks and shield discharges. It can also stop and turn in a smaller radius than any repulsorlift craft, crushing dwarf spider droids or battle droids under its treads. Nearly impenetrable armor and an arsenal of beam and missile weapons make it a match for most ground-based war machines.

Spotter

Retractable ladder rungs

Mast can telescope up or down when rungs are retracted

Observation post provides greater visibility than is possible at hull height

Clone casualties attended to by 2-1B medical droid

Ammunition loading hatch splits into separate halves for partial cover

Large dome hatch covers scanner gear

Communications dish

Spotlights

Safety blast-door separates cockpit from other sections

Commanding officer's observation hatch, often occupied by a Jedi

Clone major

Pilots wear lighter armor for better articulation while seated

Navigator

Steering pinion

Twin antipersonnel blaster cannons

Armored transparisteel viewport

Jaw lowers to reveal twin blaster cannons

Left- and right-side gunners compete over droid kill-scores

Powerful headlights scan terrain using visible and invisible beams of light

JUGGERNAUT

JUGGERNAUT! The very name of these rolling giants calls up memories of crushing defeat for the galaxy's quintillions of battle droids and their Separatist masters. Each of the Galactic Republic's HAVw A6 Juggernauts is a monstrous, ten-wheeled, armored box, built around a powerful reactor core and engine, with blasters and grenade launchers on every side. As well as being a front-line assault vehicle, these hulks provide secure shelter and transport for a company of dedicated clone troopers. The rugged and powerful Juggernauts are the well-chosen backbone of the clone armies. Under the command of Jedi Master Yoda, they form the most integral part of a dogged campaign to eject battle droid invaders from the strategic Wookiee world of Kashyyyk.

AT-RT WALKER

The All Terrain Recon Transport (AT-RT) is an armed, mobile platform for a single soldier on a patrol or reconnaissance mission. These walkers support policing actions in dense civilian areas, and are also used in cooling battle zones. A lightweight body makes it faster than the rarer one-man AT-PT (All Terrain Personal Transport). Lacking an enclosed cabin, the driver enjoys a clear view, but is exposed to small-arms fire.

The AT-RT's blaster cannon is devastating against infantry, but weak against the armor of tank, spider, and crab droids.

Enhanced helmet comlink

Comms antenna

Power cells

Exhaust baffles

Engine

Cooling vents

Steering controls

Terrain scanner

Control and navigation systems

Laser cannon

Coordination and posture controller

Laser cannon power unit

Trooper's divisional heraldic pattern denotes past battle honors under Jedi command

Upper ankle

Shoulder suspension

Upper elbow actuator and suspension

Mid-leg actuators

Cutting/ grappling claw

UTAPAUN P-38 FIGHTER

THE REMOTE PLANET Utapau, located in the distant Tarabba Sector, relies on the sturdy Porax-38 (P-38) starfighter for defensive and offensive engagements. These tough, hyperdrive-equipped fightercraft have interstellar range and are fitted with highly effective, long-distance sensor systems that provide early warning of enemy activity. Versatile thrusters, dual-reactor systems, and high-capacity deflector shielding make them a valuable asset for any starfleet. When Tion Medon, the Master of Utapau Port Administration, realizes that General Grievous's Separatist forces are about to land on the planet, he orders his outgunned P-38 forces into hiding. However, with the arrival of General Kenobi and the hope of Loyalist military intervention, Medon recalls his pilots from their concealed hangars and the cold depths of space, in a frantic, fiery bid for freedom.

Thruster branch vents direct thrust up or down for pitch maneuvers

Starboard thruster nozzle

Heat-sink fluid may be dumped into the thrust stream in an emergency—the ensuing reaction yields explosive (but dangerously unstable) additional thrust

Power distributor draws and stores energy from wing reactor and regulates power to nearby components

Small navicomputer can be loaded with charts for local sector only

Headrest

High-capacity heat exchanger cools engine

Hyperdrive motivator

Life support systems

Ion accelerator

Heat-sink cells for deflector shields

Each wing reactor annihilates up to 3.1 kg of fuel per second

Deflector shield projector web

Fuel tank

Fuel injector manifold

Capacitors accumulate power to energize laser cannon

Symmetrical power feeds deliver energy burst

Repulsorlift cells

Resonance and beam-amplification chamber

Inertial compensator band

Tibanna coolant recycler feeds

HOME FORCE

The Trade Federation protects its position in remote galactic regions by placing embargoes on arms sales to planetary governments. As a result, Utapauns rely upon self-made, downscaled ships—their biggest anti-pirate Rendili Dreadnaught is one-fifth of the size of a Trade Federation Battleship. Lacking a heavy navy, Utapauns deploy a rugged and potent starfighter force. Their large P-38 fighters are capable of independent hyperspace jumps, which enables them to defend the security of Utapau far into the Tarabba Sector. The interstellar range of these ships means they can endure longer, more arduous missions than tiny, fleet-based craft such as Separatist droid fighters, Republic V-wings, and Jedi starfighters.

Anti-static spikes

High-power laser cannon

Links between starboard comm/scan systems

Forward scanners

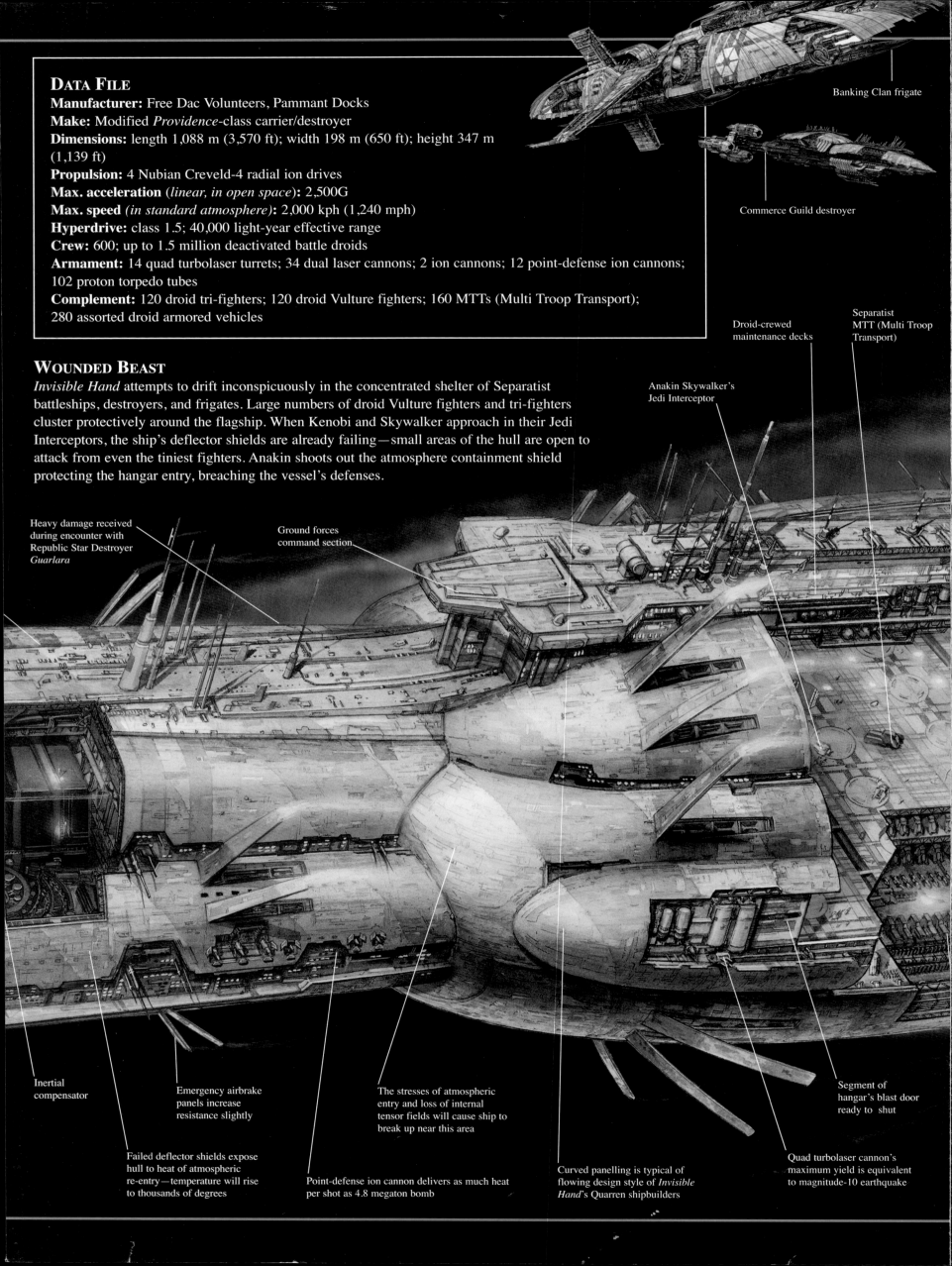

DATA FILE

Manufacturer: Free Dac Volunteers, Pammant Docks
Make: Modified *Providence*-class carrier/destroyer
Dimensions: length 1,088 m (3,570 ft); width 198 m (650 ft); height 347 m (1,139 ft)
Propulsion: 4 Nubian Creveld-4 radial ion drives
Max. acceleration (*linear, in open space*): 2,500G
Max. speed (*in standard atmosphere*): 2,000 kph (1,240 mph)
Hyperdrive: class 1.5; 40,000 light-year effective range
Crew: 600; up to 1.5 million deactivated battle droids
Armament: 14 quad turbolaser turrets; 34 dual laser cannons; 2 ion cannons; 12 point-defense ion cannons; 102 proton torpedo tubes
Complement: 120 droid tri-fighters; 120 droid Vulture fighters; 160 MTTs (Multi Troop Transport); 280 assorted droid armored vehicles

Banking Clan frigate

Commerce Guild destroyer

WOUNDED BEAST

Invisible Hand attempts to drift inconspicuously in the concentrated shelter of Separatist battleships, destroyers, and frigates. Large numbers of droid Vulture fighters and tri-fighters cluster protectively around the flagship. When Kenobi and Skywalker approach in their Jedi Interceptors, the ship's deflector shields are already failing—small areas of the hull are open to attack from even the tiniest fighters. Anakin shoots out the atmosphere containment shield protecting the hangar entry, breaching the vessel's defenses.

Droid-crewed maintenance decks

Separatist MTT (Multi Troop Transport)

Anakin Skywalker's Jedi Interceptor

Heavy damage received during encounter with Republic Star Destroyer *Guarlara*

Ground forces command section

Inertial compensator

Emergency airbrake panels increase resistance slightly

The stresses of atmospheric entry and loss of internal tensor fields will cause ship to break up near this area

Segment of hangar's blast door ready to shut

Failed deflector shields expose hull to heat of atmospheric re-entry—temperature will rise to thousands of degrees

Point-defense ion cannon delivers as much heat per shot as 4.8 megaton bomb

Curved panelling is typical of flowing design style of *Invisible Hand*'s Quarren shipbuilders

Quad turbolaser cannon's maximum yield is equivalent to magnitude-10 earthquake

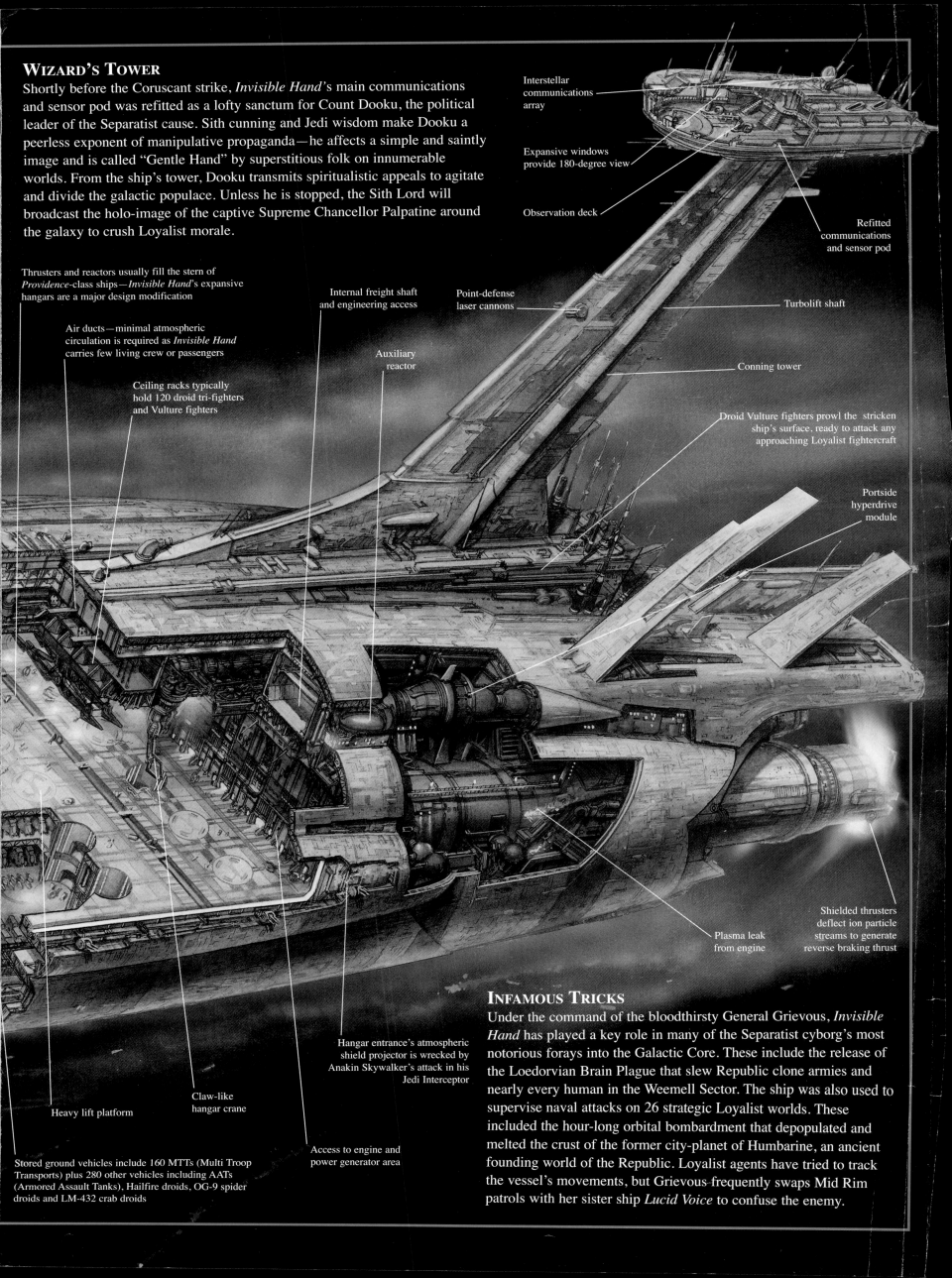

WIZARD'S TOWER

Shortly before the Coruscant strike, *Invisible Hand*'s main communications and sensor pod was refitted as a lofty sanctum for Count Dooku, the political leader of the Separatist cause. Sith cunning and Jedi wisdom make Dooku a peerless exponent of manipulative propaganda—he affects a simple and saintly image and is called "Gentle Hand" by superstitious folk on innumerable worlds. From the ship's tower, Dooku transmits spiritualistic appeals to agitate and divide the galactic populace. Unless he is stopped, the Sith Lord will broadcast the holo-image of the captive Supreme Chancellor Palpatine around the galaxy to crush Loyalist morale.

Interstellar communications array

Expansive windows provide 180-degree view

Observation deck

Refitted communications and sensor pod

Thrusters and reactors usually fill the stern of *Providence*-class ships—*Invisible Hand*'s expansive hangars are a major design modification

Internal freight shaft and engineering access

Point-defense laser cannons

Turbolift shaft

Air ducts—minimal atmospheric circulation is required as *Invisible Hand* carries few living crew or passengers

Auxiliary reactor

Conning tower

Ceiling racks typically hold 120 droid tri-fighters and Vulture fighters

Droid Vulture fighters prowl the stricken ship's surface, ready to attack any approaching Loyalist fightercraft

Portside hyperdrive module

Shielded thrusters deflect ion particle streams to generate reverse braking thrust

Plasma leak from engine

Hangar entrance's atmospheric shield projector is wrecked by Anakin Skywalker's attack in his Jedi Interceptor

Claw-like hangar crane

Heavy lift platform

Access to engine and power generator area

Stored ground vehicles include 160 MTTs (Multi Troop Transports) plus 280 other vehicles including AATs (Armored Assault Tanks), Hailfire droids, OG-9 spider droids and LM-432 crab droids

INFAMOUS TRICKS

Under the command of the bloodthirsty General Grievous, *Invisible Hand* has played a key role in many of the Separatist cyborg's most notorious forays into the Galactic Core. These include the release of the Loedorvian Brain Plague that slew Republic clone armies and nearly every human in the Weemell Sector. The ship was also used to supervise naval attacks on 26 strategic Loyalist worlds. These included the hour-long orbital bombardment that depopulated and melted the crust of the former city-planet of Humbarine, an ancient founding world of the Republic. Loyalist agents have tried to track the vessel's movements, but Grievous frequently swaps Mid Rim patrols with her sister ship *Lucid Voice* to confuse the enemy.

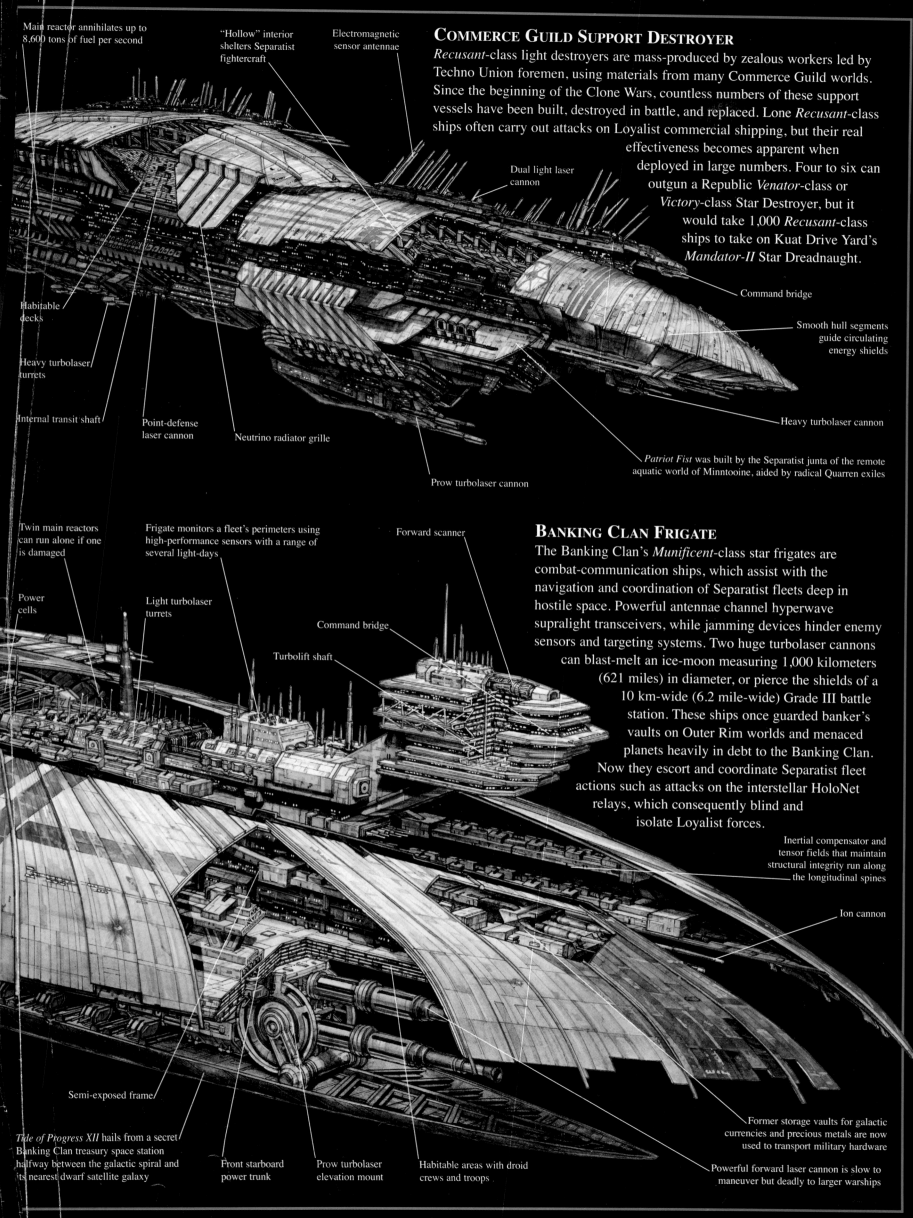

Main reactor annihilates up to 8,600 tons of fuel per second

"Hollow" interior shelters Separatist fightercraft

Electromagnetic sensor antennae

COMMERCE GUILD SUPPORT DESTROYER

Recusant-class light destroyers are mass-produced by zealous workers led by Techno Union foremen, using materials from many Commerce Guild worlds. Since the beginning of the Clone Wars, countless numbers of these support vessels have been built, destroyed in battle, and replaced. Lone *Recusant*-class ships often carry out attacks on Loyalist commercial shipping, but their real effectiveness becomes apparent when deployed in large numbers. Four to six can outgun a Republic *Venator*-class or *Victory*-class Star Destroyer, but it would take 1,000 *Recusant*-class ships to take on Kuat Drive Yard's *Mandator-II* Star Dreadnaught.

Dual light laser cannon

Command bridge

Smooth hull segments guide circulating energy shields

Habitable decks

Heavy turbolaser turrets

Internal transit shaft

Point-defense laser cannon

Neutrino radiator grille

Heavy turbolaser cannon

Patriot Fist was built by the Separatist junta of the remote aquatic world of Minntooine, aided by radical Quarren exiles

Prow turbolaser cannon

Twin main reactors can run alone if one is damaged

Frigate monitors a fleet's perimeters using high-performance sensors with a range of several light-days

Forward scanner

BANKING CLAN FRIGATE

The Banking Clan's *Munificent*-class star frigates are combat-communication ships, which assist with the navigation and coordination of Separatist fleets deep in hostile space. Powerful antennae channel hyperwave supralight transceivers, while jamming devices hinder enemy sensors and targeting systems. Two huge turbolaser cannons can blast-melt an ice-moon measuring 1,000 kilometers (621 miles) in diameter, or pierce the shields of a 10 km-wide (6.2 mile-wide) Grade III battle station. These ships once guarded banker's vaults on Outer Rim worlds and menaced planets heavily in debt to the Banking Clan. Now they escort and coordinate Separatist fleet actions such as attacks on the interstellar HoloNet relays, which consequently blind and isolate Loyalist forces.

Power cells

Light turbolaser turrets

Command bridge

Turbolift shaft

Inertial compensator and tensor fields that maintain structural integrity run along the longitudinal spines

Ion cannon

Semi-exposed frame

Tide of Progress XII hails from a secret Banking Clan treasury space station halfway between the galactic spiral and its nearest dwarf satellite galaxy

Front starboard power trunk

Prow turbolaser elevation mount

Habitable areas with droid crews and troops

Former storage vaults for galactic currencies and precious metals are now used to transport military hardware

Powerful forward laser cannon is slow to maneuver but deadly to larger warships

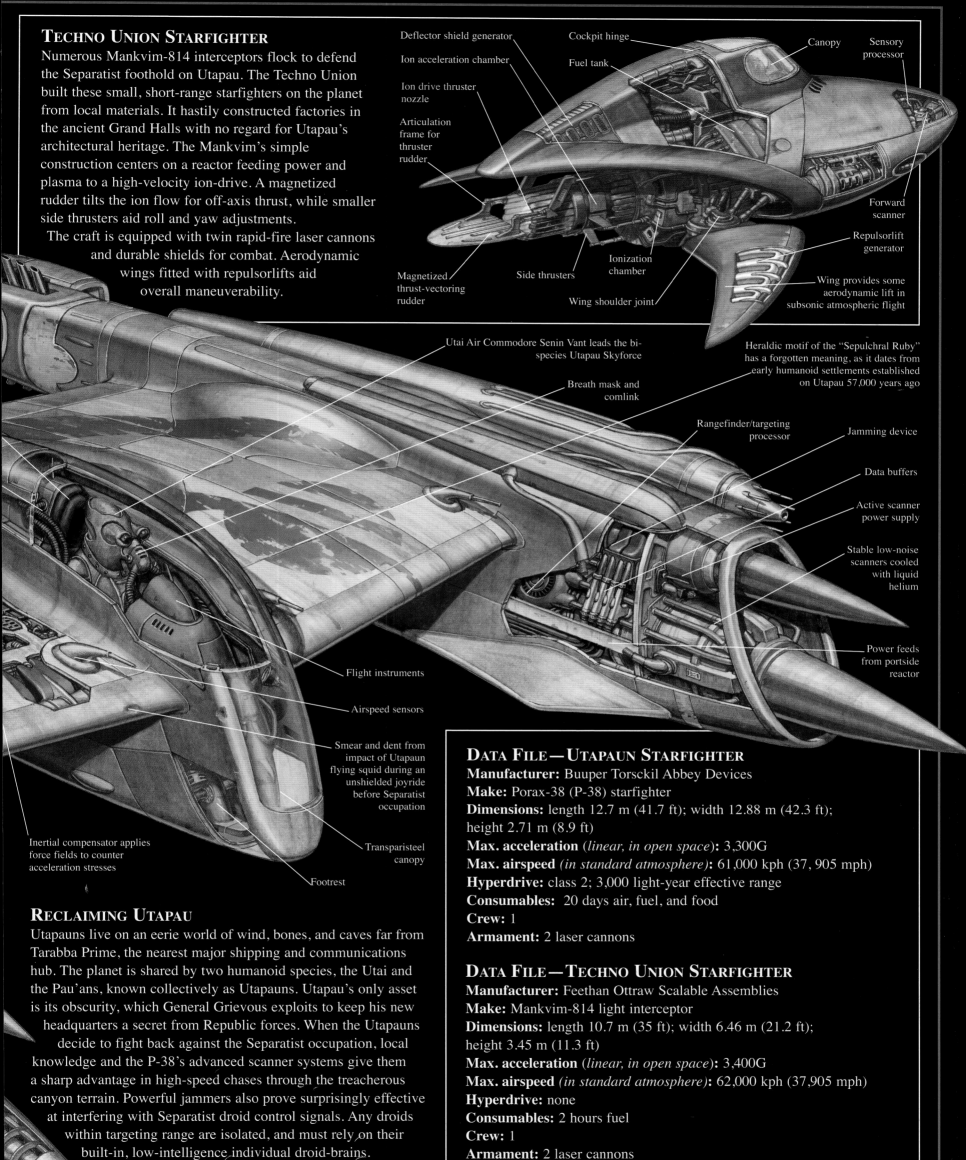

TECHNO UNION STARFIGHTER

Numerous Mankvim-814 interceptors flock to defend the Separatist foothold on Utapau. The Techno Union built these small, short-range starfighters on the planet from local materials. It hastily constructed factories in the ancient Grand Halls with no regard for Utapau's architectural heritage. The Mankvim's simple construction centers on a reactor feeding power and plasma to a high-velocity ion-drive. A magnetized rudder tilts the ion flow for off-axis thrust, while smaller side thrusters aid roll and yaw adjustments.

The craft is equipped with twin rapid-fire laser cannons and durable shields for combat. Aerodynamic wings fitted with repulsorlifts aid overall maneuverability.

Deflector shield generator

Ion acceleration chamber

Ion drive thruster nozzle

Articulation frame for thruster rudder

Cockpit hinge

Fuel tank

Canopy

Sensory processor

Forward scanner

Repulsorlift generator

Magnetized thrust-vectoring rudder

Side thrusters

Ionization chamber

Wing shoulder joint

Wing provides some aerodynamic lift in subsonic atmospheric flight

Utai Air Commodore Senin Vant leads the bi-species Utapau Skyforce

Heraldic motif of the "Sepulchral Ruby" has a forgotten meaning, as it dates from early humanoid settlements established on Utapau 57,000 years ago

Breath mask and comlink

Rangefinder/targeting processor

Jamming device

Data buffers

Active scanner power supply

Stable low-noise scanners cooled with liquid helium

Flight instruments

Airspeed sensors

Smear and dent from impact of Utapaun flying squid during an unshielded joyride before Separatist occupation

Power feeds from portside reactor

Inertial compensator applies force fields to counter acceleration stresses

Transparisteel canopy

Footrest

RECLAIMING UTAPAU

Utapauns live on an eerie world of wind, bones, and caves far from Tarabba Prime, the nearest major shipping and communications hub. The planet is shared by two humanoid species, the Utai and the Pau'ans, known collectively as Utapauns. Utapau's only asset is its obscurity, which General Grievous exploits to keep his new headquarters a secret from Republic forces. When the Utapauns decide to fight back against the Separatist occupation, local knowledge and the P-38's advanced scanner systems give them a sharp advantage in high-speed chases through the treacherous canyon terrain. Powerful jammers also prove surprisingly effective at interfering with Separatist droid control signals. Any droids within targeting range are isolated, and must rely on their built-in, low-intelligence individual droid-brains.

DATA FILE—UTAPAUN STARFIGHTER
Manufacturer: Buuper Torsckil Abbey Devices
Make: Porax-38 (P-38) starfighter
Dimensions: length 12.7 m (41.7 ft); width 12.88 m (42.3 ft); height 2.71 m (8.9 ft)
Max. acceleration (*linear, in open space*)**:** 3,300G
Max. airspeed (*in standard atmosphere*)**:** 61,000 kph (37, 905 mph)
Hyperdrive: class 2; 3,000 light-year effective range
Consumables: 20 days air, fuel, and food
Crew: 1
Armament: 2 laser cannons

DATA FILE—TECHNO UNION STARFIGHTER
Manufacturer: Feethan Ottraw Scalable Assemblies
Make: Mankvim-814 light interceptor
Dimensions: length 10.7 m (35 ft); width 6.46 m (21.2 ft); height 3.45 m (11.3 ft)
Max. acceleration (*linear, in open space*)**:** 3,400G
Max. airspeed (*in standard atmosphere*)**:** 62,000 kph (37,905 mph)
Hyperdrive: none
Consumables: 2 hours fuel
Crew: 1
Armament: 2 laser cannons

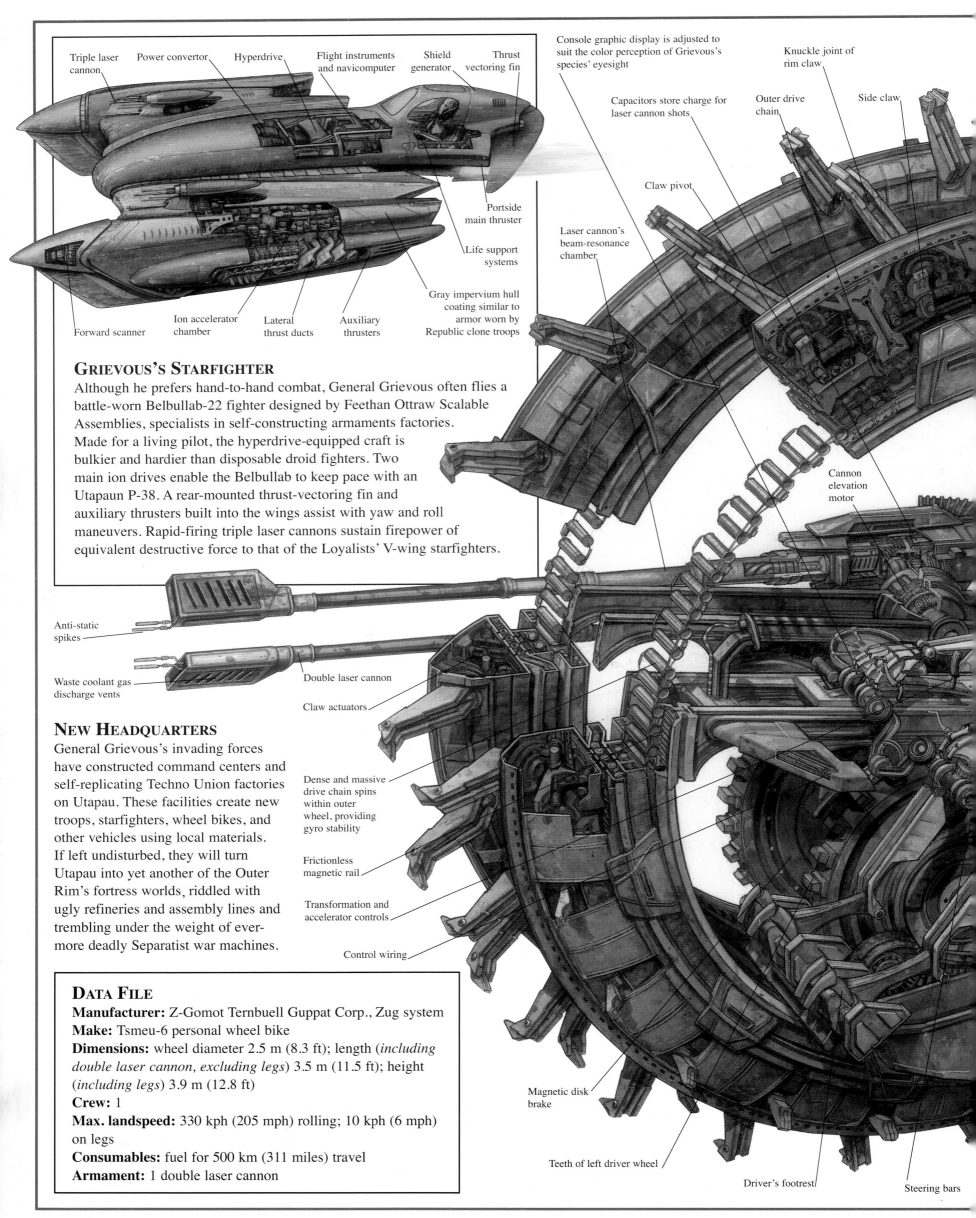

Triple laser cannon

Power convertor

Hyperdrive

Flight instruments and navicomputer

Shield generator

Thrust vectoring fin

Console graphic display is adjusted to suit the color perception of Grievous's species' eyesight

Knuckle joint of rim claw

Capacitors store charge for laser cannon shots

Outer drive chain

Side claw

Claw pivot

Laser cannon's beam-resonance chamber

Cannon elevation motor

Portside main thruster

Life support systems

Gray impervium hull coating similar to armor worn by Republic clone troops

Forward scanner

Ion accelerator chamber

Lateral thrust ducts

Auxiliary thrusters

Grievous's Starfighter

Although he prefers hand-to-hand combat, General Grievous often flies a battle-worn Belbullab-22 fighter designed by Feethan Ottraw Scalable Assemblies, specialists in self-constructing armaments factories. Made for a living pilot, the hyperdrive-equipped craft is bulkier and hardier than disposable droid fighters. Two main ion drives enable the Belbullab to keep pace with an Utapaun P-38. A rear-mounted thrust-vectoring fin and auxiliary thrusters built into the wings assist with yaw and roll maneuvers. Rapid-firing triple laser cannons sustain firepower of equivalent destructive force to that of the Loyalists' V-wing starfighters.

Anti-static spikes

Waste coolant gas discharge vents

Double laser cannon

Claw actuators

New Headquarters

General Grievous's invading forces have constructed command centers and self-replicating Techno Union factories on Utapau. These facilities create new troops, starfighters, wheel bikes, and other vehicles using local materials. If left undisturbed, they will turn Utapau into yet another of the Outer Rim's fortress worlds, riddled with ugly refineries and assembly lines and trembling under the weight of ever-more deadly Separatist war machines.

Dense and massive drive chain spins within outer wheel, providing gyro stability

Frictionless magnetic rail

Transformation and accelerator controls

Control wiring

Magnetic disk brake

Data File
Manufacturer: Z-Gomot Ternbuell Guppat Corp., Zug system
Make: Tsmeu-6 personal wheel bike
Dimensions: wheel diameter 2.5 m (8.3 ft); length (*including double laser cannon, excluding legs*) 3.5 m (11.5 ft); height (*including legs*) 3.9 m (12.8 ft)
Crew: 1
Max. landspeed: 330 kph (205 mph) rolling; 10 kph (6 mph) on legs
Consumables: fuel for 500 km (311 miles) travel
Armament: 1 double laser cannon

Teeth of left driver wheel

Driver's footrest

Steering bars

GRIEVOUS'S WHEEL BIKE

GENERAL GRIEVOUS'S fearsome reputation as a merciless military leader is reinforced by a personal fleet of specialized killing machines and vehicles. On cavernous Utapau, the cyborg General drives a wheel bike—a tumbling twin-wheel that surrounds a central motor. Grievous's military vehicle is an offshoot of the Banking Clan's hoop-wheeled Hailfire droids, designed to roll at intimidating speed on hard surfaces. It can also raise itself up on two pairs of legs to walk over the top of battle wrecks and other obstacles. A double laser cannon replaces one side seat, and Grievous can wield either a conveniently placed electrostaff, a blaster, or one of his Jedi lightsaber trophies when he rolls into battle. Flexing claws skirt the wheels to provide a smoother ride, or clutch the ground as climbing teeth. The bike's strong grip allows amazing acrobatics, an ability displayed when Grievous is pursued by Obi-Wan Kenobi.

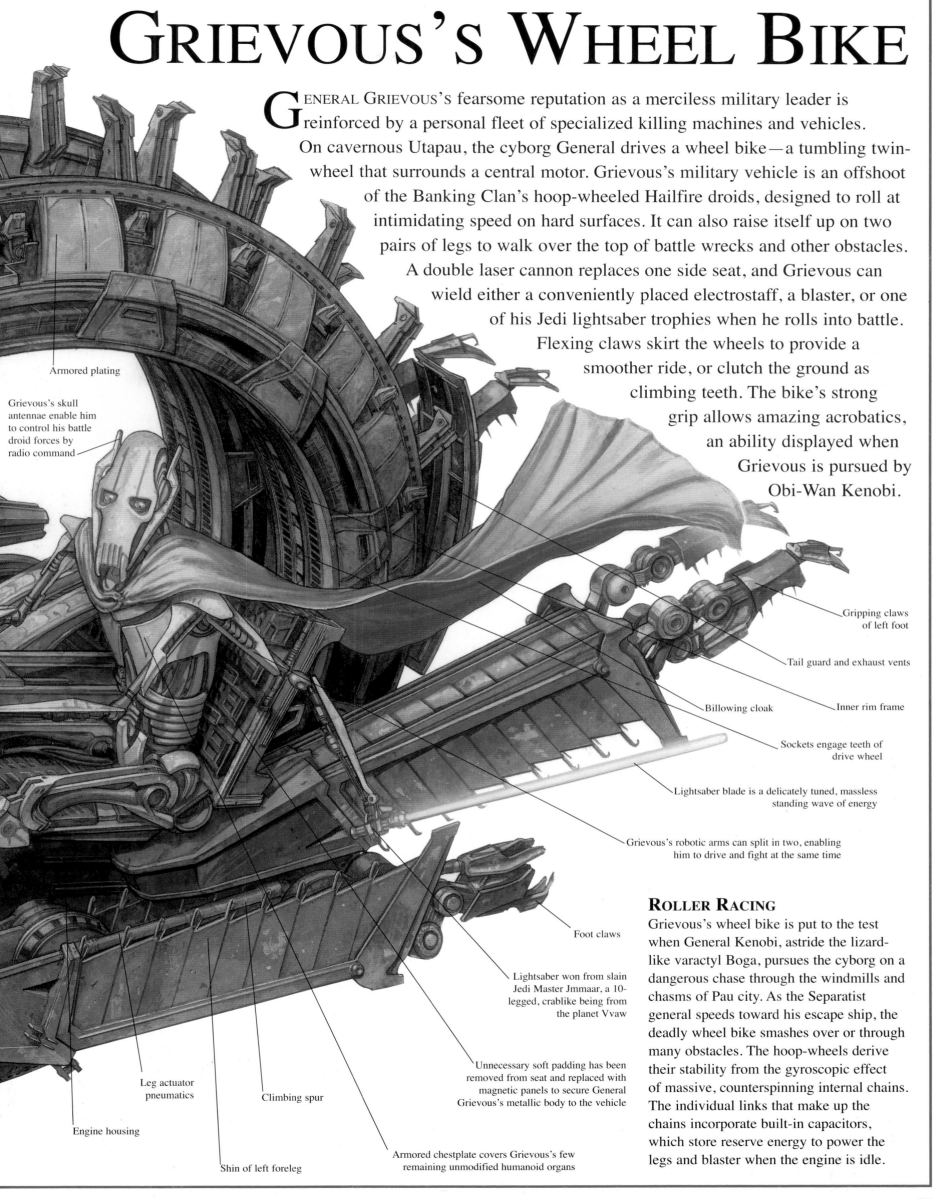

Armored plating

Grievous's skull antennae enable him to control his battle droid forces by radio command

Gripping claws of left foot

Tail guard and exhaust vents

Billowing cloak

Inner rim frame

Sockets engage teeth of drive wheel

Lightsaber blade is a delicately tuned, massless standing wave of energy

Grievous's robotic arms can split in two, enabling him to drive and fight at the same time

Foot claws

Lightsaber won from slain Jedi Master Jmmaar, a 10-legged, crablike being from the planet Vvaw

Leg actuator pneumatics

Climbing spur

Engine housing

Shin of left foreleg

Unnecessary soft padding has been removed from seat and replaced with magnetic panels to secure General Grievous's metallic body to the vehicle

Armored chestplate covers Grievous's few remaining unmodified humanoid organs

ROLLER RACING

Grievous's wheel bike is put to the test when General Kenobi, astride the lizard-like varactyl Boga, pursues the cyborg on a dangerous chase through the windmills and chasms of Pau city. As the Separatist general speeds toward his escape ship, the deadly wheel bike smashes over or through many obstacles. The hoop-wheels derive their stability from the gyroscopic effect of massive, counterspinning internal chains. The individual links that make up the chains incorporate built-in capacitors, which store reserve energy to power the legs and blaster when the engine is idle.

WOOKIEE CATAMARAN

Oevvaor catamarans are slim, twin-hulled, Wookiee-made watercraft that skid over the waters of Kashyyyk at breakneck speeds. They are lifted by a repulsorlift array and propelled by Podracer-style jet engines or propeller pods, and are steered by knife-like keels and rudders. Wookiee catamarans are normally used as fishing or sports craft, and are not equipped with built-in heavy weapons. But when Kashyyyk is invaded, hundreds of these unarmed craft are conscripted to bear Wookiee troops in small-arms attacks, darting through the lines of Separatist vehicles. The catamarans' speed and maneuverability are crucial, as Kashyyyk's defenders know that the enemy must first capture the coasts before attempting incursions into the tangled, dense foliation of the inland woods.

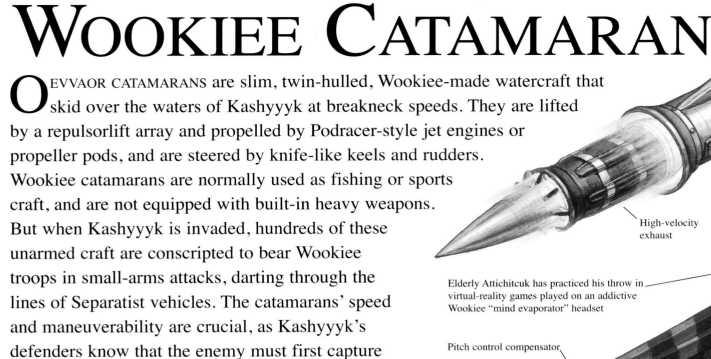

High-velocity exhaust

Elderly Attichitcuk has practiced his throw in virtual-reality games played on an addictive Wookiee "mind evaporator" headset

Pitch control compensator

Adjustable length and weight

Exhaust vent

Power generator

Heating elements liquefy fuel

Fuel in tank is solid at normal temperatures

Power cabling

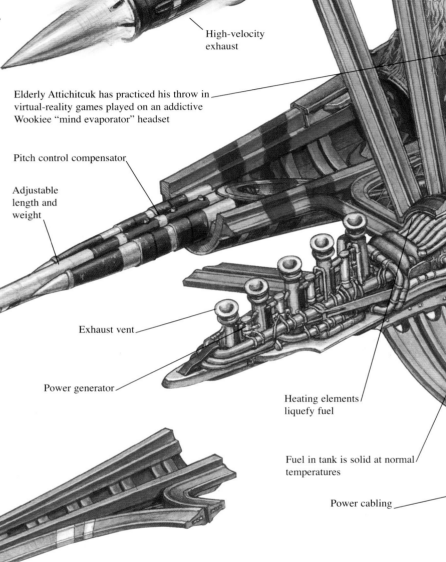

SWAMP SPEEDER

The Grand Army of the Republic bolsters the Wookiee's defensive forces with a wide variety of imported war machines. The light, two-man ISP (Infantry Support Platform) speeder is the clone troops' closest equivalent of the Wookiees' Oevvaor catamarans and Raddadugh "Gnasp" fluttercraft. The clone army's antigravity repulsorlift vehicle floats smoothly in the air without touching land or water. It is driven by a powerful turbofan, which can be reversed to fire a braking airblast when needed. Precise, controlled vectoring of the turbofan's thrust makes the ISP a highly maneuverable attack vehicle. The front-mounted pair of twin-blaster cannons are lethal to enemy infantry, but can also prove highly effective against shielded enemy gunships, fighters, and Corporate Alliance NR-N99 tank droids.

Airflow vectoring fin

100 kph (62 mph) thrust fan

Control console

Forward-terrain laser scanner

Repulsorlift

Mudshield

Seat belt

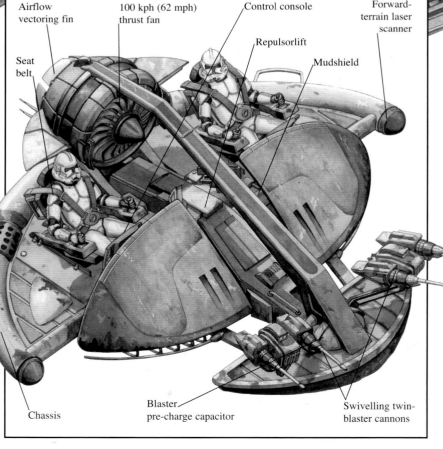

Chassis

Blaster pre-charge capacitor

Swivelling twin-blaster cannons

AGILE DEFENDERS

The Wookiee watercraft used in the defence of Kashyyyk are named after the Oevvaor, a predatory marine reptile of the Kashyyyk coasts known for its agility and territorial ferocity. The tough hulls of these aptly named catamarans are handcrafted from wroshyr timber. This light, strong, and durable wood is hewn from Kashyyyk's fabled wroshyr trees, which can grow to hundreds of meters in height.

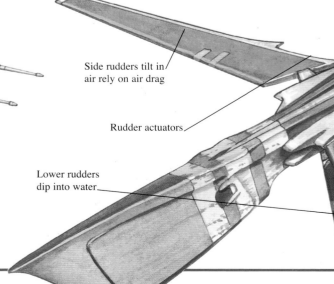

Side rudders tilt in air rely on air drag

Rudder actuators

Lower rudders dip into water

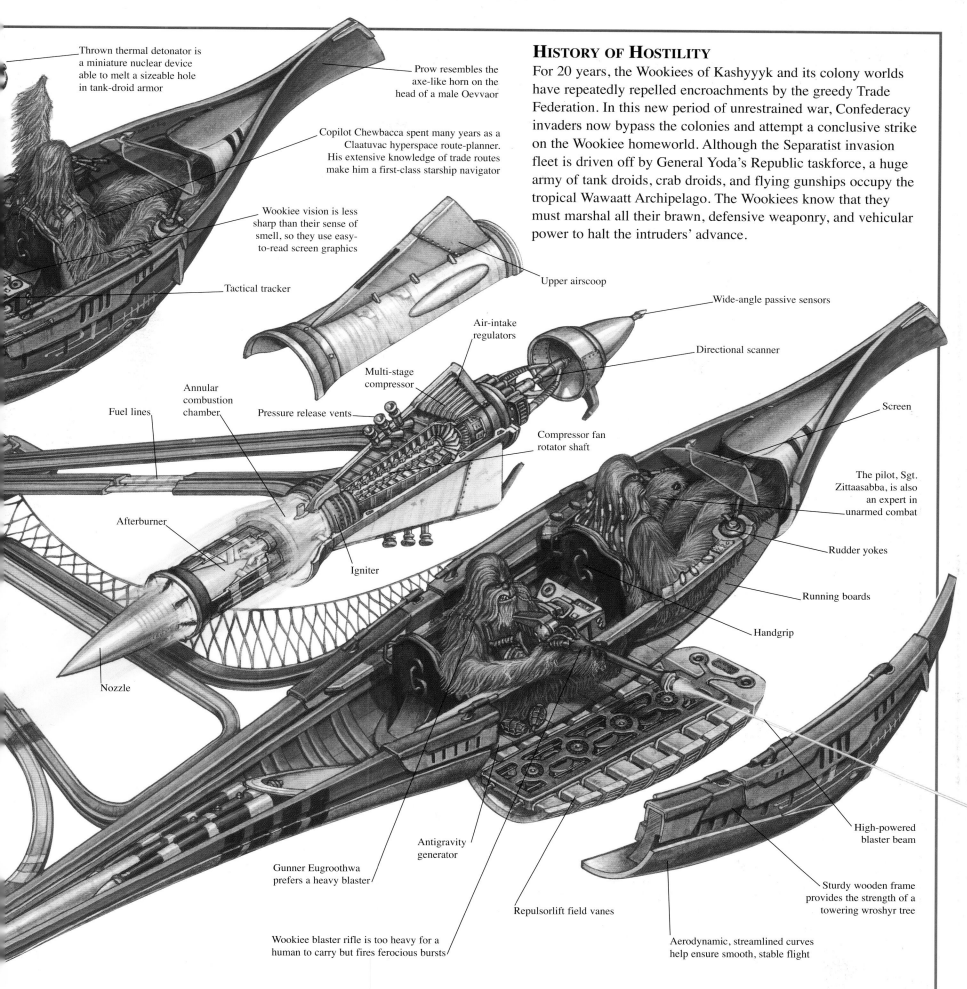

Thrown thermal detonator is a miniature nuclear device able to melt a sizeable hole in tank-droid armor

Prow resembles the axe-like horn on the head of a male Oevvaor

Copilot Chewbacca spent many years as a Claatuvac hyperspace route-planner. His extensive knowledge of trade routes make him a first-class starship navigator

Wookiee vision is less sharp than their sense of smell, so they use easy-to-read screen graphics

Tactical tracker

Upper airscoop

Wide-angle passive sensors

Directional scanner

Air-intake regulators

Annular combustion chamber

Multi-stage compressor

Fuel lines

Pressure release vents

Compressor fan rotator shaft

Screen

The pilot, Sgt. Zittaasabba, is also an expert in unarmed combat

Afterburner

Igniter

Rudder yokes

Running boards

Handgrip

Nozzle

Gunner Eugroothwa prefers a heavy blaster

Antigravity generator

High-powered blaster beam

Wookiee blaster rifle is too heavy for a human to carry but fires ferocious bursts

Repulsorlift field vanes

Sturdy wooden frame provides the strength of a towering wroshyr tree

Aerodynamic, streamlined curves help ensure smooth, stable flight

HISTORY OF HOSTILITY

For 20 years, the Wookiees of Kashyyyk and its colony worlds have repeatedly repelled encroachments by the greedy Trade Federation. In this new period of unrestrained war, Confederacy invaders now bypass the colonies and attempt a conclusive strike on the Wookiee homeworld. Although the Separatist invasion fleet is driven off by General Yoda's Republic taskforce, a huge army of tank droids, crab droids, and flying gunships occupy the tropical Wawaatt Archipelago. The Wookiees know that they must marshal all their brawn, defensive weaponry, and vehicular power to halt the intruders' advance.

STRATEGIC WORLD

Kashyyyk, or "Wookiee Planet C" as some humans call it, has long played a major role in transgalactic shipping and communications. For centuries, an elite guild of long-lived Wookiee cartographers known as the Claatuvac have maintained and updated the hyperspace route surveys that keep the galaxy navigable. It is widely believed that the Claatuvac Guild's ancient data archives contain many near-mythical, long-lost routes that do not feature on the Republic's official charts. Conquering Kashyyyk would enable the Separatists to control hyperspace route planning and to use the Wookiees' secret routes to frustrate and monopolize galactic trade and communications.

DATA FILE

Manufacturer: Appazanna Engineering Works
Make: Oevvaor jet catamaran
Dimensions: length 15.1 m (46.2 ft); width 10.2 m (33.5 ft); height 4.3 m (14.1 ft)
Max. waterspeed: 370 kph (230 mph)
Crew: 2
Passengers: 2
Consumables: 2 days' rations
Armament: none

PALPATINE'S SHUTTLE

ASSASSINATION AND ABDUCTION have punctuated every stage of the Clone Wars, and a galactic leader such as the newly self-appointed Emperor Palpatine requires a secure personal transport. The new *Theta*-class T-2c shuttle is designed to ferry important officers, Senators, and courtiers between planets and ships in safety. Capable of outgunning most starfighters, the ship is fitted with twin forward-mounted quad laser cannons and a single, high-powered tail gun. This destructive arsenal can be computer-controlled or manually operated from a combined communications and gunnery station in the cockpit. The long folding wings are designed to project powerful shielding fields, and they also aid stability during atmospheric flight.

DATA FILE

Manufacturer: Cygnus Spaceworks
Make: *Theta*-class T-2c Personnel Transport
Dimensions: length *(excluding guns)* 18.5 m (60.7 ft);
width 29.3 m (96.1 ft); height 18.5 m (60.7 ft)
Max. acceleration *(linear, in open space)*: 1,800G
Max. airspeed *(in standard atmosphere)*: 2,000 kph (1,240 mph)
Hyperdrive: class 1; 8,000 light-year range
Consumables: 60 days fuel and air
Crew: 1–5
Armament: 2 quad laser cannons; 1 aft laser cannon

ELITE TRANSPORT

Emperor Palpatine's shuttle has been upgraded by "Warthan's Wizards," the finest starship technicians in the galaxy. To provide instant transgalactic communications, they installed a hyperwave reflector akin to the secret Jedi homing devices. The shuttle is also lined with sensor masks that make the interior appear empty on conventional scanners. Palpatine's later shuttles will feature a cloaking device—making them invisible to all forms of light, gravity, and other known energies.

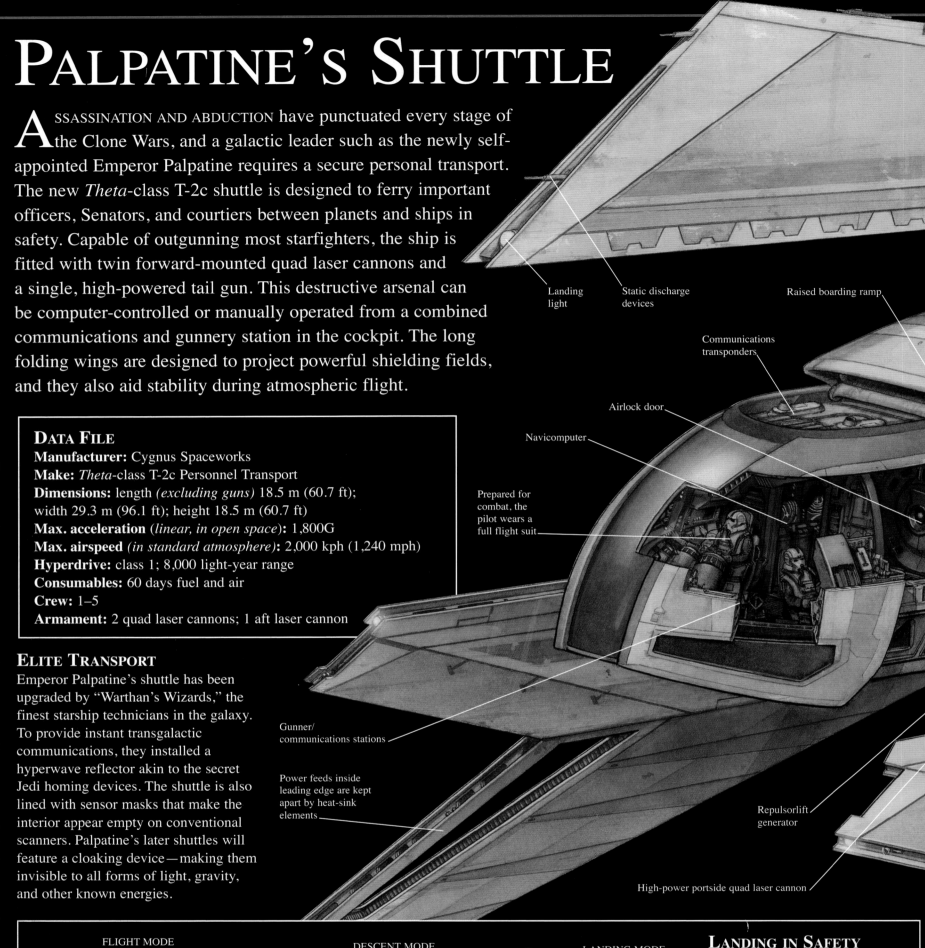

Landing light

Static discharge devices

Raised boarding ramp

Communications transponders

Airlock door

Navicomputer

Prepared for combat, the pilot wears a full flight suit

Gunner/ communications stations

Power feeds inside leading edge are kept apart by heat-sink elements

Repulsorlift generator

High-power portside quad laser cannon

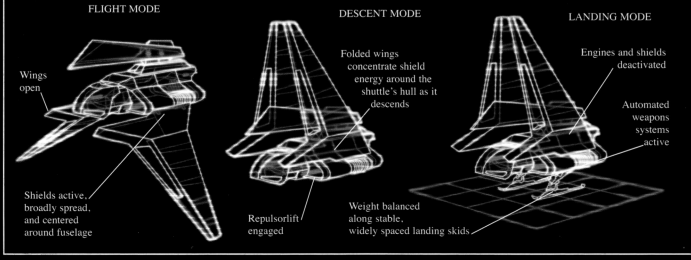

FLIGHT MODE

Wings open

Shields active, broadly spread, and centered around fuselage

DESCENT MODE

Folded wings concentrate shield energy around the shuttle's hull as it descends

Repulsorlift engaged

Weight balanced along stable, widely spaced landing skids

LANDING MODE

Engines and shields deactivated

Automated weapons systems active

LANDING IN SAFETY

When the *Theta*-class shuttle lands, its long wings fold upwards to allow access via the main hatch. The ion drive powers down as antigravity repulsorlifts guide the ship to a gentle touchdown. Scanners linked to the computer-controlled weapons systems survey the landing site as the ship descends, ready to instantly eliminate any threat to the ship or its occupants.

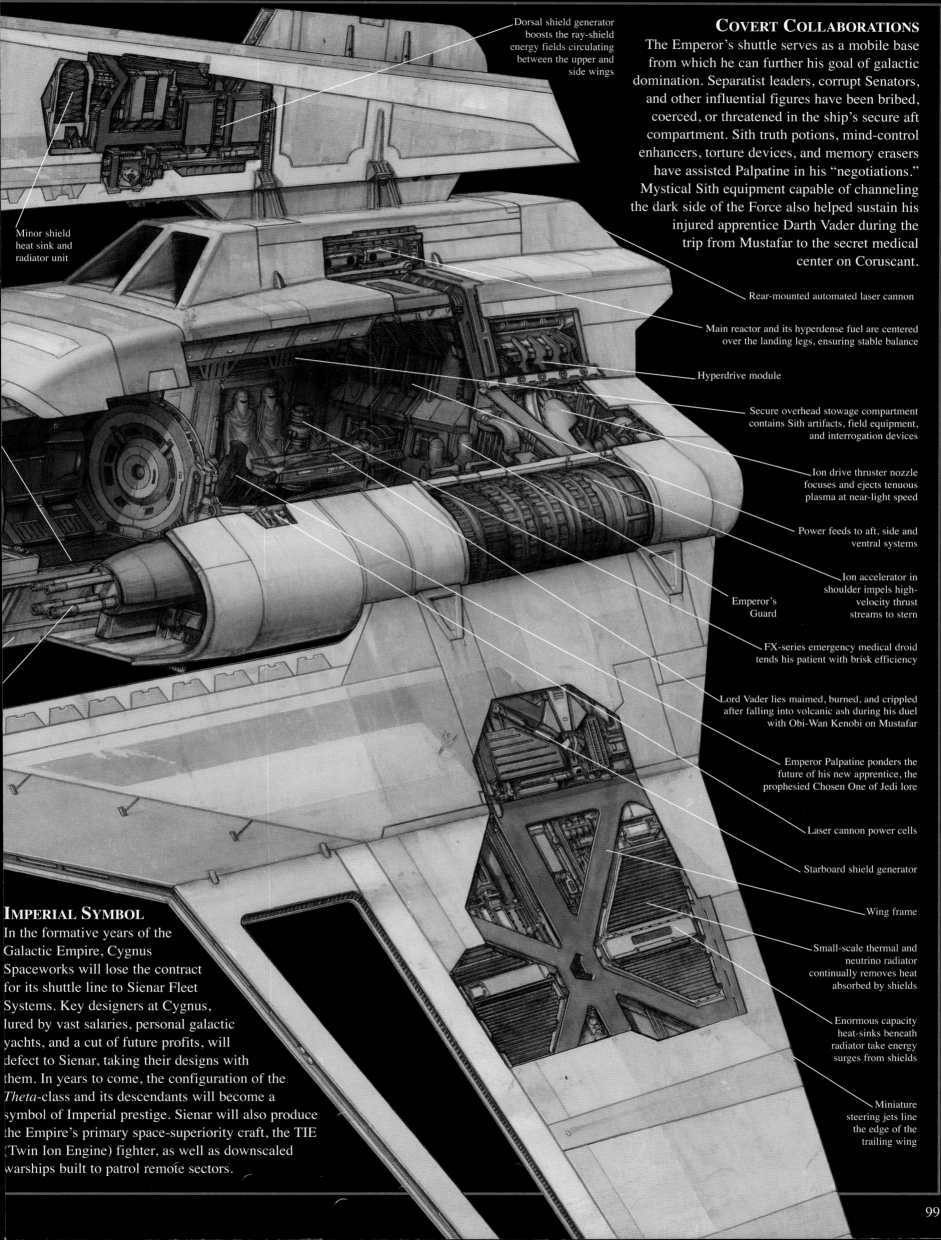

Dorsal shield generator boosts the ray-shield energy fields circulating between the upper and side wings

Minor shield heat sink and radiator unit

COVERT COLLABORATIONS

The Emperor's shuttle serves as a mobile base from which he can further his goal of galactic domination. Separatist leaders, corrupt Senators, and other influential figures have been bribed, coerced, or threatened in the ship's secure aft compartment. Sith truth potions, mind-control enhancers, torture devices, and memory erasers have assisted Palpatine in his "negotiations." Mystical Sith equipment capable of channeling the dark side of the Force also helped sustain his injured apprentice Darth Vader during the trip from Mustafar to the secret medical center on Coruscant.

Rear-mounted automated laser cannon

Main reactor and its hyperdense fuel are centered over the landing legs, ensuring stable balance

Hyperdrive module

Secure overhead stowage compartment contains Sith artifacts, field equipment, and interrogation devices

Ion drive thruster nozzle focuses and ejects tenuous plasma at near-light speed

Power feeds to aft, side and ventral systems

Ion accelerator in shoulder impels high-velocity thrust streams to stern

Emperor's Guard

FX-series emergency medical droid tends his patient with brisk efficiency

Lord Vader lies maimed, burned, and crippled after falling into volcanic ash during his duel with Obi-Wan Kenobi on Mustafar

Emperor Palpatine ponders the future of his new apprentice, the prophesied Chosen One of Jedi lore

Laser cannon power cells

Starboard shield generator

Wing frame

Small-scale thermal and neutrino radiator continually removes heat absorbed by shields

Enormous capacity heat-sinks beneath radiator take energy surges from shields

Miniature steering jets line the edge of the trailing wing

IMPERIAL SYMBOL

In the formative years of the Galactic Empire, Cygnus Spaceworks will lose the contract for its shuttle line to Sienar Fleet Systems. Key designers at Cygnus, lured by vast salaries, personal galactic yachts, and a cut of future profits, will defect to Sienar, taking their designs with them. In years to come, the configuration of the *Theta*-class and its descendants will become a symbol of Imperial prestige. Sienar will also produce the Empire's primary space-superiority craft, the TIE (Twin Ion Engine) fighter, as well as downscaled warships built to patrol remote sectors.

YODA'S ESCAPE PODS

A N ESCAPE POD is designed for just one thing: to carry a living being away from danger as quickly as possible. These basic craft roar and shake through the air, propelled by simple ion engines, while the occupant's ride is smoothed by inertial compensators and anti-gravity fields. In his escape from the forces of Emperor Palpatine's newly formed Galactic Empire, Jedi Master Yoda resorts to these devices twice in the space of one week. Yoda's first pod is a simple, Wookiee-made vessel that lifts him away from danger on Kashyyyk. His second craft, which carries him into exile on Dagobah, is a more sophisticated lander from Polis Massa. The pod can guide itself to an upright landing and touch down on its four folding legs.

A HIDDEN SANCTUARY

After discovering the disappearance of the planet Kamino from Jedi navigational charts at the beginning of the Clone Wars, Yoda discreetly scanned for other gaps. Throughout the entire galaxy, he detected 37 more "missing" star systems. He found amazing strategic resources in some, while he met fiendish foes in others. With the dark side of the Force ever more pervasive, Yoda chose to keep one lost planet, Dagobah, as his private secret. In so doing, he was able to out-manipulate the phantom menace responsible for deleting the Jedi files. By adopting Dagobah as his hiding place, Yoda now awaits a new hope for the galaxy in safe, if lonely, isolation.

Casing rings of thrusters will be cannibalised to perform a useful function in a makeshift dwelling

Engine's maximum thrust is 300G, slow even for a civilian ship

Ion acceleration chamber

Plasma feeds

Adjustable footpad

Reactor/ionization chamber

Fuel tanks are almost empty if reactant and propellant

Leg articulation socket

Fuel lines

Distress beacon, already deactivated by Yoda

Rations and survival gear

Seats are designed to be a comfortable size for an average male Massan

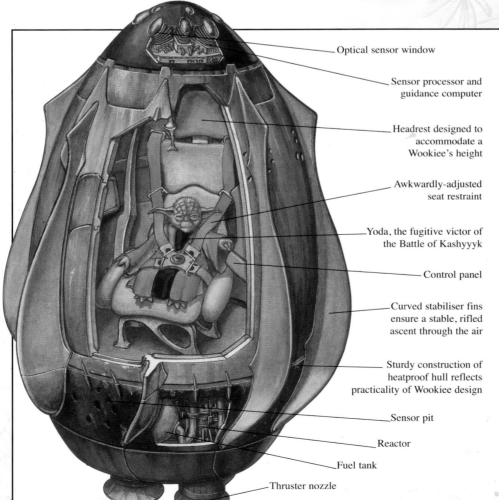

Optical sensor window

Sensor processor and guidance computer

Headrest designed to accommodate a Wookiee's height

Awkwardly-adjusted seat restraint

Yoda, the fugitive victor of the Battle of Kashyyyk

Control panel

Curved stabiliser fins ensure a stable, rifled ascent through the air

Sturdy construction of heatproof hull reflects practicality of Wookiee design

Sensor pit

Reactor

Fuel tank

Thruster nozzle

ESCAPE FROM KASHYYYK

With invading Separatist droids overrunning the forests and lagoons of Kashyyyk, Wookiee defenders prepared thousands of hidden escape pods for last-resort evacuation. General Yoda, in victorious yet unforeseeable circumstances, used the first pod. Its three sublight thrusters—cobbled together from three shipwrecks—contain just enough fuel to bear him safely into interplanetary space. Yoda deactivates his pod's tell-tale distress beacon, relying solely on his Jedi emergency transmitter. This pocket gadget reflects a tiny fraction of the supralight signals beamed between the Republic's public HoloNet relays. Encrypted modulation of these reflected signals transmits the owner's ID and location. Alderaanian agents searching for surviving Jedi on Coruscant intercept Yoda's call, leading Senator Bail Organa to his rescue.

Landing repulsorlift elements resist planetary gravity and brake the descent

Smooth hatch edge locks magnetically into frame

Egress hatch

Illuminated steps ensure visibility after a landing in dark conditions

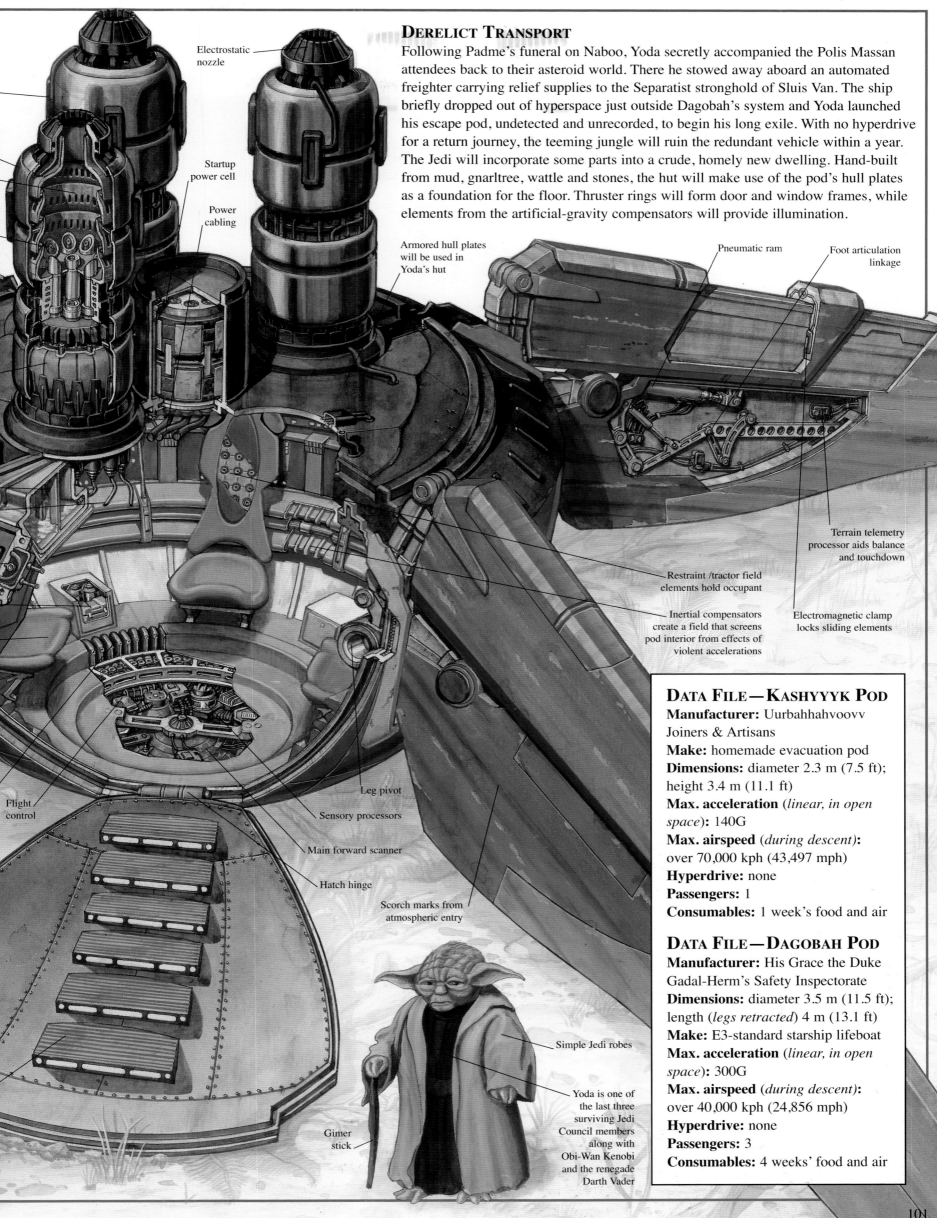

DERELICT TRANSPORT

Following Padme's funeral on Naboo, Yoda secretly accompanied the Polis Massan attendees back to their asteroid world. There he stowed away aboard an automated freighter carrying relief supplies to the Separatist stronghold of Sluis Van. The ship briefly dropped out of hyperspace just outside Dagobah's system and Yoda launched his escape pod, undetected and unrecorded, to begin his long exile. With no hyperdrive for a return journey, the teeming jungle will ruin the redundant vehicle within a year. The Jedi will incorporate some parts into a crude, homely new dwelling. Hand-built from mud, gnarltree, wattle and stones, the hut will make use of the pod's hull plates as a foundation for the floor. Thruster rings will form door and window frames, while elements from the artificial-gravity compensators will provide illumination.

Electrostatic nozzle

Startup power cell

Power cabling

Armored hull plates will be used in Yoda's hut

Pneumatic ram

Foot articulation linkage

Terrain telemetry processor aids balance and touchdown

Restraint /tractor field elements hold occupant

Inertial compensators create a field that screens pod interior from effects of violent accelerations

Electromagnetic clamp locks sliding elements

Flight control

Leg pivot

Sensory processors

Main forward scanner

Hatch hinge

Scorch marks from atmospheric entry

Simple Jedi robes

Yoda is one of the last three surviving Jedi Council members along with Obi-Wan Kenobi and the renegade Darth Vader

Gimer stick

DATA FILE—KASHYYYK POD
Manufacturer: Uurbahhahvoovv Joiners & Artisans
Make: homemade evacuation pod
Dimensions: diameter 2.3 m (7.5 ft); height 3.4 m (11.1 ft)
Max. acceleration (*linear, in open space*): 140G
Max. airspeed (*during descent*): over 70,000 kph (43,497 mph)
Hyperdrive: none
Passengers: 1
Consumables: 1 week's food and air

DATA FILE—DAGOBAH POD
Manufacturer: His Grace the Duke Gadal-Herm's Safety Inspectorate
Dimensions: diameter 3.5 m (11.5 ft); length (*legs retracted*) 4 m (13.1 ft)
Make: E3-standard starship lifeboat
Max. acceleration (*linear, in open space*): 300G
Max. airspeed (*during descent*): over 40,000 kph (24,856 mph)
Hyperdrive: none
Passengers: 3
Consumables: 4 weeks' food and air

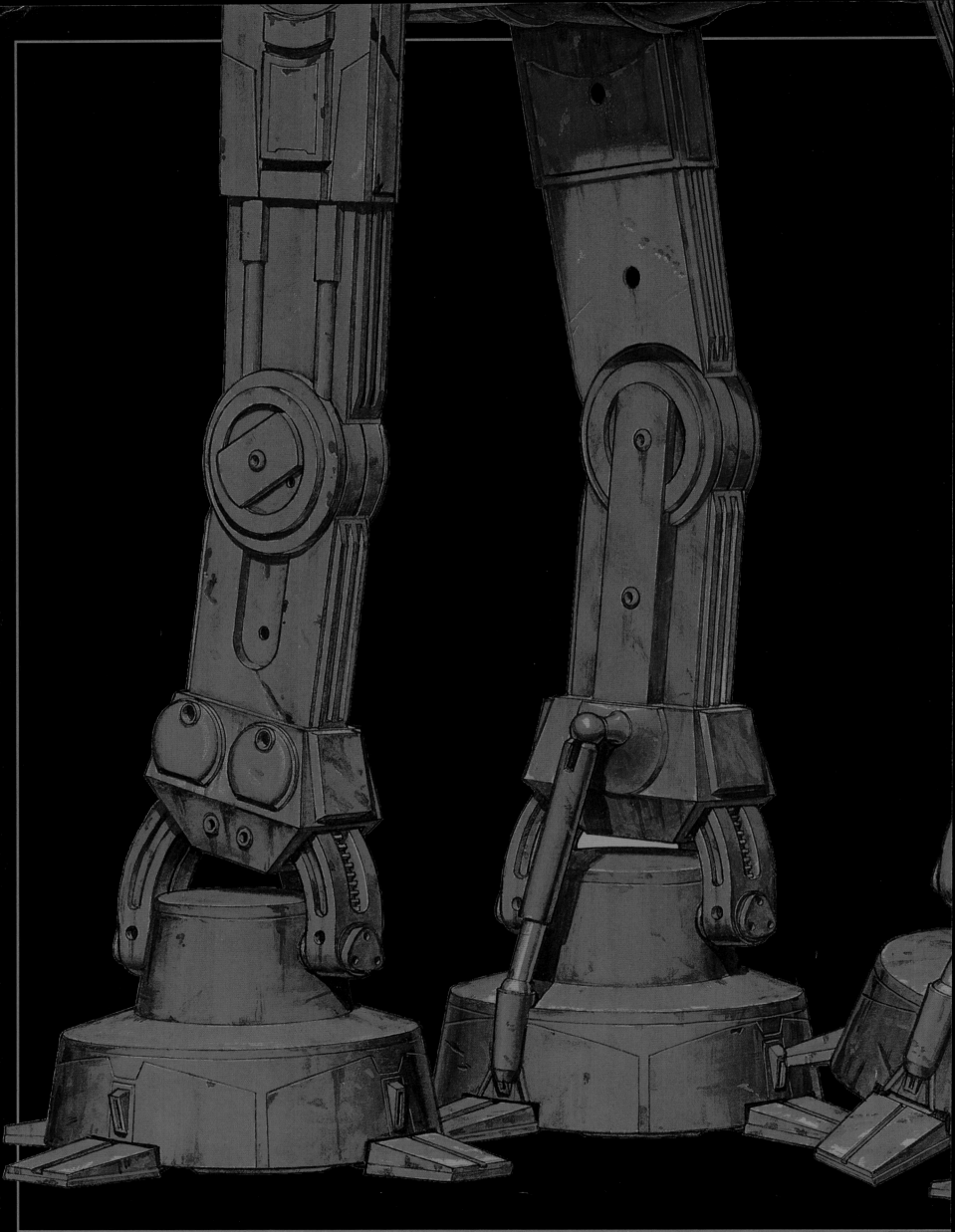

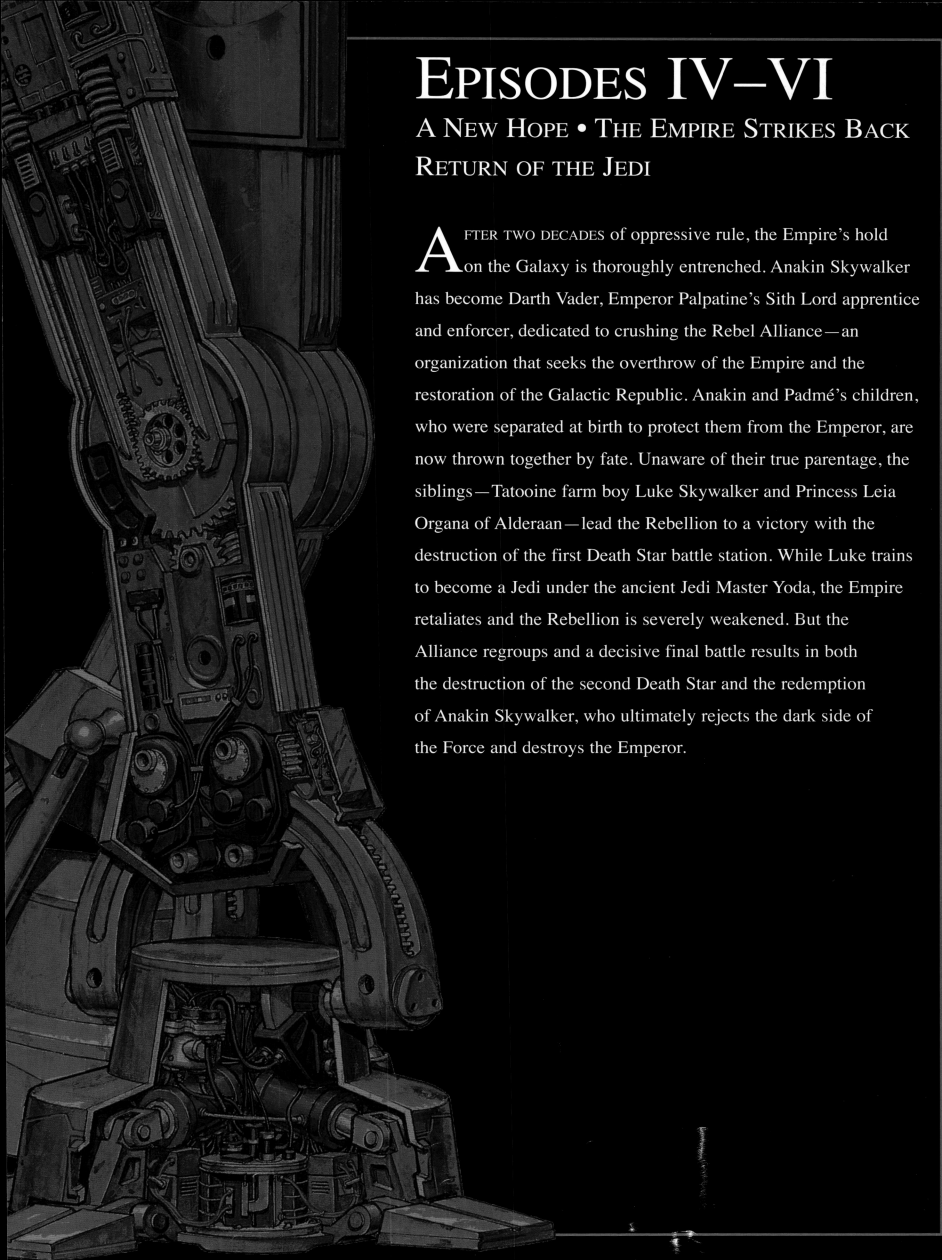

Episodes IV–VI

A New Hope • The Empire Strikes Back
Return of the Jedi

AFTER TWO DECADES of oppressive rule, the Empire's hold on the Galaxy is thoroughly entrenched. Anakin Skywalker has become Darth Vader, Emperor Palpatine's Sith Lord apprentice and enforcer, dedicated to crushing the Rebel Alliance—an organization that seeks the overthrow of the Empire and the restoration of the Galactic Republic. Anakin and Padmé's children, who were separated at birth to protect them from the Emperor, are now thrown together by fate. Unaware of their true parentage, the siblings—Tatooine farm boy Luke Skywalker and Princess Leia Organa of Alderaan—lead the Rebellion to a victory with the destruction of the first Death Star battle station. While Luke trains to become a Jedi under the ancient Jedi Master Yoda, the Empire retaliates and the Rebellion is severely weakened. But the Alliance regroups and a decisive final battle results in both the destruction of the second Death Star and the redemption of Anakin Skywalker, who ultimately rejects the dark side of the Force and destroys the Emperor.

BLOCKADE RUNNER

PRINCESS LEIA ORGANA OF ALDERAAN travels far and wide on board her consular starship *Tantive IV*, negotiating peace settlements and bringing aid to imperiled populations. Commanded by the daring and loyal Captain Antilles, Leia's *Tantive IV* is a Corellian Corvette: an older, hand-crafted ship of a make seen throughout the galaxy. Owned by the Royal House of Alderaan, this versatile craft has served two generations of Alderaanian Senators since it was first acquired by Leia's father, Bail Organa, as his personal transport. Under the cover of diplomatic immunity, the *Tantive IV* has carried out a range of missions for the Rebel Alliance, making its added armor plate as vital as its formal state conference chamber. This sturdy ship has brought the Organas through many harrowing adventures, and it is only under the pursuit of Darth Vader that the *Tantive IV* is finally overtaken and captured.

ESCAPE PODS

Spacecraft escape pods range from coffin-like capsules to large lifeboats which are small ships in their own right. The Blockade Runner carries eight small escape pods rated for up to three people, and four laser-armed pods which seat 12. More sophisticated than the smaller pods, these lifeboats nonetheless have a very limited range. None of the *Tantive IV*'s escape systems could save its crew from the *Devastator*'s guns.

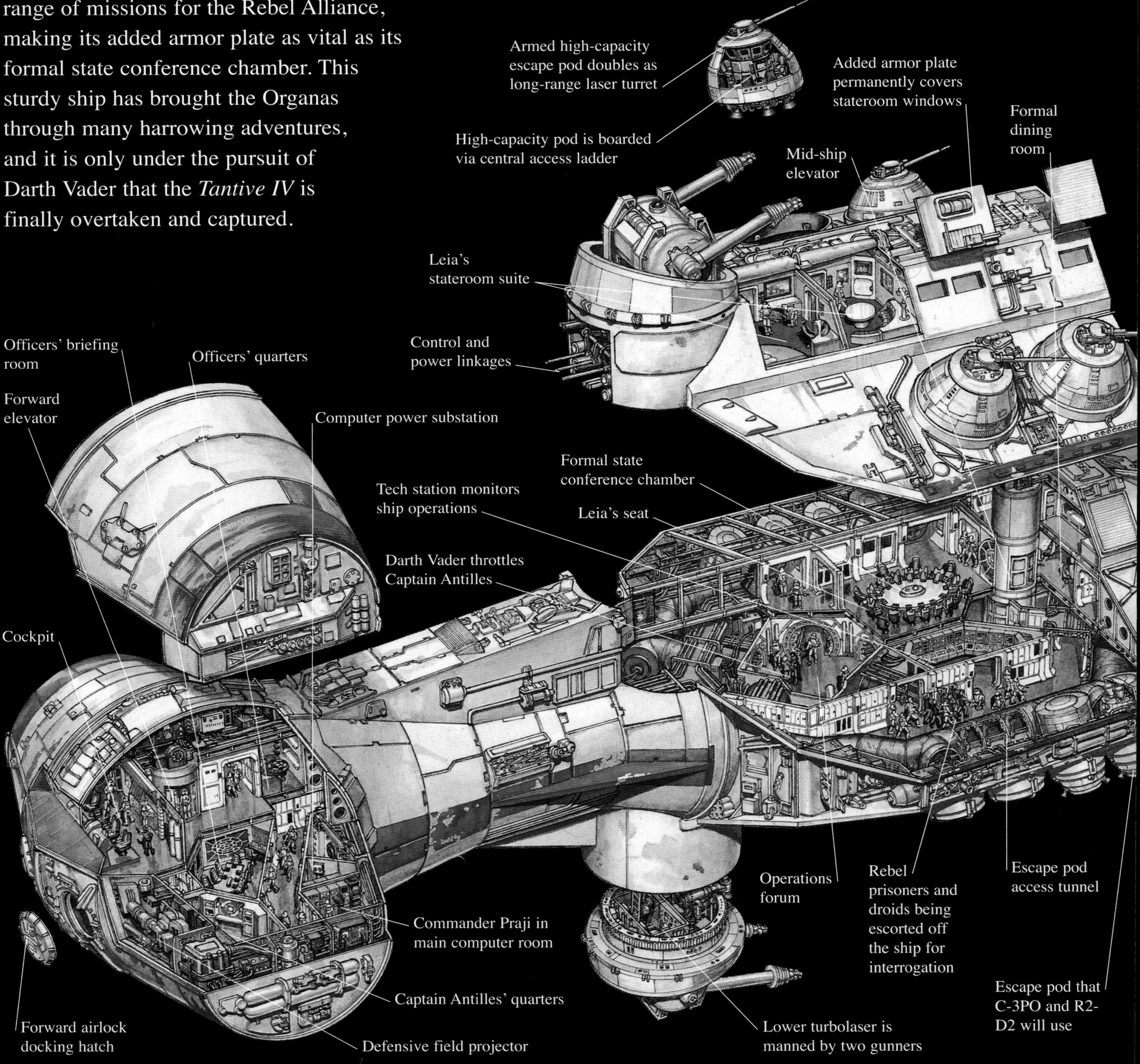

Armed high-capacity escape pod doubles as long-range laser turret

High-capacity pod is boarded via central access ladder

Added armor plate permanently covers stateroom windows

Formal dining room

Mid-ship elevator

Leia's stateroom suite

Control and power linkages

Officers' briefing room

Officers' quarters

Forward elevator

Computer power substation

Formal state conference chamber

Tech station monitors ship operations

Leia's seat

Darth Vader throttles Captain Antilles

Cockpit

Operations forum

Rebel prisoners and droids being escorted off the ship for interrogation

Escape pod access tunnel

Commander Praji in main computer room

Captain Antilles' quarters

Escape pod that C-3PO and R2-D2 will use

Forward airlock docking hatch

Defensive field projector

Lower turbolaser is manned by two gunners

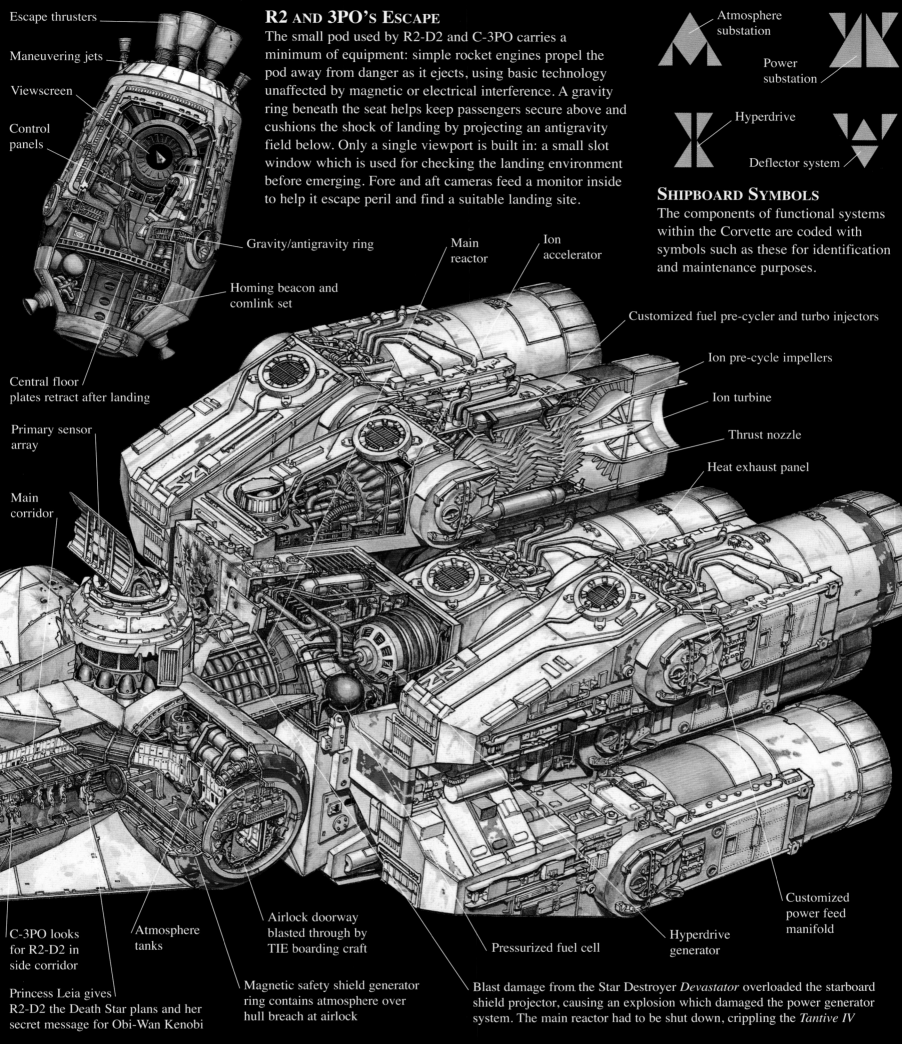

Escape thrusters

Maneuvering jets

Viewscreen

Control panels

R2 AND 3PO'S ESCAPE

The small pod used by R2-D2 and C-3PO carries a minimum of equipment: simple rocket engines propel the pod away from danger as it ejects, using basic technology unaffected by magnetic or electrical interference. A gravity ring beneath the seat helps keep passengers secure above and cushions the shock of landing by projecting an antigravity field below. Only a single viewport is built in: a small slot window which is used for checking the landing environment before emerging. Fore and aft cameras feed a monitor inside to help it escape peril and find a suitable landing site.

Atmosphere substation

Power substation

Hyperdrive

Deflector system

SHIPBOARD SYMBOLS

The components of functional systems within the Corvette are coded with symbols such as these for identification and maintenance purposes.

Gravity/antigravity ring

Main reactor

Ion accelerator

Customized fuel pre-cycler and turbo injectors

Homing beacon and comlink set

Ion pre-cycle impellers

Ion turbine

Central floor plates retract after landing

Thrust nozzle

Heat exhaust panel

Primary sensor array

Main corridor

C-3PO looks for R2-D2 in side corridor

Atmosphere tanks

Princess Leia gives R2-D2 the Death Star plans and her secret message for Obi-Wan Kenobi

Airlock doorway blasted through by TIE boarding craft

Magnetic safety shield generator ring contains atmosphere over hull breach at airlock

Pressurized fuel cell

Hyperdrive generator

Customized power feed manifold

Blast damage from the Star Destroyer *Devastator* overloaded the starboard shield projector, causing an explosion which damaged the power generator system. The main reactor had to be shut down, crippling the *Tantive IV*

THE CAPABLE CORVETTE

Sporting twin turbolaser turrets and a massive drive block of eleven ion turbine engines for speed, the Corellian Corvette balances defensive capabilities with a high power-to-mass ratio, meaning that what it can't shoot down it can generally outrun. The *Tantive IV* has been extensively refitted to suit Princess Leia's requirements, and the ship's original blue markings have been replaced with scarlet stripes to indicate the vessel's diplomatic status.

CONTRABANDITS

The Corvette's most notorious use is in the hands of Corellian smugglers. Blending anonymously into space traffic, these wily rogues pilot their vessels through Imperial security zones to avoid duties and taxes (or arrest for dealing in weapons and illegal goods). They are hard to spot, and chagrined Imperial officials have given the make its nickname "Blockade Runner."

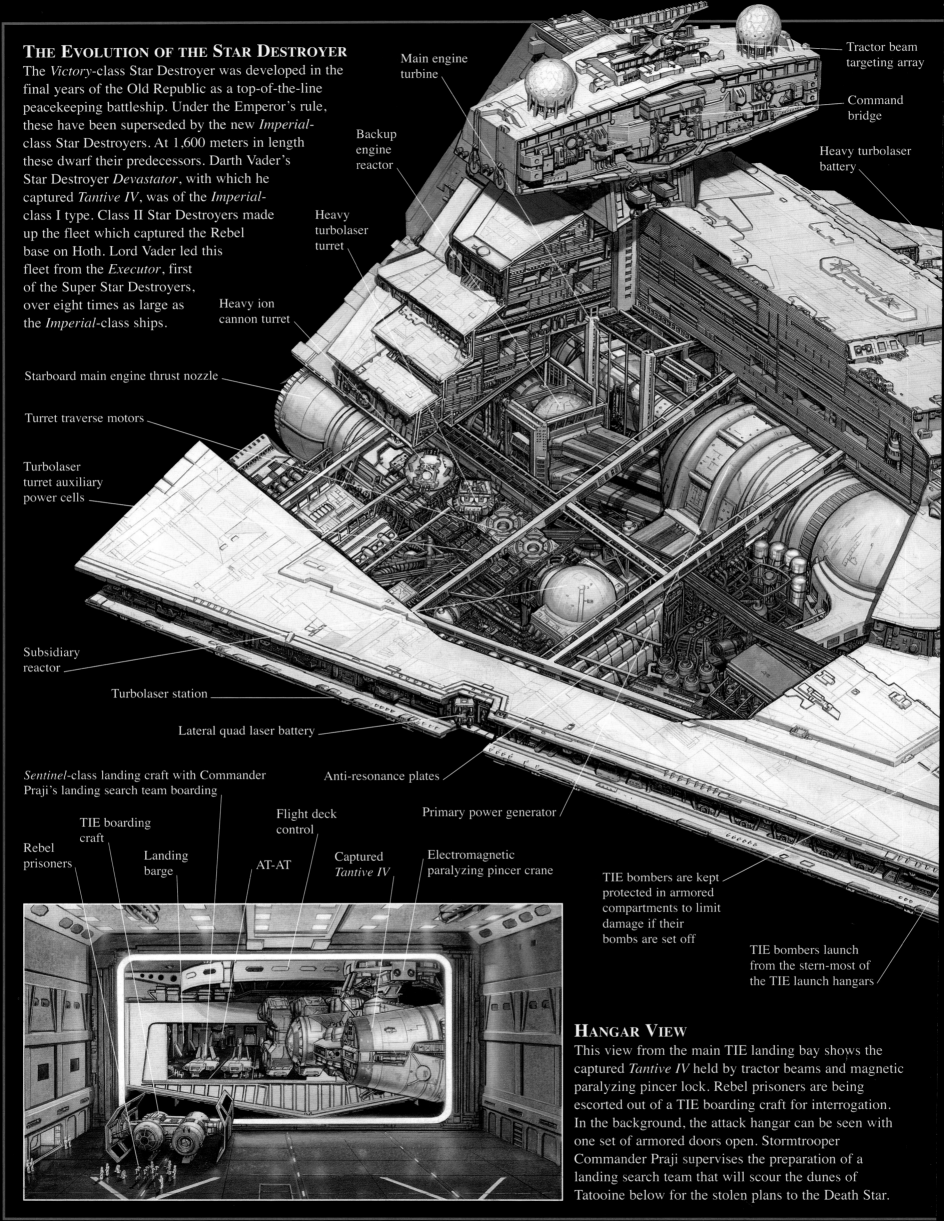

THE EVOLUTION OF THE STAR DESTROYER

The *Victory*-class Star Destroyer was developed in the final years of the Old Republic as a top-of-the-line peacekeeping battleship. Under the Emperor's rule, these have been superseded by the new *Imperial*-class Star Destroyers. At 1,600 meters in length these dwarf their predecessors. Darth Vader's Star Destroyer *Devastator*, with which he captured *Tantive IV*, was of the *Imperial*-class I type. Class II Star Destroyers made up the fleet which captured the Rebel base on Hoth. Lord Vader led this fleet from the *Executor*, first of the Super Star Destroyers, over eight times as large as the *Imperial*-class ships.

Main engine turbine

Tractor beam targeting array

Command bridge

Backup engine reactor

Heavy turbolaser battery

Heavy turbolaser turret

Heavy ion cannon turret

Starboard main engine thrust nozzle

Turret traverse motors

Turbolaser turret auxiliary power cells

Subsidiary reactor

Turbolaser station

Lateral quad laser battery

Anti-resonance plates

Sentinel-class landing craft with Commander Praji's landing search team boarding

Flight deck control

Primary power generator

TIE boarding craft

Rebel prisoners

Landing barge

AT-AT

Captured *Tantive IV*

Electromagnetic paralyzing pincer crane

TIE bombers are kept protected in armored compartments to limit damage if their bombs are set off

TIE bombers launch from the stern-most of the TIE launch hangars

HANGAR VIEW

This view from the main TIE landing bay shows the captured *Tantive IV* held by tractor beams and magnetic paralyzing pincer lock. Rebel prisoners are being escorted out of a TIE boarding craft for interrogation. In the background, the attack hangar can be seen with one set of armored doors open. Stormtrooper Commander Praji supervises the preparation of a landing search team that will scour the dunes of Tatooine below for the stolen plans to the Death Star.

STAR DESTROYER

THE STAR DESTROYER is a symbol of the Empire's military might, carrying devastating firepower and assault forces anywhere in the galaxy to subjugate opposition. A Star Destroyer can easily overtake most fleeing craft, blasting them into submission or drawing them into its main hangar with tractor beams. *Imperial*-class Star Destroyers are 1,600 meters long, bristling with turbolasers and ion cannons, and equipped with eight giant turret gun stations. Star Destroyers carry 9,700 stormtroopers and a full wing of 72 TIE ships (typically including 48 TIE/ln fighters, 12 TIE bombers, and 12 TIE boarding craft) as well as a range of attack and landing craft. A single Star Destroyer can overwhelm an entire rebellious planet. Major industrialized worlds are assaulted with a fleet of six Star Destroyers operating with support cruisers and supply craft. Such a force can obliterate any defenses, occupying or completely destroying cities or settlements.

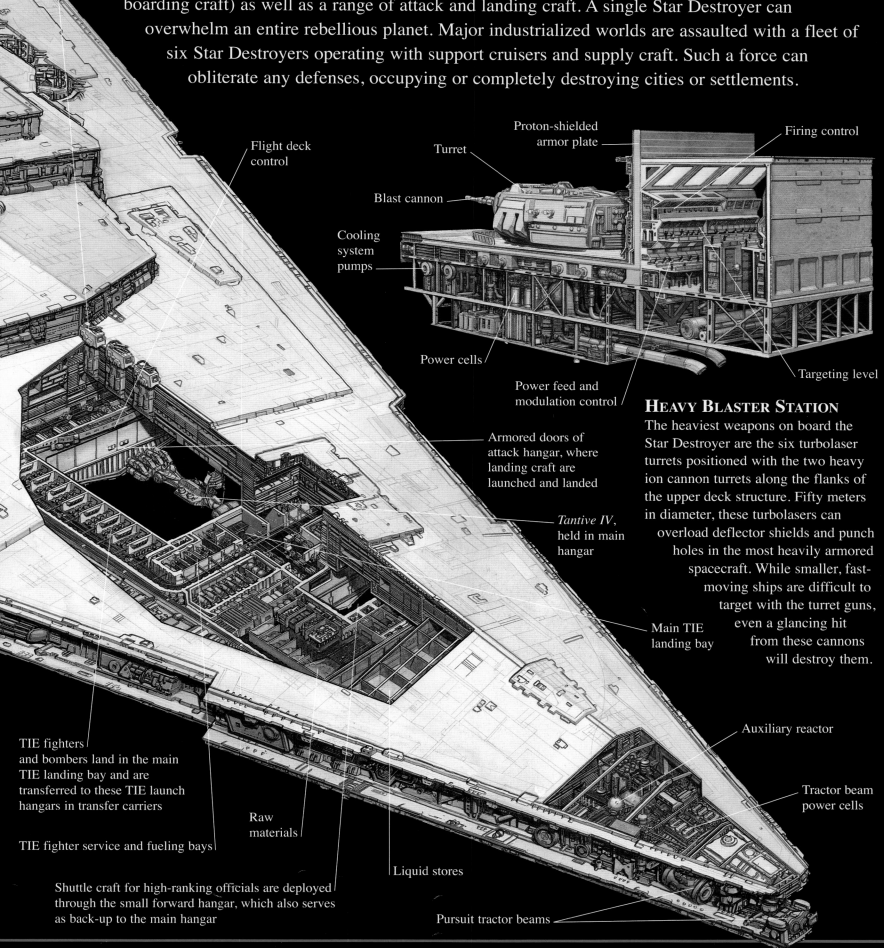

Axial defense turret

Flight deck control

Proton-shielded armor plate

Turret

Firing control

Blast cannon

Cooling system pumps

Power cells

Power feed and modulation control

Targeting level

Armored doors of attack hangar, where landing craft are launched and landed

Tantive IV, held in main hangar

HEAVY BLASTER STATION
The heaviest weapons on board the Star Destroyer are the six turbolaser turrets positioned with the two heavy ion cannon turrets along the flanks of the upper deck structure. Fifty meters in diameter, these turbolasers can overload deflector shields and punch holes in the most heavily armored spacecraft. While smaller, fast-moving ships are difficult to target with the turret guns, even a glancing hit from these cannons will destroy them.

Main TIE landing bay

TIE fighters and bombers land in the main TIE landing bay and are transferred to these TIE launch hangars in transfer carriers

TIE fighter service and fueling bays

Raw materials

Liquid stores

Auxiliary reactor

Tractor beam power cells

Shuttle craft for high-ranking officials are deployed through the small forward hangar, which also serves as back-up to the main hangar

Pursuit tractor beams

MILLENNIUM FALCON

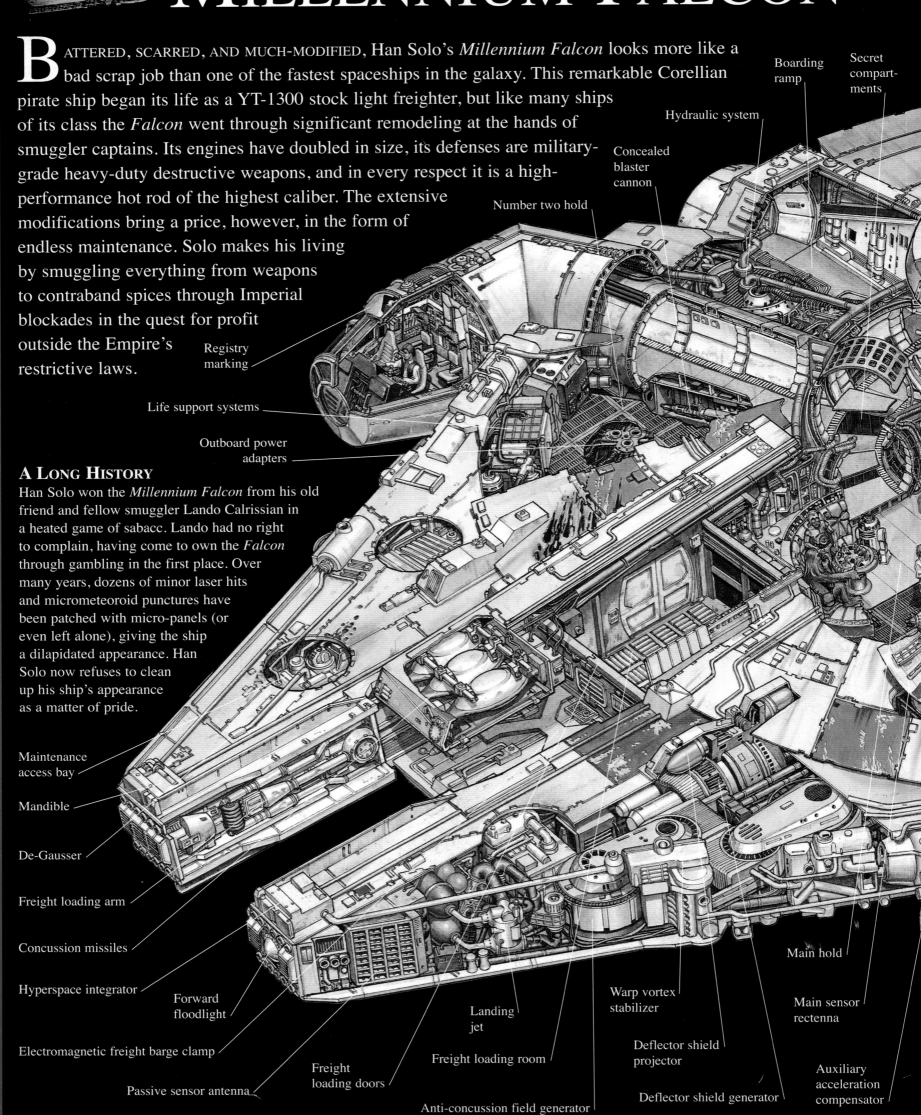

BATTERED, SCARRED, AND MUCH-MODIFIED, Han Solo's *Millennium Falcon* looks more like a bad scrap job than one of the fastest spaceships in the galaxy. This remarkable Corellian pirate ship began its life as a YT-1300 stock light freighter, but like many ships of its class the *Falcon* went through significant remodeling at the hands of smuggler captains. Its engines have doubled in size, its defenses are military-grade heavy-duty destructive weapons, and in every respect it is a high-performance hot rod of the highest caliber. The extensive modifications bring a price, however, in the form of endless maintenance. Solo makes his living by smuggling everything from weapons to contraband spices through Imperial blockades in the quest for profit outside the Empire's restrictive laws.

A LONG HISTORY

Han Solo won the *Millennium Falcon* from his old friend and fellow smuggler Lando Calrissian in a heated game of sabacc. Lando had no right to complain, having come to own the *Falcon* through gambling in the first place. Over many years, dozens of minor laser hits and micrometeoroid punctures have been patched with micro-panels (or even left alone), giving the ship a dilapidated appearance. Han Solo now refuses to clean up his ship's appearance as a matter of pride.

Boarding ramp

Secret compart-ments

Hydraulic system

Concealed blaster cannon

Number two hold

Registry marking

Life support systems

Outboard power adapters

Maintenance access bay

Mandible

De-Gausser

Freight loading arm

Concussion missiles

Hyperspace integrator

Forward floodlight

Electromagnetic freight barge clamp

Passive sensor antenna

Freight loading doors

Landing jet

Freight loading room

Anti-concussion field generator

Warp vortex stabilizer

Deflector shield projector

Deflector shield generator

Main hold

Main sensor rectenna

Auxiliary acceleration compensator

TIE FIGHTER

HURTLING THROUGH SPACE, TIE fighters are the most visible image of the Empire's wide-reaching power. The TIE fighter engine is the most precisely manufactured propulsion system in the galaxy. Solar ionization collects light energy and channels it through a reactor to fire emissions from a high-pressure radioactive gas. The engine has no moving parts, making it low-maintenance. To reduce the mass of the ship, TIE fighters are built without defensive shields, hyperdrive capability, and life support systems—so the pilots must wear spacesuits. The light-weight ship gains speed and maneuverability at the price of fragility and dependence on nearby Imperial bases or larger craft for support.

ALL THE SAME

TIE pilots may never use the same ship twice, and develop no sentimental attachment to their cr̶ as Rebels often do. TIE pilots kno̶ that every reconditioned fighter is identical to a factory-fresh ship; o̶ is the same as many thousands— another reinforcement of Imperial philosophy of absolute conformity.

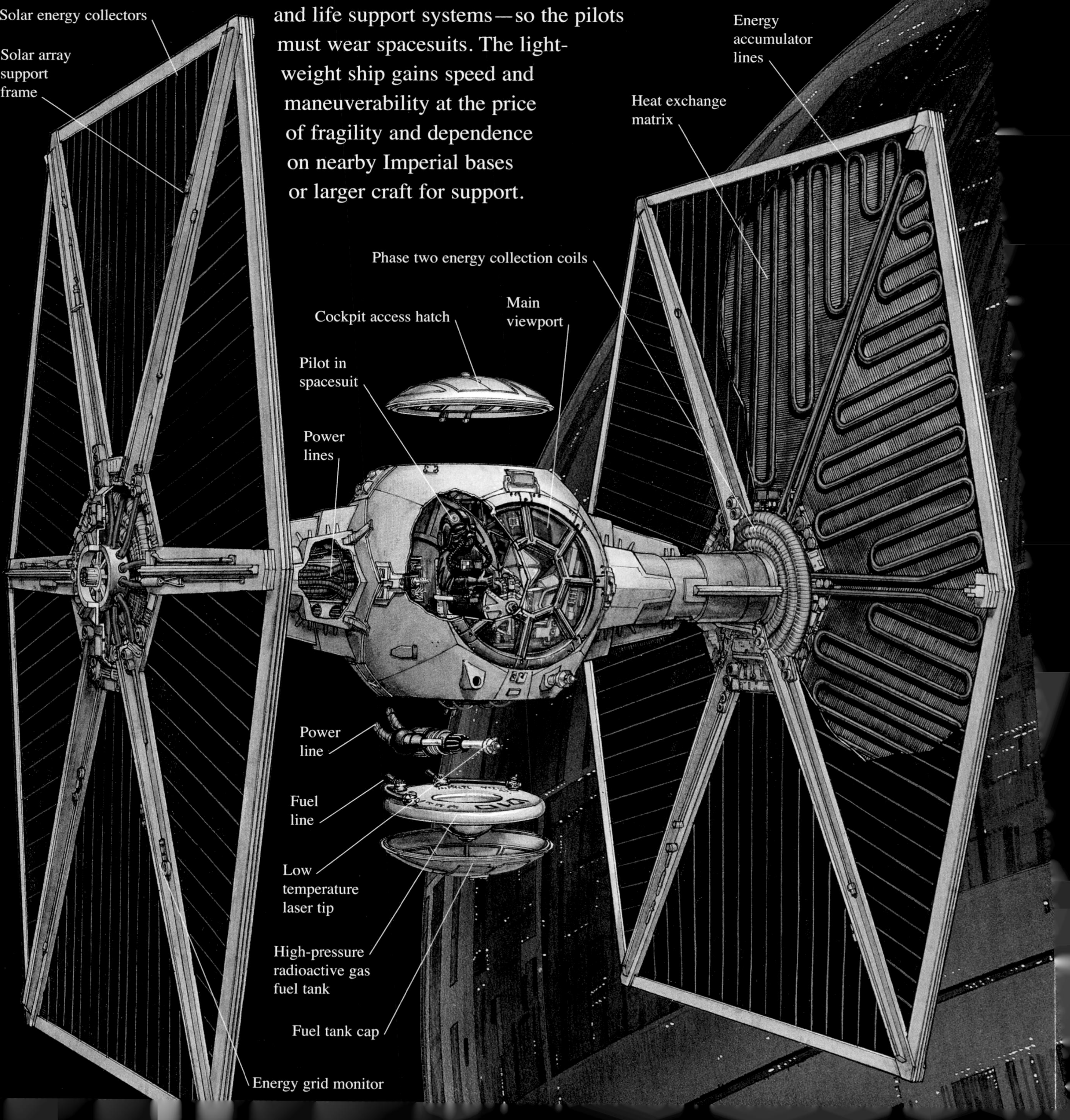

Solar energy collectors

Solar array support frame

Energy accumulator lines

Heat exchange matrix

Phase two energy collection coils

Cockpit access hatch

Main viewport

Pilot in spacesuit

Power lines

Power line

Fuel line

Low temperature laser tip

High-pressure radioactive gas fuel tank

Fuel tank cap

Energy grid monitor

DEATH STAR

THE EMPIRE'S GIGANTIC battle station code-named Death Star is 160 kilometers in diameter, large enough to be mistaken for a small moon. Credited as the brainchild of Grand Moff Tarkin, this colossal superweapon is designed to enforce the Emperor's rule through terror, presenting both the symbol and reality of ultimate destructive power. Making use of the Empire's most advanced discoveries in super-engineering, the Death Star is built around a hypermatter reactor which can generate enough power to destroy an entire planet. Designed in secret on the planet Geonosis and built by slave labor and titanic factory machines, the Death Star's vast structure houses over a million individuals and thousands of armed spacecraft, making it capable of occupying whole star systems by force. Elite gunners and troopers man the station's advanced weapons. The Death Star, once fully operational, represents a chilling specter of totalitarian domination and threatens to extinguish all hope for freedom in the galaxy.

CRUCIAL WEAKNESS

The Death Star's powerful defenses have one fatal flaw—small thermal exhaust ports that lead from the surface to the heart of the main reactor.

Main exhaust port

Thermal exhaust port shaft runs through central power column

Equatorial trench

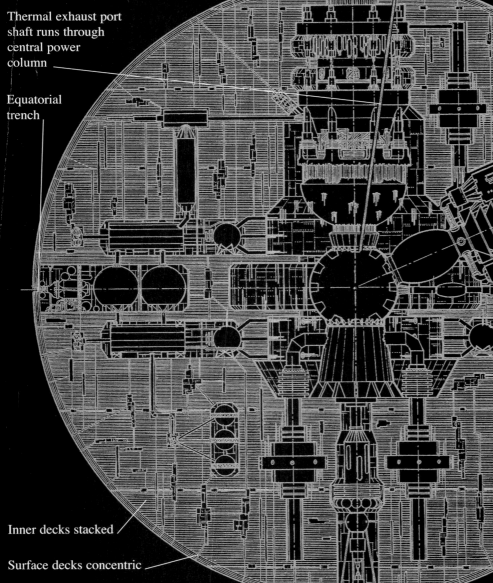

Inner decks stacked

Surface decks concentric

THE STOLEN PLANS

A complete technical readout of the battle station (left) was stolen by Rebel spies. These plans reveal the overwhelming might of the Death Star, detailing its myriad weapons systems and immense power structures. Ion engines, hyperdrives, and hangar bays ring the station's equatorial trench, while power cells over 15 kilometers wide distribute energy throughout the thousands of internal decks of the station. Air shafts and void spaces honeycomb the interior. Occupying the polar axis of the Death Star is its central power column, with the hypermatter reactor at its core.

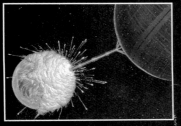

ALDERAAN DESTROYED

Without hesitation Grand Moff Tarkin orders the destruction of the peaceful planet Alderaan as the first demonstration of the Death Star's power. As the superlaser lances out at the blue-green planet, this horrific act wipes out billions of people.

SUPERLASER TRIBUTARY BEAM SHAFT

Eight tributary beams unite to form the superlaser primary beam. These tributary beams are arranged around the invisible central focusing field, firing in alternate sequence to build the power necessary to destroy a planet. The titanic energy of these beams must be monitored to prevent imbalance explosions.

DETENTION BLOCK AA-23

A desperate plan takes Luke, Han, and Chewbacca into the heart of peril as they try to rescue Princess Leia. Disguised as stormtroopers, Luke and Han escort Chewbacca, their "prisoner," into Leia's detention block. The supervisor suspects trouble, and only immediate action will save the Rebels.

TRASH COMPACTOR 32-6-3827

Escaping Leia's cell block, the Rebels dive into a garbage chute and land in a trash compactor, where refuse of every kind is collected before being processed and dumped into space.

AIR SHAFT

Throughout the Death Star are vast air shafts. Extensible bridges connect passages across the shafts, but can be disabled. When Luke and Leia find themselves trapped at one of the air shafts, quick thinking and bravery provide the only way across.

TRACTOR BEAM REACTOR COUPLING

The Death Star tractor beam is coupled to the main reactor in seven locations. These power terminals stand atop generator towers 35 kilometers tall. The air is taut with high-voltage electricity throughout the shaft surrounding the tower. It is in this setting that Ben Kenobi secretly deactivates one of the power beams to allow the *Millennium Falcon* to escape.

CHALLENGE AND SACRIFICE

Darth Vader senses the presence of his old Jedi master Obi-Wan Kenobi aboard the Death Star, and confronts him alone in a deadly lightsaber duel. Kenobi sacrifices himself to help his young friends escape, yielding to Vader in an empty victory in which, mysteriously, Obi-Wan becomes one with the Force.

Power processing networks

Navigational beacon

Control room window

Hallway overlook windows

Turbolaser turret

Ben Kenobi and Darth Vader

Landing alignment marking

Atmosphere processing unit

Ion drive reactor

Atmosphere processing substation

Equatorial docking bay

Ion sublight engines

DOCKING BAY 327

Drawn in by a tractor beam, the *Millennium Falcon* comes to rest in a pressurized hangar within the Death Star's equatorial trench. Magnetic shields over the entrance retain the atmosphere. Outboard power-feeds hook up to landed craft so that the ship reactors can be shut down while in the hangar.

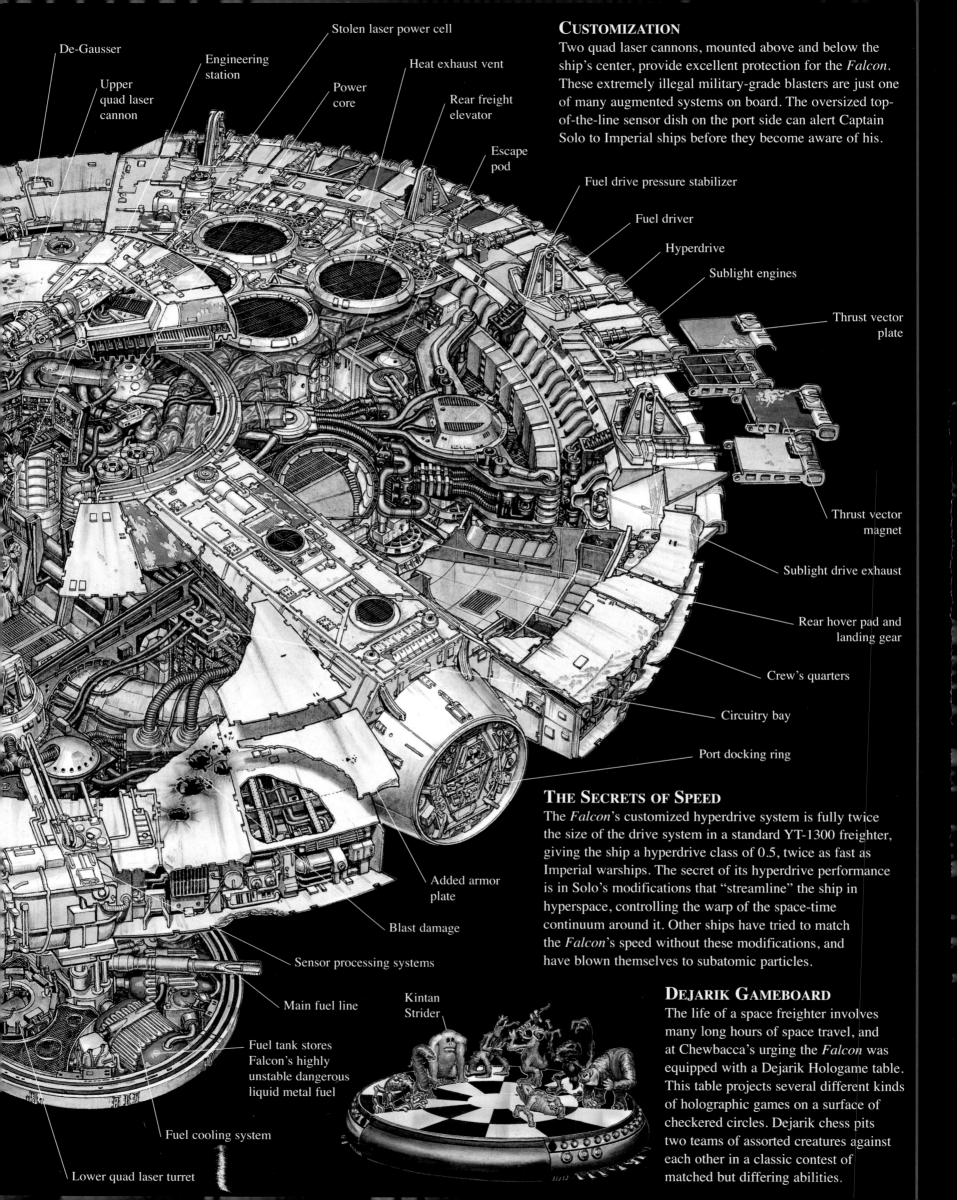

De-Gausser

Upper
quad laser
cannon

Engineering
station

Stolen laser power cell

Power
core

Heat exhaust vent

Rear freight
elevator

Escape
pod

CUSTOMIZATION

Two quad laser cannons, mounted above and below the
ship's center, provide excellent protection for the *Falcon*.
These extremely illegal military-grade blasters are just one
of many augmented systems on board. The oversized top-
of-the-line sensor dish on the port side can alert Captain
Solo to Imperial ships before they become aware of his.

Fuel drive pressure stabilizer

Fuel driver

Hyperdrive

Sublight engines

Thrust vector
plate

Thrust vector
magnet

Sublight drive exhaust

Rear hover pad and
landing gear

Crew's quarters

Circuitry bay

Port docking ring

THE SECRETS OF SPEED

The *Falcon*'s customized hyperdrive system is fully twice
the size of the drive system in a standard YT-1300 freighter,
giving the ship a hyperdrive class of 0.5, twice as fast as
Imperial warships. The secret of its hyperdrive performance
is in Solo's modifications that "streamline" the ship in
hyperspace, controlling the warp of the space-time
continuum around it. Other ships have tried to match
the *Falcon*'s speed without these modifications, and
have blown themselves to subatomic particles.

Added armor
plate

Blast damage

Sensor processing systems

Main fuel line

Kintan
Strider

Fuel tank stores
Falcon's highly
unstable dangerous
liquid metal fuel

Fuel cooling system

Lower quad laser turret

DEJARIK GAMEBOARD

The life of a space freighter involves
many long hours of space travel, and
at Chewbacca's urging the *Falcon* was
equipped with a Dejarik Hologame table.
This table projects several different kinds
of holographic games on a surface of
checkered circles. Dejarik chess pits
two teams of assorted creatures against
each other in a classic contest of
matched but differing abilities.

TIE MISSION PROFILES

TIE fighters are deployed for a variety of mission profiles. Their primary role is as space superiority fighters, engaging Rebel craft and defending Imperial bases and capital ships. Scout TIEs may travel alone to cover wide areas of space. Such individual scouts patrol the huge asteroid field left by the explosion of the planet Alderaan. Ships are assigned to escort duty in pairs, such as the twin TIEs that escort all flights of the Emperor's shuttle. Regular sentry groups of four TIE fighters patrol the space around Imperial bases, stations, and capital starships. A typical TIE fighter attack squadron consists of 12 ships, and a full attack wing consists of six squadrons, or 72 TIE fighters.

TIE VARIANTS

The basic structure of the TIE fighter has proven so successful that derivative variants use the same cockpit, wing brace structure, and drive system components. The Advanced x1 (above center) added shields and hyperdrive. The fearsome TIE interceptor (above right) features improved ion drives and electronics, and advanced ion stream projectors giving exceptional control.

Retaining claw

Launching TIE fighter

TIE in ready launch position

Pilots' boarding gantry

Transfer tunnel

Pilot boarding ship

TIE arriving from landing hangar

Service droid

Hangar control room

Elevator well

Service gantry

TIE HANGAR

TIEs are launched from cycling racks of up to 72 ships in the larger hangars; smaller hangars may contain as few as two ships. Pilots board from overhead gantries and are released to space as they disengage from the front position in the rack system. Returning ships land in separate hangars, where they are guided into receiver-carriers by small tractor beams. The receivers carry the TIE to a debarkation station where the pilot exits. From there the TIE may be serviced and refueled in a separate bay on its way through transfer tunnels to a launch hangar. In the launch hangar the TIE is cycled into the launch rack, ready for its next mission.

PILOT PSYCHOLOGY

TIE fighters lack landing gear, a measure designed to reduce mass for maximum maneuverability. While the ships are structurally capable of sitting on their wings, they are not designed to land or disembark pilots without special support. This teaches the pilots to rely completely on higher authority.

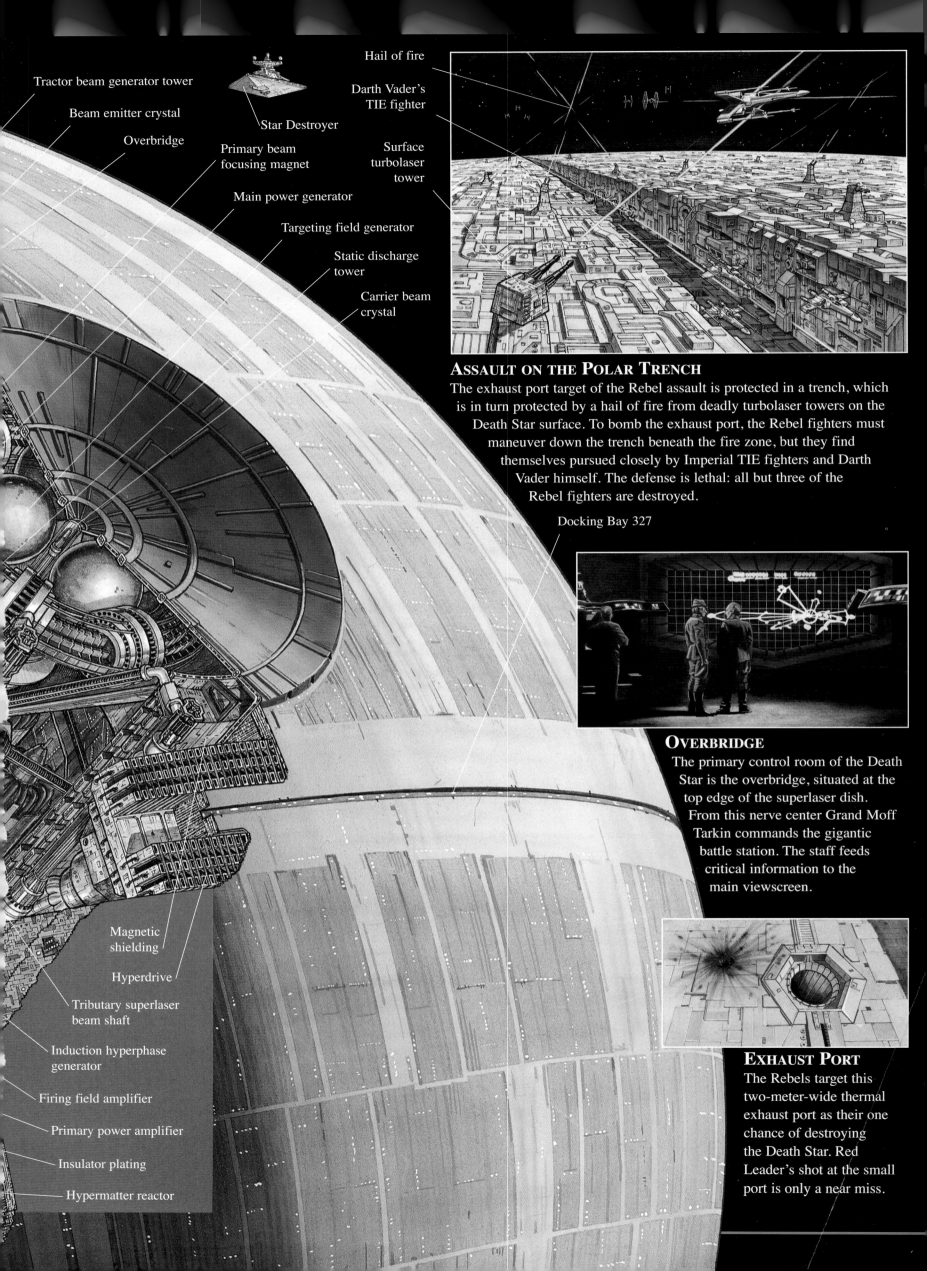

Tractor beam generator tower

Beam emitter crystal

Overbridge

Star Destroyer

Primary beam
focusing magnet

Main power generator

Targeting field generator

Static discharge
tower

Carrier beam
crystal

Hail of fire

Darth Vader's
TIE fighter

Surface
turbolaser
tower

Magnetic
shielding

Hyperdrive

Tributary superlaser
beam shaft

Induction hyperphase
generator

Firing field amplifier

Primary power amplifier

Insulator plating

Hypermatter reactor

ASSAULT ON THE POLAR TRENCH

The exhaust port target of the Rebel assault is protected in a trench, which
is in turn protected by a hail of fire from deadly turbolaser towers on the
Death Star surface. To bomb the exhaust port, the Rebel fighters must
maneuver down the trench beneath the fire zone, but they find
themselves pursued closely by Imperial TIE fighters and Darth
Vader himself. The defense is lethal: all but three of the
Rebel fighters are destroyed.

Docking Bay 327

OVERBRIDGE

The primary control room of the Death
Star is the overbridge, situated at the
top edge of the superlaser dish.
From this nerve center Grand Moff
Tarkin commands the gigantic
battle station. The staff feeds
critical information to the
main viewscreen.

EXHAUST PORT

The Rebels target this
two-meter-wide thermal
exhaust port as their one
chance of destroying
the Death Star. Red
Leader's shot at the small
port is only a near miss.

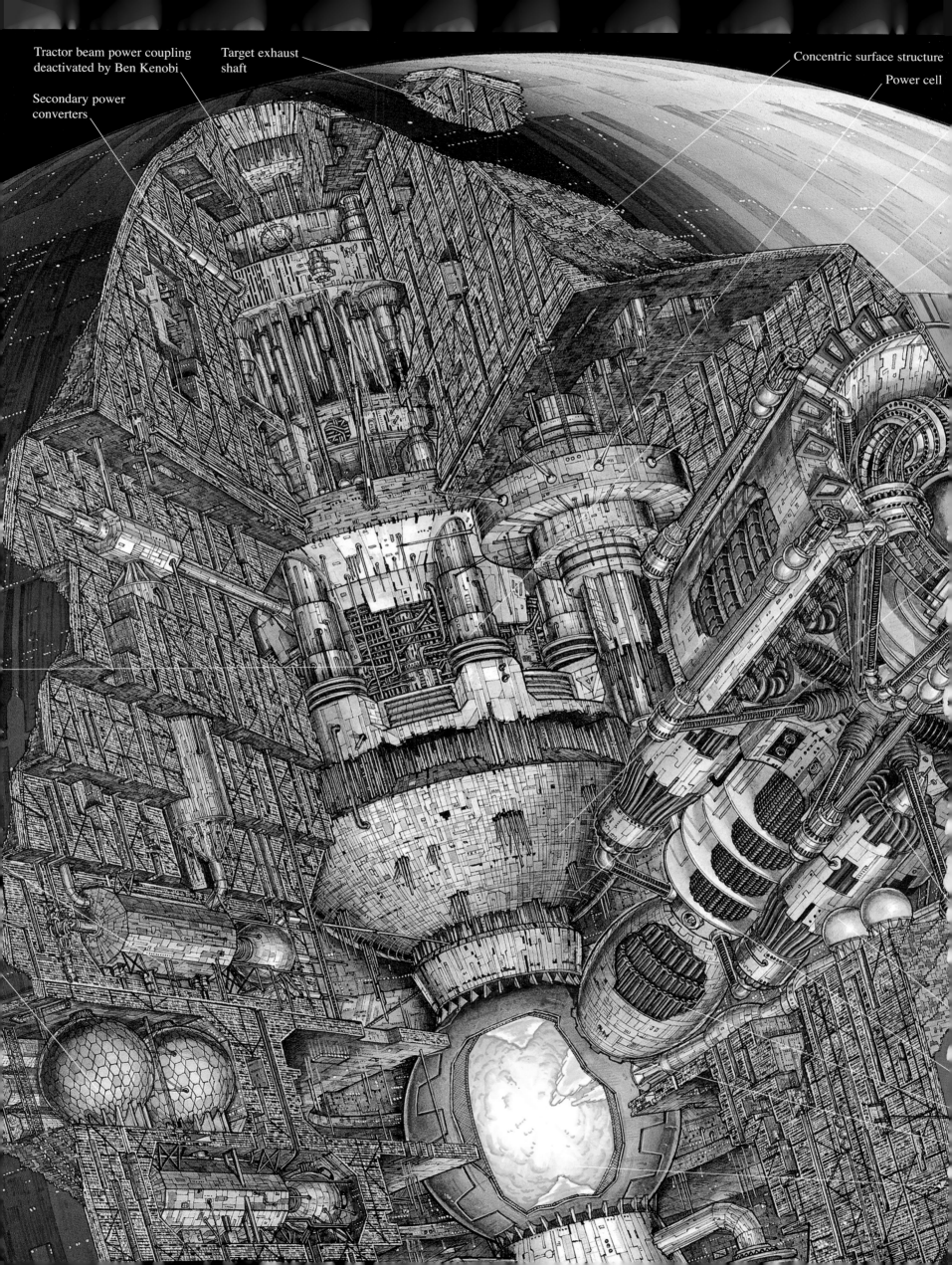

Tractor beam power coupling
deactivated by Ben Kenobi

Target exhaust
shaft

Concentric surface structure

Power cell

Secondary power
converters

SANDCRAWLER

A LEFTOVER TITAN from a forgotten mining era long ago, the Jawa sandcrawler patrols the deserts and wastelands of Tatooine in search of metal salvage and minerals. Serving as home to an entire clan of Jawas, the mobile sandcrawler makes its rounds across wide territory over the course of a year, hunting for the wrecks that dot Tatooine's surface from spaceship crashes through centuries past. Jawas also round up stray droids, junked vehicles, and unwanted metal of any kind from settlements and moisture farmers. Pitted and scoured by numberless sandstorms, the sandcrawler serves the Jawas as transportation, workshop, traveling store, and safe protection from the menaces of Sand People and desert monsters.

Case-hardened smashers crush minerals or compact metal for storage

Drill grinders

Conveyor at top of elevator

Power generators

Ore crusher

Laser pre-processor

Reactor powers entire sandcrawler

Engineering station

Maintenance passage

Reactor melts processed ore and metal into a superheated cascade

JAWA REPAIRS
Jawas are experts at making use of available components to repair machinery and can put together a working droid from the most surprising variety of scrap parts. However, they are notorious for peddling shoddy workmanship that will last just long enough for the sandcrawler to disappear over the horizon.

Power cells

Ingots are extruded from purified underlevels of slag pool

Primary drive

Rear treads non-steerable, for drive only

Electrostatic repellers keep sand from interior components

Steam-heating array

Repulsorlift tube energizer

Extensible starboard boarding gantry

Extensible repulsorlift tube

DANGEROUS PRIZES
The furious winds of Tatooine's storm season can scour ancient spacewrecks from the deep sands of the Dune Sea. Jawa sandcrawlers venture into extremely remote territories after the big storms in search of newly exposed prizes. Larger finds may cause them to call in other clan sandcrawlers to share in the processing. Field smelting factories and sun shelter awnings are quickly erected as the Jawas work to beat the arrival of the next storm. But the wastelands can hold dangers more unexpected than storms.

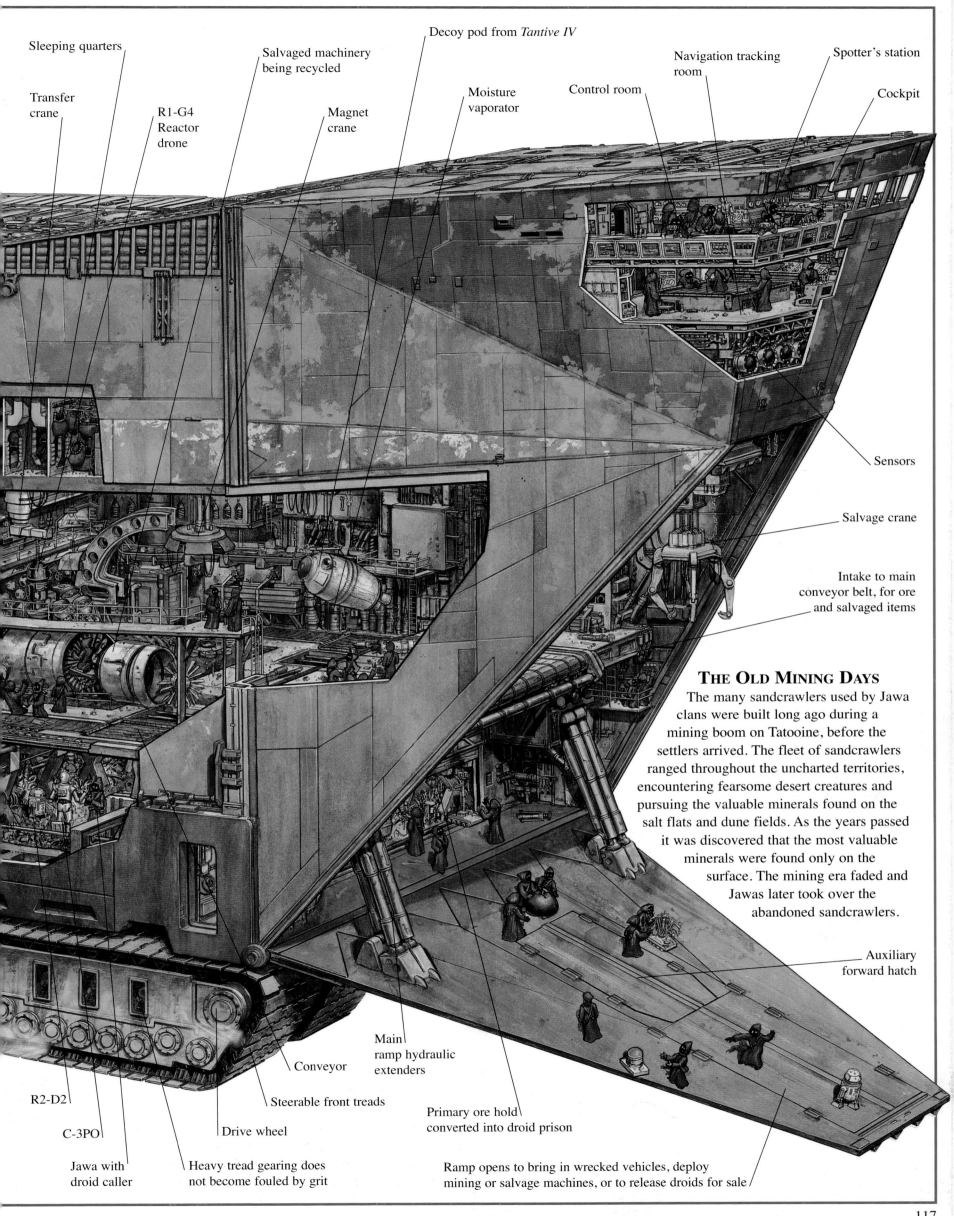

Sleeping quarters

Transfer crane

R1-G4 Reactor drone

Salvaged machinery being recycled

Magnet crane

Decoy pod from *Tantive IV*

Moisture vaporator

Navigation tracking room

Control room

Spotter's station

Cockpit

Sensors

Salvage crane

Intake to main conveyor belt, for ore and salvaged items

THE OLD MINING DAYS

The many sandcrawlers used by Jawa clans were built long ago during a mining boom on Tatooine, before the settlers arrived. The fleet of sandcrawlers ranged throughout the uncharted territories, encountering fearsome desert creatures and pursuing the valuable minerals found on the salt flats and dune fields. As the years passed it was discovered that the most valuable minerals were found only on the surface. The mining era faded and Jawas later took over the abandoned sandcrawlers.

Auxiliary forward hatch

R2-D2

C-3PO

Jawa with droid caller

Heavy tread gearing does not become fouled by grit

Drive wheel

Conveyor

Steerable front treads

Main ramp hydraulic extenders

Primary ore hold converted into droid prison

Ramp opens to bring in wrecked vehicles, deploy mining or salvage machines, or to release droids for sale

T-65 X-WING

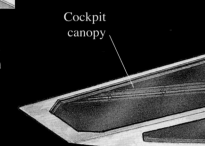

THE X-WING STARFIGHTER was a top-secret project of the Incom Corporation when the Empire began to suspect Rebel sympathies within the company and seized its assets. Key members of the design team escaped with the plans and two prototypes, destroying all other records of the ship. Hence, into the hands of the Rebellion came what would become its finest space fighter. Carrying heavy firepower, hyperdrive, and defensive shields, the X-wing is nonetheless maneuverable enough for close combat with the Empire's lethally agile TIE fighters. A truly formidable space superiority fighter, the X-wing's complex systems and rare alloys have delayed production of significant numbers of the craft for years.

Targeting scope

Primary control systems similar to those of civilian aircraft like the T-16 Skyhopper

Cockpit canopy

INSIDE THE COCKPIT
The X-wing's highly responsive maneuverability can make it a dangerous craft for new pilots to handle. In addition to the fairly straightforward flight control systems, comprehensive cockpit displays allow the pilot to monitor and control energy distribution throughout the ship's systems during combat.

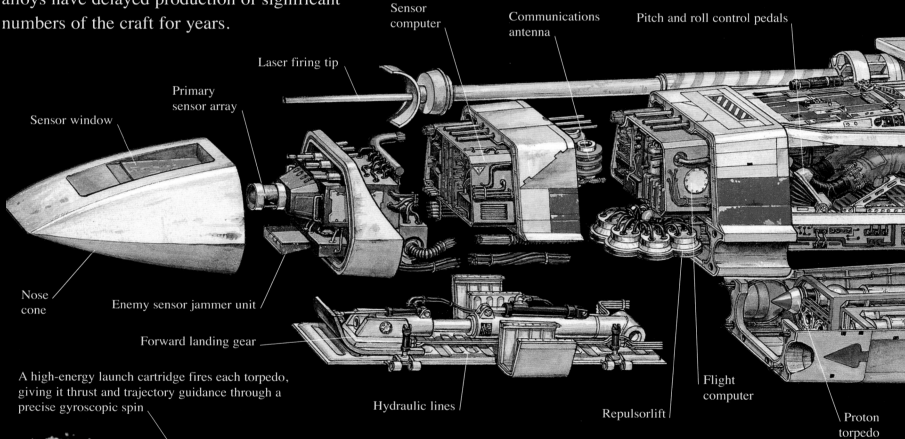

Sensor window

Sensor computer

Communications antenna

Pitch and roll control pedals

Laser firing tip

Primary sensor array

Nose cone

Enemy sensor jammer unit

Forward landing gear

A high-energy launch cartridge fires each torpedo, giving it thrust and trajectory guidance through a precise gyroscopic spin

Hydraulic lines

Flight computer

Repulsorlift

Proton torpedo

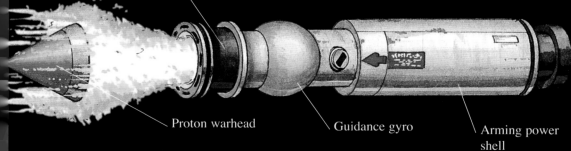

Proton warhead

Guidance gyro

Arming power shell

DESTROYER OF THE DEATH STAR
Proton torpedoes such as the MG7-As carried by the X-wing are extremely dangerous focused nuclear explosives. They are used for critical target destruction or to punch through ray shielding that will deflect laser weapons. Proton torpedoes are very expensive and available to Alliance forces only in limited numbers. Luke Skywalker carried only a single pair for his critical shots that destroyed the original Death Star.

INDEPENDENT OPERATION
Hyperdrive and the ability to launch and land without special support enable the X-wing to operate independently, unlike Imperial TIE fighters. The X-wing is equipped with life support sufficient for one week in space: air, water, food, and life-process support equipment are packed into the area behind the pilot's seat. When the ship lands, the air supply can be renewed, and the water and life support systems can be partially recharged. A cargo bay carries survival gear for pilots who land in hostile environments or remote places.

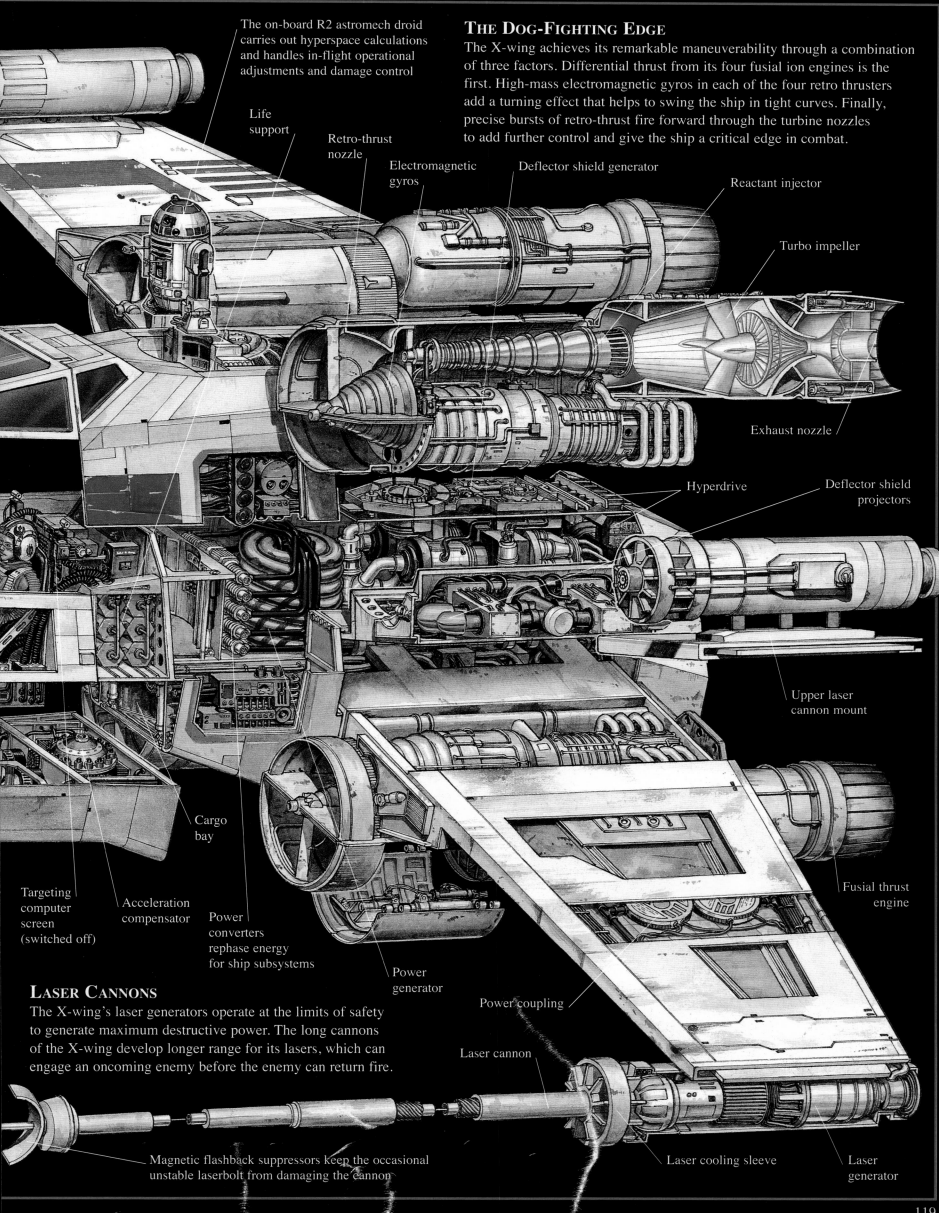

The on-board R2 astromech droid carries out hyperspace calculations and handles in-flight operational adjustments and damage control

Life support

Retro-thrust nozzle

Electromagnetic gyros

Deflector shield generator

Reactant injector

THE DOG-FIGHTING EDGE

The X-wing achieves its remarkable maneuverability through a combination of three factors. Differential thrust from its four fusial ion engines is the first. High-mass electromagnetic gyros in each of the four retro thrusters add a turning effect that helps to swing the ship in tight curves. Finally, precise bursts of retro-thrust fire forward through the turbine nozzles to add further control and give the ship a critical edge in combat.

Turbo impeller

Exhaust nozzle

Hyperdrive

Deflector shield projectors

Upper laser cannon mount

Fusial thrust engine

Power coupling

Power generator

Power converters rephase energy for ship subsystems

Cargo bay

Acceleration compensator

Targeting computer screen (switched off)

Laser cannon

LASER CANNONS

The X-wing's laser generators operate at the limits of safety to generate maximum destructive power. The long cannons of the X-wing develop longer range for its lasers, which can engage an oncoming enemy before the enemy can return fire.

Laser cooling sleeve

Laser generator

Magnetic flashback suppressors keep the occasional unstable laserbolt from damaging the cannon

119

BTL-A4 Y-WING

THE KOENSAYR Y-WING design dates back many years, as do most of the Y-wings in the Rebel Alliance space combat fleet. The ship is a combination fighter and light bomber, built to last and made to last even longer by dedicated Rebel mechanics. It has earned its reputation as the workhorse of the Rebel fighting forces, and is still the most numerous fighter in the Alliance. There are several different models, adapted for different missions, including one-man and two-man versions. Sporting heavy laser cannons, ion cannons, and proton torpedo magazines, the ship carries devastating firepower, and its solid construction weathers combat damage that would destroy lighter craft. It is neither the fastest nor the most maneuverable ship in the sky, but with its balance of capabilities the Y-wing remains a sturdy asset to the Alliance space combat forces.

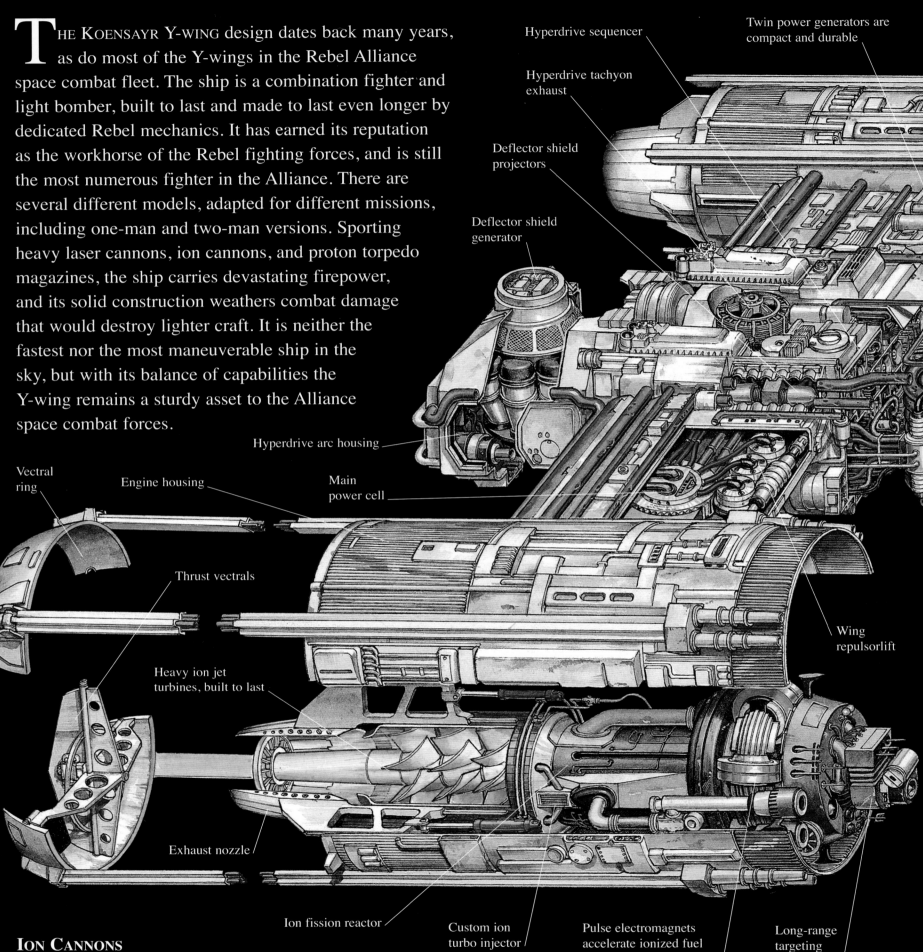

Hyperdrive sequencer

Twin power generators are compact and durable

Hyperdrive tachyon exhaust

Deflector shield projectors

Deflector shield generator

Hyperdrive arc housing

Vectral ring

Engine housing

Main power cell

Thrust vectrals

Wing repulsorlift

Heavy ion jet turbines, built to last

Exhaust nozzle

Ion fission reactor

Custom ion turbo injector

Pulse electromagnets accelerate ionized fuel for injection into turbines

Long-range targeting sensor array

ION CANNONS

Ion cannons fire an electrical charge to disrupt the control circuits of an enemy craft without destroying it. The Y-wing features twin ion cannons, but they are notoriously delicate instruments. Their crystal matrices invariably get vibrated out of alignment in flight and combat, and Rebel mechanics hate them for the time they cost in maintenance. For the attack on the Death Star, only two Y-wings in the entire Rebel force had functioning ion cannons. These proved critically useful, and one of these craft was the only Y-wing to survive the battle.

COOLING SYSTEM

The Y-wing runs very hot for a ship of its size, and employs a complicated cooling system which runs throughout the ship. Parts of this system need maintenance after every flight. Coolant tubes are often jerry-rigged by Rebel mechanics when leaks render inaccessible sections frustratingly inoperative.

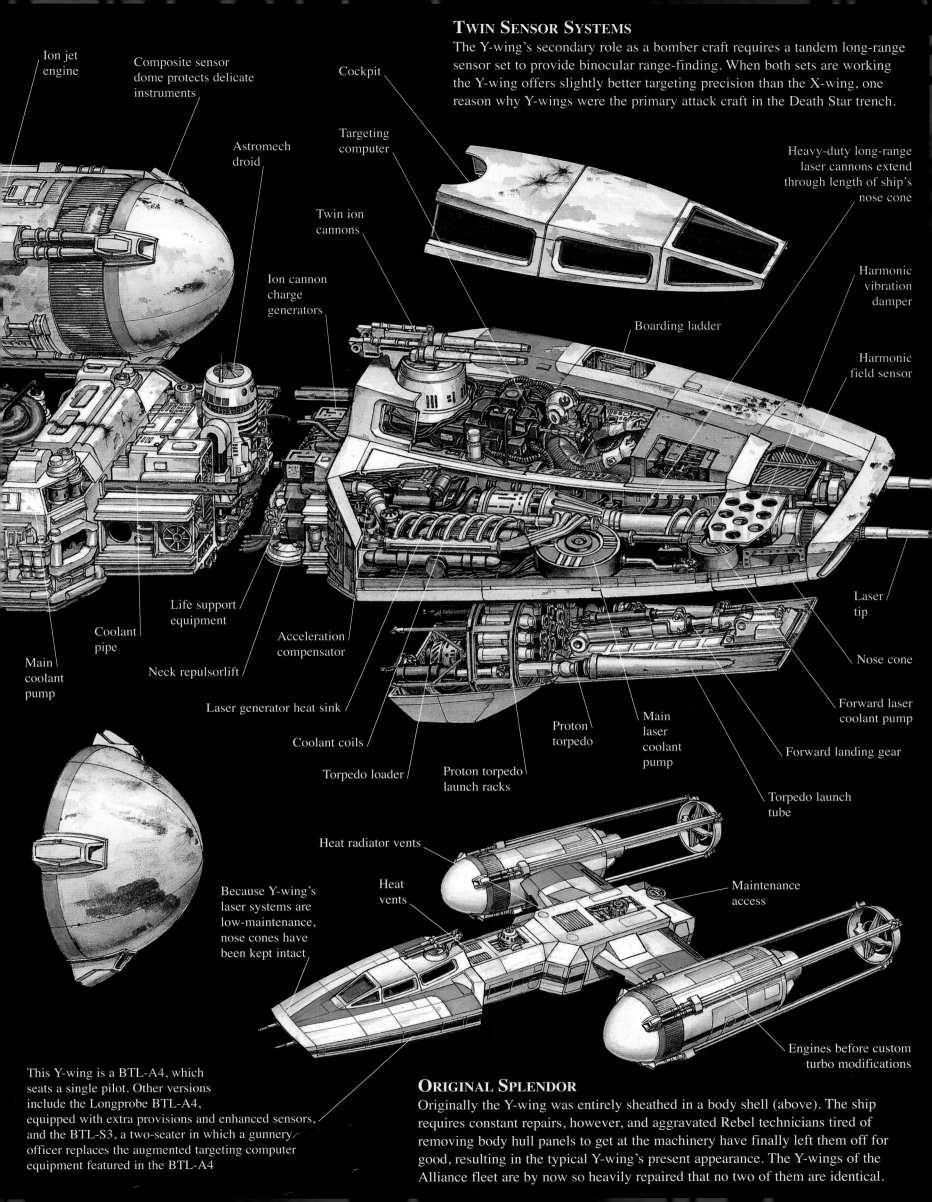

Ion jet
engine

Composite sensor
dome protects delicate
instruments

Astromech
droid

Cockpit

Targeting
computer

Twin ion
cannons

Ion cannon
charge
generators

TWIN SENSOR SYSTEMS

The Y-wing's secondary role as a bomber craft requires a tandem long-range sensor set to provide binocular range-finding. When both sets are working the Y-wing offers slightly better targeting precision than the X-wing, one reason why Y-wings were the primary attack craft in the Death Star trench.

Heavy-duty long-range
laser cannons extend
through length of ship's
nose cone

Harmonic
vibration
damper

Boarding ladder

Harmonic
field sensor

Life support
equipment

Coolant
pipe

Neck repulsorlift

Acceleration
compensator

Laser generator heat sink

Coolant coils

Torpedo loader

Proton torpedo
launch racks

Proton
torpedo

Main
laser
coolant
pump

Torpedo launch
tube

Laser
tip

Nose cone

Forward laser
coolant pump

Forward landing gear

Main
coolant
pump

Because Y-wing's
laser systems are
low-maintenance,
nose cones have
been kept intact

Heat radiator vents

Heat
vents

Maintenance
access

Engines before custom
turbo modifications

This Y-wing is a BTL-A4, which seats a single pilot. Other versions include the Longprobe BTL-A4, equipped with extra provisions and enhanced sensors, and the BTL-S3, a two-seater in which a gunnery officer replaces the augmented targeting computer equipment featured in the BTL-A4

ORIGINAL SPLENDOR

Originally the Y-wing was entirely sheathed in a body shell (above). The ship requires constant repairs, however, and aggravated Rebel technicians tired of removing body hull panels to get at the machinery have finally left them off for good, resulting in the typical Y-wing's present appearance. The Y-wings of the Alliance fleet are by now so heavily repaired that no two of them are identical.

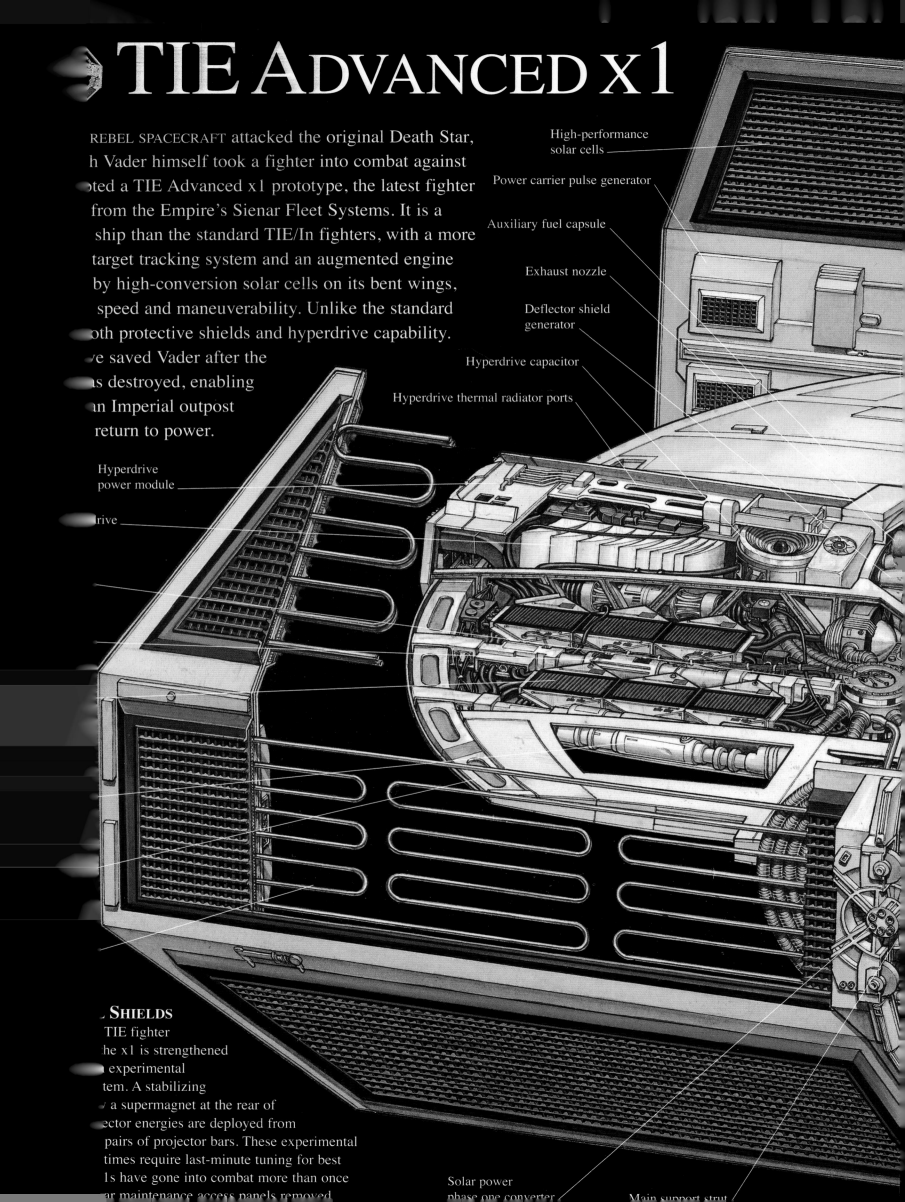

TIE ADVANCED x1

REBEL SPACECRAFT attacked the original Death Star,
h Vader himself took a fighter into combat against
ted a TIE Advanced x1 prototype, the latest fighter
from the Empire's Sienar Fleet Systems. It is a
ship than the standard TIE/In fighters, with a more
target tracking system and an augmented engine
by high-conversion solar cells on its bent wings,
speed and maneuverability. Unlike the standard
oth protective shields and hyperdrive capability.
e saved Vader after the
s destroyed, enabling
n Imperial outpost
return to power.

Hyperdrive
power module

rive

High-performance
solar cells

Power carrier pulse generator

Auxiliary fuel capsule

Exhaust nozzle

Deflector shield
generator

Hyperdrive capacitor

Hyperdrive thermal radiator ports

SHIELDS

TIE fighter
he x1 is strengthened
experimental
tem. A stabilizing
a supermagnet at the rear of
ctor energies are deployed from
pairs of projector bars. These experimental
times require last-minute tuning for best
ls have gone into combat more than once
r maintenance access panels removed

Solar power
phase one converter

Main support strut

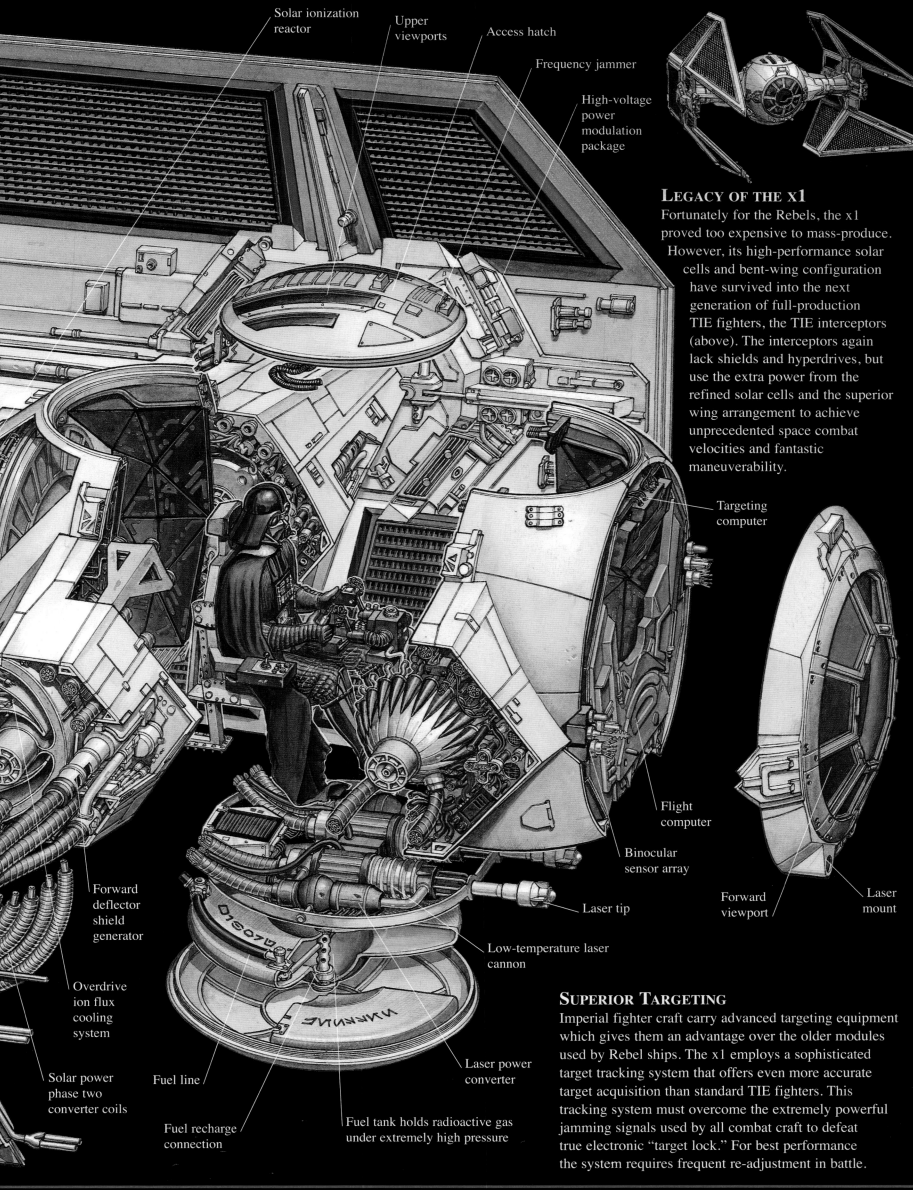

Solar ionization reactor

Upper viewports

Access hatch

Frequency jammer

High-voltage power modulation package

LEGACY OF THE X1

Fortunately for the Rebels, the x1 proved too expensive to mass-produce. However, its high-performance solar cells and bent-wing configuration have survived into the next generation of full-production TIE fighters, the TIE interceptors (above). The interceptors again lack shields and hyperdrives, but use the extra power from the refined solar cells and the superior wing arrangement to achieve unprecedented space combat velocities and fantastic maneuverability.

Targeting computer

Flight computer

Binocular sensor array

Laser tip

Forward viewport

Laser mount

Forward deflector shield generator

Overdrive ion flux cooling system

Solar power phase two converter coils

Fuel line

Laser power converter

Low-temperature laser cannon

Fuel recharge connection

Fuel tank holds radioactive gas under extremely high pressure

SUPERIOR TARGETING

Imperial fighter craft carry advanced targeting equipment which gives them an advantage over the older modules used by Rebel ships. The x1 employs a sophisticated target tracking system that offers even more accurate target acquisition than standard TIE fighters. This tracking system must overcome the extremely powerful jamming signals used by all combat craft to defeat true electronic "target lock." For best performance the system requires frequent re-adjustment in battle.

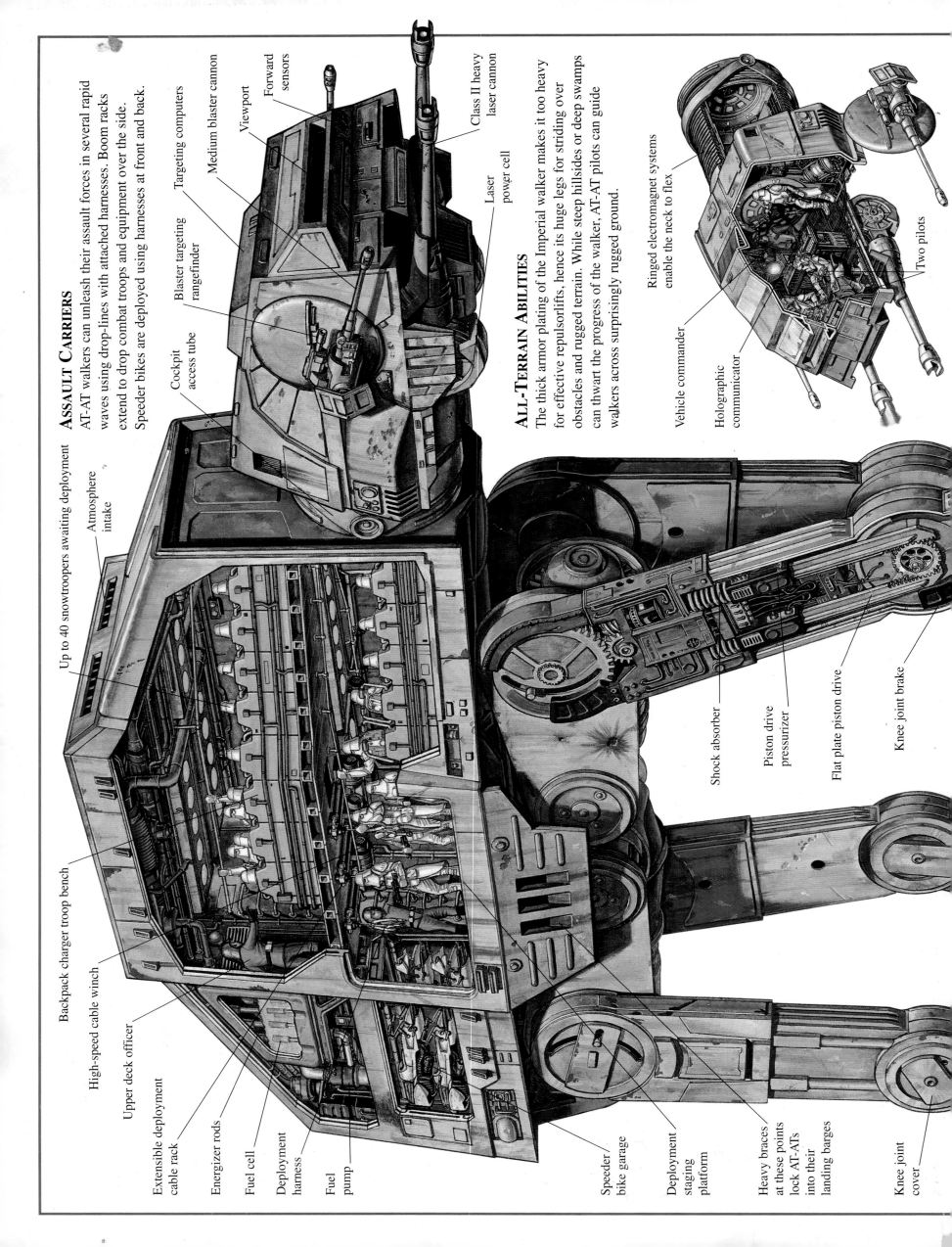

ASSAULT CARRIERS

AT-AT walkers can unleash their assault forces in several rapid waves using drop-lines with attached harnesses. Boom racks extend to drop combat troops and equipment over the side. Speeder bikes are deployed using harnesses at front and back.

ALL-TERRAIN ABILITIES

The thick armor plating of the Imperial walker makes it too heavy for effective repulsorlifts, hence its huge legs for striding over obstacles and rugged terrain. While steep hillsides or deep swamps can thwart the progress of the walker, AT-AT pilots can guide walkers across surprisingly rugged ground.

Class II heavy laser cannon

Forward sensors

Viewport

Medium blaster cannon

Targeting computers

Blaster targeting rangefinder

Cockpit access tube

Laser power cell

Atmosphere intake

Up to 40 snowtroopers awaiting deployment

Backpack charger troop bench

High-speed cable winch

Upper deck officer

Extensible deployment cable rack

Energizer rods

Fuel cell

Deployment harness

Fuel pump

Speeder bike garage

Deployment staging platform

Heavy braces at these points lock AT-ATs into their landing barges

Knee joint cover

Knee joint brake

Flat plate piston drive

Piston drive pressurizer

Shock absorber

Ringed electromagnet systems enable the neck to flex

Vehicle commander

Holographic communicator

Two pilots

COMMAND COCKPIT

The walker's heavily armored head serves as a cockpit for the two pilots and the vehicle commander. On its exterior are mounted the vehicle's weapons systems. While both pilots are fully qualified to perform all control functions, in normal practice one serves as driver while the other acts as gunner. Firing controls can at any time be yielded to the vehicle commander, who uses a periscope display capable of tactical and photographic readouts. The two pilots are guided by terrain sensors under the cockpit and ground sensors built into the feet of the vehicle. Scans read the nature and shape of the terrain ahead, assuring infallible footing.

SPEEDER BIKES

AT-AT walkers usually carry a set of high-velocity repulsorlift speeder bikes for scouting or survivor-hunting missions. The speed and agility of these bikes complement the plodding might of the walkers, making the combined assault capability thorough and overwhelming. The colossal size and nightmarish animal resemblance of the AT-AT combine with its combat strengths to give it tremendous psychological power. Until the Battle of Hoth, no army had ever fought resolutely against an onslaught of walkers, so frightening and devastating is their presence.

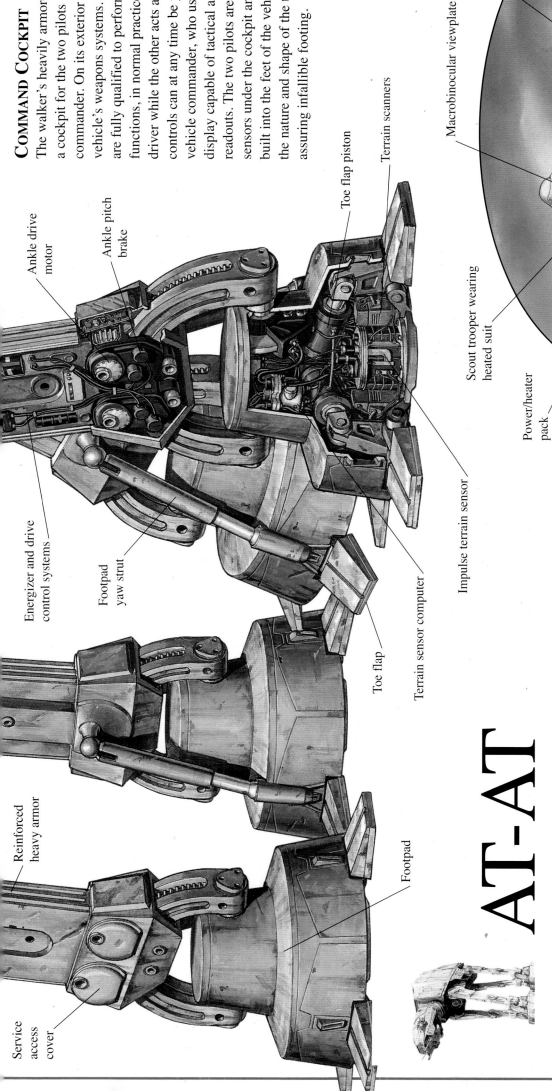

Antipersonnel pursuit gun

Macrobinocular viewplate

Scout trooper wearing heated suit

Power/heater pack

Ankle drive motor

Ankle pitch brake

Toe flap piston

Terrain scanners

Service access cover

Reinforced heavy armor

Energizer and drive control systems

Footpad yaw strut

Toe flap

Terrain sensor computer

Footpad

Impulse terrain sensor

AT-AT

Deployed as weapons of terror, the gigantic Imperial All Terrain Armored Transport walkers advance inexorably on the battlefield like unstoppable giants. These behemoth monsters are shielded with heavy armor cladding, making them invulnerable to all but the heaviest turbolaser weaponry. Blaster bolts from ordinary turrets and cannons merely glance off the walker's armor or are harmlessly absorbed and dissipated. A powerful reactor produces the raw energy needed to move this weighty battle machine. Cannons in the movable cockpit spit death and savagery at helpless foes below, cutting a swath of destruction which the mighty footpads then crash through. Breaking enemy lines with its blaster fire and lumbering mass, the walker functions as a troop carrier, holding in its body platoons of crack assault soldiers, ground weaponry, and speeder bike antipersonnel/reconnaissance vehicles. When this cargo of terror is released into the chaos and destruction a walker has created, another Imperial victory is nearly complete.

SNOWSPEEDER

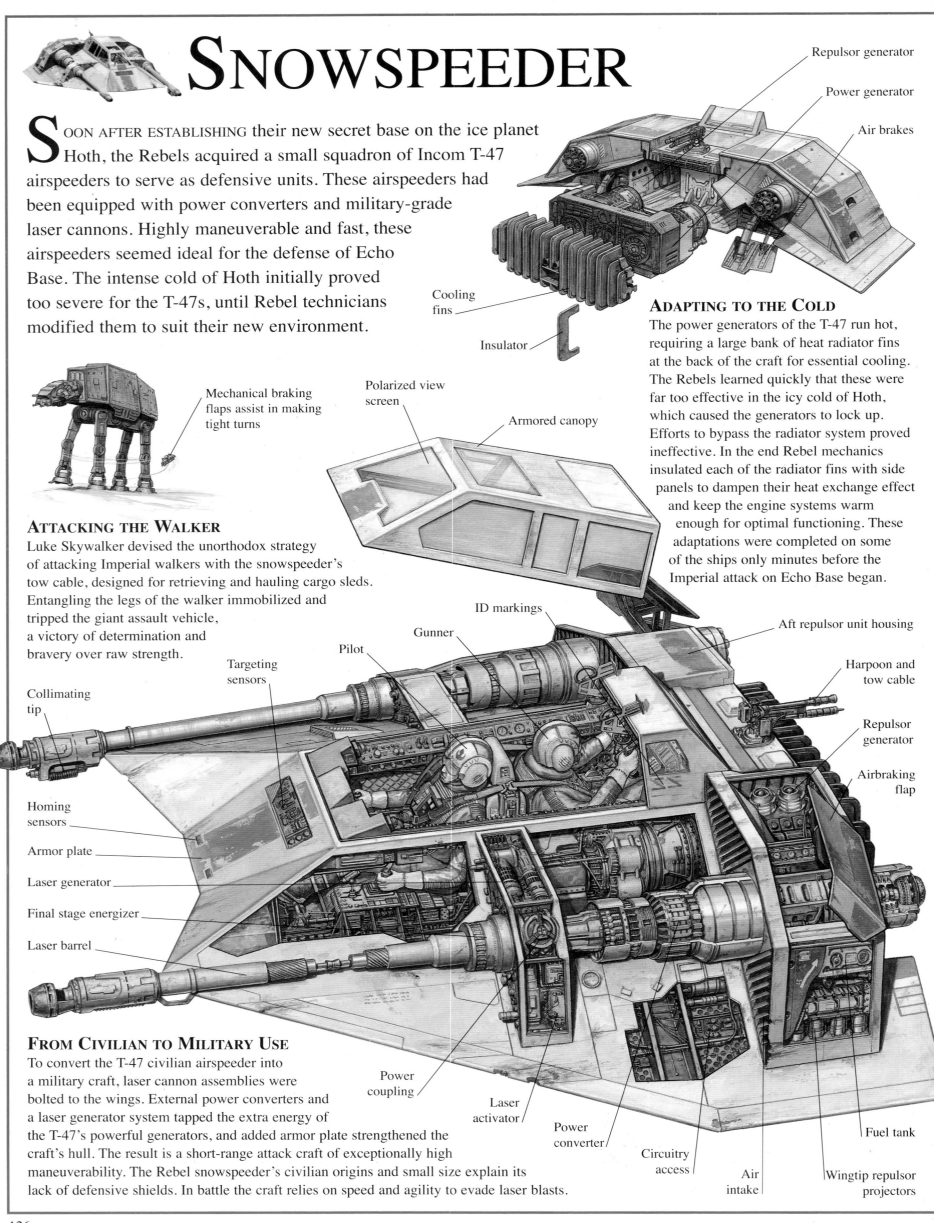

SOON AFTER ESTABLISHING their new secret base on the ice planet Hoth, the Rebels acquired a small squadron of Incom T-47 airspeeders to serve as defensive units. These airspeeders had been equipped with power converters and military-grade laser cannons. Highly maneuverable and fast, these airspeeders seemed ideal for the defense of Echo Base. The intense cold of Hoth initially proved too severe for the T-47s, until Rebel technicians modified them to suit their new environment.

Repulsor generator

Power generator

Air brakes

Cooling fins

Insulator

ADAPTING TO THE COLD

The power generators of the T-47 run hot, requiring a large bank of heat radiator fins at the back of the craft for essential cooling. The Rebels learned quickly that these were far too effective in the icy cold of Hoth, which caused the generators to lock up. Efforts to bypass the radiator system proved ineffective. In the end Rebel mechanics insulated each of the radiator fins with side panels to dampen their heat exchange effect and keep the engine systems warm enough for optimal functioning. These adaptations were completed on some of the ships only minutes before the Imperial attack on Echo Base began.

Mechanical braking flaps assist in making tight turns

Polarized view screen

Armored canopy

ATTACKING THE WALKER

Luke Skywalker devised the unorthodox strategy of attacking Imperial walkers with the snowspeeder's tow cable, designed for retrieving and hauling cargo sleds. Entangling the legs of the walker immobilized and tripped the giant assault vehicle, a victory of determination and bravery over raw strength.

ID markings

Gunner

Pilot

Targeting sensors

Collimating tip

Homing sensors

Armor plate

Laser generator

Final stage energizer

Laser barrel

Aft repulsor unit housing

Harpoon and tow cable

Repulsor generator

Airbraking flap

FROM CIVILIAN TO MILITARY USE

To convert the T-47 civilian airspeeder into a military craft, laser cannon assemblies were bolted to the wings. External power converters and a laser generator system tapped the extra energy of the T-47's powerful generators, and added armor plate strengthened the craft's hull. The result is a short-range attack craft of exceptionally high maneuverability. The Rebel snowspeeder's civilian origins and small size explain its lack of defensive shields. In battle the craft relies on speed and agility to evade laser blasts.

Power coupling

Laser activator

Power converter

Circuitry access

Air intake

Fuel tank

Wingtip repulsor projectors

Weapons power converters

Cockpit cooling system

Armor plate

Entry hatch

Locomotion computer

Handrail

Concussion charger

Gunner's station

Pilot's throttle control

Forward sensor

Command viewport

Light blaster cannon

Pilot

Face armor

Twin blaster cannons

Concussion launcher

Radiator

Gyro system

Gyro power cell

Plastron shield

Exhaust

Power cells

Drive engine

Joint shield

Knee joint

Sophisticated shock-absorbing systems within the legs of the scout walker keep it stable and feed balance data into the navigation computers

Too small to carry an onboard full-power generator, the AT-ST uses disposable high-intensity power cells to feed its power-intensive systems. These power cells limit the range of the AT-ST

Elbow joint

Shin

Shin stabilizer/compression gearing assembly

Sensors in the footpads of the scout walker offer detailed feedback on the terrain ahead, reading density and contour for precise foot placement

Footpad

Ankle joint tensioner

Foot joint

Ankle joint

Cutter actuator

Fence-cutting blade

Ground impact sensor

THE COCKPIT VIEW

Viewscreens and holo-projectors allow AT-ST crew to see ahead and behind simultaneously. While the computer can guide the scout walker over even ground, an expert human pilot must balance the wide variety of data input and control the craft's walking in difficult terrain.

GYRO STABILIZED

With an expert pilot at the helm, an AT-ST can move with remarkable agility across a wide variety of terrain. A powerful gyro stabilizer coupled with a complex locomotion system allows the scout walker to mimic the walking movements of a living creature.

AT-ST

THE SCOUT WALKER, or All Terrain Scout Transport (AT-ST) walks easily through rugged terrain to carry out its missions. Reconnaissance, battle line support, and anti-personnel hunting make excellent use of the craft's armaments and capabilities. Faster than a full-size AT-AT, the scout walker is also able to step through denser terrain with greater ease, traveling through small canyons or forest that would stop an AT-AT. While AT-ATs crush main Rebel defensive emplacements, AT-STs ferret out small pockets of resistance or the hiding places of enemy soldiers. Agile and quick, the scout walker is almost impossible to flee on foot, and the sight of patrolling AT-STs strikes fear into isolated ground troops.

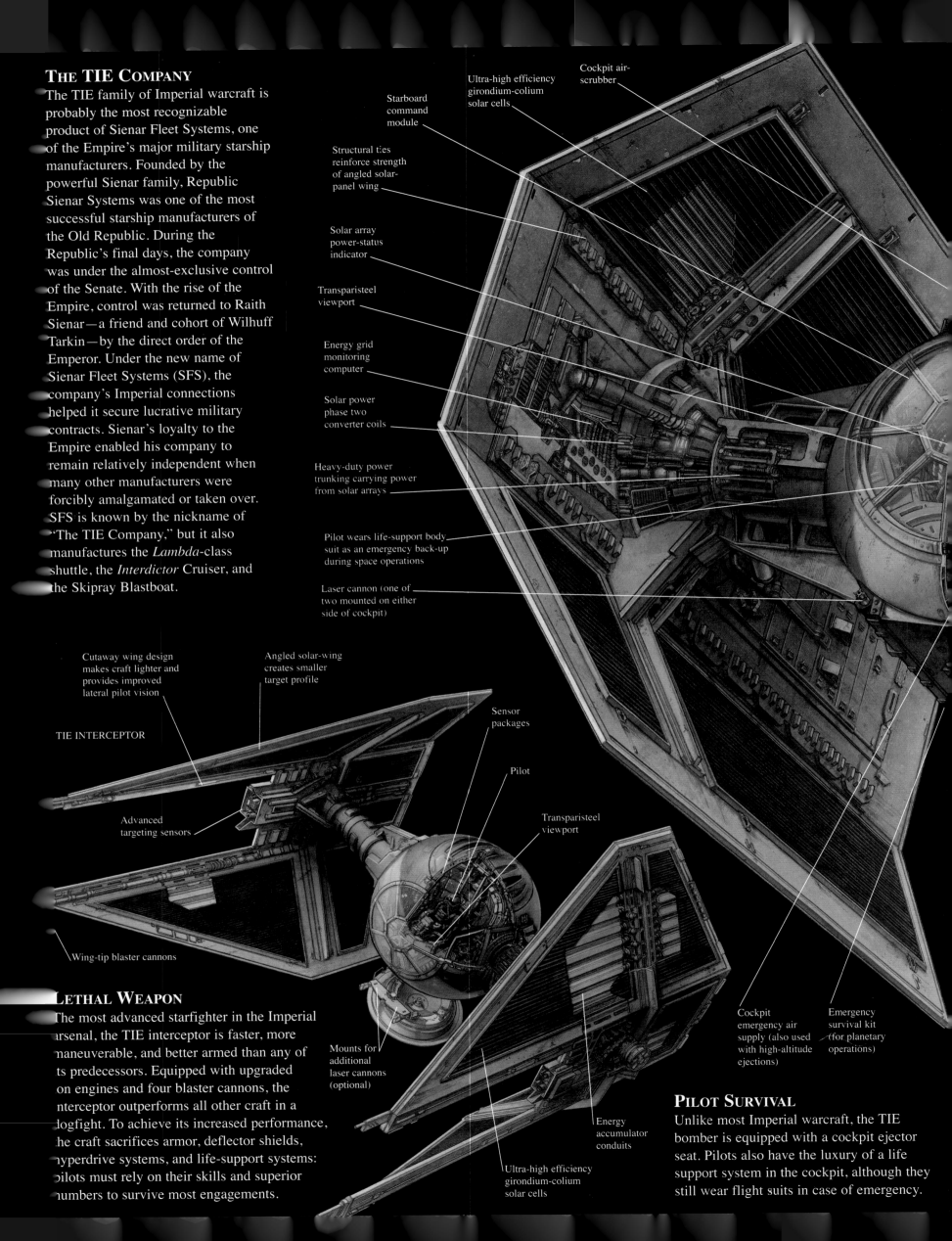

THE TIE COMPANY

The TIE family of Imperial warcraft is probably the most recognizable product of Sienar Fleet Systems, one of the Empire's major military starship manufacturers. Founded by the powerful Sienar family, Republic Sienar Systems was one of the most successful starship manufacturers of the Old Republic. During the Republic's final days, the company was under the almost-exclusive control of the Senate. With the rise of the Empire, control was returned to Raith Sienar—a friend and cohort of Wilhuff Tarkin—by the direct order of the Emperor. Under the new name of Sienar Fleet Systems (SFS), the company's Imperial connections helped it secure lucrative military contracts. Sienar's loyalty to the Empire enabled his company to remain relatively independent when many other manufacturers were forcibly amalgamated or taken over. SFS is known by the nickname of "The TIE Company," but it also manufactures the *Lambda*-class shuttle, the *Interdictor* Cruiser, and the Skipray Blastboat.

Starboard command module

Structural ties reinforce strength of angled solar-panel wing

Solar array power-status indicator

Transparisteel viewport

Energy grid monitoring computer

Solar power phase two converter coils

Heavy-duty power trunking carrying power from solar arrays

Pilot wears life-support body suit as an emergency back-up during space operations

Laser cannon (one of two mounted on either side of cockpit)

Ultra-high efficiency girondium-colium solar cells

Cockpit air-scrubber

Cutaway wing design makes craft lighter and provides improved lateral pilot vision

Angled solar-wing creates smaller target profile

TIE INTERCEPTOR

Advanced targeting sensors

Sensor packages

Pilot

Transparisteel viewport

Wing-tip blaster cannons

LETHAL WEAPON

The most advanced starfighter in the Imperial arsenal, the TIE interceptor is faster, more maneuverable, and better armed than any of its predecessors. Equipped with upgraded ion engines and four blaster cannons, the interceptor outperforms all other craft in a dogfight. To achieve its increased performance, the craft sacrifices armor, deflector shields, hyperdrive systems, and life-support systems: pilots must rely on their skills and superior numbers to survive most engagements.

Mounts for additional laser cannons (optional)

Energy accumulator conduits

Ultra-high efficiency girondium-colium solar cells

Cockpit emergency air supply (also used with high-altitude ejections)

Emergency survival kit (for planetary operations)

PILOT SURVIVAL

Unlike most Imperial warcraft, the TIE bomber is equipped with a cockpit ejector seat. Pilots also have the luxury of a life support system in the cockpit, although they still wear flight suits in case of emergency.

TIE BOMBER

Dᴇʀɪᴠᴇᴅ ꜰʀᴏᴍ ᴛʜᴇ TIE/gt variant of the TIE starfighter family, the TIE bomber was developed to take over the task of orbital bombardment from the Empire's capital ships. With its massive ordnance capacity, this formidable assault ship can be deployed against ground- and space-based targets, delivering its lethal load with pinpoint accuracy. The craft's precision targeting is an important capability—where capital ship bombardment often results in extensive collateral damage, the TIE bomber's ability to make "surgical strikes" enables specific targets to be taken out, while leaving surrounding facilities intact.

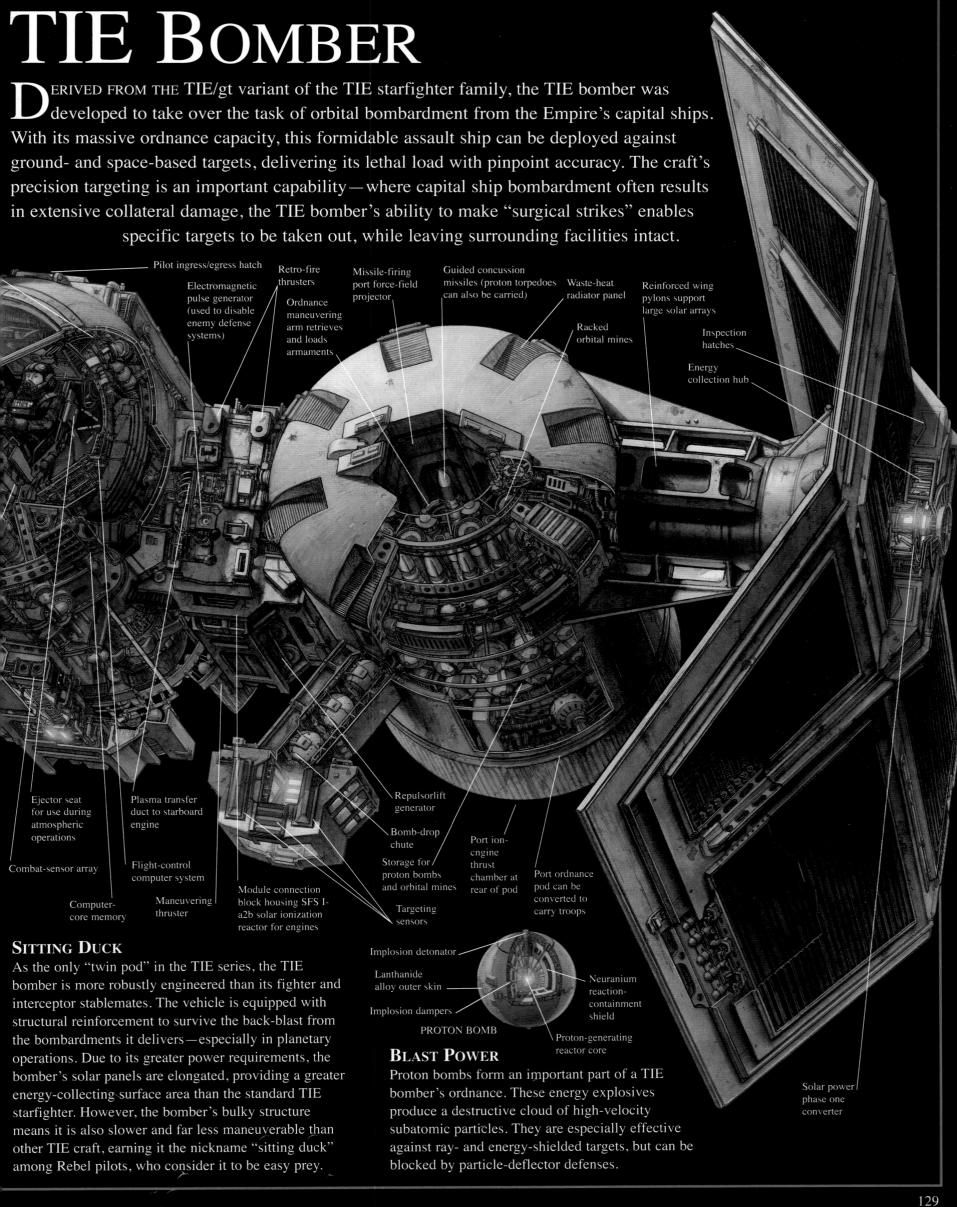

Pilot ingress/egress hatch

Electromagnetic pulse generator (used to disable enemy defense systems)

Retro-fire thrusters

Ordnance maneuvering arm retrieves and loads armaments

Missile-firing port force-field projector

Guided concussion missiles (proton torpedoes can also be carried)

Waste-heat radiator panel

Racked orbital mines

Reinforced wing pylons support large solar arrays

Inspection hatches

Energy collection hub

Ejector seat for use during atmospheric operations

Plasma transfer duct to starboard engine

Combat-sensor array

Flight-control computer system

Computer-core memory

Maneuvering thruster

Module connection block housing SFS I-a2b solar ionization reactor for engines

Repulsorlift generator

Bomb-drop chute

Storage for proton bombs and orbital mines

Targeting sensors

Port ion-engine thrust chamber at rear of pod

Port ordnance pod can be converted to carry troops

Implosion detonator

Lanthanide alloy outer skin

Implosion dampers

PROTON BOMB

Neuranium reaction-containment shield

Proton-generating reactor core

Solar power phase one converter

SITTING DUCK

As the only "twin pod" in the TIE series, the TIE bomber is more robustly engineered than its fighter and interceptor stablemates. The vehicle is equipped with structural reinforcement to survive the back-blast from the bombardments it delivers—especially in planetary operations. Due to its greater power requirements, the bomber's solar panels are elongated, providing a greater energy-collecting surface area than the standard TIE starfighter. However, the bomber's bulky structure means it is also slower and far less maneuverable than other TIE craft, earning it the nickname "sitting duck" among Rebel pilots, who consider it to be easy prey.

BLAST POWER

Proton bombs form an important part of a TIE bomber's ordnance. These energy explosives produce a destructive cloud of high-velocity subatomic particles. They are especially effective against ray- and energy-shielded targets, but can be blocked by particle-deflector defenses.

SLAVE I

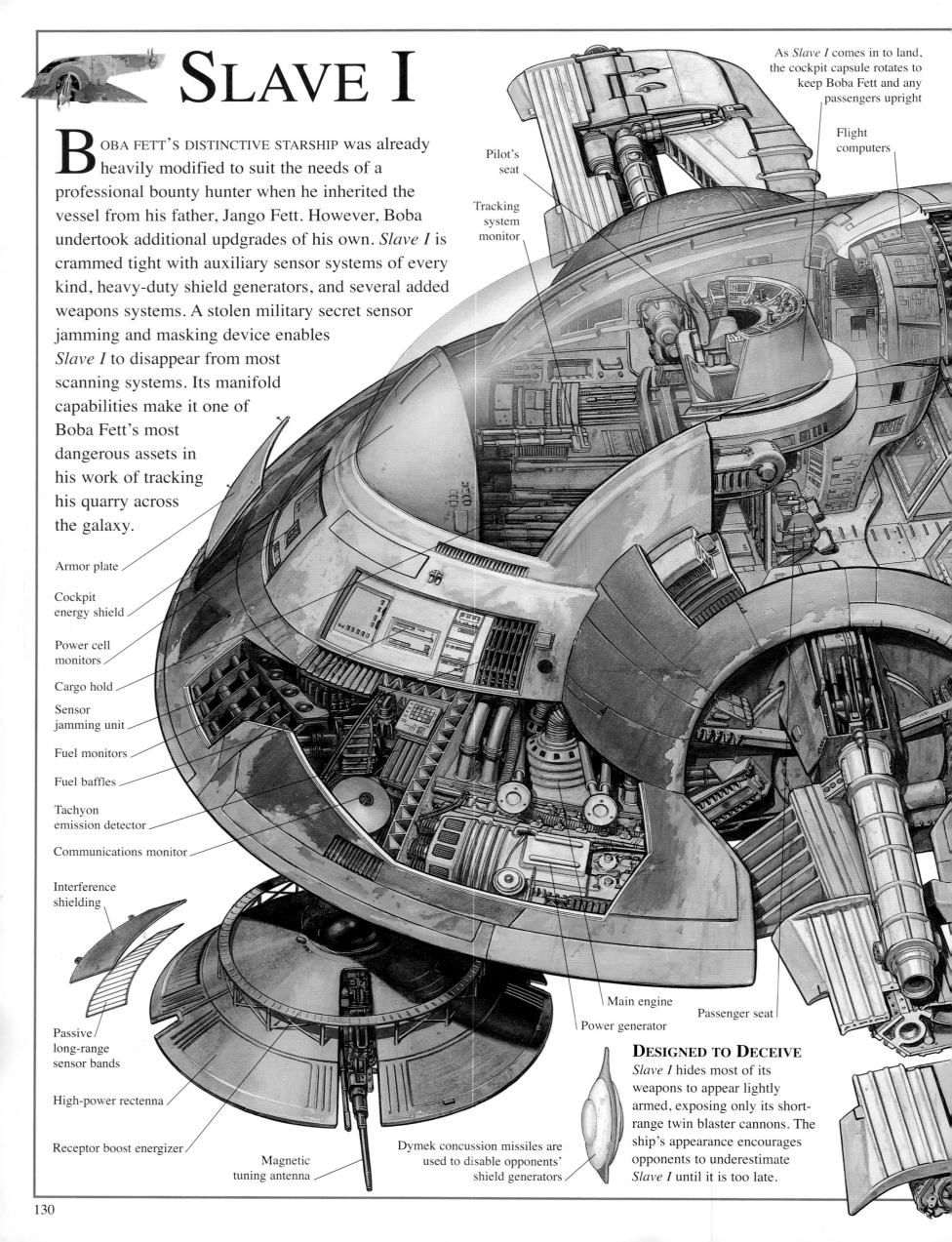

BOBA FETT'S DISTINCTIVE STARSHIP was already heavily modified to suit the needs of a professional bounty hunter when he inherited the vessel from his father, Jango Fett. However, Boba undertook additional updgrades of his own. *Slave I* is crammed tight with auxiliary sensor systems of every kind, heavy-duty shield generators, and several added weapons systems. A stolen military secret sensor jamming and masking device enables *Slave I* to disappear from most scanning systems. Its manifold capabilities make it one of Boba Fett's most dangerous assets in his work of tracking his quarry across the galaxy.

As *Slave I* comes in to land, the cockpit capsule rotates to keep Boba Fett and any passengers upright

Flight computers

Pilot's seat

Tracking system monitor

Armor plate

Cockpit energy shield

Power cell monitors

Cargo hold

Sensor jamming unit

Fuel monitors

Fuel baffles

Tachyon emission detector

Communications monitor

Interference shielding

Passive long-range sensor bands

High-power rectenna

Receptor boost energizer

Magnetic tuning antenna

Dymek concussion missiles are used to disable opponents' shield generators

Main engine

Power generator

Passenger seat

DESIGNED TO DECEIVE

Slave I hides most of its weapons to appear lightly armed, exposing only its short-range twin blaster cannons. The ship's appearance encourages opponents to underestimate *Slave I* until it is too late.

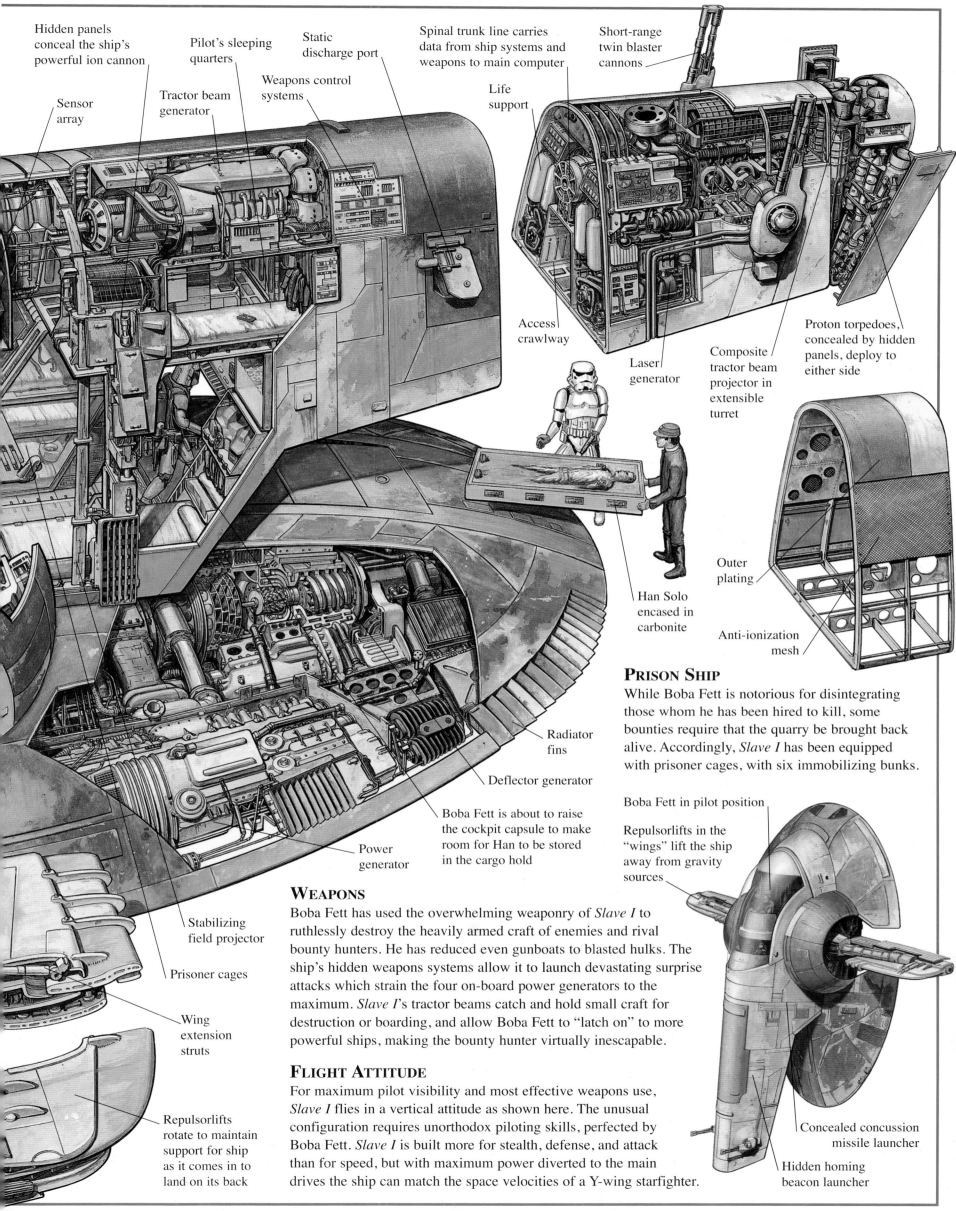

Hidden panels conceal the ship's powerful ion cannon

Pilot's sleeping quarters

Static discharge port

Spinal trunk line carries data from ship systems and weapons to main computer

Short-range twin blaster cannons

Sensor array

Tractor beam generator

Weapons control systems

Life support

Access crawlway

Laser generator

Composite tractor beam projector in extensible turret

Proton torpedoes, concealed by hidden panels, deploy to either side

Outer plating

Anti-ionization mesh

Radiator fins

Deflector generator

Han Solo encased in carbonite

Boba Fett is about to raise the cockpit capsule to make room for Han to be stored in the cargo hold

Power generator

Stabilizing field projector

Prisoner cages

Wing extension struts

Repulsorlifts rotate to maintain support for ship as it comes in to land on its back

PRISON SHIP

While Boba Fett is notorious for disintegrating those whom he has been hired to kill, some bounties require that the quarry be brought back alive. Accordingly, *Slave I* has been equipped with prisoner cages, with six immobilizing bunks.

Boba Fett in pilot position

Repulsorlifts in the "wings" lift the ship away from gravity sources

WEAPONS

Boba Fett has used the overwhelming weaponry of *Slave I* to ruthlessly destroy the heavily armed craft of enemies and rival bounty hunters. He has reduced even gunboats to blasted hulks. The ship's hidden weapons systems allow it to launch devastating surprise attacks which strain the four on-board power generators to the maximum. *Slave I*'s tractor beams catch and hold small craft for destruction or boarding, and allow Boba Fett to "latch on" to more powerful ships, making the bounty hunter virtually inescapable.

FLIGHT ATTITUDE

For maximum pilot visibility and most effective weapons use, *Slave I* flies in a vertical attitude as shown here. The unusual configuration requires unorthodox piloting skills, perfected by Boba Fett. *Slave I* is built more for stealth, defense, and attack than for speed, but with maximum power diverted to the main drives the ship can match the space velocities of a Y-wing starfighter.

Concealed concussion missile launcher

Hidden homing beacon launcher

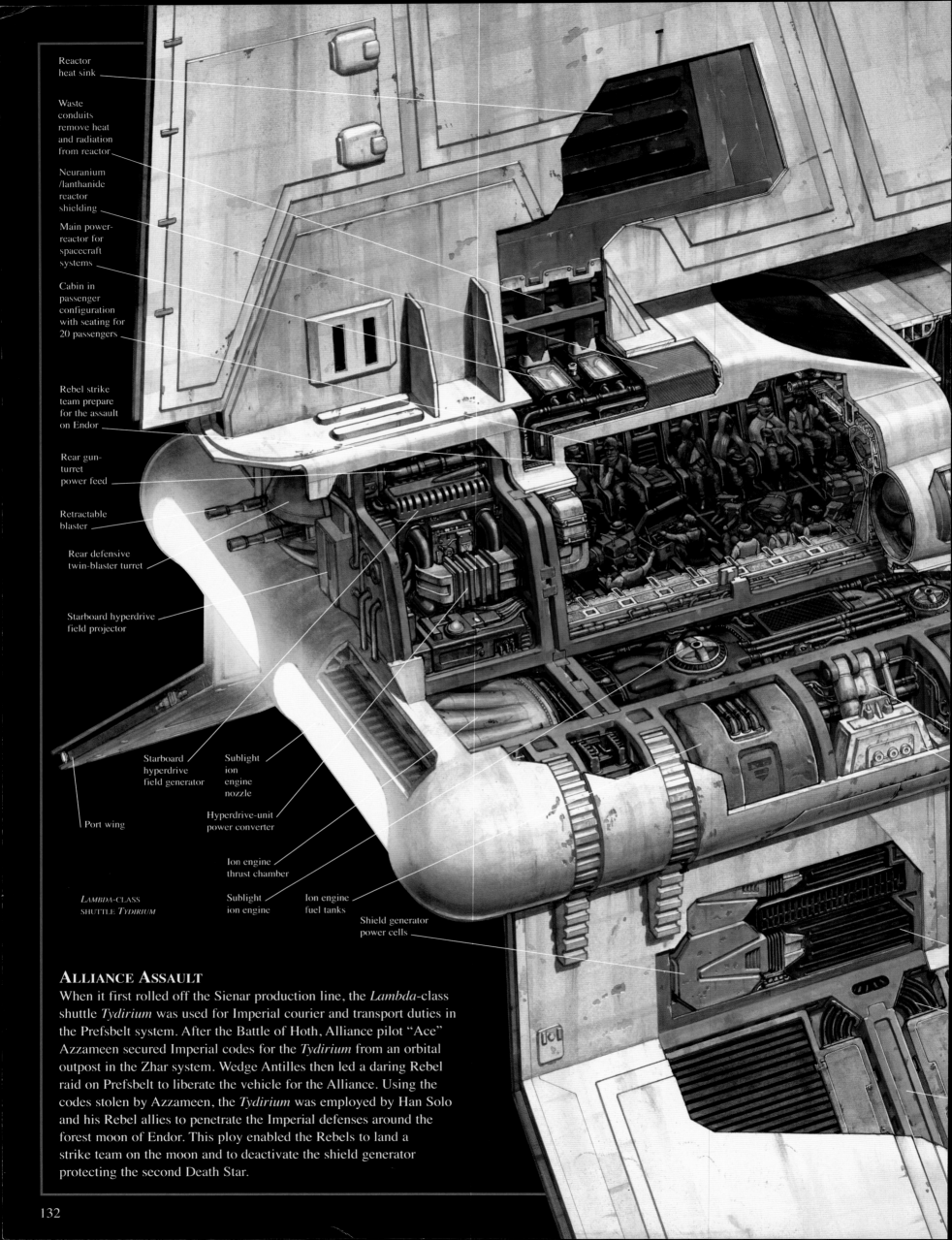

Reactor heat sink

Waste conduits remove heat and radiation from reactor

Neuranium /lanthanide reactor shielding

Main power-reactor for spacecraft systems

Cabin in passenger configuration with seating for 20 passengers

Rebel strike team prepare for the assault on Endor

Rear gun-turret power feed

Retractable blaster

Rear defensive twin-blaster turret

Starboard hyperdrive field projector

Starboard hyperdrive field generator

Sublight ion engine nozzle

Hyperdrive-unit power converter

Ion engine thrust chamber

Port wing

LAMBDA-CLASS SHUTTLE *TYDIRIUM*

Sublight ion engine

Ion engine fuel tanks

Shield generator power cells

ALLIANCE ASSAULT

When it first rolled off the Sienar production line, the *Lambda*-class shuttle *Tydirium* was used for Imperial courier and transport duties in the Prefsbelt system. After the Battle of Hoth, Alliance pilot "Ace" Azzameen secured Imperial codes for the *Tydirium* from an orbital outpost in the Zhar system. Wedge Antilles then led a daring Rebel raid on Prefsbelt to liberate the vehicle for the Alliance. Using the codes stolen by Azzameen, the *Tydirium* was employed by Han Solo and his Rebel allies to penetrate the Imperial defenses around the forest moon of Endor. This ploy enabled the Rebels to land a strike team on the moon and to deactivate the shield generator protecting the second Death Star.

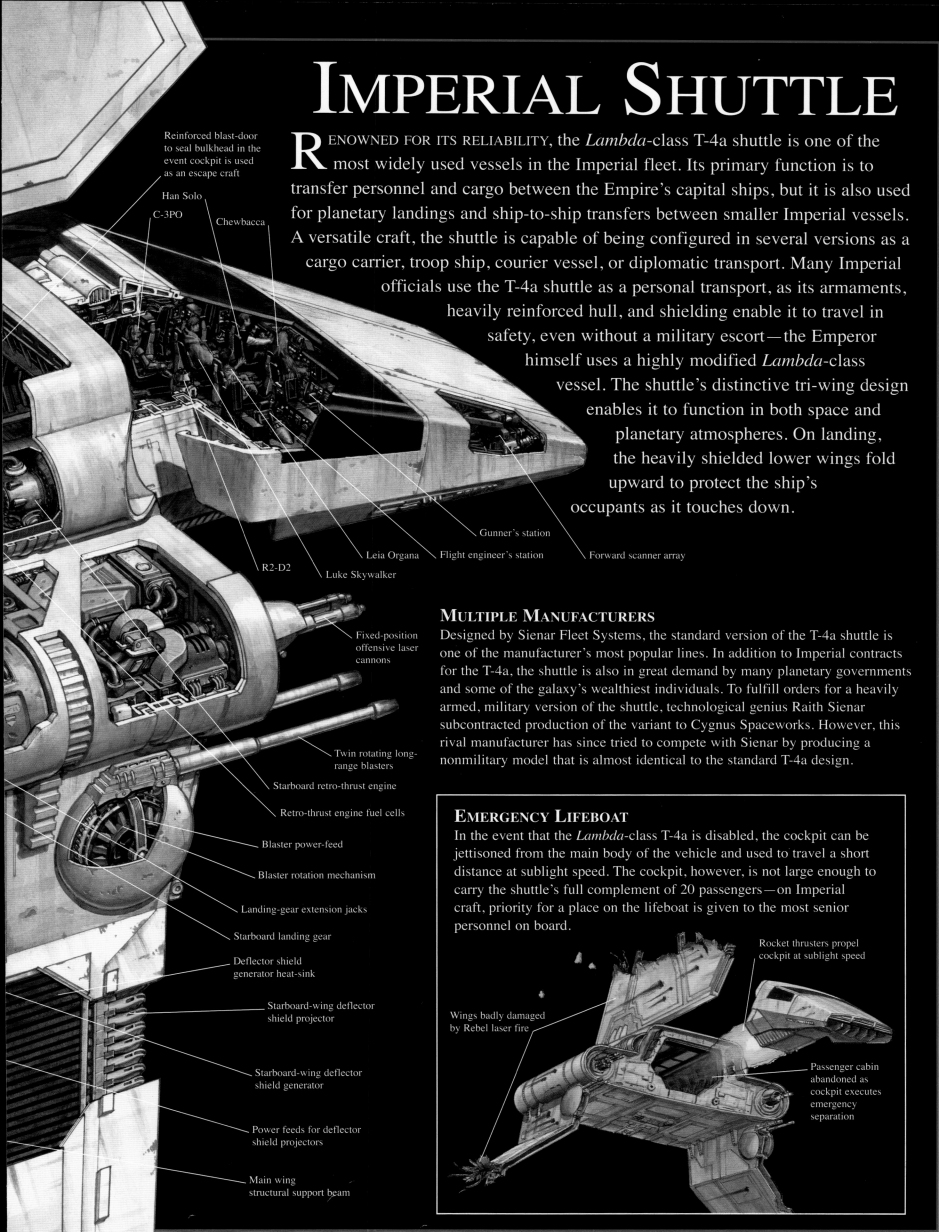

IMPERIAL SHUTTLE

Reinforced blast-door to seal bulkhead in the event cockpit is used as an escape craft

Han Solo

C-3PO

Chewbacca

R2-D2

Leia Organa

Luke Skywalker

Gunner's station

Flight engineer's station

Forward scanner array

Fixed-position offensive laser cannons

Twin rotating long-range blasters

Starboard retro-thrust engine

Retro-thrust engine fuel cells

Blaster power-feed

Blaster rotation mechanism

Landing-gear extension jacks

Starboard landing gear

Deflector shield generator heat-sink

Starboard-wing deflector shield projector

Starboard-wing deflector shield generator

Power feeds for deflector shield projectors

Main wing structural support beam

RENOWNED FOR ITS RELIABILITY, the *Lambda*-class T-4a shuttle is one of the most widely used vessels in the Imperial fleet. Its primary function is to transfer personnel and cargo between the Empire's capital ships, but it is also used for planetary landings and ship-to-ship transfers between smaller Imperial vessels. A versatile craft, the shuttle is capable of being configured in several versions as a cargo carrier, troop ship, courier vessel, or diplomatic transport. Many Imperial officials use the T-4a shuttle as a personal transport, as its armaments, heavily reinforced hull, and shielding enable it to travel in safety, even without a military escort—the Emperor himself uses a highly modified *Lambda*-class vessel. The shuttle's distinctive tri-wing design enables it to function in both space and planetary atmospheres. On landing, the heavily shielded lower wings fold upward to protect the ship's occupants as it touches down.

MULTIPLE MANUFACTURERS

Designed by Sienar Fleet Systems, the standard version of the T-4a shuttle is one of the manufacturer's most popular lines. In addition to Imperial contracts for the T-4a, the shuttle is also in great demand by many planetary governments and some of the galaxy's wealthiest individuals. To fulfill orders for a heavily armed, military version of the shuttle, technological genius Raith Sienar subcontracted production of the variant to Cygnus Spaceworks. However, this rival manufacturer has since tried to compete with Sienar by producing a nonmilitary model that is almost identical to the standard T-4a design.

EMERGENCY LIFEBOAT

In the event that the *Lambda*-class T-4a is disabled, the cockpit can be jettisoned from the main body of the vehicle and used to travel a short distance at sublight speed. The cockpit, however, is not large enough to carry the shuttle's full complement of 20 passengers—on Imperial craft, priority for a place on the lifeboat is given to the most senior personnel on board.

Wings badly damaged by Rebel laser fire

Rocket thrusters propel cockpit at sublight speed

Passenger cabin abandoned as cockpit executes emergency separation

JABBA'S SAIL BARGE

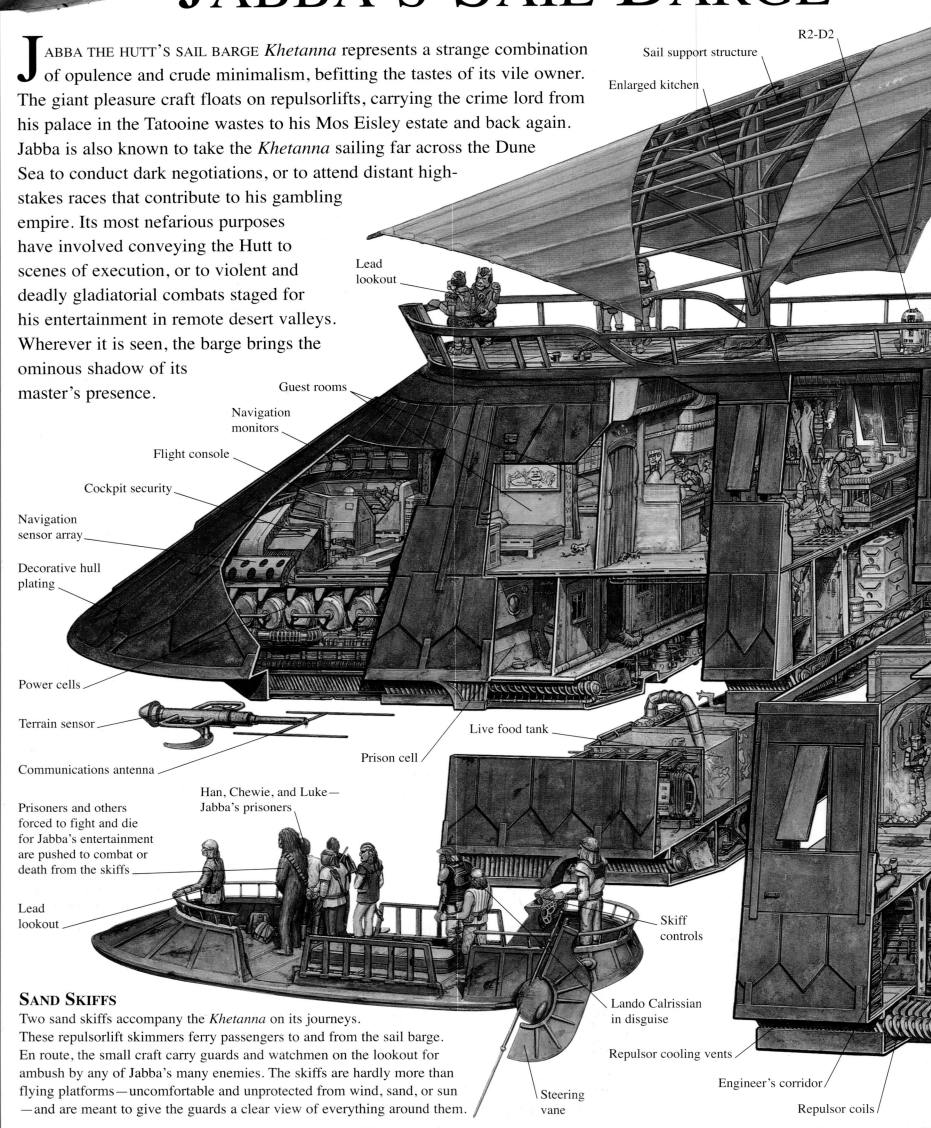

JABBA THE HUTT'S SAIL BARGE *Khetanna* represents a strange combination of opulence and crude minimalism, befitting the tastes of its vile owner. The giant pleasure craft floats on repulsorlifts, carrying the crime lord from his palace in the Tatooine wastes to his Mos Eisley estate and back again. Jabba is also known to take the *Khetanna* sailing far across the Dune Sea to conduct dark negotiations, or to attend distant high-stakes races that contribute to his gambling empire. Its most nefarious purposes have involved conveying the Hutt to scenes of execution, or to violent and deadly gladiatorial combats staged for his entertainment in remote desert valleys. Wherever it is seen, the barge brings the ominous shadow of its master's presence.

Sail support structure

Enlarged kitchen

R2-D2

Lead lookout

Guest rooms

Navigation monitors

Flight console

Cockpit security

Navigation sensor array

Decorative hull plating

Power cells

Terrain sensor

Communications antenna

Live food tank

Prison cell

Han, Chewie, and Luke— Jabba's prisoners

Prisoners and others forced to fight and die for Jabba's entertainment are pushed to combat or death from the skiffs

Lead lookout

Skiff controls

Lando Calrissian in disguise

Repulsor cooling vents

Engineer's corridor

Steering vane

Repulsor coils

SAND SKIFFS

Two sand skiffs accompany the *Khetanna* on its journeys. These repulsorlift skimmers ferry passengers to and from the sail barge. En route, the small craft carry guards and watchmen on the lookout for ambush by any of Jabba's many enemies. The skiffs are hardly more than flying platforms—uncomfortable and unprotected from wind, sand, or sun —and are meant to give the guards a clear view of everything around them.

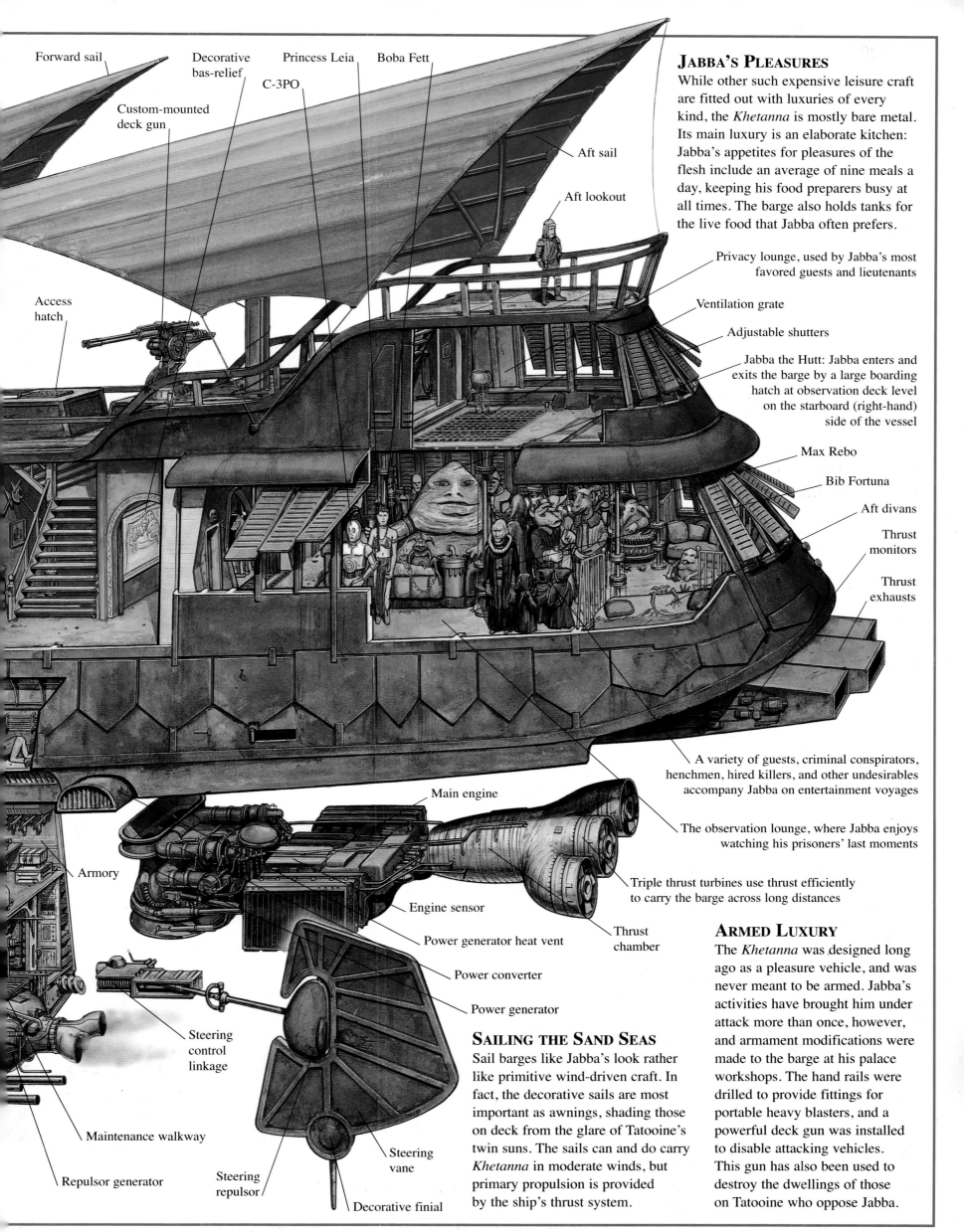

Forward sail

Decorative
bas-relief

Custom-mounted
deck gun

Princess Leia

C-3PO

Boba Fett

Aft sail

Aft lookout

Access
hatch

JABBA'S PLEASURES
While other such expensive leisure craft
are fitted out with luxuries of every
kind, the *Khetanna* is mostly bare metal.
Its main luxury is an elaborate kitchen:
Jabba's appetites for pleasures of the
flesh include an average of nine meals a
day, keeping his food preparers busy at
all times. The barge also holds tanks for
the live food that Jabba often prefers.

Privacy lounge, used by Jabba's most
favored guests and lieutenants

Ventilation grate

Adjustable shutters

Jabba the Hutt: Jabba enters and
exits the barge by a large boarding
hatch at observation deck level
on the starboard (right-hand)
side of the vessel

Max Rebo

Bib Fortuna

Aft divans

Thrust
monitors

Thrust
exhausts

A variety of guests, criminal conspirators,
henchmen, hired killers, and other undesirables
accompany Jabba on entertainment voyages

The observation lounge, where Jabba enjoys
watching his prisoners' last moments

Main engine

Armory

Engine sensor

Power generator heat vent

Power converter

Power generator

Triple thrust turbines use thrust efficiently
to carry the barge across long distances

Thrust
chamber

ARMED LUXURY
The *Khetanna* was designed long
ago as a pleasure vehicle, and was
never meant to be armed. Jabba's
activities have brought him under
attack more than once, however,
and armament modifications were
made to the barge at his palace
workshops. The hand rails were
drilled to provide fittings for
portable heavy blasters, and a
powerful deck gun was installed
to disable attacking vehicles.
This gun has also been used to
destroy the dwellings of those
on Tatooine who oppose Jabba.

Steering
control
linkage

Maintenance walkway

Repulsor generator

Steering
repulsor

Steering
vane

Decorative finial

SAILING THE SAND SEAS
Sail barges like Jabba's look rather
like primitive wind-driven craft. In
fact, the decorative sails are most
important as awnings, shading those
on deck from the glare of Tatooine's
twin suns. The sails can and do carry
Khetanna in moderate winds, but
primary propulsion is provided
by the ship's thrust system.

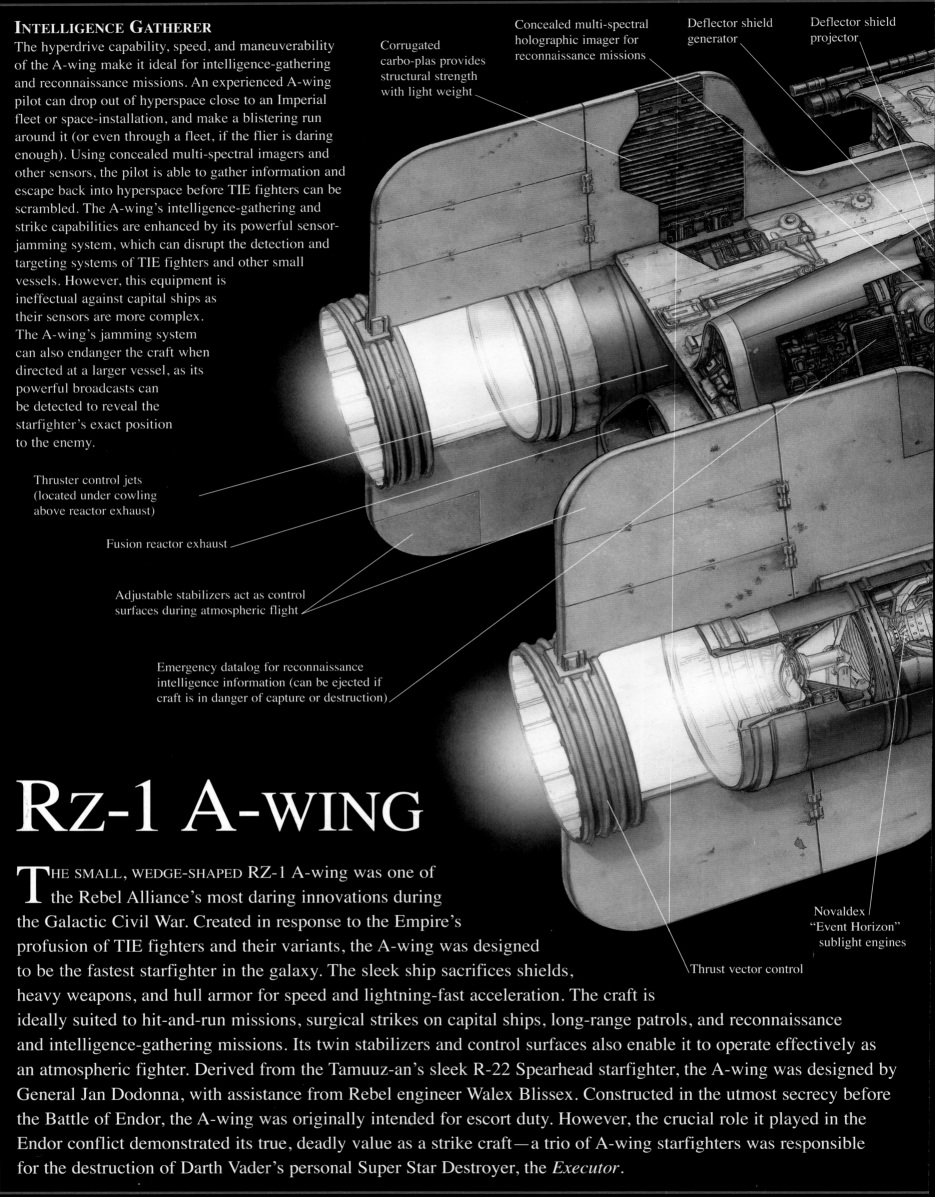

INTELLIGENCE GATHERER

The hyperdrive capability, speed, and maneuverability of the A-wing make it ideal for intelligence-gathering and reconnaissance missions. An experienced A-wing pilot can drop out of hyperspace close to an Imperial fleet or space-installation, and make a blistering run around it (or even through a fleet, if the flier is daring enough). Using concealed multi-spectral imagers and other sensors, the pilot is able to gather information and escape back into hyperspace before TIE fighters can be scrambled. The A-wing's intelligence-gathering and strike capabilities are enhanced by its powerful sensor-jamming system, which can disrupt the detection and targeting systems of TIE fighters and other small vessels. However, this equipment is ineffectual against capital ships as their sensors are more complex. The A-wing's jamming system can also endanger the craft when directed at a larger vessel, as its powerful broadcasts can be detected to reveal the starfighter's exact position to the enemy.

Corrugated carbo-plas provides structural strength with light weight

Concealed multi-spectral holographic imager for reconnaissance missions

Deflector shield generator

Deflector shield projector

Thruster control jets (located under cowling above reactor exhaust)

Fusion reactor exhaust

Adjustable stabilizers act as control surfaces during atmospheric flight

Emergency datalog for reconnaissance intelligence information (can be ejected if craft is in danger of capture or destruction)

Novaldex "Event Horizon" sublight engines

Thrust vector control

Rz-1 A-wing

THE SMALL, WEDGE-SHAPED RZ-1 A-wing was one of the Rebel Alliance's most daring innovations during the Galactic Civil War. Created in response to the Empire's profusion of TIE fighters and their variants, the A-wing was designed to be the fastest starfighter in the galaxy. The sleek ship sacrifices shields, heavy weapons, and hull armor for speed and lightning-fast acceleration. The craft is ideally suited to hit-and-run missions, surgical strikes on capital ships, long-range patrols, and reconnaissance and intelligence-gathering missions. Its twin stabilizers and control surfaces also enable it to operate effectively as an atmospheric fighter. Derived from the Tamuuz-an's sleek R-22 Spearhead starfighter, the A-wing was designed by General Jan Dodonna, with assistance from Rebel engineer Walex Blissex. Constructed in the utmost secrecy before the Battle of Endor, the A-wing was originally intended for escort duty. However, the crucial role it played in the Endor conflict demonstrated its true, deadly value as a strike craft—a trio of A-wing starfighters was responsible for the destruction of Darth Vader's personal Super Star Destroyer, the *Executor*.

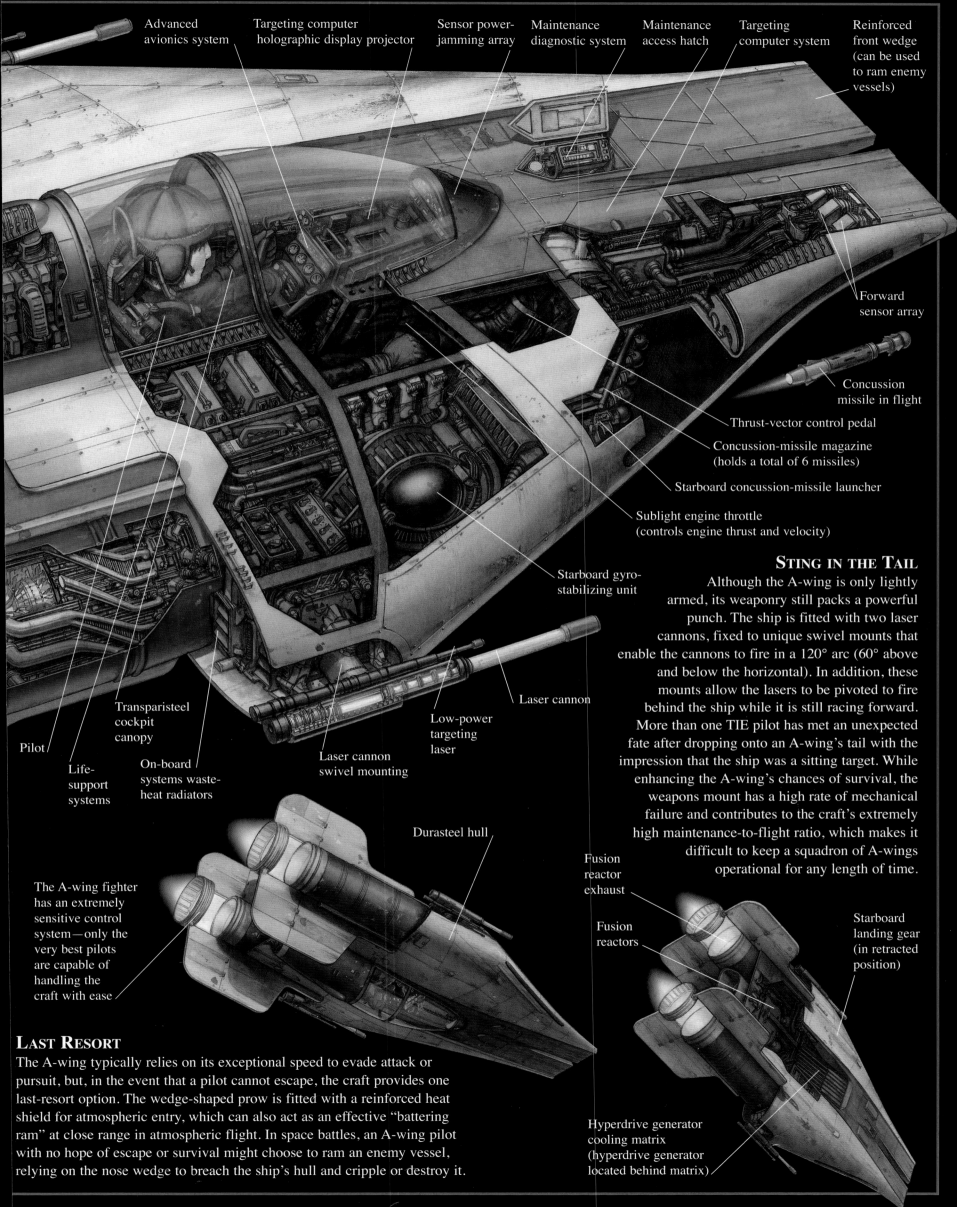

Advanced avionics system

Targeting computer holographic display projector

Sensor power-jamming array

Maintenance diagnostic system

Maintenance access hatch

Targeting computer system

Reinforced front wedge (can be used to ram enemy vessels)

Forward sensor array

Concussion missile in flight

Thrust-vector control pedal

Concussion-missile magazine (holds a total of 6 missiles)

Starboard concussion-missile launcher

Sublight engine throttle (controls engine thrust and velocity)

Starboard gyro-stabilizing unit

Laser cannon

Low-power targeting laser

Laser cannon swivel mounting

On-board systems waste-heat radiators

Transparisteel cockpit canopy

Life-support systems

Pilot

Durasteel hull

The A-wing fighter has an extremely sensitive control system—only the very best pilots are capable of handling the craft with ease

STING IN THE TAIL

Although the A-wing is only lightly armed, its weaponry still packs a powerful punch. The ship is fitted with two laser cannons, fixed to unique swivel mounts that enable the cannons to fire in a 120° arc (60° above and below the horizontal). In addition, these mounts allow the lasers to be pivoted to fire behind the ship while it is still racing forward. More than one TIE pilot has met an unexpected fate after dropping onto an A-wing's tail with the impression that the ship was a sitting target. While enhancing the A-wing's chances of survival, the weapons mount has a high rate of mechanical failure and contributes to the craft's extremely high maintenance-to-flight ratio, which makes it difficult to keep a squadron of A-wings operational for any length of time.

Fusion reactor exhaust

Fusion reactors

Starboard landing gear (in retracted position)

Hyperdrive generator cooling matrix (hyperdrive generator located behind matrix)

LAST RESORT

The A-wing typically relies on its exceptional speed to evade attack or pursuit, but, in the event that a pilot cannot escape, the craft provides one last-resort option. The wedge-shaped prow is fitted with a reinforced heat shield for atmospheric entry, which can also act as an effective "battering ram" at close range in atmospheric flight. In space battles, an A-wing pilot with no hope of escape or survival might choose to ram an enemy vessel, relying on the nose wedge to breach the ship's hull and cripple or destroy it.

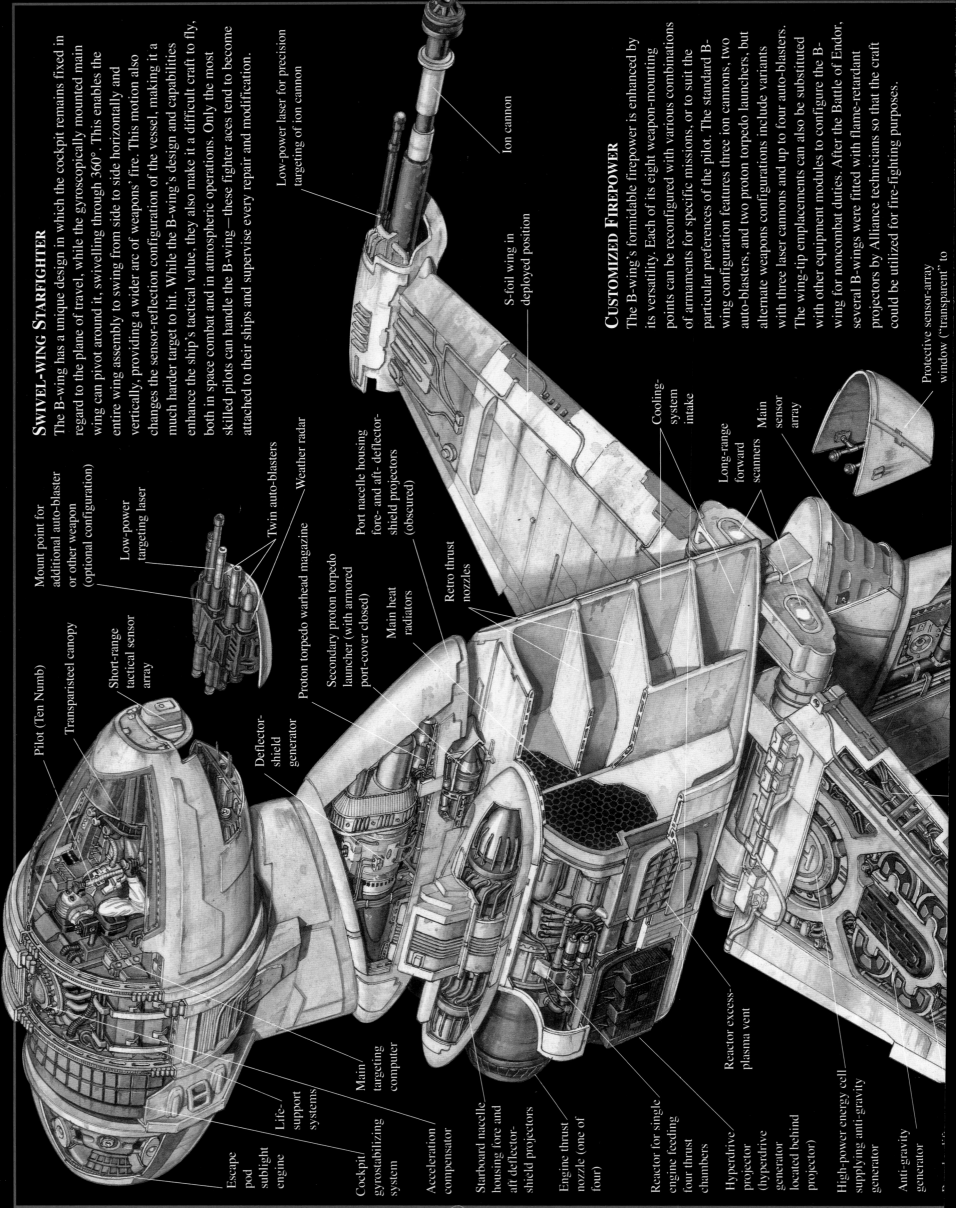

SWIVEL-WING STARFIGHTER

The B-wing has a unique design in which the cockpit remains fixed in regard to the plane of travel, while the gyroscopically mounted main wing can pivot around it, swivelling through 360°. This enables the entire wing assembly to swing from side to side horizontally and vertically, providing a wider arc of weapons' fire. This motion also changes the sensor-reflection configuration of the vessel, making it a much harder target to hit. While the B-wing's design and capabilities enhance the ship's tactical value, they also make it a difficult craft to fly, both in space combat and in atmospheric operations. Only the most skilled pilots can handle the B-wing—these fighter aces tend to become attached to their ships and supervise every repair and modification.

CUSTOMIZED FIREPOWER

The B-wing's formidable firepower is enhanced by its versatility. Each of its eight weapon-mounting points can be reconfigured with various combinations of armaments for specific missions, or to suit the particular preferences of the pilot. The standard B-wing configuration features three ion cannons, two auto-blasters, and two proton torpedo launchers, but alternate weapons configurations include variants with three laser cannons and up to four auto-blasters. The wing-tip emplacements can also be substituted with other equipment modules to configure the B-wing for noncombat duties. After the Battle of Endor, several B-wings were fitted with flame-retardant projectors by Alliance technicians so that the craft could be utilized for fire-fighting purposes.

Low-power laser for precision targeting of ion cannon

Ion cannon

S-foil wing in deployed position

Cooling-system intake

Long-range forward scanners

Main sensor array

Protective sensor-array window ("transparent" to

Mount point for additional auto-blaster or other weapon (optional configuration)

Low-power targeting laser

Twin auto-blasters

Weather radar

Pilot (Ten Numb)

Transparisteel canopy

Short-range tactical sensor array

Proton torpedo warhead magazine

Secondary proton torpedo launcher (with armored port-cover closed)

Port nacelle housing fore- and aft- deflector-shield projectors (obscured)

Main heat radiators

Retro thrust nozzles

Deflector-shield generator

Escape pod

sublight engine

Life-support systems

Cockpit gyrostabilizing system

Main targeting computer

Acceleration compensator

Starboard nacelle housing fore and aft deflector-shield projectors

Engine thrust nozzle (one of four)

Reactor for single engine feeding four thrust chambers

Hyperdrive projector (hyperdrive generator located behind projector)

Reactor excess-plasma vent

High-power energy cell supplying anti-gravity generator

Anti-gravity generator

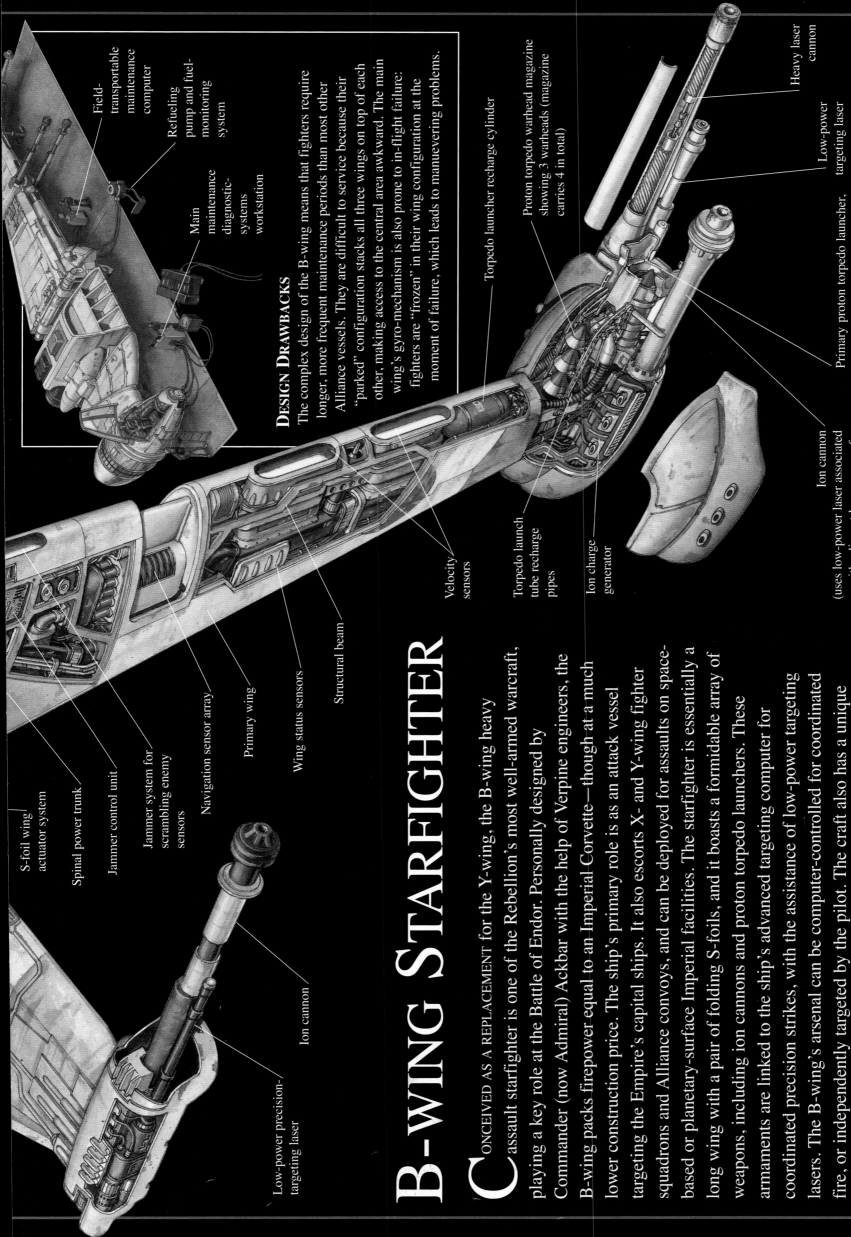

Field-transportable maintenance computer

Refueling pump and fuel-monitoring system

Main maintenance diagnostic-systems workstation

DESIGN DRAWBACKS

The complex design of the B-wing means that fighters require longer, more frequent maintenance periods than most other Alliance vessels. They are difficult to service because their "parked" configuration stacks all three wings on top of each other, making access to the central area awkward. The main wing's gyro-mechanism is also prone to in-flight failure: fighters are "frozen" in their wing configuration at the moment of failure, which leads to maneuvering problems.

Torpedo launcher recharge cylinder

Proton torpedo warhead magazine showing 3 warheads (magazine carries 4 in total)

Heavy laser cannon

Low-power targeting laser

Primary proton torpedo launcher, with torpedo in firing position (launch doors open)

Ion cannon (uses low-power laser associated with adjacent laser cannon for precision targeting)

Ion charge generator

Torpedo launch tube recharge pipes

Velocity sensors

Structural beam

Wing status sensors

Primary wing

Navigation sensor array

Jammer system for scrambling enemy sensors

Jammer control unit

Spinal power trunk

S-foil wing actuator system

Ion cannon

Low-power precision-targeting laser

B-WING STARFIGHTER

Conceived as a replacement for the Y-wing, the B-wing heavy assault starfighter is one of the Rebellion's most well-armed warcraft, playing a key role at the Battle of Endor. Personally designed by Commander (now Admiral) Ackbar with the help of Verpine engineers, the B-wing packs firepower equal to an Imperial Corvette—though at a much lower construction price. The ship's primary role is as an attack vessel targeting the Empire's capital ships. It also escorts X- and Y-wing fighter squadrons and Alliance convoys, and can be deployed for assaults on space-based or planetary-surface Imperial facilities. The starfighter is essentially a long wing with a pair of folding S-foils, and it boasts a formidable array of weapons, including ion cannons and proton torpedo launchers. These armaments are linked to the ship's advanced targeting computer for coordinated precision strikes, with the assistance of low-power targeting lasers. The B-wing's arsenal can be computer-controlled for coordinated fire, or independently targeted by the pilot. The craft also has a unique cockpit design—the pilot remains stationary while the rest of the ship rotates during flight. In the event that the B-wing is seriously damaged, the cockpit can also serve as an emergency escape pod.

TANTIVE IV

Manufacturer: Corellian Engineering Corporation • **Make:** CR90 Corellian Corvette ("Blockade Runner") • **Length:** original; 150 m (492.1 ft) after refit; 125 m (410.1 ft) • **Crew:** 85 (46 crew, 39 diplomatic/consular staff) **Engines:** 11 Girodyne Ter58 ion turbine engines **Hyperdrive:** class 2 **Armament:** 6 Taim & Bak H9 turbolasers (2 dual, 4 single)

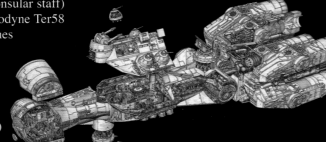

STAR DESTROYER

Manufacturer: Kuat Drive Yards • **Make:** *Imperial*-1 Star Destroyer **Length:** 1,600 m (5,249.3 ft) • **Crew:** *(standard complement)*: 9,235 officers, 27,850 enlisted, 9,700 stormtroopers • **Engines:** SFS I-a2b solar ionization reactor powering Cygnus Spaceworks Gemon-4 ion engines • **Hyperdrive:** class 2 • **Complement:** 48 TIE/In fighters, 12 TIE bombers, 12 TIE boarding craft, 12 landing craft, 20 AT-AT walkers, 30 AT-ST walkers, 8 *Lambda*-class Imperial shuttles, 15 stormtrooper transports, 5 assault gunboats **Armament:** 60 Taim & Bak XX-9 heavy turbolaser batteries, 60 Borstel NK-7 ion cannons, 10 Phylon Q7 tractor beam projectors

AT-AT

Manufacturer: Kuat Drive Yards **Designer:** Imperial Department of Military Research • **Make:** Imperial All Terrain Armored Transport • **Length:** 20.6 m (67.6 ft) • **Height:** 15.5 m (50.9 ft) • **Crew:** 3 • **Passengers:** 40 **Cargo:** 5 speeder bikes • **Engines:** 2 KDY-FW62 compact fusion drive systems **Max. speed:** 60 kph (37.3 mph) • **Armament:** 2 Taim & Bak MS-1 heavy laser cannons, 2 Taim & Bak FF-4 medium repeating blasters

DEATH STAR

Manufacturer: Imperial Department of Military Research/Sienar Fleet Systems (construction overseen by Wilhuff Tarkin) • **Designer:** Initial conceptual design by Raith Sienar, stolen by Tarkin. Further developed by Geonosian Hive engineers, with final design by Bevel Lemelisk • **Make:** Mk.1 deep-space mobile battle station • **Dimensions:** 160 km (99.4 miles) diameter; interior comprised of 84 levels, each 1,428 m (4,685 ft) in height, each level divided into 357 sublevels, 4 m (13.1 ft) in height • **Crew:** 342,953 (285,675 operational staff, 57,278 gunners) • **Passengers:** 843,342 **Hyperdrive:** class 4 • **Engines:** SFS-CR27200 hypermatter reactor powering 123 Isu-Sim SSP06 hyperdrive generators; 2 Sepma 30-5 sublight engines • **Armament:** 1 superlaser—range 47,060,000 km (29,241,719 miles), 5,000 Taim & Bak D6 turbolaser batteries, 5,000 Taim & Bak XX-9 heavy turbolasers, 2,500 SFS L-s 4.9 laser cannons, 2,500 Borstel MS-1 ion cannons, 768 Phylon tractor-beam emplacements, 11,000 combat vehicles

MILLENNIUM FALCON

Manufacturer: Corellian Engineering Corporation **Make:** Corellian YT-1300 transport (modified) • **Length:** 26.7 m (87.6 ft) **Crew:** 2 (minimum) **Passengers:** 6 **Cargo:** 100 metric tons (220,462 lbs) **Engines:** Quadex power core, powering Isu-Sim SSP05 hyperdrive generator (heavily modified); 2 Girodyne SRB42 sublight engines (heavily modified) **Hyperdrive:** class 0.5 **Armament:** 2 CEC AG-2G quad laser cannons, 2 Arakyd ST2 concussion missile tubes, 1 BlasTech Ax-108 "Ground Buzzer" blaster cannon

SANDCRAWLER

Manufacturer: Corellia Mining Corporation • **Make:** Corellia Mining Corporation digger/crawler • **Length:** 36.8 m (120.7 ft) • **Height:** 20 m (65.6 ft) • **Crew:** approximately 50 (members of single Jawa clan) • **Engines:** Girodyne Ka/La steam-powered nuclear fusion engine • **Max. speed:** 30 kph (18.6 mph) • **Cargo capacity:** approximately 50 metric tons (110,231 lbs), in addition to storage for 1,500 droids **Consumables:** 2 months' fuel and food • **Armament:** None

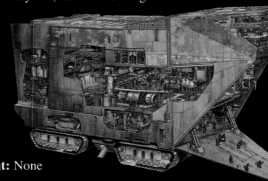

AT-ST

Manufacturer: Kuat Drive Yards • **Designer:** Imperial Department of Military Research • **Make:** Imperial All Terrain Scout Transport • **Height:** 8.6 m (28.2 ft) • **Crew:** 2 • **Cargo:** 200 kg (440.9 lbs) **Engines:** PowaTek AH-50 disposable high-intensity power cells • **Max. speed:** 90 kph (55.6 mph) **Armament:** 1 Taim & Bak MS-4 twin blaster cannon, 1 E-web twin light blaster cannon, Dymek DW-3 concussion grenade launcher

JABBA'S SAIL BARGE

Manufacturer: Ubrikkian Custom Vehicle Division • **Make:** Ubrikkian luxury sail barge *Khetanna* • **Length:** 30 m (98.4 ft) • **Crew:** 26 **Passengers:** 500 • **Engines:** 3 Karydee KD57 3-chamber repulsorlift engines • **Max. speed:** 100 kph (62.1 mph) • **Armament:** 1 CEC Me/7double laser cannon; 20 CEC Gi/9 antipersonnel laser cannons

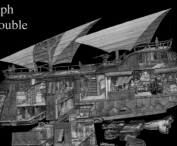

BTL A-4 Y-WING
Manufacturer: Koensayr
Make: BTL-A4 Y-wing starfighter
Length: 16 m (52.5 ft)
Crew: 1 or 2, plus 1 astromech droid
Engines: Koensayr R300-H hyperdrive;
2 Koensayr R200 ion fission engines
Hyperdrive: class 1
Armament: 2 Taim & Bak KX5 laser cannons,
2 Arakyd Flex Tube proton torpedo launchers
(4 torpedoes per launcher), 2 ArMek SW-4
light ion cannons

RZ-1 A-WING
Manufacturer: Various Alliance-linked
organizations • **Designer:** General Jan
Dodonna, with Walex Blissex
Make: RZ-1 A-Wing starfighter **Length:** 9.6 m
(31.5 ft) • **Crew:** 1 pilot • **Engines:** 2 Novaldex
J-77 "Event Horizon" engines • **Hyperdrive:**
class 1 • **Armament:** 2 Borstel RG9 laser
cannons, 2 Dymek HM-6
concussion missile launchers
(6 missiles per launcher)

T-65 X-WING
Manufacturer: Incom
Corporation • **Designer:** Vors Voorhorian
(lead designer) • **Make:** Incom T-65C-A2
X-wing starfighter • **Length:** 12.5 m (41 ft)
Crew: 1 pilot, plus 1 astromech droid
Engines: Incom GBk-585 hyperdrive; 4 Incom
4L4 fusial thrust engines **Hyperdrive:** class 1
Armament: 4 Taim & Bak KX9 laser cannons,
2 Krupx MG7 proton torpedo launchers

B-WING STARFIGHTER
Manufacturer: Slayn & Korpil • **Designer:** Commander
Ackbar (with assistance of Verpine engineers)
Make: B-wing heavy assault starfighter
Length: 16.9 m (55.4 ft) • **Crew:** 1 pilot
Engines: 1 Quadex Kyromaster engine with
4 thrust nozzles (or alternatively 4 Slayn & Korpil
JZ-5 fusial thrust engines) • **Hyperdrive:** class 2
Armament *(standard configuration):* 3 ArMek SW-7a
ion cannons; 1 Gyrhil R-9X heavy laser cannon; Gyrhil 72 twin
auto-blasters; 2 Krupx MG9 proton torpedo launchers

SNOWSPEEDER
Manufacturer: Incom Corporation
Make: Incom T-47 airspeeder
(modified) • **Length:** 5.3 m
(17.4 ft) • **Crew:** 2 • **Engines:**
2 Karydee KD49 repulsorlift drive units;
2 Incom 5i.2 high-powered ion drive afterburners
Max. speed: 1,100 kph (683.5 mph) • **Flight ceiling:**
175 km (108.7 miles) • **Armament:** 1 CEC Ap/11 double laser
cannon, Ubrikkian Mo/Dk power harpoon and tow cable

IMPERIAL SHUTTLE
Manufacturer: Sienar Fleet Systems
Make: *Lambda*-class Shuttle
Length: 20 m (65.6 ft) • **Crew:** 2–6
Passengers: 10–20 (or 80 metric
tons [176,370 lbs] of cargo)
Engines: SFS S/ig-37
hyperdrive engine;
2 SFS-204 sublight ion engines
Hyperdrive: class 1
Armament *(shuttle* Tydirium
configuration): 2 Taim & Bak KX5
double blaster cannons (forward-
mounted), 1 ArMek R-Z0 retractable
double blaster cannon (rear-mounted), 2
Taim & Bak GA-60s double laser cannons

SLAVE I
Manufacturer: Kuat Systems Engineering • **Make:** *Firespray*-class
patrol craft • **Length:** 21.5 m (70.5 ft) • **Crew:** 1 • **Passengers:**
6 (prisoners) • **Engines:** 4 Kuat X-F-16 generators powering Kuat
Engineering Systems F-31 ion engines
Hyperdrive: class 1 • **Armament:** Borstel
GN-40 twin rotating blaster cannons,
2 Dymek HM-8 concussion missile
tube launchers, Brugiss C/ln ion
cannon, Phylon F1 tractor beam
projector, 2 Arakyd AA/SL proton
torpedo launchers (3 torpedoes
per launcher)

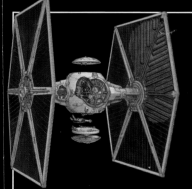

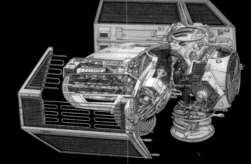

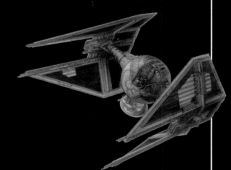

TIE FIGHTER
Manufacturer: Sienar Fleet Systems
(for all TIE variants) • **Make:** TIE/ln
space superiority fighter • **Length:**
6.3 m (20.7 ft) • **Crew:** 1 pilot
Engines: SFS I-a2b solar ionization
reactor powering SFS P-s4 twin ion
engines • **Hyperdrive:** none
Consumables: 2 days' air and food
Armament: 2 Sienar Fleet Systems
L-s1 laser cannons

TIE BOMBER
Make: TIE bomber • **Length:** 7.8 m
(25.6 ft) • **Crew:** 1 pilot • **Engines:**
SFS I-a2b solar ionization reactor
powering SFS P-s4 twin ion engines
Hyperdrive: none • **Consumables:**
2 days' air and food • **Armament:**
2 SFS L-s1 laser cannons, SFS-M-s3
concussion missiles; ArmaTek
SJ-62/68 orbital mines, ArmaTek
VL-61/79 proton bombs

TIE ADVANCED x1
Make: TIE Advanced x1 starfighter
Length: 9.2 m (30.2 ft)
Crew: 1 pilot
Engines: SFS I-S3a solar ionization
reactor powering SFS P-s5.6 twin
ion engines
Hyperdrive: class 4
Consumables: 5 days' air and food
Armament: 2 Sienar Fleet Systems
L-s9.3 TIE laser cannons

TIE INTERCEPTOR
Make: TIE interceptor
Length: 9.6 m (31.5 ft)
Crew: 1 pilot
Engines: SFS I-a3a solar ionization
reactor powering SFS P-s5.6
twin ion engines
Hyperdrive: none
Consumables: 2 days' air and food
Armament: 4 Sienar Fleet Systems
L-s9.3 laser cannons

HANS JENSSEN

THE THEATRICAL RELEASE of *Star Wars* in 1977 had a huge impact on the young Hans Jenssen. "I was just blown away by the awesome sight of the Star Destroyer flying over my head as I sat in the cinema as a sixteen year old," says the *Star Wars: Incredible Cross-Sections* illustrator. Born in Denmark, Jenssen traveled to the United Kingdom with his Dutch mother and Norwegian father as a baby and has been based there ever since. A professional illustrator for more than two decades, Hans combines his artistic skills with his lifelong interest in *Star Wars* to create realistic depictions of the interiors and workings of the saga's amazing spacecraft and vehicles. "From the time I was a kid, I always wanted to know what made machines tick and I loved cutaway art. I especially loved all the *Star Wars* vehicles: my all-time favorite is the AT-AT."

BASIC TRAINING

Hans Jenssen studied graphic design at college and specialized in technical illustration. "We illustrated boring stuff like plumbing and water pumps. You had to pay your dues…" He decided to specialize in cutaway (cross-section) illustrations, and has worked on a wide range of projects, from advertising work for shipping and aerospace companies to DK's *Star Wars: Incredible Cross-Sections* books.

CONTINUITY CLASH

When Hans started work on the B-wing artwork, he had a flash of inspiration. He wanted to depict the B-wing cockpit with a canopy hinged at the front. "I liked the old cars, like the E-type Jaguar, where the hood hinged at the front, and thought it would look good for the B-wing." However, thorough research by Lucasfilm turned up images from the *Star Wars* video games, showing the canopy hinged at the rear. So the initial front-hinged canopy drawing (left) had to be modified (right) in order to maintain continuity.

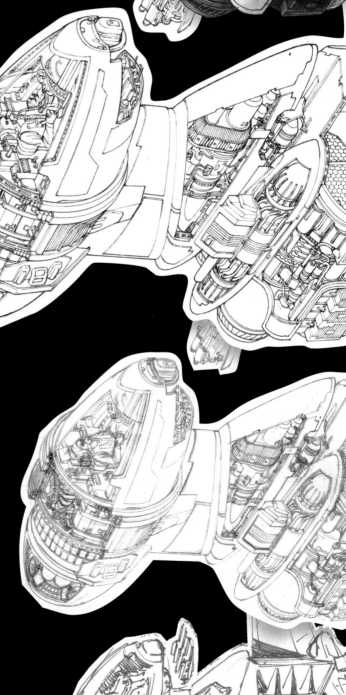

FINAL PAINTING

Jenssen uses acrylic gouache, ordinary gouache, and watercolor to color the artwork. The acrylic lays down permanent color over large areas. When the acrylic is dry, Hans can work over it with regular gouache or watercolor and scrub away areas to create worn textures.

Hans makes the artwork look as realistic as possible. "Texture is all-important to create realism: The original model-makers made everything look battle-worn and well-used, so we do the same!"

INKING STAGE

The drawing is inked using a 0.18 mm Isograph pen. Hans mixes three drops of black ink with 15 drops of brown ink, making sure that the lines are not too dark.

The eraser is a vital artist's tool!

AT THE DESK

Jenssen's "desk" is his drawing board, cluttered with the tools he needs for each stage of the illustration process.

The penciling stage can take over 200 hours on the more complex artworks

PENCIL DRAWING

For the finished pencil drawing, Jenssen uses a 0.3 mm technical pencil with an HB lead which can be erased easily. The internal detail is often reworked, based on feedback from Lucasfilm or the author, or if Hans has a new idea.

WORKING IT OUT

Getting the angle and details of each illustration right is crucial. For the shuttle *Tydirium*, Jenssen spent hours watching the *Return of the Jedi* DVD to discern cockpit detail, annotating an early sketch (top left) with suggestions for crew stations. Thumbnail sketches (middle left) were sent to Lucasfilm and the author to discuss the best angle from which to draw the ship. For some vehicles a photograph or 3-D computer model would be used to obtain the correct angle. With the shuttle, Hans had no photos from the selected angle, so he had to use his drawing skills to get the correct perspective (bottom left).

FIRST VERSION

After the rough sketches are done, Hans draws an accurate view in pencil on layout paper. This version is simple but precise and shows where the cutaway areas will be.

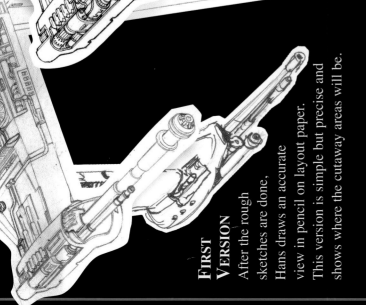

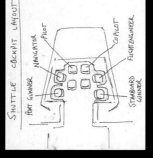

SHUTTLE COCKPIT LAYOUT
AFT GUNNER
NAVIGATOR
PILOT
COPILOT
STARBOARD GUNNER
FLIGHT ENGINEER

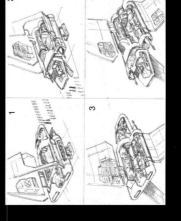

1
2
3
4

RICHARD CHASEMORE

WHEN RICHARD CHASEMORE was first approached by DK to work on their *Star Wars: Incredible Cross-Sections* books, he had a confession to make. "I'd only ever seen one of the films," says the UK-based illustrator. However, Richard, usually known as "Rich," was soon deeply immersed in the worlds of *Star Wars*. Through his work on DK's books, he has gained an in-depth understanding of the intricacies of the *Star Wars* galaxy, and is now a die-hard fan of George Lucas's movie saga. Rich and fellow *Cross-Sections* illustrator, Hans Jenssen, have a close working relationship. They have been collaborating on technical cutaway (cross-section) artworks for more than a decade, after first working with each other on the *See Inside* series of books for DK. During the production of these books, Chasemore fine-tuned his skills in creating cross-section artworks, and developed a particular interest in illustrating cutaways of armored vehicles. A man of many interests, Rich is a keen boardsport enthusiast, a hobby that often involves "perilous velocities." Music plays a major role in his life, as well: Chasemore is also an independent music producer, having co-founded his own independent record label—Superglider Records—in 2001.

TRAINING AND TEACHING

Rich completed a four-year course in technical illustration in 1992 and went on to work as an illustrator specializing in cutaway technical art. Using both traditional and digital media, he has undertaken "a huge variety of projects in publishing and advertising." Rich also likes to impart his love of drawing to others. Chasemore has run an airbrush course in St. Louis, Missouri, and has written four educational books on digital art, complete with teacher's notes.

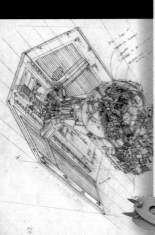

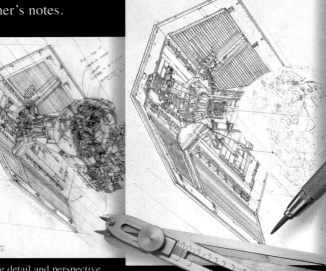

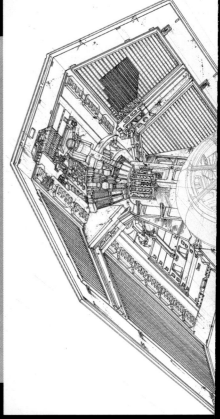

Rich's first sketch shows the key elements to be included on the final artwork.

More detail and perspective lines are added during the pencilling stage.

The final pencil drawing.

Chasemore now begins to ink in the lines on the artwork.

As the inking progresses, more fine detail is add. There is no going back now, as all of the details inked-in have been approved by Lucasfilm.

TIE bomber interior (studio-set shot)

Original Lucasfilm model of TIE bomber

BACK AT THE RANCH

To ensure that each illustration was as accurate as possible, Rich and Hans made many visits to Skywalker Ranch in California. They were given privileged access to the Lucasfilm Archives to examine in detail original models from Episodes IV to VI. They also delved into the concept files to see how individual vehicle designs were developed.

In addition, Rich and Hans had direct discussions with the prequel concept artists and designers about their visions for each vehicle in Episodes I to III.

DRAWING THE TIE BOMBER

During the pencil-drawing process, Rich makes sure that everything that should be depicted inside the craft is included. Chasemore says he "has to be mindful of the exterior shape" while making sure that the design of the internal components works in a realistic way. "You have to design the entire thing, though you will only show a part of it."

Rich has six of these "curves" for drawing accurate ellipses

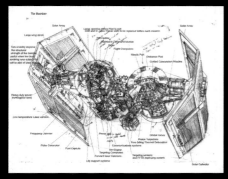

A messy paint-palette contrasts with Rich's total control of the painting process

Chasemore has had his airbrush cleaning brush since his college days

A number 1 sable brush is ideal for fine lines

ANNOTATING THE ILLUSTRATION

While Rich is working out what to include in the cutaway drawing to ensure continuity with the *Star Wars* movies, the author works with him and Lucasfilm in deciding which parts of the artwork to annotate with technical information. Drawing on many different sources, the author develops a draft set of annotations for Lucasfilm approval.

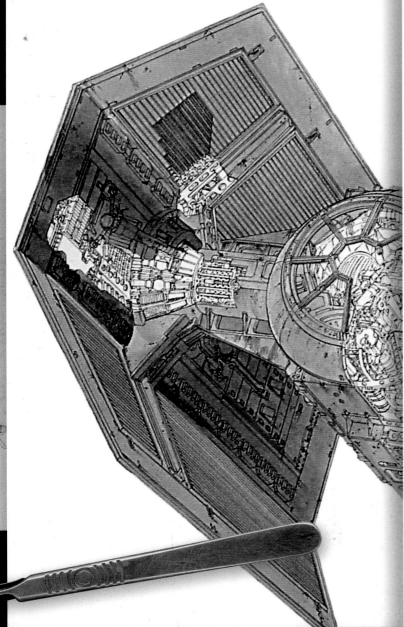

The first "wash" colors the main parts of the craft and indicates the direction of light and shadow in the artwork.

PAINTING THE ARTWORK

According to Rich, "Painting is where the fun really starts." Making sure the direction of the light is right and adding appropriate streaks and blemishes in the "dirtying down" process can "help make the ship jump right out of the page." Colors are often the most difficult part of the painting process, so Rich constantly has to make careful decisions about which colors to use to paint the different parts of the craft.

The TIE bomber artwork is shown above in relation to Rich's favorite number 7 brush, highlighting the size of the artwork and the incredibly detailed work that went into it.

With the paint added, the TIE bomber is nearly complete (above, main image). Chasemore uses dry-brush techniques to scrub dirt into the corners and around the base of shapes, to depict the realistic wear and tear a craft would suffer. "I try to think how real-world objects get dirty and reproduce the effects."

Rich uses gouache paints, as they are opaque; this makes them ideal for use in detail work

GLOSSARY

ACCELERATION COMPENSATOR

A device that generates a type of artificial gravity, which helps to neutralize the effects of accelerating to high speeds aboard medium- and larger-sized spacecraft, such as the *Millennium Falcon*.

ASTROMECH (DROID)

Multipurpose utility droid, designed primarily for use in spacecraft. Many starfighters incorporate an integral astromech droid to assist with astronavigation.

BLASTER CANNON

Limited-range, heavy artillery weapon fitted to starships for defensive use. Blasters utilize high-energy blaster gas to produce a visible beam of intense energy, which can cause tremendous damage to structures and organic tissue. Although their destructive power is considerable, blaster cannons are not as powerful as laser cannons.

CAPITAL SHIP

A large military starship designed for deep-space warfare, such as an Imperial Star Destroyer or Mon Calamari Star Cruiser. With crews numbering in the hundreds or even thousands, capital ships have numerous heavy weapons and shields. They often carry shuttles, starfighters, and other craft in their huge hangar bays.

CLOAKING DEVICE

Used to render a starship invisible to electronic detection systems, a cloaking device disrupts the electronic signature normally emitted by a craft's various systems and sensors.

STAR DESTROYER–
VENATOR CLASS

CONCUSSION MISSILE

A projectile that travels at sublight speed and causes destructive shockwaves on impact with its target. Concussion missiles are capable of penetrating the armor of a capital ship.

DROID

Generic term for any form of mobile robotic system that has at least some of the capabilities of locomotion, manipulation, logic, self-aware intelligence, communication, and sensory reception. Droids are usually fashioned in the likeness of their creators, or else are designed for functionality. Programmed with varying degrees of artificial intelligence and powered by internal rechargeable cells, droids are the workhorses of the galaxy. They are employed for an incredibly broad range of tasks, from field and manufacturing labor to use as soldiers, assassins, mechanics, diplomatic aides, and doctors. Many cultures treat droids as slaves or second-class beings. There are over fifty billion droids in current service in the galaxy.

TRADE FEDERATION
DROID STARFIGHTER

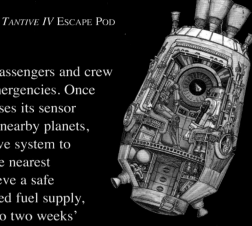

TANTIVE *IV* ESCAPE POD

ESCAPE POD

A space capsule used by passengers and crew to abandon starships in emergencies. Once launched, an escape pod uses its sensor systems to collect data on nearby planets, then utilizes its simple drive system to enter the atmosphere of the nearest hospitable world and achieve a safe landing. Pods have a limited fuel supply, but are equipped with up to two weeks' supplies to aid passenger survival.

HEAT SINKS & RADIATORS

Devices designed to draw away heat generated by spacecraft or vehicle systems and dissipate it into the surrounding environment. Removing this "waste heat" keeps the system's components within their normal operating temperature, preventing malfunctions and breakdowns.

JEDI INTERCEPTOR WITH
HYPERDRIVE BOOSTER

HYPERDRIVE

The "faster-than-light" drive that allows a starship to enter the alternate dimension known as hyperspace, where the normal laws of space and time no longer apply. By traveling through hyperspace, vehicles can cross vast distances of space in an instant.

HYPERDRIVE CLASS

Hyperdrives are rated by "classes": the lower the class, the faster the hyperdrive. Most civilian ships use relatively slow hyperdrives rated at Class Three or higher. Government, diplomatic, and military vessels have Class Two or Class One hyperdrives, while some experimental or "rogue" craft, such as the *Millennium Falcon*, use even faster classes.

ION CANNON

A weapon that fires powerful bolts of ionized energy designed to overload a target's systems or fuse its mechanical components. It is used to disable an opposing starship without causing lasting damage.

REBEL ALLIANCE
SNOWSPEEDER

ION DRIVE

An extremely common form of sublight drive, employed to transport starships into orbit from planetary surfaces and through local space. Ion engines produce thrust by projecting a stream of charged particles. There are many ion engine configurations, but one of the most successful designs is the twin ion engine utilized in the TIE family of starfighters.

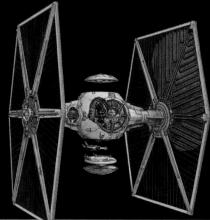

IMPERIAL TIE FIGHTER

LASER CANNON

The dominant weapon in the galaxy, found on both military and civilian spacecraft and vehicles. Laser cannons are a more powerful form of blaster, firing bolts of concentrated energy. They can range from low-grade models—which are only slightly more powerful than blaster rifles—to military versions capable of destroying starfighters with a single blast.

PROTON BOMB

A form of particle weapon that can be dropped onto spacecraft or planetary-surface installations. The bomb creates a cloud of high-velocity protons that can penetrate defensive shields. There are several types of proton bombs in the Imperial arsenal.

PROTON TORPEDO

A high-speed projectile weapon that destroys its targets by releasing a wave of high-energy proton particles on impact. It can bypass standard deflector shielding but can be stopped by particle shielding.

PROTON TORPEDO

QUAD LASER

Laser weapon consisting of four linked laser cannons which fire alternately in pairs. Quad lasers are very powerful in comparison to many ship-mounted weapons, but more affordable than turbolasers. They are commonly used on small- to medium-sized starships.

REPULSORLIFT

Antigravity technology used by planet-based vehicles. Repulsorlifts create an antigravity field which repels a planet's gravity, providing lift that enables a craft to hover over the surface or fly in the atmosphere. Most starships also use repulsorlift technology for planetary landings and atmospheric flight.

BATTLE DROID & STAP
(SINGLE TROOPER AERIAL PLATFORM)

SENSOR ARRAY

A suite of information-gathering instruments fitted to a spacecraft or vehicle. A sensor array is composed of a number of different scanners and other detection instruments that provide data on the environment surrounding the craft.

SHIELDS

Also known as deflector shields, these protective energy fields absorb laser blasts and deflect physical projectiles. Almost all spacecraft and some vehicles are protected by shields. The strength, radius, and endurance depend upon the available power supply. There are two main types of shields: ray shields, which absorb radiation and raw energy; and particle shields, which repel solid objects, from proton particles to concussion and proton weapons.

REPUBLIC ISP (INFANTRY
SUPPORT PLATFORM)

SPEEDER

Generic term for a ground vehicle that uses repulsorlift technology to hover and fly above a planet's surface. Variations for different environments include landspeeders, airspeeders, and snowspeeders.

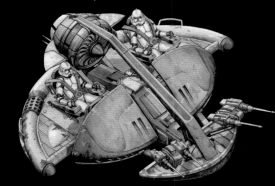

SPEEDER BIKES & SWOOPS

SITH SPEEDER BIKE

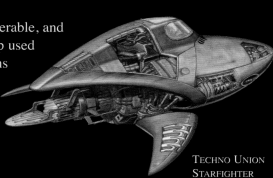

Personal ground-transport vehicles that use the same repulsorlift technology as speeders to travel across a planet's surface. Designed to carry one or two passengers, speeder bikes are in use throughout the galaxy for both civilian and military transportation. Swoops are high-powered versions of the speeder bike that are faster and more difficult to control. Swoop racing is a common sporting event throughout the galaxy.

STARFIGHTER

A small, fast, maneuverable, and heavily armed starship used in direct confrontations between opposing forces. Most space battles are fought between squadrons of starfighters.

TECHNO UNION
STARFIGHTER

SUBLIGHT DRIVE

A form of propulsion used for non-hyperspace travel. Spacecraft use sublight drives to lift off from planetary surfaces and travel into orbit. They can also be used to travel into deep space, where a vessel can engage its hyperdrive if necessary. During space battles, all starships engage their sublight drives.

TRACTOR BEAM

Modified force field capable of immobilizing and moving objects in space. Tractor beams can be used by spacecraft and space stations to guide spacecraft into landing bays, move cargo or salvage, or capture enemy vessels for boarding or destruction.

TRANSPORT

A starship used to carry cargo or passengers. The term is usually applied to civilian vessels, but can also refer to a ship that ferries troops and military supplies.

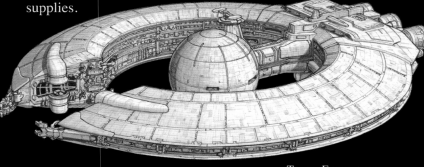

TRADE FEDERATION
DROID CONTROL SHIP

TURBOLASER

A high-powered form of laser cannon developed for use on capital ships. Turbolasers require large generators for power and multiperson crews to operate, but can penetrate the shields and armor of opposing capital ships. They are also effective against planetary targets.

REPUBLIC STAR DESTROYER
TURBOLASER TURRET

INDEX

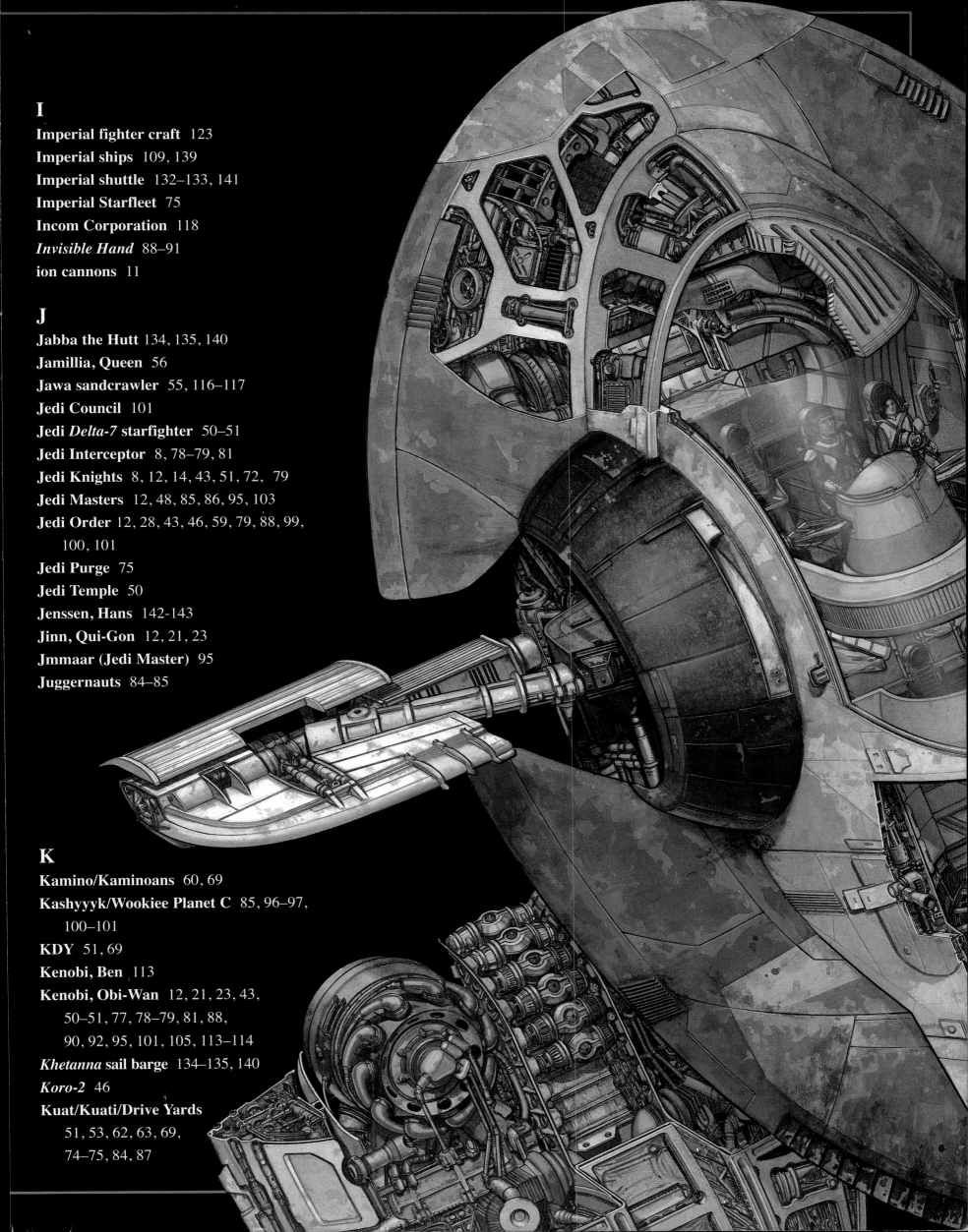

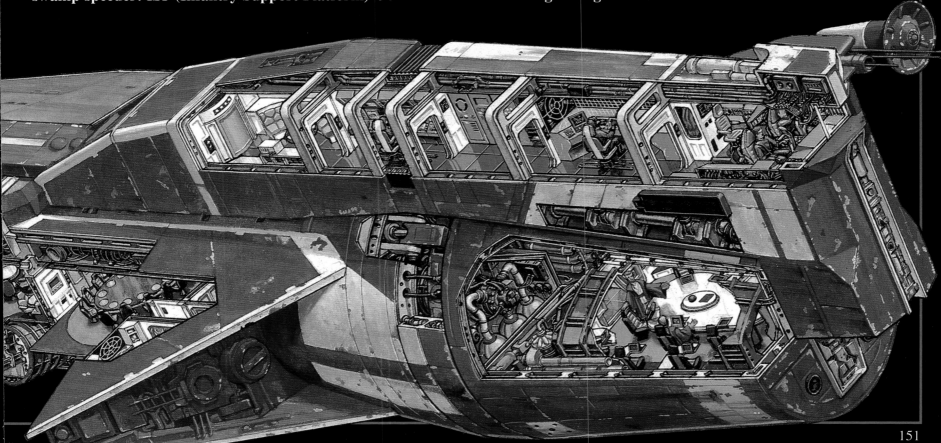

LONDON, NEW YORK, MELBOURNE,
MUNICH, and DELHI

DK PUBLISHING

PROJECT ART EDITORS Ron Stobbart, John Kelly,
Iain R. Morris, and Mark Regardsoe
PROJECT EDITORS Neil Kelly, Simon Beecroft,
David Pickering, Joanna Chisholm, and Nicholas Turpin
BRAND MANAGER Lisa Lanzarini
PUBLISHING MANAGER Simon Beecroft
CATEGORY PUBLISHER Alex Allan
DTP DESIGNER Hanna Ländin
PRODUCTION Rochelle Talary and Nick Seston
INDEXER Marian Anderson

LUCASFILM LTD.

EXECUTIVE EDITOR Jonathan W. Rinzler
ART EDITORS Iain R. Morris and Troy Alders
CONTINUITY SUPERVISOR Leland Chee

First American edition, 2007
Published in the United States by
DK Publishing
375 Hudson Street
New York, New York 10014

12 13 14 13 12 11 10 9 8 7

016-SD263–02/07

Material in this book was previously published in:
Star Wars: Incredible Cross-Sections ®, ™, and Copyright © 1998 Lucasfilm Ltd.
Star Wars Episode I: *Incredible Cross-Sections* Copyright © 1999 Lucasfilm Ltd. & ™
Star Wars Attack of the Clones: *Incredible Cross-Sections* Copyright © 2002 Lucasfilm Ltd. & ™
Star Wars Revenge of the Sith: *Incredible Cross-Sections* Copyright © 2005 Lucasfilm Ltd. & ™

DK Books are available at special discounts when purchased in bulk for sales promotions, premiums,
fund-raising, or educational use. For details, contact: DK Publishing Special Markets,
375 Hudson Street, New York, New York 10014, SpecialSales@dk.com

A catalog record for this book is available from the Library of Congress.

ISBN: 978-0-7566-2704-1

Color reproduction by MDP, UK
Printed and bound in China by L. Rex Printing Co. Ltd.,

DK Publishing would also like to thank:

Stacy Cheregotis, Tina Mills, Amy Gary, Sue Rostoni, Chris Gollaher, Steve Chianesi, Paul Ens, Pablo Hidalgo, Fay David,
Aaron Henderson, John Searcy, Heather Scott, Jane Mason, Cara Evangelista, Joanna Devereux, Cathy Tincknell, Cynthia O'Neill
Collins, Kim Browne, Jill Bunyan, Lauren Egan, Steve Lang, Lauren Britton, Nicola Torode, Louise Barrett, and Katy Holmes